Blue Moon Island

By Jack Durham

To my long-suffering Jude, with whose help all things are possible.

With special thanks to Margaret York.

Set in the South West of England.

An expensive painting by Édouard Vuillard is taken to Tuscany to complete the art collection of a prominent Italian.

Art and artists involvement in the proceedings move the action eventually to Christchurch in Dorset and the beautiful harbour.

Boats feature in the proceedings when a body is revealed, but that is only part of the story.

Problems after a French connection across the Channel lead to further complications and searches for reasons and answers.

The detectives in charge of the case are caught up in confusion and deception.

The outcome is not really intended, or is it?

Sometimes crime pays……sometimes.

Table of Contents

PROLOGUE

George Manion, as he was known in England, was born in Italy. His Italian birth name was Giorgio Manini. His mother, Louisa, was a cleaner and servant to an Italian family on the South-eastern coast of Tuscany. At this time, she was young, around nineteen years of age. She was quite attractive and had a number of boyfriends but nobody who really suited her. She wanted a family, someone who would look after her, with a good job and plenty of money. Her infatuation with the head of the Italian family eventually led to her becoming pregnant by him.

A pregnant and unmarried young woman in Tuscany was not in a good situation; she asked for help and support from this man when her son was born. He agreed to give her money on the imperative condition that she never divulged the identity of her son's father or the consequences would be dire. She had found out that the man she looked up to, was, in fact, a Mafia member and very high up in the hierarchy. All Italians knew instinctively what 'consequences' meant. This condition included her never being able to tell her son who his natural father was either. She was told only to call him 'Signore' and she never tried to find out his full name for fear that doing so would cause his help to disappear completely. Something she did not want to compromise under any circumstances.
She did find a man named Luigi who would marry her and accept the boy although Georgio was never completely accepted by him. The problem was that this mans' idea of 'looking after' was not the same as hers. Although he had money, he did not appear to do a lot of work. Quite soon, his personality became clear to her when she realised that he was quite a violent person. Louisa was still employed by the family and the feelings between her and the head of the household, still simmering. He remained kind to her and continued to give her money - something which her husband seemed unable to supply in sufficient quantities, except of course, for his drinking which had increased substantially. His personality became even more evident when he turned increasingly violent towards her following his drinking bouts and although she'd suffered physical abuse for many years, there came a time, when Giorgio was about 14 years old, that things came to a head.
Giorgio had become quite a strange child, affected one must suppose, by the attitude of the man he thought of as his father. Giorgio showed little emotion and seemed quite introverted. He was cold and suspicious with an expressionless gaze and found things without joy, which, for a child in his early years, was not considered to be normal. He had very few friends and would exhibit extreme reactions when criticised. He became quite hostile and consequently, he lost the few friends he had. Perhaps the worst trait was that he showed no guilt or emotion when he saw an animal die or when someone was hurt. In fact, he had often shot an animal or bird with his catapult and although this was something that perhaps most boys would do during their early years, Giorgio would be very cold and actually quite liked watching them die but felt absolutely no remorse at this outcome. When he had seen an injured dog or cat, he would be the first one to 'put it out of its misery' but in truth, he liked doing it.
After so long suffering abuse at the hands of her husband, Giorgio's mother turned for help to the man at the head of the family who had shown her such kindness. The day came when this man she knew only as 'Signore', asked to see Giorgio. The conversation which transpired showed 'Signore' that Giorgio was not a normal boy; he could see that he had traits which he thought might be

useful to him if the boy were 'cultivated'. 'Signore' was a Mafia boss.
He asked Giorgio just how much he disliked his father or at least, the man 'Signore' knew that Giorgio thought was his father. The resulting answers gave 'Signore' all the fuel he needed to 'control' Giorgio and prepare him for future use.
"Giorgio, you say you dislike your father so much you could kill him. Just how much do you mean that?"
"I would, but I don't know how."
"Let me explain. Does your father come home drunk very often?"
"Nearly every night and when he does, he usually beats my mother. He has done this for years."
"And do you think you could stop this beating?"
"Just tell me how. I know I could do this."
The general reaction to this conversation caused 'Signore' to realise that Giorgio had in fact, not only psychopathic but sociopathic tendencies too.
There followed a very serious discussion during which Giorgio was left in no doubt whatsoever that whatever he did, would remain a secret between him and 'Signore' because any action would help Giorgio's mother and stop the abuse. He was given detailed instructions as to how to resolve the 'situation'.
"I will have someone show you exactly how you will do this Giorgio. He will show you how to do what you have to do and how to keep things secret so that no-one will know that you had anything to do with the resolution of the problem. Do you understand?"
"Yes Signore, I understand and this will keep my mother from any more beatings?"
"Permanently," said 'Signore'.
His mother was perhaps the only person he really liked or cared anything for because she never criticised him. Critiscism made him extremely angry and usually when someone did, they received a beating.

"Then, I will do this. It will be easy for me when I know how to do it." In the end, Giorgio would feel neither guilt nor emotion, and he would leave no traces.
What Giorgio did not know was that in reality, 'Signore' was his father. This fact was kept entirely and firmly secret, except that 'Signore', now knowing just what sort of boy Giorgio was, did not really care for the boy except for the possible uses he would have for him and was happy to keep this knowledge to himself.
Giorgio went on to kill this man, his 'father', a man who had so brutally abused his mother, with absolutely no guilt, other than feeling pleased that he had been able to do it so easily, without emotion and without remorse or repercussions from the one person who knew exactly what he'd done – the 'Signore'.

CHAPTER 1

The unmarked delivery truck from the shipping company 'ArtCare – Fine Art Handling' was nearing the end of the journey from London as it followed the coastal road from Genoa. The scenery was beautiful and the driver had taken the 'scenic' route along the coast for the final part of the journey. It was rewarding after a very long and tiring drive through France and across the Italian border, where he took the road through Torino and then turned south to follow the coast. At every turn there were spectacular views and the sea was an azure blue. This made a very welcome change from the grey skies and continual damp of London. George, the driver said to his colleague, "I think we'll take the long way back. I want to take a better look at where I came from, some twenty years ago. I want to see the beautiful countryside of Tuscany once again before heading back home, if that's okay with you."
"Fine by me mate. I'm in no hurry. Nice place."
"I think 'nice' is an understatement, given where you come from."
"There's nothing wrong with London - just a bit overcrowded - innit?"
"Yeah, but I bet you just can't wait to get back can you?"
"Just take as long as you like. Anyway, it's all right for you, 'cos you live on the south coast and it's nice down there."
"I think we might take the route back through Chamonix and see the mountains."
"That'll be magic, mate," said his partner. "We don't have many mountains in London – just snow sometimes but I'd like to try skiing. Looks like a bit of fun."
"You'd never make it up the slope," George said, looking at his bulk.
They had taken the route close to Lyon and two days to complete the trip, employed to bring a special consignment personally, rather than have it shipped by air. The van was unmarked for security reasons as the cargo was particularly valuable. George had decided to take the last part of the journey to their destination to follow the coast. This road had the most spectacular views and at every turn on the twisty road, high above the coast, there were new vistas. The sea was a deep blue and so different to where they lived in England. George's co-driver said, "Bloody hell George, the sea's never this colour when I go down to Southend." George just looked at him with a very slight smile. "Never mind, you'll soon be back to your fish and chips and fry-ups."
"Yeah, 'cos I reckon this Italian food is too weird for me, all that olive oil and stuff, spaghetti and things like that."
"Perhaps that's why you're overweight and unfit," countered George, who was healthy and had a powerful physique.

Finally reaching their destination the truck pulled up at the large and beautiful villa overlooking the sea at Castiglioncello on the Tuscan coast. They removed a wooden crate and took this to the side entrance of the villa and rang the bell. A maid answered the door. "Buongiorno Signores"
"Buongiorno Signorina." My name is George and we have a delivery for Signore Tosco Scarpetti.
"Yes," she said, "*Signore Scarpetti* is expecting this. Please follow me." She took the two men through the entrance room and directed him where to put the crate. "Please sign for the delivery," he said and George passed her a large envelope which she duly signed on behalf of Signore Scarpetti and returned the sheet to George. They walked back to the truck, looking around at the immaculate garden full of multi-coloured flowers and shrubs.
"Can't grow stuff like this in my garden George."
"I've seen your garden and I'm not surprised. The flowers would need to grow through bricks and stones"
"Yeah, well, I'm working on it ain't I?"
"You've been saying that since we started doing these deliveries, and that's about two years now."
"Well, I don't have much time do I?"
"No. You spend too much time down the pub I reckon."
"Well, it's thirsty work this gardening."
"How would you know, you lying sod? Anyway, job done, so shut up and let's get going. I've got plenty to do when I get back. Come on; let's just get on the way. I need some food."
"Yeah, those lousy sods didn't offer any did they?"
"They don't mix with the likes of us, anyway, don't worry, we'll get some in the town.
They set off on the return journey.
The crate contained a painting which Scarpetti had bought through a gallery in England. The large envelope contained the Authentication Certificate and all the relative documentation.
The maid called Signore Scarpetti on the internal phone, informing him of the delivery. "Will you ask Guiseppi to come and open the crate, please Rosina"' said Scarpetti.
Guiseppi was the gardener-cum-handyman. "Tell him to be extremely careful when he opens this as it contains my new painting which I have been waiting for over a month to receive."
After Guiseppi had opened the crate and carefully removed the considerable packing, Scarpetti just looked in silence at the painting. He just said "*Magnifico*!" The new work was to be hung in a special place where the lighting was installed to perfectly illuminate and enhance the work. The light only falling on the painting, and isolating it from the surroundings, showing it in the best possible way. This was taking place in Tosco Scarpetti's palatial Italian villa on the Tuscan coast. This villa was furnished with impeccable taste that comes not with just money, which Scarpetti had a very plentiful supply of, but taste and knowledge.

It would be hung in a long gallery and the position that Tosco had reserved was mid-way along one wall which was not opposite any of the high windows which lit the gallery. This would mean that the work would be isolated and just the newly restored piece would be viewed, accentuating its integrity, and virtually completing his collection.
Tosco Scarpetti had paid £250,000 for the painting by ÉDOUARD VUILLARD. It was bought as an original and was an impressionist painting with an unusual oval mount and was painted using a distemper made with boiling hot animal glue. The sale was arranged through a connection of his in England and subsequently, a gallery in London. Prior to the completion of his purchase, he was advised that as the painting was not in the best condition, due to the unusual material used by the artist, it would benefit from cleaning which would take about a month. This was agreed upon.
Scarpetti had an extensive collection of paintings and most of them were relatively expensive, but this one was by far the most he had paid for a work of art. He was extremely pleased with his purchase and was looking forward to showing it to his many business friends and associates, although to say they were friends would be rather stretching the truth a little far.
Once this was in place, he stood and admired his new work of art, with a glass of wine in his hand and a satisfied look of pleasure on his face. During the next few weeks, Tosco would have numerous dinner guests and parties for his many acquaintances. This new addition would be greatly admired, as well as his other artworks.
He was a very cultured man who had invested a great deal of money into his collection. Perhaps the way he had acquired his money was less obvious, as he was a member of the Mafia. In fact, he was a 'Don'. He lived in a spectacular villa surrounded by so many objects which bore witness to his status in the Mafia suggesting that his wealth was gained in some very questionable ways, maybe drugs; prostitution; gambling; protection – and other unsavoury ways. He had managed to be untouched by accusations and arrest because he never involved himself in 'actual crime' but by always having others to do the deeds, whilst he reaped the rewards.
Following the period after the painting was hung he had invited his influential contacts to view this latest addition and about a month later, Tosco invited Augusto Canzano, a business associate.
Augusto arrived at the villa and he was about to pull the 'Lions Head' bell-pull beside the large and imposing main door. But before he had chance to do this, the door opened and the maid Rosina was standing there. She was slim with a really good figure. Her hair was tied back from her face and fell below her shoulders in a long black plait. She was dressed in a black skirt covered by a white apron and a white blouse. Very attractive with delicate pale skin, her eyes were black and she appeared to be about twenty-five years old.

Augusto, who was in his fifties, gave her a look which she realised was quite lascivious but she smiled, although she avoided his eyes. Tosco offered Augusto a drink and they sat on the terrace overlooking the sea.
Augusto ventured, "Tosco, your maid is very beautiful. She seems a charming girl."
Tosco replied, "She is, and you are right, she is very attractive. It is so nice to have someone so pretty close by whenever you need her." As he said this, he was looking at Augusto who realised exactly the implication.' That is what being a 'Don' means', thought Augusto,' you have whatever you want, whenever you want it'. But he also knew that under his urbane exterior, Tosco was a very hard man - certainly dangerous. It would not be wise to do him some wrong.
Eventually, Tosco said, "Please, I have something to show you."
"What have you bought now Tosco?"
"Come and see Augusto, I think you will like this." He took him through the villa to the large room in the centre of the house where the light was quite subdued. On the main wall, was the new painting, lit by a light which just put a soft light directly onto the painting but nowhere else, so that it was completely spot-lit and showed it off in the best possible way?
They looked at the painting by Éduardo Vuillard and Augusto said, "My friend, this is magnificent! I love impressionist work and I have seen many of his paintings, but never in a private home. There are some in the Tate Gallery in England. He has a very individual technique and in this work I know he used a very unusual material for the medium. If my memory serves me well, it was made from boiling hot animal fat."
"That is what I understand Augusto, and that is why I was advised to have this cleaned before delivery. It was in quite a bad state but now that it looks so much better, I hardly recognised it. I have waited a long time but now it is finally here, I am so proud. I have the Authentication Certificate to show that it is the genuine painting, so I have insured it which cost a great deal. I think it's necessary."
Augusto nodded. "That is certainly true Tosco."
They stood and looked at the work for some considerable time with Augusto looking very closely at the painting. He said little and became quite thoughtful but eventually, he turned to Tosco. "I am so sorry but I have to go now, I have some things which cannot wait any longer. Thank you so much for inviting me to see your new work. You have a superb collection."
"It is my pleasure and you will understand how much I value this masterpiece. I am indeed lucky, although I have to tell you that it did cost a great deal of money, in fact more than I wanted to pay, but I think it is worth everything I paid, for such an original."
"I can understand what you are saying," said Augusto, who had strangely become quite reserved. Putting down his unfinished drink

he said, “I am so sorry, but now I must wish you goodbye and thank you once again Tosco. I have some pressing engagements which will wait no longer.”
“Of course my friend, I understand. You must go now.”
Augusto left and Tosco went back to his painting with a glass in his hand and stood for a long while, admiring the work.
He went back to his office and made a number of phone calls, all to do with 'business'.

CHAPTER 2

The following afternoon, there was a telephone call and Rosina, the maid, took the call.
"Signore Tosco, there is a call for you."
"Who is it Rosina?"
"It is Signore Augusto."
"Ciao Augusto.' Come sta?"
"Sto bene grazie. Tosco, I need to speak with you."
There was something about Augusto's tone which rang warning bells for Tosco.
Augusto said to Tosco, "Midi spiacetanto per dirvi Tosco, che hoa vuto unos guardo molto attento al vostro nuovo dipinto e sono quasi certo che si tratta di una copia."
He said that he'd had a very careful look at the new painting and he was very sorry to say, but was almost certain that it was a copy.
"Che cosa! Non puoies sereserio! Come fai a essere cosìsicuro? What! You must be mistaken! How can you be so sure?"
Tosco knew that Augusto was much respected for his knowledge of art, especially impressionist paintings and he himself had a comprehensive collection of copies of many famous works.
Augusto said, "As I said to you yesterday, I have seen this artists' work before. There is another painting by him which depicts a couple eating oysters and drinking champagne which I have seen and studied carefully. I am now firmly of the opinion that the work you have is similar to another by Édouard Vuillard called *'Maison a Gauche – Paysage'*. Comparing the brushwork and all the other factors and similarities, I have to say that I consider that the one you have is a very good copy, but not an original."
Tosco was astounded. "But I have an Authentication Certificate. That proves that it is an original, surely?"
"You may have a certificate and I'm sure that it applies to the original and is authentic, but somehow I think perhaps they could have been switched - the copy for the original. May I suggest that you have it examined again for a second opinion?"
There was a long silence, then Augusto said "Tosco, are you there?"
"Yes," came the reply. "I am thinking. I respect your knowledge and I know you are giving me your best advice, but I am sure you are mistaken. However, I will do as you say and contact a specialist in Florence. There will be a suitable person there of course."
"A good choice my friend; I do hope that he can prove me wrong."
"Si," said Tosco, "I have to do some thinking Augusto. I will make some telephone calls and I will take your advice, although again, I sincerely hope that you are mistaken."
"I hope this also and I am so sorry to bring you this news but I think I am correct."
"Very well, I will be in touch with you later. *Parlerò con voi presto.*"
Tosco sat very still and slowly sipped his drink. He was deep in thought with an expression on his face that was of deep concern.

Eventually, he said to himself, "*Questa azione devo prendere*. This action I must take!"
He called an art specialist in Florence and explained that he had recently acquired a work by Éduardo Vuillard, and that he would like to have the authentication of this piece verified.
He asked if it would be possible to do this as soon as possible. He was told that this would not be possible as there were many appointments, but he was asked for his name and this made the specialist pause a little. "Signore, please allow me to check my appointments and call you back." The specialist made some discreet enquiries regarding Tosco. Based upon what he had heard from his contacts, he returned a call to Tosco. "I will re-arrange my schedule and call you back with a time for my arrival." Tosco was pleased that he was considered important enough to have influence as far as Florence. "*Gracias Signore*."
Two days later, the specialist came to the Villa. He was shown to the artwork and was invited to take as long as necessary to inspect the work.
Following some two hours of very close and detailed inspection of all aspects of the work - the brushwork; the material on which the painting was made; the medium used - and other complex aspects of a work or art such as this. He eventually stood back and looked at Tosco.
"May I ask what sum you paid for this piece?"
"250,000 Euros."
"This would be the expected price for a piece such as this. You will understand that I am a qualified appraiser, experienced in the paintings of the period of this artist. I am very sorry to have to tell you, but this is a copy, a very good copy, but regretfully not the original."
"Mio Dio, questo è incredibile! Qualcuno pagherà a caroprezzo per question ganno." 'My God, this is incredible! Someone will pay dearly for this deception.'
He expressed his amazement to the expert but refrained from saying too much as he was thinking that his next move would not be for general knowledge. Although not a hardened gangster, he was a Mafia 'Don' and he had many connections. He was known as Tosco '*Collettore*' Scarpetti, because of his collection and love of art.
His appetite for restitution and revenge had bubbled to the surface. "*Nessuno fa gioco di me. Questo saràpunito.*" 'Nobody makes a fool of me. This will be punished.'
He made an international telephone call. He was calling Giorgio Manini. The call went on to an answering machine and Tosco left a message. "*? Buongiorno Giorgio, come stai? Hobisogno di fare unlavoro per me. Siete disposti a soddisfare una richiesta di me l'Inghilterra?*"
A few minutes later, his telephone rang. It was Giorgio returning his call, saying that he was just coming into his house and he had heard his phone ringing, so he called back as soon as he could.

Tosco had asked if Giorgio could carry out a 'request' in England. Giorgio and Tosco exchanged the usual pleasantries and then Tosco switched to good English as he knew that Giorgio had lived in England for many years and was almost word perfect. In England, he was known as George Manion.
"George, as you know, I have recently bought a painting from a gallery in London. I need you to find the address of the woman who arranged the purchase of my painting. Do it quickly, I need to find her, pronto. I can tell you my problem, but you must keep it to yourself and tell nobody what you are doing and why. Do you understand?"
He then went on to explain what had happened and that he needed to have the money he had paid returned to him, 'with interest'. He could not allow his reputation to be brought into question in this way should the truth be discovered. He would have to keep the fraud a total secret. He had asked the specialist from Florence to assure him of his complete discretion and to divulge the problem to no-one. Thanks to the enquiries which had already been made about Tosco, there were no illusions as to what might happen if he was 'crossed'.
"Of course, you know my discretion only too well Tosco. Do you have the name of the gallery?"
"Yes, it was the 'Arcadian Gallery'. It is in Wimbledon, near London. They will tell you what you need to know, but don't tell them why you need the address."
"Sì Tosco, faro immediatamente."
With that, Tosco said, "I need to have answers quickly and to have the matter cleared up in the shortest possible time. Do you understand?"
"Absolutely Tosco. I understand your feelings and need for restitution completely. You may rest assured that I will clear up this matter. As you know so well, that is what I am good at and what you pay me so handsomely for and you know I leave no traces!"
"I do George. I know you will take whatever action is necessary to protect my reputation."
"Tosco, I will say goodbye and take action as swiftly as I can."
"Keep me informed George, and you will be suitably rewarded on a good outcome."
"As ever Tosco, thank you. *Buongiorno*."
George then set about finding the phone number of the gallery on the internet. A search on the internet for 'Arcadian Gallery' soon brought up the details.
He called the number which was promptly answered. "Good morning, this is the Gallery Arcadian. How may I be of assistance?" was the greeting from Rebecca Connors.
"Yes, I think you may. I am speaking on behalf of a colleague of mine from Italy who is interested in possibly purchasing another painting. He has asked me to speak only to the person he dealt with

on a previous occasion. Can you tell me who that might be, yourself perhaps?"
"Was this a recent sale, as it could have been myself or perhaps an assistant?"
"The previous purchase was about two or three months ago, I am not completely sure."
"And the buyer was from Italy you say?"
"That is so, yes."
"Then, that would have been one of my assistants. As I have not personally concluded any sales in Italy for perhaps six months, this would be her sale."
"In that case, if I may speak to her, as this matter is quite urgent."
"I am afraid that will not be possible as she is not here in the Gallery today. Can I try to help you?"
"Thank you, but my colleague has insisted that I deal only with the person who finalised his previous sale, so you see I must ask you for her address. My instructions are that I must see her today as I am only in London until this evening. I realise this is probably most unusual but you see, my situation is very difficult. Without this information, my colleague will be most displeased. This is not something I would like to happen, if you understand my meaning."
"I am afraid that I simply cannot give you her address as this is very private. However, as you say this matter is very urgent, and you obviously need to keep your colleague happy. What I will do is to call my assistant and ask if I may give you her address so that you may meet. If I could have your name and a contact number I'll let you know as soon as I have an answer from her."
"I would be most obliged, thank you. My name is George. I will be in a meeting for a few hours so I'll not be able to contact you, but I will phone you again as soon as I am out of the meeting, if that is possible."
"Of course Mr George. I will have an answer for you then."
"You are most kind, thank you."
"It is my pleasure Mr George, goodbye."
Rebecca had the impression, correctly, that this 'Mr George' was acting on 'orders' and he sounded as though a refusal would be out of the question. However, asking her assistant would absolve her from any problems regarding disclosure of personal information, which would not please the gallery owner at all, were she to find out that personal information had been disclosed without permission.
However, when Rebecca phoned her assistant, there was no reply, so she called the gallery owner and sought her advice.
"Good afternoon Mrs Harrington-Thorpe. I have just had a phone call from a man who has asked for Yaren's address and I told him that this was not possible but that I would seek permission. I have tried to contact Yaren but she does not answer her phone. I would not give him any information before I contacted you. He says that it is urgent that he talks to Yaren as she handled the previous sale to

his boss and he said that there was a further sale to be made if he could contact Yaren. Do you think this would be in order?"
"This is quite unusual Rebecca and I am a little dubious but I suppose if there is a further sale to be made, then it would be permissible in this instance. Was it urgent or could he wait until Yaren is back at work?"
"He said that he was only in London for one day and that he had a meeting so I couldn't call him but that he would call back later."
"I think in this case we could give him Yaren's address. I suppose he will go to see her?"
"I would think so, yes."
"In that case, go ahead and give it to him and leave a message on Yaren's phone to expect him when she gets back."
"I did try to leave a message when I phoned her before but it seems the answering 'thingy' wasn't switched on."
"Never mind, you've done the right thing by asking me and I'm sure it'll be alright."
"Thank you Mrs Harrington-Thorpe.' Rebecca said, thinking how she really does like being called by her 'full title'."
"Goodbye dear."

CHAPTER 3

Mark Jordan was a drug dealer. He was on his way back to Christchurch from London with a load of cocaine which was concealed in his Porsche. The drugs had been kept in the flat he shared with his girlfriend. She had become very unhappy that they were there and had been asking him to get them out of the flat for quite some time. Mark had told her that they would be taken 'very soon' and after that there would be nothing for her to be worried about.

He had a passenger with him. This was a man called Jason Chandler. They were on their way to a place on the south coast where they would take a fast boat across the Channel to France to deliver the drugs. They would 'borrow' this boat from the Marine Auctions at Christchurch where his father owned a business selling all manner of boats and equipment via sales and auctions.

On the way, Mark had collected Jason from Newbury and they had taken the A34 south to pick up the M3 at Winchester. As they came to the services at Winchester, Jason said, "I need a piss. Can we stop and get a coffee as well, I'm parched."

"Okay, but we'd better be quick or we'll be leaving it tight for the tide."

As they pulled into the services, they saw a lot of police vehicles where there were a number of HGV trucks being checked. As they took the lane into the car parking area, they saw that there were also a line of cars being checked by police as well.

"Oh shit!" said Jason. "I just hope they don't pull us over to the check line." Just as he said this, a uniformed officer in his hi-vis jacket motioned to them to pull over to the left, indicating they should join the line of vehicles being checked."

"Oh, bollocks!", we don't need this 'Jase', I just hope to Christ that they don't have any sniffer dogs around here - I saw some as we passed the trucks."

"Nah, they wouldn't check out cars surely? It's the trucks they check. Why would they do routine checks on private cars?"

"You muppet, this is the direct line to Southampton and Portsmouth, you know, links to Europe - where are we going, huh?"

"Yeah, s'pose you're right so let's just hope they don't have any reason to get too nosey. But, if they have sniffer dogs, they're going to pick up the stuff pretty damn quick. If they do, we're going to be deep in the doo-doo."

Looking smugly at Jason, he said, "Don't worry matey, they won't smell anything except rubber and mushrooms."

"Eh? Rubber I can understand 'cos I know you've got it all in bags inside the spare tyre but mushrooms! Is your boot damp then, growing mushrooms?"

"No, you pillock! Mushroom compost apparently stops the sniffer dogs from making out the smell of coke. All the packets are covered in compost."

"Oh yeah - and where did you get that piece of priceless information then?" said Jason, looking sceptical.
"I looked it up on the internet."
"And does it work?" Jason looked confused.
"How the fuck should I know, I've not tried it yet but I bloody hope so because we're about to find out. Keep smiling at the 'nice' policemen," he said as two approached.
As one appeared at the drivers' side, Mark lowered the window.
The police officer said, "Good day Sir, do you mind if we take a look around? We are doing spot checks; just a general look to make sure that all vehicles are in good condition - you know lights and such. Nothing to worry about."
Mark smiled at the police office, giving him one of his best charming smiles, although parts of his anatomy were tightening......
While one officer took a quick check of the tyres and other points, the first one looked through the driver's window and said "Nice car sir. What's it like to drive? Quite fun I'd imagine."
"It is, but the problem is I can't go over the speed limit and give her full throttle can I?" said Mark with a disarming but impudent smile.
"I'm sure you never exceed the speed limit sir," the officer replied with just a hint of irony. "Would you mind opening the boot so I can take a peek inside, just to check for any drugs and so on?"
Mark thought, "Drugs – he said they were just checking that the usual things were in good order. He didn't mention looking for drugs."
With that, Mark experienced a further clenching of the bowels but he operated the boot-lid catch as the policeman moved towards the back of the car. Hesitating, he turned then looked at Mark and gave a wry smile and with a nod, he just said, "Hmm, 'Porsche'."
Mark thought the better of giving a smug smile.
Then the officer moved to the front of the car where he opened the boot-lid and peered inside.
The packets had been loaded inside the spare wheel tyre. The cocaine was inside Ziploc ® sealed bags. Any possible smell which may have been discovered by 'sniffer' dogs, Mark hoped, would be concealed by the very strong mushroom compost which surrounded the packages. He had seen sniffer dogs working around the trucks but he was hoping they'd not be brought over to the private vehicles.
He was wrong. Out of sight, the surly looking officer had motioned to the dog handler to come over. The dog handler walked over with his sniffer dog. Mark spotted this in his mirror and said to Jason, "We're about to find out if this mutt can find our stuff. I really hope to Christ that the mushroom compost does what it's supposed to, or we've had it."
They'd made three trips before using the method of taking the drugs by boat over to France, but the previous trips had been with only relatively small amounts of drugs. However, this time they were into some serious money. Mark had taken all the precautions

he could think of and he had a confident outlook on the face of it, but inside he was really worried. Not because of the drugs, but really the fact that if they were actually found, not only would they be confiscated but the money for the drugs had come from a painting which had been bought by a very wealthy client in Italy. Although it was sold as an 'original', it was in fact a copy. What he didn't know was that it had been bought by a member of the Mafia!
While both police officers were looking carefully at the tyres, lights and inside both the car and the boot, Mark and Jason said nothing to each other but Mark could see that Jason was sweating slightly.
"Keep your cool for Christ's sake, whispered Mark. The last thing we need is for you to actually look guilty. These guys will spot that immediately."
"Yeah, but the one this side is a hard-faced looking git. I'm sure he'll find something just to bag some brownie points.
"Stop worrying will you. You just look guilty; they'll spot that for sure."
"I know, but these fuckers give me the willies." Jason whispered.
It was with an inward sigh of relief that Mark heard from the policeman who had spoken earlier, saying – "Everything is fine sir, thank you and we apologise for keeping you."
As they drove off, Jason said, "'I told you Mark, that other bastard looked disappointed that he hadn't found anything."
"Never mind him; I was shitting myself when they brought those dogs over. Thank fuck they didn't find anything!"
"So you'll never know whether your mushroom compost muck did the trick and confused the dogs or not?"
"It must have worked but that's not the way I wanted to prove it because I may want to do this again."
"Sod it; let's get a coffee and a piss."
"Okay, but no time for coffee. We have to get to that boat because if we miss the tide, we'll have a bitch of a passage to get to Caen before the water goes. If that happens, we'll be stuck in the channel all night, and I for one do NOT want that!"
"Is that where we are heading?"
"No, we're heading for the Cape of Good Hope. Of course we are, you prat!"
"Is there a good landing away from authorities there then?" asked Jason.
"Yep, it's all arranged. There is a landing stage just a way down the port channel away from Ouistreham ferry terminal – this is the other name for Caen ferry terminal by the way. It's only for small craft and there's a brasserie just there which is where we'll meet our contact. We'll give him a call as we are nearing the coast; he'll be expecting our call. We give him the goods, he gives us the money and we leg it back to our side. No-one is any the wiser."
"But if the ferries can get in there, why can't we, there must be plenty of water?"

“Yes, but not our last bit down the channel you dork. It’s not that deep, that’s why it’s only for small boats. I don’t know why I bring you sometimes, do you know that!”
“It’s all right for you, you know all about boats and stuff; me, I’m just a landlubber.”
“I’ve got another word for it but you just do what I tell you and we’ll be okay, Okay?”
“Aye aye Skipper.” Jason winked as he saluted Mark in jest.
“You cheeky sod.”
They both went into the services and found the gents toilets. On the way, Jason said, ‘I know we can’t get a coffee but can we get something to drink, I’m parched?’
"Bloody hell Jase, just now you needed a piss and now you want some more liquid."
"You know what I mean, I must keep hydrated."
"I tell you what, if you need to get some liquid inside you, how about I chuck you over the side on the way over? You’ll get pretty hydrated then."
"You’ve got a weird sense of humour Mark."
"Who says I’m joking? Anyway, be bloody quick and get something to stop you bleating. Let’s get the hell down to the boat and get this stuff sorted."
“How are we going to take the coke? It’s in the tyre and we can’t really take a spare wheel to deliver to someone, it’ll look a bit dodgy.”
“Don’t worry about that. I’ve got a special tank for the coke so that if we get any trouble, we can put it over the side and it’ll be on a rope and it will be down under the boat. Not that anything’s going to happen. We’ve had our share of bad luck for today. Anyway, it’s very rare that boats are intercepted, especially small boats crossing the channel. “

CHAPTER 4

As they arrived at the Marine Auctions Boat yard in Christchurch, it was getting dark and the car was parked out of sight of the main road. Mark and Jason got out of the Porsche and walked into the main buildings. "We've no time to lose Jase, so can you get the spare wheel out and put the right one back in the boot, it's over there under that bench. Take the one with the drugs in over to the workshop and I'll get the packages out just leave that to me, then we can stow them in the boat; I'll be there in a couple of minutes.'
Mark went into the office where his father Frank Jordan was waiting for him. "I thought you'd never get here; where the bloody hell have you been?"
"We got pulled over by the plod for a spot check at Winchester services."
"Christ, you were bloody lucky you didn't have anything like a busted light or they'd have done you and given the car a really deep check."
"I know, I was crapping myself to be honest but I'd taken precautions."
"Precautions, what precautions?" asked Frank.
"I'd packed the tyre with mushroom compost."
"What!' he exploded, "you did what?"
"Yeah, mushroom compost. That's what they use to confuse the sniffer dogs - it apparently confuses their poor little snouts so they're not sure what they're sniffing."
"And this is your 'perceived wisdom' is it? I think you've been eating those bloody mushrooms and the wrong sort as well! It's addled your brain you little prick. If you think that a little mushroom compost will keep you safe, you'd better get a good lawyer ready for when you do get pulled. You've been bloody lucky son."
"I know, but anyway we've gotta go, I've a big shipment to unload and I want this to go without a hitch. Is the boat ready?"
"Yes, it's that 'Jeanneau Prestige 42' - she's all fuelled up and the engines have been checked. Everything is working well. At least the owner of this one looks after it, it's in great nick. For Christ's sake don't go and do anything to make this guy suspicious when he gets back and wants to go for a spin in it. It's worth around £160k."
"What sort of speed will she do?"
"Around 16 knots but top end 25. For pity's sake don't go revving the guts out of it. It's got twin diesels so if you do get any engine trouble, and I hope to hell you don't, you've got another one. Just be bloody careful, right."
"I do know how to handle a powerful craft Dad, I should do by now after all the racing we've done."
"I know, but this is a bit different. There's much more at stake than a belt to Torquay and back. Don't forget, if anything goes 'tits up', I have no idea what you're up to, right - just keep me right out of it. Understood?"

"I've been making sure that we're staying clear of any snooping police in the area; we can't take any chances with this lot."
"How much is this delivery worth then?"
Mark replied with a little hesitation, "Around 250K I reckon."
"Jesus Christ, you take more chances every time don't you? One day you're going to come unstuck and then what's going to happen? You've already had a taste of prison; do you want a really long stretch, 'cos that's what you'll get next time?"
"That won't happen. I've taken every precaution to make sure that this shipment is pretty near undetectable."
"Oh yes," said Frank, "and what makes you think you're cleverer than all the other muppets who have said the same thing - the ones sitting in their cells wondering where it all went wrong."
"This time, I made sure that everything is watertight, quite literally."
"So how have you secured the 'cargo'?"
"I've used a weighted aluminium fuel tank and made sure that it sinks when it's in the water. If we get any problems, all we do is chuck it overboard on a rope and it will hang under the boat until we can get it back. If it's only a rope going over the side attached to a cleat, then it will look like a fender rope."
"I hope you know what you are doing, so you'd better get the hell out of here now or you'll be sitting on your arse on a mud-bank all night."
For the exit from Christchurch Mark had checked the tide times at the Harbour and he said "We've got a high water at 11.36 and it's a 1.7 metre high so we'll be okay."
Mark went and found Jason and together they boarded the boat with the cargo, slipped the moorings and set off down the river towards the harbour, where they would set a course for Caen.

CHAPTER 5

Monday 17th August 2015
They made their way down the river Stour and into Christchurch Harbour coming to the 'Run' at the entrance to Christchurch Harbour, which sometimes had a fast flowing current. After negotiating that with care, they set a course across the channel towards Ouistreham, better known as the Caen ferry terminal. There was a channel to the port side of the harbour entrance and this is where Mark was heading to deliver his cargo, in return for a very large payment.
They were having an uneventful crossing and Jason was enjoying the fast cruising in the Janneau. It had an open deck above the main bridge known as a fly-bridge and with the twin engines running nearly flat-out, they were making around 23 knots on a sea that was fairly smooth with just a little swell. Sometimes they met a slightly heavier swell and this made Jason feel somewhat concerned. As a particularly big swell came into view, Jason looked at Mark and said, "Aren't we going a little bit fast for this one Mark? We're going to hit it full on."
"Stop worrying, you big Jessie - you should see the waves that we've run into on some of the races that Dad and I have been on!."
"It's alright for you, you've done it before, but to be honest it's scaring the shit out of me when I see a wave that blocks out the horizon. Why are they so big anyway, because it's not as if there's a strong wind or anything and most of the time, the sea is pretty flat?"
"Did you see that bloody great tanker that crossed ahead of us in the distance about ten minutes ago?"
"Yes, sodding great thing but it didn't seem to be going very fast."
"It would have been doing about fifteen knots but with around 120,000 tons of water being displaced, it's caused a great wave in its wake and that's the wave we're about to take."
As Mark smiled, he said, "Hang on, here we go," and with a mighty "whomp" the boat reared up and almost stopped as it crested the huge swell.
Jason was hanging on for dear life and he shouted, "You mad bastard, you're going to sink this fucking boat. You drive this thing like it's a rally car!" Mark however, was laughing and enjoying the feeling of exhilaration of conning a powerful craft, doing what it was built to do.
Jason was scared. "For Christ's sake, don't forget that we have to get this thing back to the dock in one piece so that the owner doesn't know we've been out on a 'jolly' with his toy."
"Will you stop worrying Jason and get the radio switched on to channel 16. We're getting fairly close to the coast now, so make

sure you keep your eyes open for all the ships, especially small fishing boats as we get nearer to the coast. We can see the bigger stuff, but the last thing we want is to drive straight through a small boat which might be hidden by a wave. With this little baby weighing around five tons and doing about twenty-five knots, we'd probably go straight through one and they wouldn't stand a chance."

"OoohSheeeit, that's all we need! Why don't you slow down a bit?"

"We'll slow down as we get within about half a mile of the coast because we have to make the tide. This place we're going to doesn't have a lot of water and we have to get up to the landing stage to meet our contact. Now will you shut up and just listen out for the radio Jason?"

"What do I do if someone calls us?"

"No problem. As soon as they spot us on their radar, they'll call us - just give me the handset when they do."

"When we see the *Phare de Ouistreham*, we keep to the port channel."

"What's that in English?'

"That's the port lighthouse and we have to keep to the left channel, ok?"'

"Got it."

"Good. Now shut up and keep your eyes peeled for small boats, it's going to get a bit dodgy 'cos there'll be a fair amount of stuff chugging around. We're heading for a place called *Face Baie",* said Mark. "That's where there's a landing stage and our bloke will be waiting. I'll just give him a call to say that we're nearly there. Take the wheel for a mo' while I call him."

"Ooooh, goody, playtime," said Jason.

"Stop being a clown, this is serious now so behave yourself and don't take any chances, understood!"

As they passed the Ouistreham lighthouse and turned into the channel, Mark made the call on his mobile and spoke briefly to someone. Jason couldn't hear what was said and anyway he was concentrating on steering the boat. As Mark finished the call, the radio sprang into life.

« Bonjour, ceci est la Capitainerie, Ouistreham. La petite embarcation sur le point d'entrer dans le canal Orne, identifiez vous s'il vous plaît. »

"Oh shit," said Jason, "I don't speak French; do you Mark?"

"Only a bit." With that he pressed the transmit button and said, "Pardon monsieur, Je n'ai pas beaucoup français, donc en anglais s'il vous plaît."

The voice changed to heavily French accented English. "Bienvenu, zis is ze 'arbour Mastaire of ze Port of Ouistreham. We 'ave your small cwaft on our wadar.Pleeze can you schange to schannel cent-cinquante-six point six. Vous comprenez? You understand zis?"

Mark said, *"Oui Monsieur, je comprends*. I am changing to channel one-five-six-point-six."

He changed the channel setting on the handheld VHF transceiver. The Harbour Master called again. This time he said, “Small cwaft, you weel identify ze name of your vessel pleez?”
Mark was about to reply but didn’t press the transmit button. Instead he turned to Jason and said, “What’s the name of this boat Jase?”
“How the fuck should I know Mark?”
“Well don’t just stand there, shit for brains, take a look over the stern and see what she’s called. We should’ve known this. Quickly, for pity’s sake.”
Jason ran to the stern and hung over as far as he could to see what the name was.
The harbourmaster repeated his request. Mark thumbed the ‘transmit’ button a couple of times to cause what he hoped sounded like interference and make the harbourmaster think he was having a little transmission trouble.
“You are ‘aving a little probleme wiz ze radio, no?”
Jason shouted back, “It’s called *Lady of the Mist*. This time he pressed the transmit button and said, “*Pardon Monsieur*, we are called *Lady of the Mist*.”
Judging by the state of the female company the boat owner had with him when they had met, Mark thought the boat should be called more like *Lady on the Piss……..*
“Merci. Pleez be standing by for ze ferzer instwuctions.”
Hello, what’s this? thought Mark. A bit unusual, we’re only a private boat.
The ‘further instructions’ were soon forthcoming, this time in much better English, although with quite a heavy accent.
“*Lady of the Mist*, this is Caen Customs, please be advised that we are conducting routine searches of small vessels entering the port of Caen. As soon as you have entered the port channel, please ‘heave to’ and wait for the arrival of the port customs vessel which will meet you within the next few minutes. Please confirm your understanding of this message.”
“Message received and understood,” replied Mark. But even as he said this, his heart was hammering away inside his chest. Jason had heard the conversation and was looking at Mark with his mouth gaping open.
“This cannot be happening,” said Mark. “I just don’t believe our sodding luck - not only do we get pulled on the way down here but now this - I can’t believe this is just coincidence. Why would they stop a piddling little boat for a ‘random check’?”
“We are going to get nicked and this means a long stretch in choky,” moaned Jason.
“Not if we are quick off the mark, I’ve taken precautions. I’ll just get the tank with the stuff in, you make sure the rope’s tied off to a cleat amidships, while I keep watch for the customs boat. Before you do though, let’s wait until we see which way their boat comes from and then we’ll throw the tank over the other side, out of sight.

With any luck, it'll just look like a rope holding a fender hanging over the side. In fact, I'll put a fender over the side nearest the customs boat as well."

When he had prepared the fender to put over the side, Mark went below to get the aluminium tank which held the drugs and took it back up into the wheelhouse. He gave it to Jason and said, "Tie it on very securely, we don't want this to sink without getting it back." Jason picked up the end of a rope which was in a pile on the deck and tied the tank with a couple of knots to be sure it would be secure.

Mark looked back down the channel towards the landing stage which was getting closer but couldn't see any craft that looked like an official launch. The engines were still running but with the propeller disengaged and in neutral, they were drifting very slightly. When he looked round towards the port entrance which they had just passed, he was horrified to see the customs boat closing quickly from their port side.

He called to Jason, "Quick, chuck it over the starboard side Jase."

"Which one's that Mark?"

"The right hand side for Christ's sake," he yelled and quickly threw a fender over the port side. Jason hastily threw the metal tank over the starboard side away from the boat, which was coming from their port stern quarter.

The tank went in with a splash and quickly sank from view. It was moving towards the stern and Mark saw that the splash would not have been seen from the customs boat, especially as the topsides of the Jeanneau were fairly high which would have screened it. He gave a sigh of relief and said, "Let's just be very polite to them and let them search every nook and cranny. No clever remarks or attempt at humour because the French don't have our sense of humour and they could take anything the wrong way which could land us in even deeper shit than we might be."

"Right, I'll keep schtum," said Jason.

Finally, the customs boat pulled alongside and the Captain called to them in his quite heavy accent. "Bonjour messieurs, as we are so close to the landing stage ahead, I request you to make for this and tie up there. We will conduct a routine search at this place."

Mark replied, "Would it be possible to do the search here as there is no other traffic and the tide is about to run?"

"As I said, monsieur, please proceed to the landing stage. We have to be quick as we need to complete this inspection before we have not enough draught to return to base. It will be quicker to do this at the landing stage."

Mark was about to ask again, but Jason said, "Don't piss 'em off Mark, for Christ's sake - let's do what he wants."

"Very well, we will proceed to the landing stage," said Mark to the Captain.

"Merci monsieur, we will be ahead of you, please follow."

Mark then engaged the engines and put the throttles ahead slightly to follow a little astern of the customs boat.
As their boat began to move and gather speed, there was a dull heavy 'thud', followed by a shudder from the stern. The starboard engine warning light came on indicating that an engine had stalled.
"What the hell was that?"
"I don't know but it doesn't sound good Mark," said Jason. "Have we hit something?"
"Unless we've caught some piece of driftwood or something like that, I don't know what that was. Hang on Jason and just make sure that the tank is ok on that rope. Don't make it obvious though and I'll just keep moving without rushing."
Going to the starboard side, Jason pulled the rope attached to the tank. It was tight and would not come up when he pulled; "it's stuck on something," he said.
"What do you mean, *stuck on something*?"
"I can't pull it up, that's what I mean," Jason answered.
"For fuck sake Jason, pull it harder - we have to get that tank back. It can't be stuck; it's only hanging over the side." Realising that it would have been trailing toward the stern, Mark just let out a long, painful groan, "Oh noooo, don't tell me it's caught round the prop! How long was the rope you tied on to the tank?"
"I don't know - it was quite long; it was the one lying by the side of the tank when you brought it up."
"You mean that thick one or the fender rope....?" After saying this, Mark looked across to where the rope he had prepared earlier was still lying on the deck. "YOU STUPID - FUCKING - IDIOT!" cried Mark whilst trying to keep his voice down. You've gone and tied it on to the mooring rope, you fucking dork! Couldn't you see the fender rope I'd left out? If that thicker mooring rope's gone round the prop, it's no wonder the bloody thing has stopped the engine."
"Well I don't know which rope is which, do I?" whined Jason. "How am I supposed to know the difference?"
"Oh Christ -.Just take over the wheel, keep the bloody boat straight and I'll go and take a look."
Mark went to the stern and looked over at the starboard side where there was no turbulence coming from the stationary propeller. He leaned over as far as he could and then he noticed some rope snaking out from under the stern.
The rope was idly wafting around in the water with a frayed end, but no tank – gone, sunk, lying on the sea bed most likely!
Mark was completely stunned. His whole body went cold. His head buzzed and his blood pressure rocketed.
"What's the problem?" shouted Jason. He had a worried look on his face as he knew that Mark was in a really bad temper this time.
"Oh nothing," said Mark with an idle shrug. "Just that the fucking tank has gone! You tied the tank to the long mooring rope which got sucked into the prop and that thud we heard was the tank being smashed against the hull and then ripped off. Thanks a fucking

million you stupid half-witted, shit-for-brains moron. We've just lost a quarter of a million quid's worth of coke and you say, 'what's the problem'?
"How was I to know it was the wrong rope, I'm not used to boats am I?" And... what's more, you never fucking told me which one to use so it's not all my fault Mark!
Mark couldn't answer him, partly because he was so appalled by what had happened and partly because he actually realised that it was his fault for not checking something which he knew he should have done. Jason had no idea which rope to use. He'd not made it clear to him. This didn't help the situation one little bit.
They had a stalled engine and had, in all probability, a propeller with yards of rope tightly packed around the shaft. Not to mention the likelihood that the tank had whipped up against the hull, hence the 'heavy thud' they'd heard.
"Now what do we do?" said Jason, looking to Mark for answers.
"You mean after I fucking kill you?" snapped Mark. "We'll have to get to the landing stage and do what they say. We've nothing to hide now, have we?"
Jason then said, quietly, "You don't want to look over the back Mark."
"Why, is there someone else coming after us?"
"No, but I think the tank must have split, 'cos there are packets floating on the surface."
Looking over the stern, Mark was totally horrified to see a number of white coloured polythene packets floating to the surface in the boat's wake.
"WHAT THE FUCK! This can't be happening! We'd be better off just giving ourselves up now because we've had it. They're bound to see them and I don't think they'll be saying, *"ello, 'ello, wot is zis zen'*?" It's bloody obvious to anybody. So, not only have I lost the whole shipment worth two hundred and fifty grand, but if those are spotted, there's a bloody good chance that we'll be banged up for bringing in drugs and if, with a very big IF, we're lucky and they don't spot them, this boat is not ours remember. Not only that but the prop is probably jammed-to-fuck and we're going to have one hell of a job to get it cleared, if at all. We're supposed to get it back to the pontoon tonight as if nothing has happened. If by some chance we don't get nicked, we may have to get back there on one engine. So no problem then!"
"Hold on Mark, look over the back. The packets, they're going towards the sea aren't they?"
Mark looked carefully and judged the movement of the packets that were now littering the surface and realised that Jason may be right.
"The tide must have turned and it's running now. With any luck at all, and we sure as shit need some, by the time these *Frenchies* have finished checking things, they'll have gone back out of the channel towards the coast and they won't see them. Thank Christ they went ahead of us!"

"We'll just have to keep them nattering a bit longer or hold them up somehow," said Jason, "that'll give more time for the tide to take those packets further out to sea."
"You could be right for once Jason. That's probably the only sensible thing I've heard you say," said Mark.
By this time, they were approaching the landing stage and when they had come alongside the pontoon and put the mooring lines in position, the coastguard officers came up to Mark and they shook hands. Mark said as nonchalantly as he could, "Please take all the time you need to check everything. I realise you have a job to do to catch possible drug smugglers and other illegal goings on."
Looking at both Mark and Jason standing in the cabin, the customs officer said, "*Merci Messieurs*, we will check the boat thoroughly including the engine compartment now that they are turned off?" It is better, because sometimes we can be burned when there is not much space and the engines are hot."
"Of course, *bien sur messieurs'*," said Mark throwing a couple of French words that he actually knew the meaning of. "Can we offer you a coffee, we don't have anything else I'm afraid?"
"*Mais non, Monsieur*, it is kind of you but we do not have time to accept your offer. As you can see, the tide has turned and the flow is increasing."
Mark had indeed seen this and was hoping like hell that the flow was taking the incriminating packets which were now quite a way behind them, out to sea. It was his only chance to get away without becoming a victim of the stringent laws against drug smuggling. He thought, disconsolately, at least we won't be caught with any drugs on the boat. After that, he had an even brighter thought; they can't prove that they came from us. Not that it was much consolation considering he'd just lost a fortune but it would sure as hell have made them suspicious if they'd seen them floating away from the vicinity and out to sea.
The customs officers made a thorough search of all parts of the boat and when they had finished, the Captain came up to Mark and said, "*Merci Monsieur,* everything is completely in order. We are sorry to have held you up. You may now continue your voyage and we wish you a very pleasant stay in France. Are you berthing overnight or moving on?"
"We have not decided yet. We may stay or perhaps we will move to another port."
"If you do decide to move, then perhaps you should not leave it too long as the tide is running, although I think your craft does not need too much depth."
"We will meet our friend at the Brasserie and then decide," said Mark.
"Very well *monsieur*, whatever your decision, we wish you *Bon Voyage."* He then returned to the customs boat, which then left the landing stage and made its way towards the port entrance.

Mark thought, 'just don't go too bloody fast and catch up with those packets...'

When the customs boat had disappeared behind the ferry port sea wall, Mark turned and said, "Right Jason, get your kit off and jump over the side. Take this knife with you and cut that rope off the prop."
'DO BLOODY WHAT!' shouted Jason. "You're mad, I can't go in that water, it's fucking freezing!"
"Right, now that would be a blessing," said Mark, "so stop being a tosser and get over the stern. We've got to clear this prop or we'll be chugging around in the middle of the channel being chucked about at half speed and trying to avoid all those sodding great tankers. If we don't get back, just to complete the picture, we could face a charge of boat theft."
"Yeah, but they're big enough to see and they have lights on don't they?"
"Don't be a complete muppet, they wouldn't see us - they're probably too busy playing with their iPods or PlayStations to be looking out for a small boat. Anyway they wouldn't stop for us or rather, they can't anyway. You don't do an emergency stop with a sixty thousand ton ship going at fifteen knots so stop moaning and get over the side and cut that bloody rope free. I'm going to the brasserie to meet our contact and tell him the 'good news' - I don't think he'll be too pleased and I'll be lucky if he doesn't beat me to a pulp thanks to you! At least I'll be in a restaurant with other witnesses if he does try anything so be prepared for me to be back here bloody quickly if he does," and with that, Mark left for the brasserie. He walked up to the where his contact would be waiting who, as soon as he saw him, immediately recognised Mark as he approached and gave him a welcoming smile. *"Ah, mon ami, bienvenu, eet is so good to see you! You 'ave somsing for moi, oui?"* As soon as his contact spoke, Mark knew this was not going to go well. These people expect things to be done properly and things were sure to be going downhill at a rate of knots! Mark could imagine that the welcoming smile with the big white teeth would soon manifest into a snarling smile with even bigger white teeth.
"You 'ave som of ze trouble wiz ze Douanes je pense but zey go so you 'ave not ze trouble, oui?"
"Let us just say that I 'had' something for you and no, the Customs did not find anything because there was nothing to find."
"Wot is zis? You 'ave ze drugs but zey do - I am not 'ow you say, 'of ze comprennez' – zey do not find zem, oui?"
"Yes, no, er, *oui*, they didn't find them because they are at the bottom of the sea."
"Wot? Zey are not wiz you? Mon dieu!"
"No, and I can't explain, it is too complicated. I have lost the drugs because of a problem with ropes."

"You 'ave ze probleme wiz ze ropes. You do not 'ave ze packages zat we agree? Merde!"
"No, I mean yes, they are lost. I am sorry but I cannot deliver them so I must go back and get another supply. I will contact you again when I have this problem fixed. Do you understand?"
"Oui, I sink I understand, but Monsieur, I tell you, I am not 'appy. You give me big problem.'
"Believe me, your problem is not as big as my problem but I will make things right again, I will contact you soon."
"I sink you are in 'mauvaise humeur' monsieur, so I go now to my people an' tell zem ze problem."
With this exchange, Mark made his way back to the boat to see what progress Jason had made with cutting the rope free under the stern.
Jason had taken a large cork-handled floating knife and looked over the stern at the green water. He could see quite a way down and it seemed clearer than the typical water colour back home but he was still not looking forward to being in it.
He climbed over the stern and, very reluctantly, dropped into the sea. Taking a deep breath he pushed himself down to the propeller, holding his breath as long as he could. He held on to the rudder to keep himself down while desperately trying to cut away the rope which was, as they suspected, very tightly compressed around the propeller shaft. It took him a great many tries and repeated resurfacing for fresh, deep breaths to cut away small sections of the 1 ½" mooring rope.
During this diving and cutting, he noticed a deep gash on the hull just forward of the propeller shaft where it entered the hull and thought to himself, 'This must have been when the metal tank was smashed against the hull – that must have been the noise we heard. Doesn't look too bad I suppose. I won't mention it to Mark 'cos he'll just give me another bollocking and anyway I'm too bloody tired.'
After about half an hour, completely exhausted and extremely cold, he finally managed to cut the rope from the propeller and surfaced for the last time. He looked up at the boat from the waterline and then realised that he could not get back up the topsides. It was too high for him to reach the coaming strake which ran along the edge of the deck and would give him a handhold. 'Oh Christ, he thought, I'm going to die of cold - where the hell is Mark?' He swam around and eventually realised that he could actually climb on to the landing stage. 'Thank fuck for that,' he said to himself' Finally back on to the boat and shivering uncontrollably, he had great difficulty in putting his clothes back on over his damp body as there was no towel on board. Feeling really sorry for himself, he just wanted to be back home as soon as he could.
He had just managed to get some clothes on but was still shivering when Mark came back looking. like thunder. "Chummy was not pleased, to put it mildly," growled Mark, "but then it wasn't his fucking money that's been lost. It's mine! He's got to take the dosh

back to his dealer and tell him what's happened. I don't know what the hell to do now."
All they could do now was to make passage back to Christchurch and try to find some way of obtaining another supply of drugs to repair some of the damage that had been done to his reputation.

CHAPTER 6

Setting a course for Christchurch, Mark and Jason left the port at Ouistreham on a sea that was noticeably rougher than their initial crossing and which caused their speed to be somewhat reduced this time as they were only making around 20 knots. Visibility was considerably reduced too. The tide change had affected their course so to overcome a potential drift towards the Atlantic, they had to take a diagonal heading which made the crossing longer than they'd anticipated.

After about an hour, Mark said to Jason, "She seems to be making hard work of this, the speed is dropping and now we're only doing about 15 knots - I'm going to take a look at the engines. Take the wheel and for pity's sake just keep your eyes open everywhere and make sure you keep to the compass heading that I've set it to. If you see anything at all, and I mean anything, that you don't like the look of, for fuck sake give me a yell - we've got enough trouble as it is without anything else happening."

"Got it Mark. Don't worry; I'll keep my eyes open."

"It's not your eyes that worry me, it's your wits," retorted Mark.

Mark opened the hatch and stepped down into the large compartment where the two big Cummins engines were roaring. Although these big diesels were giving out something like 450 hp, Marks' experience with powerful boats told him this boat was not performing as expected. Everything seemed to be ok but as he was about to go back up to the cockpit, he saw water sloshing about at the stern of the engine space. 'What the hell is that' he thought. 'There shouldn't be water here.'

He opened the small hatch to the stern section where the propeller shaft exited the hull and the rudder gear was located, and he got a shock. There was a significant depth of water there which meant that they had a leak! No wonder the boat didn't seem right; she was now well down at the stern, with the weight of water which had been taken on. Realising that they may have a leaking stern gland where the propeller shaft exited the hull. That's all we need! That could've been caused by the rope round the prop shaft. He thought quickly; let's get the bilge pump operating and keep it on automatic. That should keep things ok until we get back. 'What the heck could have caused the?...hold on...the tank. Of course! That was the loud thump and bang that we heard when the tank and rope got snarled up.

Shit, shit, shit, shit!' yelled Mark. He quickly went back up to the helm, closing the engine hatch behind him. Switching on the bilge pump, he said to Jason, "I hope to Christ this thing can keep sucking out the water that's coming in below or we'll have to swim back."

"What do you mean Mark – we're sinking? Water coming in below? Christ Almighty - you know I can't swim!" shrieked Jason.

"Then you'll have to learn bloody fast, won't you. We've got a leaking hull now and I thought things couldn't get worse. I guess the

tank was smacked against the hull, and it's caused either a hole or a split in the hull – I just hope the bilge pump will take care of it but I'll have to keep checking it. I wish to fuck I'd kept to stamp collecting! Surely things just can't get worse, we've had it all now; I've lost all the coke, I'm now up to my eyeballs in debt and now we've got a sinking boat. What the hell else is there?"
"I meant to mention it to you earlier," said Jason.
"Mention what?"
"Well, when I was underwater trying to cut the rope free, I saw this big mark in the hull."
"'A big mark on the hull'. What sort of A BIG FUCKING mark Jason - how big was it?'
"It was about two feet long, a sort of split. It looked like it could have been the tank that banged into it."
"About two feet long and how deep was it?"
"I couldn't really see but it was quite deep and there were little bits of what looked like netting or fibres coming out of the split."
"You stupid-fucking-idiotic-twat!" yelled Mark. "Let me get this straight - you saw this damage to the hull and you didn't think to tell me - just what sort of lunatic are you? You do realise don't you that we could actually sink with damage like this. If you saw stuff coming out of it, it's a fucking HOLE! Jesus wept! If that bilge pump can't handle the water coming in, this sodding boat will fill up, the engines will stop, we'll have to send out a Mayday signal and we'll be sinking in the middle of the English bloody Channel. Either that or we just let her sink with us in it! Fucking wonderful! You must be the most stupid bloody twonk in creation! I just cannot believe that anyone can be so short of any sort of common sense as you. I have decided on something and I won't tell you what, but you'll bloody soon find out, believe me."
"I'm sorry Mark."
"Sorry, SORRY!" screamed Mark. "Sorry is something a banker says to his customers who have lost their pensions because he's been a twat but he still manages to walk away with a nice fat golden handshake, but you - you, my friend, are going to walk away with something very different, just you wait and see. Christ Jason, I'm so fucking angry with you!"
Jason had been dreading Marks' reaction and now he was very worried indeed. He had seen Marks' temper but was now seeing a side of him that had been previously hidden by his usual easy-going attitude to everything. Now things were completely different and Jason was becoming worried; in fact, he had become really scared of Mark and with good reason.
As Mark knew the entrance to Christchurch Harbour well, he was able to find the marker buoys without a problem. He said to Jason, "At least I know this entrance. The sandbars keep changing with the tides and the marker buoys aren't always showing the right channel. It would be just our final piece of bad luck to be stuck on a sandbar looking like complete twats, ready for the police to spot us and

make enquiries. Then they'd find out that this boat was stolen and we'd be nicked."
"At least we'd be nicked in England," said Jason in a meek attempt to placate Mark.
"Have you ever been strangled before Jason?" said Mark.
Jason made no reply, choosing instead to try and keep Mark off his back.
Eventually reaching Christchurch Harbour without further mishap, although very late due to their reduced speed, they slowly motored up the river Stour to Tuckton and manoeuvred to berth on the pontoon at the Marine Auction.
With Mark carefully approaching the dock, Jason jumped onto the floating pontoon, and made the mooring ropes fast to the bollards.
Switching off the engines and bilge pump, Mark left the boat and went into the office and, finding Keith, one of the employees, said, "Have you seen Frank around, is he here?"
"No Mark, he went out this afternoon with another bloke and I don't know when he'll be back. Sorry mate."
"Thank Christ for that. Never mind, just get the heavy-lift crane out and take that Jeanneau out of the water; take Ben with you. There's a bloody great hole under the stern which needs some very quick repairs before the owner comes down. The last thing I want is trouble from him now, so get to it pronto," ordered Mark with not a please or thank you in sight.
"We'll have to get a fibreglass specialist in to see to it Mark - we don't have the gear for those sorts of repairs."
"I don't care if you have to hire a troupe of dancing girls and a herd of elephants, just do the fucking job Okay!"
Saying nothing, Keith knew Mark well enough not to argue with him when he was in a bad mood and marched off to find Ben.
He found him at the end of the large auction shed and called to him.
"Hey, Ben, leave whatever you're doing and come with me straight away. We have to lift the Jeanneau out and get some repairs done, '*tout bloody suite*', Mark's in a bad mood. Can you get the heavy crane to begin lifting the boat? I'll get the support frames ready"
"Okay Keith, on my way. I'll get the big slings ready."
Ben went to move the heavy crane while Keith moved the hull supports into place on the concrete hard-standing.
After fitting the large slings around the hull of the Jeanneau, they attached them to the crane's lifting gear and she was carefully lifted out of the water and onto the support structure so that they could make their inspection of the damage to the stern.
"What the hell caused that?"' said Keith.
"It must have taken a hell of a whack to cause that sort of damage and it can't have been from hitting anything or it would be at the bow not the stern."
"You're right there Ben. I don't think I'll ask Mark just at the moment, he's in no mood to talk about it by the sounds of it."
"Yeah, I think I'll give him a wide berth as well."

When the boat was safely cradled on the dock and Keith had contacted a fibreglass specialist to arrange for urgent repairs, he saw that Frank had arrived back at the Office. Frank had already seen Mark...

CHAPTER 7

"Oh, you're back - I was wondering where you'd got to. How'd it go?" Enquired Frank
"You'll never believe what happened Dad! You know we had that stop on the motorway on the way down? That wasn't a problem, we were actually sound on that. After we left you, we got to Caen with no more trouble but when we were about to get to the landing stage by the brasserie where we should have met the courier who had the money to pay for the 'goods' the damn port office called on the radio telling us that there was a bloody French Customs boat on its' way to meet us. Can you believe that?"
"And did they get to you or were you quick enough?"
"Quick? - Quick? We had no time; they just appeared from round the end of the port sea-wall. They were there in less than five minutes. I was crapping myself! We had only just enough time to throw the tank with the 'cargo' in, over the side."
"So they didn't get anything then, the boat was clean?"
"It was, but then that stupid twat Jason had only gone and tied the tank to a fucking mooring line hadn't he? Big enough rope to hold a bloody tanker, not the proper one I'd put out to use."
"And did you check it first?" asked Frank.
"You have to believe me Dad, there was no time."
"Well, never mind, at least you didn't lose the cargo, so what's the problem?"
"The Customs boat people told us to go ahead to the landing stage because the tide was dropping. I did ask if they could do the search where we were but they said no, so we had no choice but to go ahead and follow their orders. Then, because dopey bollocks had tied the wrong rope, the tank trailed behind the boat and the rope was sucked into the prop and wrapped around the prop shaft. This must have caused the tank to smash into the hull, splitting it and the hull open."
"So you lost the tank then?"
"Yes, it probably dropped to the sea bed," said Mark.
"But they didn't get any drugs then - if they didn't find anything, you're in the clear."
"But can you believe it? The packets had floated to the surface for Christ's sake!"
"But the French Customs didn't see this or you'd be in their hands right now, wouldn't you?"
"No thank God because they'd gone ahead of us. I can't tell you how much we were shitting ourselves with a dozen or so packets floating out on the tide."
"So how come they missed them?" pressed Frank.
"The tide had changed and they just floated away from us, past the harbour wall and off out to the open sea. The Customs blokes didn't see them - the only piece of 'luck' I've had today."

"You were bloody lucky there son," ventured Frank, so tell me how much you've lost on this deal."
"I was in for £180,000 and was due to get £300,000."
"But you've just done a deal with that painting haven't you? That must have put you in the clear."
"Yeah, but I cleared £200,000 after expenses, so I'm down to £20,000."
"Then you're in the shit aren't you, my son?"
"At the moment, but I have another painting being copied and Yaren should be finalising the sale on that so when that's done, I should get back on track."
"You're a lucky fucker, aren't you?" said his father. "I think it sounds like you have a problem with Jason though."
"I know. I think we must do something about him, he's a liability and he knows far too much about our trips to France."
"Does he know about the paintings scam as well Mark?" said Frank.
"Yes, but I don't know exactly how much although I think he has a pretty good idea."
"How's that then - have you been opening your mouth? I told you to keep that side of things to yourself, didn't I?"
"I know, but he was with me once when I went to see Yaren on my way back from London and I think she must have said something to him when I wasn't in the room. I can't be sure, but he made a remark to me later which made me think he knew something about it."
Frank said, "I agree. He knows too much. He's a problem that has to be sorted; leave that to me. I know someone who might be able to help, and while we're at it, what's that Jeanneau 25 doing up on the dock?"
"Oh that, I asked Keith and Ben to lift it out of the water to see what damage was caused when the metal tank I told you about was smashed against the hull. It definitely put a split in it, so I'm getting it fixed pronto before Mr 'weekend secretary shagger', Fortune comes down to use it again."
"Christ, can you do anything else wrong? You're a walking disaster. That's all we need, a very irate customer who has left his very expensive boat with us and we, or rather you and that twat Jason, have buggered it up."
"He won't notice a thing when it's repaired and covered in anti-fouling paint. He won't even see any damage once it's back on the water."
"That's if he doesn't decide to come down for another dirty weekend with his secretary, or a different one for that matter, just get it fixed. We don't need any more problems - you just seem to create them by the bucket-load! Get out of my sight; you're nothing but trouble at the moment. Just piss off and get it sorted."
Mark went off with his tail between his legs, mentally working out what he had to do. He had to return to London to do some 'business' to try to rectify the problem of the drugs loss. There was

another painting copy which had to be shipped and until that was completed and paid for, there was a definite 'cash flow' problem.
***
What Mark did not know was that a local birdwatcher was on the beach opposite where all the action in Caen was happening. He became interested in what was going on and took some photographs of the boats involved. He had a telephoto lens on his camera and then he also noticed the packets floating away from *The Lady in the Mist*. He took several shots of these thinking it was unusual, especially as the Customs boat was there and the men in charge of each boat seemed to be having a dialogue. As a result, when he went into a local bar, he later remarked to a friend who was a local police officer what he'd seen. The officer thought this was unusual as well and asked the birdwatcher if he would email the photographs he'd taken to his local station for them to look over just in case they might show anything of interest. He did this when he returned home, downloading the digital photographs to his computer. The photos he had taken very clearly showed the white packets floating away from the boat, as well as showing the name on the stern of the boat. The local policeman realised the implications of these photographs and subsequently, these details were passed to the authorities in England as a matter of course.

CHAPTER 8

She was making some lunch at her flat when there was a knock on the door. She was expecting her boyfriend at some point during the day, but he had a key, so she was wondering who that might be.
As she opened the door, a man with dark brown hair and looked perhaps around 50 years old with a dark complexion stood there.
He was wearing a black leather jacket and blue jeans. He did not look pleasant.
"You are Yaren Ganim?'
"Yes, she said, who are you? What do you want?"
"Is anyone else here?"
"No, my boyfriend lives here but he is out at the moment, he will be back very soon."
"When is he coming?"
"I said, very soon. Who are you? What is this all about?"
"That does not matter. It is you I want to see."
"Who are you? What do you want with me?"
His manner became very aggressive and he roughly pushed her back into the flat. She was very worried now. "Leave me alone. Get out now"
"Where is the money?"
"I don't know what you mean. I don't have any money. I don't know what you are talking about."
"My boss wants his money back. This was paid in cash and I need to have the money back."
She became suddenly really scared. She had no idea who this man was. He was a complete stranger. It was her boyfriend who had despatched a painting shipment to Italy. He had received money from this to buy drugs. Having just been over to France and he had come back in a very bad mood. Perhaps something had gone wrong. Maybe that was why they had been rowing recently. She did not want to become more involved. Knowing that he was dealing in drugs and there had been a large quantity in the flat just recently and now this had gone. She also was involved because she knew of his activities. Things were beginning to make sense now.
The stranger was now very angry. "Don't give me that, I know you have the money. Where is it kept?"
"I've told you, I don't know about any money. What money? There is nothing here."
'The money you were paid for the painting.'
"There is nothing here," she said again.
"I don't believe you," he said and pushed her onto the sofa.
"I'm going to call the police," she said in a tremulous voice.

"I don't think that would be wise, just sit there and shut up."
"You can't keep me here," she said, "I don't know what you are talking about."

"Oh, I think you do,' he said, 'I know very well that there is a very large sum of money which you took, and it was in cash so I know it wouldn't be in the bank, so where is it, where is it hidden ?"
"I keep telling you, it isn't here, I don't know where any money is."
He grabbed a dining chair and moved it across the room. He had spotted a roll of packing tape on the desk in the corner of the room where it looked as though some parcelling had been done recently. He said, 'Sit on this chair.'
"No, you can't make me, I won't."
With that, he reached out and punched her hard on the side of her head. She reeled under the blow, her head ringing. As she fell to the side, semi-conscious, he caught her and pulled her onto the chair. He quickly wound some of the strong tape around her body so that she was firmly strapped to the chair. He bound her ankles together, then tore off a strip, and roughly put this over her mouth. She gave him a terrified look as she realised that this man was not going to treat her well.
He left her strapped to the chair and completely immobilised while he ransacked the flat, looking in all the likely places that a large amount of money might be hidden. He ripped out the drawers from a chest at one side of the room and pulled all the books off the shelves, together with all the various items that were displayed. There were several sculptures which were not the usual sort of tatty bits and pieces that would be found on shelves, but she was an art lover and she had built up a substantial collection of ceramic sculptures. As they smashed to the ground, she was sobbing and had a terrible headache. She was groaning at the sight of her collection being destroyed but no sound came out as the tape over her mouth prevented any escape from her lips.
He was systematically destroying her flat by ripping up anything that he could. She desperately wanted her boyfriend to come back but she had no idea where he was or when he might come.
The intruder came back to and ripped the tape from her mouth in one swift and violent movement. This was painful, "I will ask you one more time, where is the money?"
She was a very tough woman, coming from a harsh upbringing in Turkey, but now she was very afraid of this violent and aggressive man and she realised that she had no way of escaping his rage.
"I can't tell you anything. I don't know anything."
He took out a short length of what looked like steel tube from inside his jacket pocket. "This might convince you to tell me."
She looked at the bar and realised that she was going to be hurt. This man will not take 'no' for an answer. She said, "Please, I know nothing about the money."
He grinned. "Ah, you said 'the' money. That means that you know about it, so just tell me where it is and I can leave you alone. If you don't tell me, I am going to hurt you."
"If I knew, I would tell you. How many times do I have to say this, I don't know where it is."

With that, he hit her hard across the thigh with the bar. She screamed with the pain. "Tell me or I will do that again."
"I can't," she said crying. He hit her again but this time, much harder. Her leg was numb but she screamed as the pain coursed through her body.
"Tell me; is it here in this flat?"
She was mumbling almost incoherently now, "I don't know, Ben Tanrı aşkına, bilmiyorum, bilmiyorum."
"What did you say? Was that where the money is?"
"No, no, no," she said, "I just said, for God's sake I don't know."
"But you said something I couldn't understand, what was it?"
"I've just told you what I said, it was in Turkish. I just said I really don't know."
He hit her again, with the iron bar. This time, on her side. She felt and heard a rib crack. The pain shot through her like a bolt of lightning. She screamed again with the pain.
"You still won't tell me?" he growled.
"I don't know, I can't tell you anything," she cried, moaning with the pain.
He hit her again, this time on the other side of her body. The pain lanced through her as a crack meant another rib had shattered. She was on the point of passing out with the pain.
"You must know something. I will give you one more chance. Where is your boyfriend, was he involved with the painting?"
She could barely speak, but she said with great difficulty through the haze of pain, "All I know is that he is out on business but he did have some involvement with the painting but I don't know about any money."
She felt that she was betraying her boyfriend, but she was so terrified that she was now telling whatever she knew to stop this man from hurting her any more.
"So where is your boyfriend now?"
"I keep telling you, I don't know. All I know is that he goes down to the South Coast where his father has a business."
"Give me the address and phone number of this business."
"I don't have the address or the phone number, he has never given me this but I know that it is a Marine Auction business in Christchurch, near Bournemouth."
"Enough, I have no more time to waste on you. You are of no use to me." He smashed her across the face again with the steel bar. This snapped her head to one side and left a deep bruise to her once-beautiful face.
She was semi-conscious and turned her head and his eyes locked on to hers with an ominous hardness to them. He reached into his jacket and he pulled out a handgun. She froze completely at this. He took from a pocket a black cylinder about 8 inches long. This was his favourite 'toy', a silencer or a suppressor. Slowly screwing this on to the muzzle of the Glock 30SF .45 calibre pistol, he stared at her with cold, hard eyes.

Now she was completely terrified and the look on her face was of utter disbelief at what was about to happen. She did not even have time to pray to her God, as he pointed the suppressed gun at her. Without pausing, he shot her at point black range. He was using sub-sonic ammunition and there was a quite gentle sound, almost like a sharp cough.
Her head jerked backward sharply. A small entry wound in the centre of her forehead was insignificant compared to the haze of blood, bone and brain matter which had sprayed from the large exit wound on the back of her head. She slumped sideways on the chair and toppled over.
"Che spreco di tempo," he said, "what a waste of time." Not in the least bit concerned that perhaps the gunshot may have been heard, although very unlikely, and with a final check around to make sure that there would be no trace of him and then, without a backward look he went out of the flat, closing the door quietly behind him and removing his gloves as he did so. He walked casually down Enmore Road turning right into Birchanger Road.
This was a different way to how he'd found her flat after leaving Norwood Junction station. He considered that he was non-descript enough to not stand out if anyone had seen him and, the likelihood of being noticed on both routes was small, and as he had not used a taxi, he could not be traced.
That was how he worked, leaving no traces. Now he needed to get down to Christchurch and was making his way back to the station where he knew he could get a direct train. George Manion, or Giorgio Manini, which was his real name, was keen to bring this part of his task to a close. He just wanted to find the money and return it to his Boss in Italy.
Once he was on the train, he had time to think back to what had just taken place. He felt no remorse – 'why should I', he thought to himself; 'this is my work, it's what I do – it's what I've always done since I was a child, only then it was just practicing.'
***
As a young boy, Giorgio was considered a 'different' child, and he was at odds with the world he lived in. He found it difficult to relate to the friends few he had and was often left alone because these friends didn't know how to be with him, often feeling intimidated by, and frightened, by his strange behaviour. To Giorgio, this was nothing to him. He had only one person he cared for and that was his beloved mother. Unfortunately for her and for Giorgio, her husband was an abusive man; Giorgio hated him and believed that one day he, Giorgio, would save his mother from this abusive, drunken beast.
He had a thing about injury, pain and death – somehow it thrilled him, it gave him pleasure! Often, as a child, he would use his catapult to fire at small animals and birds. Then, if he hadn't killed them, he would finish them off with his bare hands or tread on them. Here was pleasure, here was the control that he had over a

living thing and during those moments, he could imagine himself having control over his father in such a way that it would give his mother some peace.
As he reached puberty, he was thinking more and more about how he could achieve this. But his family life was not what he thought it was; in reality, his 'father' was not his true father. He did not know this and in fact, he never knew the truth about his parentage.
Louisa, his mother, was 19 at the time of Giorgio's birth and to be a young girl, unmarried with a young son, was a shameful situation.
An attractive woman living in southern Tuscany, she worked as a cleaner, for a rich Italian family. What she needed now was the stability of a husband who earned good money and who would take care of her and her baby.
Eventually, she found Luigi who promised he would look after her and her son and, although not particularly good looking and quite a bit older than her, she saw the potential of him giving her the security and home she needed. They married and settled into his small *casa*, which was really an apartment in the house where he was born. Very quickly, her idea of him being the one to look after her became the stuff of nightmares. She never knew what he did for a job but he certainly had money although his work was not regular. Unfortunately, he was not about to share any of it with her and she was made to do things for him that she had never even heard of, before he would allow her to have money for shopping of any kind. His drinking became worse and his beatings more severe.
As time passed by, her life became unbearable and she feared for her now, 13-year old son.
She had returned to work as a maid for the family she had worked for when she became pregnant. When Giorgio started school she went back and spoke with the head of the family, whom she had always known as 'Signore Collettore' as he was an avid collector of art and ceramics. She explained her situation. He had shown her much kindness over the years about her marriage; Luigi's drinking, his tormenting of her and their son, the regular abuse. One thing led to another; she told him about her worries over her son's behaviour. It always shocked her to see that when a cat or a dog had been hurt, he would always rush to put it out of its misery. Even more worrying was that he seemed to enjoy doing it. She also felt that he would like to do something to his father, just by the cold, steely look he gave him whenever his father was close by.
"I'm sorry your marriage is not what you hoped for but I don't know what I can do to help. What I will do Louisa, is to talk to Giorgio; see if I can help him in some small way. You know, don't you Louisa, that you are important to me. Despite our secret, I still have feelings for you and this is why I have supported you with money for all this time...you have told no-one have you?"
"Never, never. Thank you so much. You have been so kind to me but I often wonder what would have become of us if I was not who I am, and you were not who you are; the secret between us would

not exist and Giorgio would know his father; but promises were made to protect us both. I will say no more except that I hope you will be able to talk well to Giorgio and help him to overcome whatever demons he may have. I will go now and continue to endure my marriage for his sake until he able to whatever it is that he will do in his life." With that, Louisa turned away, and trailing the other hand as if she was giving him a gentle wave. 'I still love him,' she mouthed to herself as she left the room, closing the door behind her.
Watching her leaving the room, Giorgio's father felt a pang of sadness, knowing that it was never really over between them. His sadness turned into an ache which he instantly dismissed – he knew he could never take things any further, and now he must try to help her son – his son, a boy he found difficult to like, let alone love. He still had feelings and for her sake he must try and help; he could no longer bear to see the pain and anguish she carried every day that she spent with that bastard of a husband. He had an idea that would be useful to him as well, and he knew that his plan would give the boy the strength he needed.
Giorgio was called to attend the big house on the cliff, high above the sea. When he reluctantly turned up at the very grand house full of paintings and sculptures, he was overawed at what he saw. Compared to the very small house he lived in and the conditions that he had to endure, this was another world.
His demeanour was surly to say the least and he'd made it obvious that he did not really want to be there.
"Would you like me to help you to give your mother peace and stop her being hurt?"
"Yes, of course. My mother is always being hurt by my father, especially when he is drunk. And he is always drunk.
"Very well then Giorgio, if I am to help you and your mother, you must call me 'Signore Collettore', will you do that?"
"Si, Signore Collettore."
There followed a very involved 'interrogation' of Giorgio. Signore Collettore was very patient and seemingly kind to him and the answers he received gave a particular insight into Giorgio's demeanour and way of thinking, the reasons why he seemed to like having the power of life and death over creatures and why he felt no remorse or emotion. What Giorgio absolutely did not know was that 'Signore Collettore" was actually Tosco Scarpetti, his biological father, the result of the clandestine affair he and Louisa had had when she was nineteen and was working for Tosco. The secret they shared was sworn on a solemn oath which had been adhered to and Louisa had been made to understand the full consequences should this secret ever be divulged.
Tosco was a very educated and intelligent man and this enabled him to bring insight and understanding of Giorgios physche. He formed the impression that Giorgio had in fact sociopathic tendencies and

revelled in inflicting pain, even to the point of watching something die, showing no emotion whatever.
As Tosco was a mafia 'Don', he had occasion to use 'encouragement' or perhaps force to obtain cooperation from some of the more 'reluctant' people he dealt with. This meant that someone, not himself, had to get their hands dirty to enforce this cooperation. He now was realising that Giorgio had a huge debt to repay for helping his mother over the years and now his plan was to further and strengthen this debt.
"Your father beats your mother doesn't he?" said Tosco.
"Yes Signore Collettore."
"When he has been drinking."
"Yes Signore Collettore."
"And when he is drunk, is he really drunk in the way he might fall down or not be able to do anything?"
"Yes Signore Collettore, he usually falls asleep after beating my mother. She has to go to her bed, usually crying badly. Sometimes she is bleeding and I help to clean her cuts and bruises."
"And do you hate your father?"
"Yes Signore Collettore. I hate him so much, but I don't know how to stop him from hurting my mother."
"And if you could stop him, how would you do it Giorgio?"
"I would kill him. He is so bad. He does not give mother any money and she is always very poor. He spends everything on drink and she has nothing for herself. She never has new clothes or any money to buy me anything. He is a monster to her but nobody seems to care."
"So you would kill him, do you really mean that?"
"Yes. I hate him so much but I don't know how to do it, I am not strong enough."
"Oh, but you are Giorgio. You just need to know the way to do this without anyone knowing. I can help you if you would like me to. Would you like me to help you to have some peace for your mother?"
"Signore Collettore, I would be so grateful and this would make me happy."
Tosco thought, 'I doubt that anything could make this child really happy, but what I am about to suggest will be very useful to me.' Tosco was thinking like a true Mafia 'Don'.
"Very well then, I will have someone come to teach you how to do what you know you have to do to your father for your mothers' sake. He will show you exactly what to do and how to do it, without leaving any traces. That is so important, that you leave no traces. Remember that and you will stay safe."
"Yes Signore Collettore, I will remember that. I will leave no traces."
Tosco arranged further clandestine meetings together with a mafia 'specialist' who trained Giorgio in certain methods of dealing with his 'problem'. When this tutoring was finished, Giorgio had shown that his 'talents' had been very correctly assimilated and confirmed Tosco's thoughts.

Giorgio subsequently carried out that act which freed his mother from her continual abuse and his fathers' death was noted by the police as an 'accident whilst in a drunken stupor'. This meant that Giorgio had indeed left no traces.
Tosco now had a perfect 'hit man' at his beck and call with sworn allegiance whom he could call on for the more 'necessary' actions, wherever and whenever they were needed.

CHAPTER 9

Mark called at Yaren's flat on his way back from London following a few days of negotiations. He had been to see his drugs supplier. As the consignment he had taken to France had been lost he'd had to do some serious explaining as to how this had happened. Not only was his supplier most annoyed but he was extremely reluctant to give Mark any further supplies without payment up front. Explaining about the paintings and that there was another about to be shipped to an unsuspecting customer, the supplier had, albeit reluctantly, agreed to let Mark have a further shipment which he would again move to his dealer in France. This time, he was left under no illusions as to what would happen if the drugs were not paid for when promised. With this in mind, he made his way back to South London where Yaren lived in the flat which Mark had rented for her. He was going to spend the night with her and then go on to the Marine Auctions in Christchurch.
Parking his Porsche not far from the flat, he unlocked the door and went into the vestibule. Climbing the single flight of stairs, he was looking forward to a relaxing night, with a nice Turkish meal, Mardin Köfte, one of his favourites, made with minced lamb with spices. After that, he hoped for a night of relaxation and lovemaking with the girl he was really fond of. He'd had many girlfriends over his adult years and had really fallen for Yaren as she was so different from the usual 'London' girls that he dated. She was intelligent and had a great sense of humour as well as being extremely attractive and very knowledgeable about art, gaining a degree in art history at university.
University was something which had either passed Mark by or perhaps he had passed University by. For whatever reason, Mark was a little further down the education scale and he had learned closer to the 'street', possibly due to his father being who and what he was.
As he entered the flat and went into the hallway, he called out, "Yaren, hi, it's me." No reply. Strange, he thought. Putting his briefcase down and walking through to the lounge, he was stunned as he took in the sight of the room which had been completely wrecked. Furniture overturned and drawers emptied, as well as lamps smashed and the glass coffee table shattered and was now lying in broken shards. All this paled into insignificance when he saw her body lying on her side, strapped to a chair. There was a large 'flower' of blood sprayed onto the wall behind where she must have been sitting.
"Oh my God!' He shouted. 'No, NO! Not Yaren. Not my girl. What have they done?" He moved over to her and bent down to look at her face. It was obvious to him from the blood on the wall that she was dead.
"What the hell is going on?" He pulled back the long hair which had fallen across Yarens face and saw the small hole in her forehead.

There was only a trace of blood but there was a black sooty ring around the hole. He realised that this was a bullet fired from very close range. This was not done in anger, thought Mark, this was done very deliberately. This is murder. Why? What were they looking for? What's been going on, why would they kill Yaren? He'd said 'they' but was it one or more people? He didn't know. She didn't know anything beyond his involvement in drugs and even then, she didn't know much about it. 'That's it', he thought. It must be the drugs; but then there is nothing in England that would lead to this. Then, another thought struck him. Perhaps it wasn't the drugs, with all that had happened over in France and even then, they were not caught. He'd lost the drugs and therefore didn't have the money they would have made. Perhaps it's something else. He sat down on the only chair that was still upright. He had to think. Trying to overcome the nausea he felt at seeing his girlfriend in such a way, he realised that he had to get a grip on himself and think carefully, as things had taken a completely unexpected turn. He would never in a thousand years have expected this to have happened. I did not get involved with murdering thugs, he thought, just drug dealers. But then again, they could turn nasty. After a few moments of deep thought about the reasons for someone to kill Yaren, the realisation struck him like a thunderbolt. It must be that painting that went to Italy. She was involved in the sale. If the buyer had found out that it wasn't a genuine work, he'd be pretty mad. Italy – That's where the Mafia are isn't it? If they get mad, they take revenge don't they? Mafia – Mad – Revenge - Yaren. Who's next? Me? But he doesn't know me does he?
That thought scared him thoroughly. There was no time to waste. Rushing out of the flat, he called the marine auctions and the phone was answered by one of the hands. 'Ben, is Frank there, I need to speak to him urgently?'
"Who's that?" said Ben.
"It's me, Mark, you dozy bugger. Where's my Dad?"
'He's not here; there was some bloke who came down to see him. Didn't like the look of him, he didn't look friendly. They went off together."
"Right, I'll call him," ending the call and dialled Frank's mobile number.
"Frank Jordan here, who's calling?"
"It's me Dad, Mark. Something's happened and I need to speak to you about it."
"I already know about Yaren.'"
That stunned Mark. "What! How the hell do you know? I've not spoken to anyone about it. I've just been into the flat and found her. She's been shot, murdered, Dad, she's dead!"
"I know, and the man who did it is standing beside me."
"What!' he shouted. Mark's voice was getting higher. "You mean to say he's with you, a killer, and the one who killed Yaren. For fuck's sake dad, what's going on?"

***

The man Frank was referring to had 'appeared' and introduced himself as 'George', nothing more. He had explained exactly why he was there and what he had done. He said this in such a cold, unemotional and relaxed manner without any sort of aggression, that Frank realised this man was very dangerous. He had admitted to having killed Mark's girlfriend as though it was of little concern. 'George' had gone on to explain who his 'boss' was and that he wanted restitution for the fake painting, saying that he would do whatever it took to get this money so that he could take it personally to his boss.

"You will understand that to take a person's life is nothing to me as it is what I do. It is just a job to me. You will get the £300,000 very quickly. I do not have much patience."

Frank had regained a little composure and had realised the full implication of the situation. He said "Give me some time to think." Frank was a smooth talker and said to George, "If I am to get the money, then the body of the girl must be disposed of so that there will be no connection with us. Mark may be a drug dealer and involved in fraud, but he would never do what you do. Besides, you have just killed his girlfriend, so he will not be too happy to see you. I don't want to see him get violent and finish up like his girlfriend. He's my son, so we have to cover our tracks, and quickly!"

"Perhaps Mark has a problem with this, but I do not. Do not waste time, or there will be further consequences."

"But, there is also a further problem. Mark has a friend, Jason who knows too much, so he has to be silenced. You are the only person who can do this. You certainly seem to have the stomach for 'getting rid of people'.

I appreciate that your boss wants 'restitution' and I don't blame him, but I don't have that sort of money here and the only way I can get the money quickly and for that matter, at all, is for me to go to see the Gallery owner and get the money arranged, and in the meantime for you to dispose of the body and then sort out the 'Jason' problem however you wish, but permanently.

"But why should I do this and not you?' said George, I'm not your lackey."

"Because no-one knows you. You have not been seen by anyone who can identify you and I can arrange things while you do this to get what you need for your boss. You are not known here. It is the only way. There will be no way that anything can be traced back to you."

"If I do this, you will have all the money, £300,000 for me when I get back? If not I will certainly make someone suffer badly, it is nothing to me."

"It was £250,000 that was paid."

"I was told to get £300,000. The extra is the 'interest. My boss is not greedy."

"I'll get the money. I don't want to be involved any further than this. Any connections stop when this 'contract' is complete. We can make up our losses by other means, but for now we have to borrow and quickly. We have a code of practice just as you do in Italy. If we don't give the service which we've promised, we also receive retribution. Maybe not the same as you give, but just as effective, believe me."
***
After Marks outburst, Frank said, "Calm down and listen carefully. Don't interrupt. This is a very delicate matter. This man has explained everything to me. It seems that you sent a dodgy painting to a bloke in Italy. This man just happened to have a friend who was an art expert and he spotted that the painting was a fake, so he had this verified by a specialist who confirmed that it was a good copy, but not the original he paid a load of money for. And I guess it was you who collected the money, right, and then used this for the drugs. He's kind of pissed off, understandably. He reckons he's out of pocket to the tune of £300,000 and wants it back - now." Mark realised that he'd been right about the painting.
"But he only paid £250,000" said Mark.
"I said don't interrupt. You don't listen, do you?" Anyway, this Italian chap who bought the painting just happens to be a Mafia 'Don'. People you just do not piss off, do you get the picture? He wants his money back with interest. He sent the gentleman standing next to me, over here specially to collect the cash which he paid, and I guess it was you that the money went to."
"But how the hell did he find Yaren?"
"I don't know how, but he did. My guess is that he somehow found out from the gallery she worked at that she'd handled the sale. The buyer would know where he bought it from and anyone with a grain of common sense would get onto the gallery and get her address. He went to Yaren for information and she said she didn't know, but he didn't believe her, so he knocked her about a bit. She kept saying that she knew nothing and when she refused to tell him about her 'boyfriend', and threatened to go to the police, he shot her. Do you get the picture now?"
"Oh my God, so how did he find out about us then?"
"Apparently, she said that all she knew was that your father ran a boat auction business in Christchurch. He is not stupid and found out about this place and, well, he turned up. He has told me everything that happened and I can assure you that he is not a person who you would want to annoy, if you get my meaning."
Mark took some while to let this information 'sink in'. To have the man who killed his girlfriend actually with his father and not only with him, but waiting for Mark to get back, with the money, but only empty pockets, just didn't bear thinking about.
Mark said nothing.
Frank said in an exasperated tone, "Are you there?"
"Yes, but I don't have the cash."

'Well, where is it then?' said Frank. "You've just been to France with a load."
"I was to get it from the drugs shipment I've just tried to make, but I've explained what happened and how we lost everything. Now I have virtually nothing left."
"So you don't have the money and you expect me to get you out of the hole, is that it? I think we can say that you are in as deep as you can be, don't you?"
"I don't know what to do, Dad."
"I don't know what to do dad. I don't know what to do dad," he repeated. "Stop whinging and now listen to me and do exactly as I say. I'll tell you what is going to happen. You told me that Jason knows too much about the drugs and he's about as much use as a chocolate fireguard, so he's a liability. We have a body to hide and I have convinced this gentleman; who has chosen not given me his name yet, but who is listening to this conversation; that what has to happen is that you get Yarens' body, and bring Jason with you down to Christchurch soon and it will be dumped where it will never be found. We'll 'package' the body so it won't float to the surface, ever.'
Mark was hurting, but he began to see the impossibility of any alternative. There was too much at stake.
"But Dad, Jason will be there, he won't want to be part of that will he? Anyway, he's a mate."
"You don't get it do you? He knows too much. He will be 'taken care of'. He has caused trouble before. Anyway, he does what you tell him, doesn't he? We'll tell him that there are a load of guns that we have been asked to 'dispose of'. He'll buy that. Don't you want to save your skin?"
"Fucking hell, do you mean that he will be permanently silenced? But he'll be missed; someone will be looking for him."
"But didn't you tell me that his parents were killed some years ago, in an accident?"
"That's right," said Mark.
"You said he's always away from where he lives, Newbury isn't it, to go with you on your little jaunts? In that case, there'll be no one looking for him will there?"
"I suppose not. But he's not such a bad bloke really. I can't be a party to this."
"Mark, you're not listening to me. He is a liability and we must put a stop to all the fuck-ups that keep happening. We have to keep Mr Mafia Don happy or the shit will really hit the fan. These guys just do not give up. Do you get me?"
"Yes, I hear you. I suppose."
"Yes, well you suppose right for a change. Now, put her body in your car, at night, obviously. Make bloody sure you're not seen. Bring it straight down here and I'll make arrangements to prepare the body. Do you think you can manage that without cocking up as well?"

By this time Mark was actually trembling with the enormity of what had happened and what was about to happen, but he realised that this was probably the only way of keeping himself out of the line of fire of both the police and now the Mafia.

CHAPTER 10

Mark was in London. It was far too early to go back to the flat. He was hoping that no-one had called, but then why would anyone call. Even if they did, there would be no answer, so what am I worrying about, he thought to himself. Instead, he went to a coffee bar quite a way from anywhere he would be recognised, even though this would have been highly unlikely.
He waited until about one thirty in the morning, before driving back to her address. It took him two circuits of the area to find a parking space he thought was close enough to the flat. It was not directly outside the door but it was as close as he could get. He went to the door after checking that the road was clear. He let himself in and went directly to the room where she still lay. He was almost overwhelmed by grief until the reality of his situation welled up. This is something I have to do, he thought. I did love you Yaren, but I will get my revenge on the bastard who did this to you. I'll find a way.
With great care, he wrapped Yarens' body in a blanket he had taken from the bed they had shared and carried her quietly down the stairs. She was not heavy, and the thought that this would be the last time he would hold her was almost choking him. He got to the door and then suddenly realised that the car was quite a distance along the road, someone was bound to see him loading the car. He took a chance and put the body down very quietly in the vestibule of the flat and hoped that the other occupant of the flat was not given to early morning dog-walking or something equally bizarre. Carefully checking the road in both directions, and making sure that there was no-one and nothing in sight. He went back to the flat entrance and picked up the body. She was not a heavyweight but he had a difficult job to lift her onto his shoulder. He carried her out of the door and stopped. Carefully looking around again, he saw that there was no-one in the street. Moving swiftly to his car, he lifted the bonnet at the front, thankful that he'd had the foresight to open the catch. Putting her into the small space was not easy and he had to bend her body tightly. He said under his breath, "I'm so sorry Yaren. I didn't mean this to happen." He shut the boot lid as quietly as he could and once again checked the street. A light came on in a window of a flat nearly opposite. He froze. He realised that with lights on in a room, it was unlikely that a person could see out. He relaxed just a little and crouching down beside his car, he tried to keep calm. If anyone sees me, that'll be the end. They'll have plod down here in no time. Mind you, that's probably not going to happen. They seem to be doing more and more to catch speeding drivers than dealing with important stuff. Nothing happened. No-one opened a door or window and no-one showed themselves. After about five minutes, the light went out. Mark heaved a sigh of relief, opened the car door, got in and quietly closed it again. The he thought, 'Oh shit!, Porsche. When this little baby starts up it's going

to wake half the street. Then he had an idea. As Enmore road was on a slight slope, and he was actually pointing downhill, he wondered if he could let the car coast down the hill before starting the engine. Worth a try, he thought. Releasing the handbrake, the car began to roll slowly down the slope and gathered momentum. The car was rolling slightly to the left side of the road. Mark steered to the right. Or rather, he tried to steer to the right. As the car had power steering, this was not working with the engine being off, therefore the steering was extremely heavy and it caught him by surprise, as he could hardly turn the wheel. He wrenched it to the right, but by the time he had moved the wheel a little, the car had mounted the kerb and was heading towards a fence. He braked to a stop and, with his heart pumping furiously; he had no option but to start the engine. Without this, he couldn't get the car back on to the road. The engine started with a gentle but quite loud roar. With his heart in his mouth, he put the car into gear and moved slowly off the pavement and back onto the road. However, a Porsche is a very low car, and as the front wheels rolled back onto the road, the left-hand sill of the bodywork hit the kerb and scraped along the granite kerbstone, with a very loud grinding noise. The sort of noise that woke several people, one of whom was actually about to get back into bed, after a trip to the loo. In the dark, this man moved quickly to the window and saw the Porsche, being silver, gleaming in the streetlight, moving off the pavement, dropping off the kerb and pulling away down the road. As the car disappeared, he saw the registration number, but could only make out the first three letters.

CHAPTER 11

Turning at the end of the road, Mark made his way to the main road to Croydon and then on the M25 back to the South Coast via the M3.
His mobile phone rang. He saw that it was Frank calling. "What?"
"Where are you now?" said Frank.
"Nearly on the M3," Mark said in a very clipped voice. "I was going to take the A3 via Guildford."
"Have you got Jason?"
"No."
"I told you to get him. Why the hell can't you do anything right? Just stay on the M25 and go over to the M3 and get him. Bring him with you. We need him here."
"But he won't want to come at this time of night,' said Mark"
"I don't care what he says, don't take no for an answer. Make him. I don't care how you do it, but get him here. Understand?"
"Right. I can see you won't change your mind." Mark was used to his father and he recognised the tone of voice. He knew better than to question him. Mark took the detour through Basingstoke towards Newbury and called Jason on the mobile. "Jase, we have a job on."
"What now?" said Jason "'Do you know what bloody time it is? I was asleep."
"Of course I do, you prat. Just get yourself ready, we have to get down to the yard as soon as possible. Don't tell anyone where you're going, Okay?"
"Who the hell would I tell? You know there's no-one to tell. You keep telling me I'm a lonely git."
"Good, just get ready, I'll be there in about 15 minutes."
"Oh, all right, but I'm not happy about being woken out of a lovely sleep. You know I need my beauty sleep. I hope there's something in this for me."
"Don't you worry, there certainly is," said Mark, and ended the call.
When he got to Jason's address, he saw a light on and Jason was waiting. Coming out of his flat, it was obvious that he was not in a good humour. He got into the Porsche and said, "What's all this about then?"
"Never mind, there's a bit of a flap on but you'll find out when we get there, so be a good boy and shut up while I concentrate on what we'll have to do, Okay?"
The rest of the journey was silent and Jason quietly nodded off.
Mark began to relax and kept to the speed limit as he was a sure target for police out on the hunt. He had an uneventful journey back to Christchurch as there were so few cars on the road.
He turned into the Marine Auctions and parked out of sight at the back of the main shed.
He found Frank waiting for him.
"What do we do?" asked Mark.

"Right, the plan is that we parcel the 'you know what' and make it so that it will never come to the surface and then this 'George' will take that 'Fairey Christina' owned by Michael Fortune, and go through the harbour and drop it somewhere where it will never be found, somewhere off the usual channel, but for fuck's sake, he'd better not go aground. He tells me that he's done some boating and knows how to handle one and the tide should be okay. He'll have Jason with him, so it should be straightforward. They'll dump the boat somewhere and George will come back here. Then we'll get him back to Italy, where he will give the money which YOU owe, to his boss. Get it?"
"But Jason won't agree to this, he doesn't know about Yaren and he won't want to be dumping a body. He'll kick up about it."
"He won't know what it is. You and George will be doing the 'packing' and Jason will be told that it's a load of stolen guns that have to be 'lost' It'll feel heavy, so that should fool him.'
"So where will you get the money from?"
"The less you know at the moment the better; let's just say that I know someone who will have that sort of money to hand, so shut up and get to work. I'll keep Jason busy while you two do what you have to do, while I get YOU out of the 'you know what'."
"Hang on, this 'George', is he the one who killed Yaren?"
"Yes."
"Oh Christ! That's incredible and why is he here?"
"He's here because of you and your involvement with the art scams and believe me; you do not want to annoy him. As you probably saw, he beat the shit out of your girlfriend before he killed her. He is very dangerous and that is why I'm doing exactly as he says. We're in deep enough trouble as it is without getting even more involved. This way, everything is kept quiet and nobody is any the wiser. No-one knows about George and that's the way it has to stay.'
"But he killed Yaren. She was my girl. She meant a lot to me and...."
"Shut up Mark. You are so deep in this and she is dead now. We didn't expect this but it's happened and there's nothing we can do to bring her back. Now listen to me, if this comes out and we don't get rid of the body, everything is going to come apart. It'll just seem as though she was burgled and abducted. As there'll be no body, the police will assume that the killer has taken the body and dumped it somewhere. That will keep them busy for a good while but at the moment, no-one knows her killer and if we play this right, he'll go away and we'll be in the clear. No trace. Nothing that can be traced back to you or me, now that you've dragged me into this, thanks to your dodgy dealings, so shut up and get on with things."
Mark thought about this for a short while and stared at Frank, who stared back. Nothing was said, but finally Mark said, "I guess there are no choices now, are there?"
"Well, there are choices, but you really don't want to know the other one. It'll get you and me back in the slammer again, and you've had a taste of that haven't you?"

“Yes, and I don’t want that again, that’s for sure.”
“Neither do I so now you’re beginning to understand it; get moving. I’ll tell Jason to get the ‘Christina’ ready for the trip and make damn sure that he doesn’t see what we’re doing.”
“Tell him to make sure there’s a tender so that he can get away,” said Mark.
With that, Mark went into the boat shed where all the smaller craft were kept and saw ‘George’ for the first time. This was the man who had killed his girlfriend. He was seething underneath, but realised that if this man could kill once, he could do it again. It must have been nothing to him, actually beating her half to death before killing her, so not only was he a murderer but he was sadistic as well. In other words, if he could torture and beat a woman, he wouldn’t hesitate to do it again, to anyone. Presuming that ‘George’ still had the gun, he held himself in check. ‘When he comes back I’ll find a way to do him some real damage’, he thought.
George said, “So, you are Mark. Under different circumstances, I would be pleased to meet you but I suppose you are not pleased to meet me.”
“That would be an understatement,” said Mark through gritted teeth, trying to keep his temper. Taking a long hard look at ‘George’, Mark realised that any sort of attack on him would be hopeless, as ‘George’ was much heavier, taller and more muscular. Taking Mark’s stare, George gave him a malevolent look. ”Do not annoy me I urge you. I didn’t want the body down here but circumstances have changed and we now have a job to do to conceal any evidence and we must hurry. Get the body and bring it here. Put it on the table.”
Mark thought, ‘‘it’, put ‘it’ on the table. This guy hasn’t a shred of feeling.’
George then said, “There’s a concrete post lying just outside. I saw this as I came in. It will do to weight the body. Bring it in here.”
‘I can’t believe I’m taking orders from a murdering fucker this time`, thought Mark. ‘But I guess I’ve no choice right now, but just give me a chance, that’s all I want’. Inside he was fuming but a plan was forming.
Mark went to the Porsche and tried to lift Yaren’s body out, but he’d had to bend the body so tightly to get it into the car, that he had to go back and ask George to help. It was much more difficult to lift the dead body than to drop it into the car in the first place.
‘At least rigor mortis has not set in,’ said George, ‘so we can straighten it out.’
“You disgusting bastard”
“Not at all, I’m used to it. It is what my people pay me for. I have no feeling in the matter. It is work. No matter, just get on with it. Pass me that roll of heavy duty tape over there.” He was pointing to a roll of thick tape that was used for repairs to inflatable dinghies, so it was waterproof and unlikely to become detached.

When they had put the body on to the table and it was lying straight, George said, "Roll her over so she is face down. You lift her up and put a block of timber under her shoulders, so we can pass the tape round."
They lifted the concrete post on to Yaren's back and George wound the first band of tape tightly round the body. This was repeated until there were about six bands of this heavy duty waterproof tape holding the post in place.
"We'll wrap the body. Once it is in the boat, it will stiffen when rigor mortis sets in"
"Oh for God's sake, shut up. I'm going to throw up soon," said Mark.
While the body was being wrapped, he said to Mark, "Does this Jason know what we're doing?"
"No way, he'd have nothing to do with it. I'm only doing what I'm told, believe me I really don't want any part of this but I've no options."
"Then we'll have to disguise the feet so that when the other person holds them, he doesn't know what he's holding."
Mark replied, "Just do what you have to do. Remember, this was my girlfriend you've just killed, and I'm supposed to go along with whatever you say. I'm not going to argue with you. I just think you are a sadistic bastard who shows no remorse for what he's done."
"That's right. It's what I do for a living and I'm good at it. No-one knows who I am and I leave no traces. After this, I will disappear, but that's after I have collected the money you owe my boss. The money had better be here when I get back or there will be more suffering, if you realise what I mean? And one other thing, please don't even think about informing the police about any of what is going on or I can tell you that you have no idea just what could and would happen to you all."
"'I have no intention of telling anyone anything, certainly not the police. I have too much to hide myself."
"Good. So we understand each other, yes?"
Mark replied gloomily, "Yes."
"We roll the body in the polythene sheet just to keep it covered, but when we drop it overboard, we take it off. The weight will hold it down until it decomposes and then there will be nothing except any bones which are left may wash away with the tides."
At this last remark, Mark ran outside and threw up behind the shed.
After a few minutes, Mark went back into the shed looking very pale and vulnerable.
'Good God Almighty', thought Mark, how does this ghoul live with himself? I know I deal with some dodgy things, but this is a whole new ball game. I really don't like it. But then I don't have a choice, do I'?
"Come on," said George, "we don't have time for this."
When the body was wrapped, George said, "Right, now let's get it onto the boat. Is it ready?"
"Hang on, I'll go and make sure that the coast is clear,"

Mark went outside to the pontoon where the 'Christina' cruiser's engine was gently burbling away. Jason had prepared the craft as Frank had instructed. With fuel and some food and drink, Jason said to Mark, "Why am I doing this? Frank said we have to get rid of some 'dodgy armaments' that should not be found. Are we involved in that sort of stuff now? Because if that's the case, then I don't want to know."
"Well, you don't know anything about this, so don't worry, it's just a one-off. It won't happen again, but I think Frank owes someone a favour, so we just do this once and we're clear of any 'debt'. Do you know what I mean?"
"I suppose so, but why me? And who's the bloke over there, is he coming with me?'
"Yes, that's George. Don't know his surname and he won't give it apparently. And, a word to the wise, don't cross him, he's a mean bastard. They're probably his guns and he want to make sure that they are 'disposed of' correctly and the job is done."
"But why aren't you coming with me?"
"Because I have to stay here with Frank to tie up the loose ends and make sure everything is clean and clear. Does that make sense?"
"I suppose it has to. Oh well, let's get on with it. Anyway, how do I get back?"
"I guess you'll come back here once the stuff is dumped, so don't worry about that part. Just do what 'George' tells you and there should be no problems."
"Oh, Okay then," said Jason.
"Just go and tell Frank that we're ready to go and when you're aboard, I can cast you off."
"Won't we be noticed?" said Jason, "you know, going out on the river in the dark?"
"No, some of the locals sometimes go down after dark and have picnics on the banks of the harbour. There're some quite inaccessible places there, only reached by boat. They can get up to whatever they want, if you know what I mean?"
"Oh, right, a bit of night-time nookie then?" said Jason, with a smirk and went to find Frank.
As soon as he was out of sight, George said, "Let's get the 'armaments' on to the boat. You take the lighter end."
Mark held Yaren's legs and George took the weight of her torso. She was very heavy with the added weight of the post and although Mark was fit, he did not have the sheer 'heft' that George had. Another reason not to tangle with him, thought Mark. They got the body on to the boat and it was lying on the engine cover, near the stern section of the cockpit. "This will make dumping it easier when we get to a suitable spot," said George.
Jason came back and boarded the boat. Mark went to the stern and released the bowline knot on the mooring bollard and then went to the bow to do the same.

“Okay, you’re clear to go now,” he said and with George driving the boat, they went gently out on to the river and headed downstream towards Christchurch Harbour.

CHAPTER 12

During the short journey down the river Stour to Christchurch Harbour, Jason tried to make small talk and asked 'George' what he did for a living. George said 'Mind your own business. It is of no concern of yours what I do. Just shut up and let me concentrate on driving this boat without getting stuck on the mud, the rivers' very narrow here.'
"How come you know so much about boating? Do you know this area?"
"I've been living in England for many years and I have known boats for a long time, now will you shut up and be quiet?"
The tone of voice he used made it very clear to Jason that conversation was not on the menu. Miserable bastard, he thought although he kept his comments and questions to himself. It was not too long before they passed the confluence of both rivers, the Stour and the Avon and shortly after this the water broadened out into the harbour. It was quite dark by now and Jason said, "Shouldn't we be showing navigation lights?"
The surly reply was,"We are not here to be seen. We just have to do what we have to do and get out of the area without being noticed. We are not putting any lights on, got it?"
"Right," said Jason, "but where do we go from here, back to the boatyard?"
"You don't listen do you? We're going to dump the boat somewhere and get back to shore where it's quiet and no-one will see. It's supposed to have been stolen, right? It's what would happen to it if it had been. They'd hardly expect it to be taken back would it, dummy?'
Slightly puzzled, Jason said nothing.
When they were in the middle of the harbour, George pointed, "That looks like it's a good place over there and it's outside the marked channel, so no chance of a boat fouling this package. That'd be the last thing we need."
He swung the boat over to port and throttled back almost to a standstill. "This will do," and he disengaged the drive sot that the boat was completely stopped. "Give me a hand to roll this overboard. Be careful you don't get it caught between the davits."
There was a small inflatable tender hanging between the davits, but there was sufficient clearance to get the package through without it snagging, by pushing first one end and then the other, over the stern. As there was only about a two foot drop to the water, there would not be too much of a splash.
As they were about to push one end over, George said, "Stop. We have to be careful. Hold on to your end while I push this out so that we clear the stern-drive unit or it will catch on the prop. Just hold on to the edge of the polythene sheet and the package will roll out."

Jason was holding what he thought was the end of a bundle of guns, while George pushed what was, unbeknown to Jason, the head of the body, out as far as he could. He held on to the edge of the polythene sheet and as the body 'unrolled', it entered the water at a slightly downward angle, resulting in hardly a splash. Because it was rolled in several turns of plastic, the body was completely hidden from view as it unrolled and sank immediately.

"I don't think that will ever be discovered, unless someone dredges the harbour, but I don't think that's at all likely, if ever," said George.

CHAPTER 13

George went back to the helm and after checking around to see that there were no other craft in the vicinity, he engaged the drive and they moved forward, gathering speed to about 10 knots, so that the engine noise was minimal.
"Let's get out of here,' said Jason. 'I'm not happy about this at all. It all seems very dodgy to me."
"Nothing to worry about, it's over now and we're in the clear."
They increased speed slightly to about 15 knots and as they approached Mudeford they should have taken a straighter line, but where they had dropped the body was to the shoreward side of the harbour and consequently not on a straight line to the 'Run'.
***
The 'Run' is the very narrow channel at the entrance to Christchurch Harbour and the current through there is very strong, sometimes as much as 8 knots. With two tides a day along this stretch of the coast, due to the presence of the Isle of Wight causing the tides to actually run up against the Island and 'bounce' back, the harbour filled and emptied four times a day. The 'Run' was very aptly named as the amount of water running through this narrow channel was very considerable.
***
What George and Jason didn't know was that there was a sandbar on the port side of the entrance to the Run.
As they crossed this to take a line into the Run, the propeller hit the sandbar. The boat gave a shudder, slowed almost to a stop and the engine speed dropped almost to zero and then picked up again as the boat slowly cleared the sandbar.
"What the hell was that?"' said Jason.
"I think that was the sound of our propeller being fucked," said George.
"Great, now what do we do?"
"We appear to still have way on but if, as I suspect, the prop blades are bent, that's going to slow us down and make any distance very unlikely. I was going to go head towards Southampton, but that's out of the question now."
"Oh, so now we're going to get caught in a stolen boat. That's fucking great. This has been a really shit week for me."
"Stop whinging will you. I'm told the owner of the boat will not be down again for at least another week, so that's not a problem. Nobody will realise the boat has gone. We have to get this prop repaired so that we can finish what we started, and I have other things to take care of."
"What things?" said Jason.
"Never you mind, just 'things'. You just mind your own business."
"Can't we just leave the boat here and go back to the boatyard?"

"Are you some kind of dimwit? If we left the boat here, there would be all sorts of questions and that would lead to investigations. Do I really have to spell everything out to you?"
"'No, I suppose not. So where do we get the propeller repaired."
"There's a place in Poole that I know about, they repair propellers. We'll head to Poole Harbour, take up a mooring buoy and we can get the prop off: I can take it over there and get it sorted."
"And how long will that take, about a week."
"No way. I'll make sure that it's fixed pretty bloody quickly, believe me."
Jason thought, somehow I believe him.
They went on through the Run and turned to starboard, making for Poole. However, the engine was labouring and the temperature gauge went up, so they had to throttle back because there was a very noticeable vibration coming from the stern.
Jason said. "That doesn't sound good. Will it damage the boat?"
"Not unless some sort of idiot was driving this boat and tried to go faster, then it might wreck the stern drive bearings and then they'd have to paddle this bloody thing back."
They made their way, at a much reduced speed, towards Poole Harbour, without further mishap.
As they approached Sandbanks and the chain ferry, Jason said, "I know this place, I've been here with Mark when we watched the race boats coming out. He wasn't racing that day and they were belting out through this part at one hell of a speed."
"That's all very well if you don't get 'wind over tide' as this narrow gap takes all the water from the harbour as it empties and I believe it's about 60 feet deep. That makes for some very hairy boat handling. I suppose you know that this harbour is probably the largest coastal harbour in the world and when all that water runs through a narrow gap like this, it makes the current very fast, up to about 8 knots on an ebbing tide."
"How am I supposed to know that, I live in Newbury; anyway, what does 'wind over tide' mean?" said Jason.
"I'd have thought that was pretty obvious, but then you are a bit lacking in the brain department. It means that when the wind is coming one way and the tide is going the other, waves are created and for small boats this can be very dangerous. Thankfully tonight, everything is calm."
When they finally arrived in the centre of the harbour, they were able to find an empty mooring buoy. It was by now, very dark, but there was still sufficient ambient light to see a buoy.
"Right, I'm going to approach that mooring buoy very slowly. You get the mooring hook and catch the line."
"Sorry?"
"Christ, give me strength! The pole with a hook on the end, it's fastened beside the port rail. As we get to the buoy, I'll stop the

boat and you can hook the line below the buoy. Pull it up and we'll attach our line to it. Can you actually understand all that?"
"Yes," was the sullen reply from Jason.
"We can't get the prop off until there is some light, so we'll get some sleep and do what's necessary at dawn."
They were awake by the time the morning sun had appeared. George said "You'll take the prop off and I'll take it over to the repair place in the tender. There's a metal case next to the engine and there'll be a large spanner in there."
"Why don't we just go to the quayside, it would be much easier?"
"Because we're bound to be seen and being seen is not an option. Just do what I say or you'll be sorry."
"Anyway, how do we get the prop off?"
"*We* don't, *you* do."
"How?"
"You'll see. George operated the hydraulic lift to bring the stern drive out of the water which made the propeller accessible. "If I'd known about that bloody sandbar, I could have raised the drive and this wouldn't have happened." But then, he was a pragmatist and accepted the situation.
Jason had opened the engine casing and reaching inside, found the toolbox. Leaning back out, he held up a large spanner saying, "Is this it?"
"If it looks big and heavy, and it looks like a spanner, it probably is, you dumb fucker."
Handing it to George, this prompted a very cold look. "Don't give it to me; it's you who needs it. Right, now is the time you get to take the prop off. Go over the stern and stand on the stern drive unit. I'll lock the engine in gear so that the prop won't turn. Unscrew that large 'boss' holding the prop on and be very careful. When you've got it off, hand it to me, and then pass me the prop."
"But the water's cold, in fact it's bloody freezing!"
"Stop your moaning; you won't be there for long, and in any case you won't be in the water unless you fall in. You'll be standing on the fins just above the propeller. You'll have to reach down. It's only a few turns and it'll be off. Don't be such a wimp. Anyway, you are lighter than me and that stern-drive is not really meant for standing on, so shut up and get working. The sooner we can get this fixed, the sooner we can get everything sorted and get the job finished."
Jason grudgingly, did as he was told and carefully climbed over the stern, standing on the drive unit while George handed him the spanner.
Putting this in place, he put pressure on to the bronze boss which held the propeller in place. It wouldn't move. He put muscle behind the spanner, but it still refused to budge. He said, "It won't move."
"Do you know, it's strange but I can see that," he said with heavy sarcasm, "so just put your foot on the spanner and push gently. Push slowly and harder but not suddenly or you'll slip and lose the spanner."

Jason put his foot on the spanner, bending over to hold it with his other hand. Pressing hard, he felt it begin to move slightly.
"Now just use your hands and pass me the spanner," said George.
Jason passed over the spanner and went back to the propeller to unscrew the now loosened boss. Finally, the boss came loose and Jason began to unscrew it. After several turns it became free from the propeller shaft. He turned to hand it to George, but he slipped on the weed covered metal of the stern-drive, and overbalanced. He reached out instinctively to hold on, but in doing so, let go of the boss. It dropped with a gentle 'plop' and instantly disappeared into the brown water of the harbour.
George saw this happen saying very slowly and menacingly, "You fucking, stupid twat! You do realise that we can't get the prop back on without that?"
"It's not my fault, it's slippery," Jason said in a whiny voice.
George thought quickly. "Right, shut up whingeing and get the prop off and give it to me, but if you drop this I *am* going to kill you. Then get back on board quickly."
Jason managed to remove the propeller and hand it back to George on the deck. It was obvious that it had suffered serious damage and the blades were bent out of shape.
As Jason clambered back on deck, George said "Now listen *very* carefully, and do exactly as I tell you." He took a visual bearing on a factory chimney to the left of Poole quay, and then took another visual bearing on a dockside crane. He then took a third bearing on a landmark on his right, a large white building on Evening Hill. He explained these bearings to Jason very carefully. When he thought it was getting through he said, "While I'm gone, you can get over the side right where we are now and find that boss."
"What?' do you mean I have to go into the water? It's freezing."
"You dropped it, so you will find it, and you *will* find it. Stop whining and get over the side. If you get over now you stand a better chance of picking it up because the boat won't move far as we are in a standing tide. If you wait, it'll swing as the tide comes in and you'll be under the water for longer, so I suggest you shut up and get started. Just keep checking your bearings so you stay in the same place. The longer you take the more the boat will move, but you will stay in the same place no matter where the boat goes."
"Oh Christ, this means that I'll be stuck in the middle of the harbour and it's too deep anyway."
"It's only about four feet deep here; we're not in the channel. Just go or we'll be stuck here, or rather you will be stuck here and yes, it is a long way to the shore."
Having said that, George freed the small inflatable tender from the davits on the stern and set off with the propeller towards the shoreline.
Meanwhile, Jason very reluctantly got over the stern of the boat and dropped into the water, full of trepidation. Thinking back to Caen, he thought, 'Here we go again, I'm really sick of this'. It was a

little deeper than George had said, and the water came up to his chest. He carefully checked his position with the sightings that had been very forcefully explained. When he was sure that he was in about the right position, he began searching the sandy seabed with his foot. He touched something hard, which was not sand. He ducked under the water with his eyes closed as there was no visibility. He reached down and grabbed, but it was only a large pebble. This happened again and again. He was getting very cold and said out loud, "This is bloody ridiculous. I'll never find it." Once again he checked his position and repeated the 'foot-tip' searching. Repeated tries underwater, only succeeded in finding many large pebbles. He was becoming more and more desperate. Again, he checked the bearings and was sure that he had the correct place and had not moved. He was getting extremely anxious and said to himself, 'One more time and I've had it.' As the boat was drifting slightly, it had moved away from the position where he had taken the bearings. He looked around and although he'd not moved, the boat was quite a distance from him. He became very anxious and felt very vulnerable. Oh shit, the tide's coming in and I'm going to drown. He was becoming very nervous and once again he took the visual bearings and when he was sure that he was in the right place, although his head was now only just above the water he ducked down again. His foot hit something big and hard. 'Fuck, not another one,' he groaned. Ducking down for what he had vowed, was the last time, he reached out to the sandy bottom and picked up something much heavier than the dozens of other pebbles. When he surfaced and stood up to look at what he held, he could not believe his eyes.
"YES!, YES!", he shouted, at the top of his voice, holding it up as high as he could, looking just like the Lady in the Lake holding Excalibur, the sword from Avalon to be given to King Arthur – although Jason probably would have no idea what Excalibur was.........
Throwing the bronze 'boss' onto the deck, he very thankfully climbed back on to the stern-drive and then back onto the boat, where he tried to somehow dry himself and struggle back into clothes. Not easy on wet skin, and he literally ran in circles to try to get some circulation going. He inwardly said, 'That's it. I've had it. I'm going back as soon as he gets here. I don't care what he says.' Unfortunately for Jason, that was not really an option, as George had other plans.

CHAPTER 14

George had gone back the next day to the workshop where the propeller had been repaired. Having collected this, he made his way back to find the inflatable tender where he had concealed it. From there, he paddled back to the boat where Jason was waiting, cold and hungry. As George boarded the boat, he handed the repaired propeller to Jason and gave him a carrier bag with some food and drink inside. "Thank heavens for that, I thought I'd die of hunger."
"Hang on, before you eat that, get this propeller put back on the stern-drive and make bloody sure that this time you don't drop anything or there will be 'consequences,' if you understand me."
"Oh bloody hell, George, whoever you are; I'm still freezing after having to dive down for that propeller nut yesterday."
"That was your own stupid fault, so don't go moaning about that; just get it done then we can get out of here."
"Oh, and by the way, don't even think about who I am, that's for me to know and NOT for you to try and find out."
Reluctantly, Jason went over the stern once again and George handed him the propeller. He managed very carefully to get on to the stern drive unit, replaced the propeller and boss and then tightened it securely.
Now even more cold, hungry and thirsty, Jason clambered back over the stern, saying to George, "Now can I get some food? You were gone for so long, I thought you'd never come back."
"Go on then, but we have to get going as soon as possible. I don't want to stay here any longer than I have to." Starting the engine, he said to Jason, "Right, you can untie the mooring buoy so we can get going. It was dark by now and without navigation lights; they were able to exit Poole Harbour by using the marker buoys to find the channel. Once they were through the narrow channel by the Sandbanks Chain Ferry and past the 'Training Bank', they turned to port and headed along the coast. George had decided to make for Lymington as there was more chance of a mooring place and it would be easy to make an escape from there.
Their passage along the coast was uneventful except for a time when they had passed Hurst Point where the Solent narrows dramatically and the currents are very strong. There was enough moonlight for them to see their position. George had taken notice of the direction of the current and realised that it was heading away from the Solent area; this suited his purpose well.
He slowed the boat almost to a stop and Jason, who was eating some bread and cheese, looked out of the cabin and said, "What's going on, have we got a problem."
"We haven't, but you have. Get up here, I need you."
Jason came out of the cabin and saw that George was holding a gun which was pointing directly at him. "What the FUCK?" shrieked Jason. "Don't play with that thing, I nearly crapped myself when I saw that."

"Who told you I was playing with it? Just strip off and throw your clothes in the corner over there."
"Don't be fucking stupid George, what the hell do you think you're doing?"
"One thing you should know about me is that I am not stupid. Don't argue, just do what I tell you or I'll shoot you in the legs and then I'll have to take your kit off myself."
"But why? What the hell do you want me to do that for?" Jason was shaking now, but not from the cold anymore, just fear.
"I have my reasons, just do it before I really lose my temper and then you'll be in a lot of pain, believe me."
"But why have you got a gun? We've done what we set out to do and dumped those guns back in the harbour and now you're waving that thing about. Just what the hell is going on? We should just get back to Christchurch as soon as we can."
"Just get your clothes off and stop yakking. I don't have the time to explain things to you. Do it or you will suffer pain like you've never known before. I am not joking; this is what I do for a living."
"Whaddya mean - 'What I do for a living'?"
"I am an 'enforcer'."
"Yeah, but that's in the movies innit?"
"Actually no, because I am exactly that; I work for the Mafia in Italy."
Finally, it had dawned on Jason what was about to happen and for George; this was all part of the pleasure. Seeing the terror on the face of his intended victim accessed his sadistic tendencies which had been a part of his psyche for his entire life.
Jason was now really terrified. "Just DO IT" shouted George.
George had not moved the gun from its focus on Jason who finally began to undress, but slowly.
George shouted, "FASTER" and lunged at Jason, swiping his head with the gun barrel.
The pain from the barrel gave him the incentive to do what George wanted. He quickly took off his shirt and trousers and threw them into the corner of the cockpit. Jason found from somewhere the will to fight. He was scared, badly scared, but this gave him the necessary incentive to try to fight back. He lunged at George and tried to wrestle the gun from him. George was nearly taken by surprise but managed to stop the swinging right arm which Jason had thrown at him. George blocked this move and then pushed Jason very firmly away from him. Jason almost lost balance and managed to grab hold of a stanchion on the edge of the cockpit. Just as he managed to hold on, George had reached into his pocket and drawn out the steel bar which he'd used on Yaren. He swung at Jason's arm which was holding onto the stanchion. The force with which he brought this bar down on Jason's arm, simply shattered it with an audible 'crack'. Jason screamed with the pain and instantly released his grip. As Jason fell to the floor in agony, George hit him again. "That'll stop you from grabbing anything else," he said as he

broke Jason's other arm, this time the upper arm. The pain was absolutely intense and now and there was nothing he could do to stop George, who was enjoying the 'sport', as he saw it, of inflicting pain.
George then said, "Thanks to your stupidity, you now can't take your clothes off, so I'll just have to rip them off myself, you silly little fucker. Just like the girl; if you'd done as you were told you would still have two working arms."
With that, he roughly pulled Jason to the floor in a 'face-down' position and began to rip his underclothes off. Once Jason was naked, he then literally bundled Jason down into the cabin. He threw Jason onto the forward bunk, propping him up against the cabin side. Jason was moaning with the pain from his broken arms.
"Look at me." Jason turned and looked into the face of the man who had caused him such pain and suffering and mostly, fear.
"Why are you doing this?" said Jason.
"Because I have to. Anyway, it's good fun. Anyway, this way there are no traces, no clues."
"What do you mean no clues?" Jason was visibly shaking and sweating with fear now.
"No DNA, no clothes because I'll set them adrift on the dinghy and when they are found, it will be assumed that someone was swimming and drowned.
"Oh my God, NO! You are a sick fucker. You're not going to...?" Jason was trying desperately to control his knotted stomach and was about to lose this ability.
Jason looked at George in blind terror. His face was white and he was sweating in fear, although it was quite cold in the cabin.
Without any delay and with absolutely no feeling whatsoever, George shot Jason at close range. A small hole appeared in Jason's head and he fell sharply backwards against the cabin side.
Moving quickly, George removed the blue mattress from the bunk in the bow of the hull. He roughly pushed the body to the front of the boat onto the bunk, pushing Jason's body into the void underneath. He had to really tuck the body into this small space by folding it as much as he could. When the contorted body was pushed down, he replaced the mattress. Having done that, he gathered up the discarded clothes from the corner where he had thrown them. Moving to the back of the boat, he threw all the clothes into the inflatable dinghy, which was hanging on the davits. Releasing the dinghy, he let it drop to the water. It was Georges' intention that this little dinghy would be found by someone eventually after the current had taken it back along the coast. He thought that when the empty dinghy was found with just clothes in, it would be presumed that someone had probably been swimming and drowned after getting into difficulties. George didn't care. He had already put Jason out of his mind. The job was done and he was clear, with no evidence and no witnesses. Satisfaction for George in more ways than one...

He went back up to the helm and selected 'drive', pushing the throttles full ahead the boat surged ahead, making about 25 knots. Continuing along the coast, eventually, the marker buoys for Lymington came into view. The channel was very well marked because it was also the Isle of Wight ferry route into Lymington.
He manoeuvred the boat toward the mooring pontoon where all the private craft were berthed, spotting a space right at the extreme end of the first pontoon. He drew close to this, briefly reversing the boat to bring it to a stop. Jumping onto the pontoon, he very hastily tied the mooring ropes to the bollards, first the stern and then the bow.
As soon as this was done, he looked around, saw no-one and quickly walked along the pontoons and past the yard office, where there were no lights showing. Going up the slipway he walked quickly through the entrance barriers to the road outside.
He now had to get back to Christchurch but had to cover his tracks. He was thinking about the ways of getting back as he approached the main road at the end of the boatyard access road. He saw what looked like a restaurant or bistro. A thought occurred to him; he walked into the bistro and over to the bar. With no hint of politeness, he asked the barman if there was any chance of a lift back to Poole. He said Poole, because he needed to make sure there was no chance of his movements being traced back to Christchurch.
The barman was not used to people not showing some degree of courtesy, but had the sense not to question this man. "I don't know Sir. Can I ask why you need a lift, I take it you don't you have a car?"
George thought, 'This guy has brains. If I had a car, would I be asking for a lift?'
"Actually, I've been out on a boat and we've had some engine trouble, so I have to get back to our base to get some spares. I thought perhaps there might be a chance of a lift from someone here. If not, I'll just walk to the main road and maybe I can get a lift there with a bit of luck."
"We could call you a taxi, Sir."
"I don't have enough money on me, to be honest. It would cost an arm and a leg from here I imagine."
'You're right, it wouldn't be cheap, and that's for sure at this time of night."
Just then, a customer who had been sitting a little way along the bar said, "Excuse me, but I couldn't help overhearing. I am just about to go across to Wareham to stay with a friend and I can give you a lift if you'd like. I can take a slight detour and go via Poole; it's not much out of my way."
"That's very good of you, thank you, that'll get me out of this problem; after my last couple of days, a bit of good luck."
"Right then, if you're ready, let's go - I was just about to leave anyway. My name's Bob by the way."

Ignoring the introduction, he said, "Fine, let's go." By telling this that he was going to Poole, George was covering his tracks and he now had the means of 'doubling' back to Christchurch. He had realised that he could catch a train from Poole station to Christchurch. By walking from Christchurch station back to the Marine Auctions, he was sure this would overcome any possibility of being followed. He knew that there were CCTV cameras around, but It was doubtful that they would be covering a suburban housing area. However, there were far more CCTV cameras around than he had thought.

CHAPTER 15

Two canoeists were paddling towards the 'Run' at the entrance to Christchurch Harbour.
The current was speeding up as they headed for the narrow harbour exit and some of the shallower parts of the harbour were becoming apparent. Just ahead of them, Simon saw a hump of sand becoming more obvious. A small island......
"That's funny," he called to his brother, Pete, "I've never seen that before and we've canoed here loads of times."
There was something dark lying on the sand. "What do you reckon that is Pete?" said Simon.
"I dunno, looks like some driftwood or junk that's drifted down from that load of nutters from the rowing club at Wick; they're always dropping oars or bits of tackle."
As Simon was closer, he could see that it was not driftwood. It actually looked more like a body lying face down and partly buried in the sand.
"Oh Christ," said Simon, "can you see that?"
"Yeah, but I wish I hadn't," said Peter, "because if it's what we think it is, we can't just ignore this, we'll have to report it."
"Maybe it's already been done although I doubt it. If it had, there would be people here, probably the lifeboat crew and police.'
"Do you think he's dead?" said Peter.
"I can't see it properly just yet but unless he can breathe through sand as, I'd say yes, as he's face down, but, hang on Si, I can see now - judging by the hair, it's not a 'he' mate, it's a 'she'."
Realising this was serious; they paddled hard to the island, and dragged their canoes onto the sand. They stood back and looked at the body with feelings of complete unease. Wearing blue jeans and a black or dark blue sweater, her hair was long and dark. The body was lying in a strangely 'straight' position with her legs together and her arms beside her. There appeared to be some sort of black straps around the body.
"How long do you think she's been here Pete?" said Simon.
"I dunno," said Pete. "I wouldn't know how to tell except that she's fairly well buried in this sand but that might be the tidal flow, so we can only guess; that'll be for the cops to check out."
"Should we get to Mudeford Quay and report this?" said Peter.
"Yeah, but with the speed of the tide in the 'Run', it's going to be difficult on the outgoing tide to stop. It runs around 7 knots at full flow, doesn't it? At the speed we'll be going, we'll have to veer off to port away from the main flow pretty early and land on the slip. Come on, there's nothing we can do here, let's go and report it."
Clambering back into the canoes, they launched themselves off the sand and paddled hard. Very soon they were landing on the slipway

at Mudeford and Peter, being the elder brother, would take responsibility for reporting their gruesome find.
"What do you reckon Si, the pub or lifeboat station?"
"The lifeboat first then the pub, I reckon," said Simon. "After finding that, I don't know about you but I need a drink anyway."
They pulled their canoes up the slip and ran to the lifeboat station but there was only an emergency telephone outside the building. Picking up the phone, Peter had an immediate response. Explaining to the operator his 'find', he was told that this information would be passed directly to Bournemouth Police because the local station was only manned part-time. The operator also said that the information would be passed to 'RNLI Control.
Simon and Peter waited anxiously and they decided not to mention their find to anyone as it would only cause problems. They would leave it up to the police and lifeboat crew to handle things.
Shortly after the emergency call ended, a dark blue van with RNLI emblazoned on the side drew up and a man in a dark blue sweater with the RNLI logo, walked quickly over to Peter and Simon who were waiting beside the lifeboat station and were obvious in their canoeing gear and lifejackets.
"Hi guys, I'm Andy, the local contact for the station. Are you the guys who reported a body - can you tell me where you found it?"
"It's back there on that small island which you can only just about see looking towards Christchurch Priory tower which is only just visible. We've never noticed this island before although we've done loads of trips here in the harbour."
"I'm not surprised," said Andy, "it's hardly ever exposed unless, like today, it's an exceptionally low spring tide. I think it stands at about only half a metre and that's probably why it's become exposed."
"The inshore crew will be here very soon as they've been alerted and I expect the police won't be far behind."
As soon as he said this, three other cars arrived.
"I see the cavalry have arrived," said Andy. "That's our lads now and plod will be hard on their heels."
Sure enough, a local police car drew up a couple of minutes later. The arrival of vehicles drew more people who were rubbernecking which grew to become quite a small crowd of mostly holidaymakers.
"They'll soon have the RIB launched although the full name is a 'rigid Inflatable Boat'; but from what you say, there's no real hurry," said Andy. Reflecting on his earlier thoughts, he said, "All these police and RNLI vehicles turning up is bound to attract attention. It's amazing to me how some people just have to gawp when they think something horrible has happened. You should see them when something as obvious as a dead body is brought in – they'll have a field day later on, that's for sure!"
After giving the details of their find to a Police Constable, they were told that two detectives from Bournemouth Police Station would

arrive very shortly as it was only about a ten minute drive with the blues-and-twos on.
"Perhaps you should wait here as the Atlantic will probably take you all over to the site," said Andy.
"What the heck is an 'Atlantic'?" asked Peter.
"The Atlantic is the Atlantic 85 R.I.B.Inshore Lifeboat," answered Andy, "It's a bit on the big side for this little harbour, but there should be enough water to get close and you can always walk the rest of the way," he said with a grin. "Oh, and don't worry, I'll make sure that your canoes are safe."
"Thanks, I was going to ask about that," said Peter.
Another car quietly pulled up. A man just over six feet tall unfurled himself from the passenger seat, followed by a dark-haired woman who was nearly a foot shorter who had been driving. Peter guessed her to be about 35 years old, pleasantly attractive and had a distinct air of authority. That was Peter's appraisal.
She came over to the two canoeists and said, "My name is Detective Sergeant Anna Jenkins," and pointing to her co-passenger, introduced him as Detective Inspector Alex Vail."
Looking at the two young men, Anna said, "Can you give me your names and the circumstances in which you discovered the body please? We'll take a full statement later on." In an aside to her DI, she said, "It's a pity our bloke didn't make a more subtle approach, this only attracts more gawpers – just look at them."
"You're right Anna," said DI Vail, looking at the growing crowd.
Turning to Peter, she said "So, you two are?"
"This is my brother Simon Simpson and I'm Peter."
"And are you here on holiday?"
"No, we're local and we often canoe down here to the harbour. Today, we were canoeing from Tuckton and were going to make a fast dash through the 'Run' then try to get back again on the outgoing ebb tide against the strong current, just for the experience and to show off to the grackles, you know, the holiday visitors, but on the way over, we saw this little island and found, well, you know what we found, a body." Peter suddenly felt a tingle down his spine as he recalled what they'd seen out there.
"I see, not a very pleasant experience for you both I imagine," said Anna.
"You're telling me - I'll probably have nightmares now."
The crew had gone into the lifeboat station building as soon as they'd arrived to put on their regulation gear. Then the lifeboat was brought out of its building on a large, wheeled cradle and, with the crew manoeuvring this down the slipway, the large RIB was ready for launching and the crew were soon waiting for instructions.
DI Vail turned to the three lifeboat crew waiting by the big inflatable and asked, "Can you take us all over to this island so that we can make an initial inspection?"
The reply came from the crewman who introduced himself as the coxswain. "Of course, but you may have to walk a bit as this beauty

is a bit big for this puddle," he said looking at the big 'Atlantic' RIB lifeboat, "but she'll get us most of the way. Don't worry, the water's warm and we have towels.....
This did not seem to impress the DI.
They were handed two life jackets to put over their smart working clothes. Both Anna and Alex did not seem particularly thrilled at the prospect of salty spray. However, with the help of small steps, the crew, together with the two detectives, Peter and Simon, all boarded and the large RIB was launched quickly and efficiently. The two 115hp Yamaha Outboards growled into life, and with a burst of tremendous acceleration, they headed out to cross the short distance over to the island.
Very shortly they came to the small island which by now was quite dry. It had emerged from the water by no more than about three or four feet but had an overall surface size of some forty feet by twenty-five feet - enough space to hold the body of a dead woman lying face up in the soft sand of the harbour.
The problem was that the large RIB could only get to within about thirty feet of the island.....
The helmsman throttled back and the twin motors settled to a muffled roar on tick-over while the propellers were raised slightly. The bowman jumped overboard, taking an anchor as a precaution.
DI Vail said, "Anna, I don't really see that it needs two of us to confirm that this person is actually dead, so perhaps you could just hop over the side and make sure?"
Anna said, "But sir, it's not too easy to 'hop over the side' with a skirt on so I think it might be better if you rolled up your trouser legs and 'hopped over the side' instead...Sir."
"Oh, don't worry Anna; I'm sure these husky lifeboat men will be only too pleased to give you a hand."
"I'm sure they would sir, but it's giving me a 'hand', that makes me more worried!"
"Ah, but I have a problem as my trouser legs aren't built like sailors flares and they can't be turned up. So I think the final words should be, 'off you go Detective Sergeant'."
By this time, Simon, Peter and all the crew were trying to hide smirks at this exchange but not really succeeding. Looking over to Peter, Simon said, "So that's pulling rank if ever I saw it."
Asking everyone to look away, Anna grudgingly and discreetly removed her shoes and tights and, gripping her notebook, submitted to the indignity of being hoisted over the side of the boat rather like a sack being offloaded from a barge. "I don't think this is what I signed up for," she muttered to herself.
Once on the tiny island, she was joined by Peter and Simon and two of the crew who carefully looked over the body lying on the sand. Straight away Anna noticed that not only was the body lying in a straight position with her arms beside her, but that there were bands of what looked like either strapping or plastic banding around

her arms, legs, torso and neck: These bands were very tightly tensioned around the body.
She called over to Alex, "Sir, can you see these bands?"
"Yes, I can but they'll have to be removed later on in the morgue."
Anna quickly realised that there was another problem. She turned to one of the lifeboat men and said,"The tide is out now but when does it come in again?"
In a heavy Dorset accent he said, "Well now 'missy', you'll be aware that there be four tide changes a day hereabouts an' not the usual two. That's thanks to the 'hydriodynamics' of this 'ere part of the coast, what's unusual; the tides do come in an' out very quick. As this tide flowed some time ago now, I reckons that this 'ere little island will be covered over again in 'bout twenny minutes, so maybe we should take 'er back to our station and do what 'as to be done there. I don't think you'll get any footprints or tyre tracks for your forensics people to look at, do you?"
Anna chose to ignore this rather inappropriate humour and shouted over to Alex, "Sir, the tide will cover her in 20 minutes. Should we take her back?"
"I don't think her getting wet again will matter too much but it'll make the forensic examination bloody difficult if we leave her, eh? They'll want us to preserve as much evidence as there may be so we'd better get her off of there."
'Another feeble attempt at 'black' humour', she thought. "Ok, we, or rather these beefy lads will bring her over."
With that, the two crewmen and Peter gingerly tried to ease the body out of the gripping sand.
"Bloody hell, she's stuck in the sand," said the big crewman as he tried to roll the body over. "I think there must be something holding her down underneath." Scraping the soft sand away from under one side of the body with his hands, he said, "Oh Christ - there seems to be a log or something under her and she is strapped to it!"
"Can you see or feel what it is?" asked Anna. The others looked on without saying a word while he continued to scrape away more sand along the length of the body.
He stopped, and slowly stood up. Looking very pale, he stared into Anna's eyes and said very slowly and quietly, "Can you bloody believe this, she's only strapped to a damn great concrete post!"
Simon said very softly to Peter, "I guess that rules out suicide."
"Oh, for God's sake Si, don't be such a twat," said Peter.
"I was only saying Pete, I didn't mean it sound like a joke... I was only saying," his voice trailing off, as he realised it would be best to keep quiet.
Anna called over to the DI "Sir, she is actually strapped to a concrete bar or something. She's going to be too heavy to get her out of this sand so shall we cut these straps?"
"Bloody hell, no Anna!." said Alex. "Just try the best you can to free her. If it's really not possible, then you'll have to. If you've got your

phone, you can take some shots of the body while they try to move her.
"Ok, will do." Turning to the others, she said, "Lads, can you do your best to lift her as she is. It will be important for the forensic examination. It might be possible as there are four of you."
Anna took a number of photographs, some of them shots of the actual body and some of the body being moved.
They carefully managed to free the body but when they tried to lift it, it became apparent that she was indeed strapped to a concrete post - something like a fence post.
It was very difficult, as the body and the attached post made everything very heavy. With much grunting, they managed to lift her; however, it was extremely difficult to move the body with any dignity due to the strange nature of the corpse.
However, with great effort and care, they did manage to get their burden to the high, rounded inflated edge of the RIB and with the combined help of the coxswain and Alex who had remained in the boat; they managed to carefully slide the body and attachment aboard.
Anna looked at the high side of the craft and said "I'm sorry I couldn't help but I'm not tall enough to reach the side of the boat."
"Don't worry. As long as you have some good shots of the body in situ, that should help," said Alex.
Anna had to suffer the repeated indignity of being 'handed' back in to the craft. She thought, 'This is really not in my job description'.
When the body was safely covered and the anchor stowed back on board, the boat was pushed back off the shallows.
Peter was visibly shaken by the experience as he had never seen or had to touch a dead body before.
Quietly, Simon said, "How old do you reckon she was Pete?"
"Dunno mate, I suppose about mid-forties but hard to tell 'cos her face was all bloated and wrinkled - not surprising really. I think I'd be bloody wrinkled if I'd been lying face down like that for days. Christ knows how long she'd been there. As the island is only visible so rarely, she could have been lying there for bloody weeks, who knows? I don't know when it would have last been exposed but that's something for the lab techs I suppose, along with the police to find out."
"Yeah, but Pete, if she'd been there for that long, you wouldn't have been able to pick her up, she would have dissolved by now and would have been just a bag of slime."
"Shut up Si, you can be a ghoulish bastard sometimes. I don't even want to think about it; it was bad enough lifting her up. I'm probably going to have nightmares now, thanks a lot....."
***
The brothers really didn't know much about what happens to the human body when it's immersed in water; most of what they thought they knew came from programmes like CSI and, whilst this

type of programme was fairly accurate, they make the forensic work look so simple.
Although a body usually is bloated by bacterial action in colder water, the skin undergoes changes which make the corpse become 'available sea life food'.
In this case, the body was still quite 'intact' and this fact would be borne out during autopsy.
***

CHAPTER 16

They all arrived back at the lifeboat slipway at Mudeford Quay by which time there was a far more sizeable group of onlookers, curious to see what had been going on as the boat could be seen at a distance from the lifeboat slipway.
There was bound to be a reporter or, for sure, people with video recording on their mobile phones and they would be only too quick to get these onto Facebook and Twitter or even sell them to the newspapers. Unfortunately, that was only too accurate - nothing was sacred these days with the advent of smart phones, iPads and CCTV.
There was an innocuous guy standing a little way back from the gathered crowd of people who were craning their necks to see what the commotion was about.
He was the reporter for the local rag, the Bournemouth Echo, who was having a day off at the coast but, as ever, he was on the lookout for some interesting activity.
With a strong eye for a good news story, he quickly realised that a body had been recovered by the inshore Lifeboat and briefly saw the covered corpse being taken into the lifeboat station.
The detective sergeant asked Andy, the lifeboat station representative, to get the people to disperse as there was nothing more to see.
He managed to get them to leave, all except for the reporter who approached Andy and asked for more details.
Andy said, "Sir, it really isn't for me to give information and besides, I don't know who you are and why you should be interested."
"My name is Bert Metcalf and I'm a reporter with the Echo," he said with an air of importance. "Anything you can give me would be much appreciated," he said as he dug out his reporter's notepad and pen from his coat pocket.
"Well, I don't know much except that it was a woman who was found on a small island in the middle of the harbour." Andy replied. Beyond that, there's not much else I can tell you.
"Do you know how old she was?"
"No idea, sorry. I've not seen the body but she'll be taken directly to Bournemouth Hospital I would imagine, or at least to the mortuary for the medical and police examination - that's what normally happens when our boys retrieve a body."
"Okay and thanks anyway. I guess I'll have to get on to my contacts at the hospital for some more info - maybe see if there is a story here, cheers mate." And with that, he walked off to find his car, eager to make contact with one of his sources for this kind of thing.

The dark unmarked coroners' vehicle came through the car park and passed the 'Ship in Distress' pub, pulling up beside the lifeboat station.
Anna was talking to Alex as the body was moved quietly into the coroners' van. "Where do you think she came from sir, she surely can't have been washed there by the tide?"
"I don't know much about the tidal flows and currents here, but I'm sure it can't be strong enough to carry a weight like that even though the Avon and the Stour both run into the harbour. Perhaps there was a flash flood or something which gave an unusually strong flow recently; we'll have to check that out. My gut feeling is that she was deliberately placed there."
Peter and Simon asked Alex if they could go now. He told them that they would be contacted in due course by the local police for a formal statement, but yes, that would be fine and thanked them for their help. He also asked them not to discuss the details until they were cleared to do so by the police as the matter was not common knowledge and, obviously, they had yet to establish identity and other important facts.
"Okay thanks," said Peter, "we'll be in the pub for a while if you need anything else from us. After this we need something a little more than a watery beer!"
"I'm sure it can't have been easy, especially as, I'm sure you've realised, it's obviously not a simple case."
With that, the two brothers walked round to the 'Ship in Distress' pub on the quay which had stacks of lobster pots and other gear in rows outside and there were also a couple of small fishing boats tied up alongside the quay.
"Come on Si, let's get a couple in before we set off home. It's put the kybosh on our day but it's a damn sight worse for that poor woman."
"Do you know what Pete, I reckon she must have been dumped there because there's no way that she just ended up there by accident - there just isn't enough current or flow for that to happen."
"I think you're right mate, but you know what, someone must have known about the island and put her here there deliberately. If that's the case, then they'd either thrown her out of a boat or waded across with all that weight - bloody near impossible, I'd have thought."
Simon said, "Yeah, but hang on Pete, why put her on an island where she could be seen? Surely if you are going to try to hide a body, you'd put it somewhere pretty deep, wouldn't you? Perhaps she was just dumped and it's a coincidence that the island was there and they didn't know about it. We've never seen it before in all the times we've been here, have we?"
"Yeah, I think you're right bruv."
"Damn right I am!" said Simon. "Come on, let's get that drink and leave this to the police."

CHAPTER 17

At the 'Ship in Distress', they ordered a couple of 'fortifying' drinks and sat at a table near some fishermen. They were quite weather-beaten and were dressed in seagoing gear, so obviously not tourists.
As they sat down, one of the fishermen who had a large beard and wore a heavy sweater looked across and said, "Would you two lads be the ones what found that there body on 'Blue Moon Island' then?"
"Yeah, unfortunately," said Peter, "gruesome that was. Buggered up our day, but we can always come back – she can't."
"You be right there and no mistake," said the bearded fisherman.
"So why do you call it 'Blue Moon Island'?" asked Simon.
"Well, see lad, what we calls a 'Blue Moon' only occurs once every two years or less and it do give a very big tide rise and fall. So this little island t'will only be uncovered when the tide be very low as in 'Spring Tides', so this is why we call it 'Blue Moon Island', 'cos 'tis only seen very rarely. You know the saying "Once in a Blue Moon," and today being a low 'Spring' see."
Simon and Peter gave an understanding look to each other.
"Have you seen any unusual activity or boats recently?" asked Peter.
"Not much was there Daniel?"
"Not much truth be told, but I do 'member what we was a sittin' 'ere after we'd stacked them lobster pots, having a quiet beer afore goin' home, 'an you 'member Zak, that biggun what came through t'other day. We did see 'um cumin outa mist late on Monday last. She were only going slow like, stoppin' and goin' agen."
"What boat was that then?" said Peter.
"T'was that blue and white one, a bit like an old Fairey 'Huntsman', wannit Zak?" said the second chap. "She were quite a pretty craft, an' didn't she seem to bump that bloody sandbar just 'afore the Run. That would've done summat bad to 'er prop, I'll be bound."
"'T'would that Daniel," said Zak, "now you mention it. I'm thinkin' 'twas the craft what I did see up at that place on the river at Tuckton, where we do buy our cordage and the like, and they sell boats too. You know that auction house. Well I'm sure I saw that boat there some while back, when I was a getting' that new anchor. I think I heard someone call it a 'Christina'. Quite a nice boat, about three tons I reckons. Take a lot of lookin' after tho', being built of meogany like. P'rhaps 'twas that boat what we saw?"
"Aye, mebbe," said Daniel. "Anyway lads, we've to be a getting' away home 'but I don't suppose you'll be a forgettin' today for a while, eh?"
"That's for sure. Good talking to you both. Good fishing."
With that, Daniel and Zak left and Pete said, "I guess we'd better go and find Andy. He said he would take us and the canoes back to our

van at Iford when we were ready. Nice bloke. I bet the police will be knocking on our doors tomorrow wanting more details."
"Yup, s'pose you're right; let's go."
As good as his word, Andy loaded both canoes into his van and took them back to their starting point at Iford Bridge to collect their vehicle.

CHAPTER 18

The next morning, back at Bournemouth Police headquarters, Anna and Alex are given the sole responsibility for the case by their Detective Chief Superintendent James Gordon, who said that this was a strange and disturbing case as there had never been a body found in such a way in this area. "I'd like this wrapped up as soon as possible please - a case like this will affect the tourist trade which it will do when it's plastered all over the press and on the TV news programmes."
"Mind you Sir," said Alex, "I wouldn't be surprised if there were a lot of 'interested' people just itching for more bits of gossip about this; you know what people are like, anything macabre and juicy..."
"Unfortunately, I think you could be right Alex, but all the same, I'd like this to be cleared up as soon as possible – as quickly as you and your team can bring it to a close would be good result. Let's hope that it's just a simple case."
"Of murder, Sir?"
"Yes, of course Alex, you're right, there's usually more to a murder than 'simple' though, isn't there? Anyway, do your best please. What we don't need is for this case to drag on which could risk the press firing up the public by making it look as though we're not doing our job properly if we don't solve it quickly."
"Agreed and understood Sir." Alex responded.
The DCS left the room and Alex turned to Anna saying, "I hope you're ready to get stuck into this one Anna. I think it's going to be difficult to find out who she was."
"My thoughts exactly, sir."
"Firstly, can you get over to the mortuary and see what they've found out about the cause of death?"
"Yes sir but maybe they won't have done much yet so perhaps I should go and talk to Peter and Simon Simpson to see if they can throw any more light on how they came to find her."
"Okay, good idea Anna. There's not much else I can do for the time being, so I'll get on with other matters for now. Keep me informed if you find anything worthwhile."
"Will do sir," she said and left to pick up a car from the pool.
Alex sat looking at the door after Anna left and was quietly thinking to himself that Anna was becoming a very useful member of his team. She was very easy to get on with and had a good sense of humour as he had seen during her interaction with other colleagues. He was quietly looking forward to working with her, as he also found her rather attractive but he put that thought to one side - for a while...!
Arriving first at Simon's address, Anna knocked on the door. The door was opened by Simon who had a rather solemn look as he invited her in.
"Didn't sleep too well last night," said Simon stifling a yawn. "Would you like a coffee?"

"That that would be very welcome, thanks. I can't get going until I've had a strong coffee first thing."
"Me too," said Simon, "milk and sugar?"
"Just milk please," she said, sitting at the dining table so that she could take notes
"I'm not surprised you didn't have a good night," said Anna. "In the police, we are expected to take death in our stride and we often do, but when something as sadistic as this turns up, it's a 'game changer' to say the least. Someone has gone to great lengths to make sure she stayed in one place, as you must realise."
"Yes, to have gone to the trouble of taping the body to a bloody great concrete post obviously meant that they didn't want it found, I'd say."
"Can you give me any more information about your movements before you found the body? You know, where you came from and so on? - By the way, do you mind if I call you 'Simon'?"
"No of course not."
"Thanks."
"Well," he said, all I can tell you is that we 'put in' up at Iford Bridge as that's the end of the tidal run of the river but beyond that, we are not allowed to navigate. It's a nice easy place to launch and retrieve plus we can leave our van in the car park there."
"By 'put in', I guess you mean put your canoes in?"
"Exactly."
"For clarification, by 'we', you mean yourself and your brother Pete?"
"Er, yes, sorry, I wasn't thinking about you having to take notes – a combination of shock and tiredness I s'pose."
"No problem, I completely understand." she said in a sympathetic tone.
"How far is it down to the harbour from there would you say?"
"At a guess, I'd say about five miles or so there and back."
"Did you hear or see anything unusual on your trip?"
"Nope, nothing at all, just the usual things like people being on holiday or fishing and some of the posh houses along the river had garden parties going on but no, nothing out of the ordinary."
"Was the current strong or anything to make you aware or alert you to any potential problem?"
"No, nothing at all, it was a very pleasant. That is, up until we saw, you know, 'Her', well; I actually thought it was a bloke at first as I was ahead of Pete, so I could see the hair which was covering her face. The rest you know, as you arrived there very soon after the call was sent from the lifeboat station; about ten minutes I'd say."
"You said yesterday that you had never seen this small island before, is that right?"
"That's right, never. We've canoed around here many times but this is the first time we've actually come down on such a low tide."

"Okay Simon, I don't think I need to ask you anything more for now, but can I ask you to go to the main Bournemouth police station as soon as you can to make a formal statement?"
"Okay, I'll go over after work today. Peter and I took a day off yesterday so we need to show our faces for at least part of the day."
"And what do you do Simon?"
"I'm a mechanic. Peter and I both are, although we work at different garages."
"I see. Well thank you Simon. I'll go and see your brother now to see if he can throw any more light on his memory of what happened, although somehow I doubt it."
Anna was soon at Peters' address. When he answered the door, he was also looking rather drawn – red-eyed, ruffled hair and unshaven.
"Peter, I've talked to your brother Simon and he has given me a pretty complete picture of what happened yesterday but I was wondering if there might be anything more you can add to what we already know; something which might help our investigation."
"Well, I don't know what Si has told you, but I imagine that it can only be the simple facts of our short trip from Iford Bridge down to the harbour. Nothing happened on the way there until we found the body."
"That's what Simon has said, but is there anything which you can elaborate on?"
"Well," said Peter, "the only thing that might be helpful is that after the body was taken away, we met a couple of fishermen from the lobster boats at Mudeford while we were having a drink in the 'Ship in Distress'. They were telling us that they saw a boat in the harbour on Monday evening a week ago, with two men on board. They said it was about 10 o'clock and it was quite dark and misty."
"What sort of boat did they say it was?"
"I know they said it was a cabin boat, 'a bit like a Fairey Huntsman', a blue and white one."
Anna made a note of that name. "Did they say how big it was?"
"The chap called Daniel said it was about 30 foot and would have been around 3 tons."
"Did he say anything else about this boat, Peter?"
"Well, the other chap, his name was Zak, said that he thought he had seen this boat at the marine auctions at Tuckton when he was there a while ago as he was buying an anchor. He thinks it was called a 'Christina'. I suppose that is the type of boat design rather than a name, or he would have said 'it was called Christina'. I've never heard of this type before but I'd imagine the auction people or the owner would be the best people to help with this. I guess if it was on the water, then they'd have either sold it or were taking it for a test run or something like that. Anyway, you could look it up on the internet, there's bound to be pictures of this type of boat."

"Good idea, Peter. Did these men say anything about the boat's movements?"
"Yeah, actually they did; they said that it was 'stopping and starting' and 'coming out of the mist'."
"Oh, so it was misty on the Monday evening?"
"As I think I mentioned that's what they said but I don't know, I wasn't out and about that night."
"Did they say anything else about what happened to this boat, did it go back towards Christchurch?"'
"No, they said it went out through the 'Run' but just before it did, they said it seemed to slow down quickly and they reckoned it looked like they'd hit 'that' sandbar just before the entrance to the 'Run' and that it could have damaged the propeller."
"Do you think that's what happened?"
"Well with a boat that size, your prop is going to be quite a size and it's made of aluminium, so to hit a sandbar would be more than likely to distort the blades out of shape."
"Would that affect the boat very much then?"
"I know that it would cause them some problems and, thinking about it, if I'd been on that boat, I would have turned back and gone back up to the mooring, taking it slowly. It's not that far and Tuckton is about the last place for mooring a boat that size, as the river is too shallow beyond there. Of course, I'm presuming that it had come down the Stour."
"Could it have come from the other river, the Avon?"
"Absolutely not, although it's just possible as there are moorings just before the bridges on the Avon, but certainly not beyond there. In any case, the bridges are too low for anything other than a very small boat. Anyway, they said that they thought they'd seen it up at the Marine Auctions on the Stour."
"Yes, I see. But these fishermen you spoke to said that they went out through the 'Run', have I got that right?"
"That's what they said and, thinking about it now, it does seem a little strange."
"Why's that Peter? Is it okay if I call you Peter?"'
"Yeah - I wouldn't know who you were talking to if you called me Mr Simpson'."
Anna smiled at that.
"Well, I've had a few boats over the years and I know that if you have that sort of problem you don't go any further than you absolutely have to. You want to get moored up and check out the damage."
"Where do you think they might have gone, towards Southampton?"
"I very much doubt that." Peter shrugged.
"Why's that then?"
"Well, to get to Southampton or anywhere in that direction, such as Lymington, you'd have to go through the 'Narrows' at Hurst Castle -

the currents there are very fierce; there are even whirlpools ! The last thing you'd want there is a lack of power. Very dangerous!"
"Ok then, where else do you think they might have gone?"
"Given that they didn't go back upriver, or at least the fishermen didn't say they saw them head that way, they only saw them go out of the 'Run' and then lost sight of them in the mist. I reckon they could have made for Poole harbour."
"Why Poole particularly, Peter?"
"Because that's probably the best place to have a prop repaired. Some years ago, I had a propeller refurbished for an outboard of mine. I had a twin hulled fishing boat with a 120 hp outboard; it had a prop about 20 centimetres diameter which got damaged. This specialist re-shaped the blades and rebalanced it. Without that being done properly, the vibration caused by an unbalanced prop will cause incredible damage very quickly."
"So, if this boat had a damaged propeller, how would that have affected the speed do you think?"
"Well, given the size of the boat, and those guys said it was about 30 feet long, I would imagine it had something like a Mercruiser Stern Drive. If that's the case then, yes, it would have severely affected the speed."
"Hang on..... What's a 'Mercruiser Stern Drive'? Don't forget you're talking to a landlubber here."
"Sorry, that's the bit sticking out of the back of the boat with the propeller on. Unlike an outboard motor which has the engine outside the boat, the stern drive is simply the bit that takes the drive from the engine which is inboard, and transmits that to the propeller."
"The mists are clearing a little now. It's always very helpful to know a little more about the technical aspects of some of the things we have to deal with."
"Another thing about the stern drive is that because this part can be raised and lowered, it isn't just so that the 'trim' of the boat can be adjusted. It also means that it can be raised right up so that the propeller is away from the sea-bed and out of harm's way."
"You've got me again I'm afraid. What's the 'trim'?"
"Well, you know when a boat accelerates, the bow raises up?"
"Yes, I've seen that happen."
"Well, to make the bow ride at the proper height, the stern might have to be raised slightly, and that's when you 'trim' the boat by adjusting the stern drive leg to give the boat the correct aspect."
"Enough, enough! Information overload! Thanks Peter, I think I understand but I think we are going to have to have a talk with those two fishermen, don't you?" said Anna. "Can you give me their names?"
"I can only tell you that they were called Zak and Daniel. They'll certainly be able to confirm what I've told you and they can give you a better description of the boat and what they saw."

“Thanks Peter, you’ve been a great help giving us something to follow up especially as we have very little to go on at the moment. I don’t suppose you know where they live or where they might be found?” She asked
“Well, I guess as they have boats here and they are fishermen, they’ll be around here most of the time and I’m sure the local people will know them. They’ll most probably be in the pub.”
“Okay, that’s all for now. As I’ve already asked your brother Simon, can you get over to Bournemouth Police HQ and give a formal statement as soon as you can.”
“Of course, I’ll go after work tomorrow.”

CHAPTER 19

Anna went back to Police Headquarters and immediately gave DI Alex Vail a detailed summary of the details of the information from Peter and Simon Simpson including their conversation with the two fishermen.
"Great," said Alex. "You've done well with a very comprehensive report; at least we have a start. Do you think that this boat could be the one from which the body was dumped?"
"I think it's very likely, as it would've had to have been sometime when whoever dumped the body was not going to be seen."
"Do you have any idea of when they saw the boat?" Alex asked.
"According to the Simpson brothers, they were told by the two fishermen that it was the previous Monday evening - that would make it the 31st of August."
"OK, then we need to look up the state of the tides at that time because that might be important. I know you were going to get to the mortuary after seeing the boys, so can you get over there right away. We need the cause and time of death urgently."
"I'm on my way," said Anna. Alex was very impressed with Anna's report. He knew that she was a very conscientious and she always paid a great deal of attention to detail. She was also very pleasant to work with and, although she was very serious in her diligence, she was outgoing and had a good sense of humour too; he liked her a lot.
At the mortuary, Anna talked to the pathologist who was actually carrying out the post-mortem. He told her that the coroner had instructed a forensic autopsy as this was not a natural death or a suicide which was obvious from the way she was found, making it a criminal matter.
George Matthews was a very experienced pathologist. He was 55 years of age and was quite taciturn and had a rather 'dark' humour as was often the case with this sort of work. It was a kind of 'protection' against the very morbid nature of the pathologists' work.
George had just begun the examination as Anna arrived.
"Hi Anna, nice to see you again, it's been a while hasn't it?"
"It has George, we must stop meeting like this," she said with irony.
"I understand that you've been promoted and moved to Bournemouth nick. Congratulations."
"Thanks George. Yes, Detective Sergeant now and my new boss seems a really nice guy, quite dishy in fact."
"I'll tell Alex that when I see him again," said George with a smile.
"Don't you bloody dare?"
"Moving on," said George. "This one is a just a bit unusual. Someone was rather determined that she wouldn't float to the surface.... sticking that bloody great concrete beam to her."
"You're such a bundle of happiness George."
"I know Anna, it goes with the job."

The 'heavy duty strapping' surrounding the body had been cut and laid to one side as the concrete post prevented its' complete removal. The assistant photographed everything and George's notes were recorded through the microphone hanging just above the dissection table. The strapping was actually industrial tape about two inches wide, which had held the body very tightly to the concrete.

"Is this tape unusual?" said Anna.

"Not really, it's pretty standard. I think it might be the sort of tape that is used to repair inflatables and other such things that need to be kept waterproof but we'll get samples off to forensics and they can give you a better idea. They'll have to get someone to come and collect the concrete post though."

The body was lying face down with the post on top. With the help of his assistant, the heavyweight sealing tape was removed and the post put on the floor. Then the clothing was cut along the length of the body and removed, then carefully folded and put into evidence bags for further inspection.

"Are there any obvious signs of how she died?" said Anna.

"Not at the moment but let's have a closer look."

As the body was turned over and the long dark hair was moved back from the face, a small hole in the centre of her forehead was revealed. It became very evident as to the cause of death.

"Oh my God!" Anna exclaimed, "she's been shot!"

"It looks to be a small calibre gunshot but bigger than a .22 I think," said the pathologist. "Death would have been instantaneous. It was probably close range as there are no powder burns."

"Wouldn't these have been washed off by the tide?"

"I don't think so, the residue may have been but there would be burn marks, so I would guess that the shot was from certainly no more than five feet away."

"If we turn her back, we can find the exit wound which was probably hidden by the matted hair."

The two men rolled the body back to the 'face down' position. George carefully lifted the hair to search for the exit wound.

"There you are," he said, "as I thought, it does look larger than a .22 calibre and more than likely a .38 or similar but ballistics will give us more precise details. The bullet has expanded on impact and when this happens, it takes a great deal of bone and 'matter' with it." This was evidenced by the large area of skull missing from the back of her head. This had initially been obscured by her hair.

"So would this leave traces at the murder site, when we find it, so that we can confirm the location?" Anna asked.

"Indeed - there will be quite a lot of 'splatter' and 'blood haze' which will be easily identifiable I would imagine. I would also say that I think, although I'm not an expert by any means, that by using that sort of ammunition, the perpetrator is a very dangerous person."

"Why do you say that George?"

"Because it would appear that they have used a type of 'hollow point' ammunition which causes immense tissue damage. Normally, that sort of bullet will stop inside a body, but when fired from such close range, it will pass through as we see here, with the resulting devastation. A truly horrible injury."
"Excuse me George; I need to phone the boss." Anna stepped outside and quickly phoned her DI.
"Sir, she was shot in the forehead, from close range, George thinks."
"And George is..."
"Sorry sir, George is George Matthews, the pathologist. I know him from my contacts with him while I was at my previous station."
"Okay, I see; actually I do know George slightly; we've met a few times. But his has to be murder," or... perhaps an execution?" said Alex pausing.
"An execution would seem to me to be more than probable as George is of the opinion that the bullet could have been what he called a 'hollow point' bullet. One that opens out on impact, to cause more damage. He also said that the killer must be a very dangerous person, to use that sort of ammunition. It's unbelievable sir, who the hell can hate someone that much to be so callous?"
"Does it have to be hate? There is a possibility that it could be something else."
"What do you mean sir?"
"Well, there is the possibility that it could have been carried out by someone who was paid to kill her - a hired killer..."
"Jesus Christ, that's unheard of around here."
"I know Anna but until we know who she is and where has she come from, we cannot move on. Have they found any identification or any clues as to who she might be?"
"We're still checking. I'll get back to you as soon as I can if there is."
"Okay Anna, keep me posted."
"Sir," She said ending the call.
Going back in to the pathologist, she asked, "Do we have any ID or other information from her clothes?"
"I don't think they'll be much help actually as the jeans are just like millions of others and the sweater is one you could probably buy in any large supermarket. She is wearing a T-shirt but again, just a bog-standard one with some sort of pattern."
Looking at the T-shirt, Anna saw quite a distinctive design which she thought could be traceable and have possible significance.
As the T-shirt was removed, a number of heavy bruises to each side of her body became evident. They were dark purple in colour and were in the form of straight lines about 15 centimetres long; there were some on her upper legs and thighs too. There were other marks on her chest, arms and legs.
"What do you make of these George?" She said pointing at the bruises.
"The dark bruises look to me as if they were made by a bar of some sort. Perhaps an iron bar or a heavy wooden stick, maybe a

truncheon. Someone's given her a heck of a beating. There will be a number of broken bones here, I'm sure."
"Do you think that maybe the killer was trying to get some information out of her?" said Anna.
"Either that, or he or she, was very vindictive but in my experience, it's usually men who use the gun. I suppose it is possible that there were two people involved, a man and a woman. The woman giving the beating and the man actually shooting her, although I would suggest that a woman wouldn't usually have the strength to do this. Who knows?"
"Would she have been tied up?"
"Well, she has some marks around the upper chest and arms suggesting that she might have been restrained or something similar but that's far from definite at this stage."
"But it seems likely?"
"I'd say that to sustain the injuries that she has and in the places that she has them, she could well have been tied or strapped to a chair and beaten on the sides of her body and thighs, whilst she was restrained. Looking at those marks, I would suggest that it could have been a sort of tape, as they are not deep but the bruising is superficial and quite wide. That says to me something like packing tape, you know the sort that is used when strapping up big parcels."
"It's all pretty brutal," said Anna.
"Indeed," said George.
"I'll leave you to the rest of the autopsy now George and get back to you later unless you find anything 'startling'."
"Okay, I'll get everything to forensics as soon as I've finished here and made my notes."
"Thanks George; it was nice to see you again. This can't be the best of jobs but even worse when you see how this poor woman died, and we don't know why or where or even who she is."
"It's certainly a strange one - 'bye Anna."
As she left the mortuary suite, her mind was caught up with the strange design on the T-shirt.
As she was driving back to HQ her mobile rang.
Driving back to HQ, her mobile rang.
"Hi Anna, it's George. I just thought you might like to know but we missed a fairly small tattoo on the body. We were so busy looking at the head that we didn't see it on the inside top of her thigh, close to the groin."
"Oh; thanks for letting me know George. What sort of tattoo is it - can you describe it?"
"Well no, not really as it seems to be some sort of script. I would say it looks either Arabic or Syrrilic - something like that. I can send you an email of it if that would help."
"That would be great, thanks George. It may well get us going on tracing her. It will narrow the search to about ten million tattoo artists!"

By the time Anna got back to her desk at Police HQ, there was an email from George waiting on her PC.

From ADC Matthews@hotmail.com
To: DS Jenkins Bournemouth CID
Hi Anna..... This is what I found.... hope you can find someone who can decipher this, whatever it means. Rgds, George”. ناشناختنی من

CHAPTER 20

Anna then went to find Alex to update him on the latest situation. She showed him the photo of the tattoo and his reaction was,
"What the hell is that language, that's not
something I've ever seen, have you?"
"Nope, I thought at first it was something like Arabic but I really don't know."
"Get onto that will you Anna? Find someone who can tell you what language that is and what it says; then get her fingerprints run through the Police National Computer, the PNC, you never know, she may have some form. If you can, also try to get some idea of the design on her T-shirt - that might give us a lead."
'Actually, I did know that PNC meant the Police National Computer Alex', Anna thought. 'I am a sergeant now'.
Alex went to try to find a witness who might have seen the boat or recognised it. He searched on-line for a picture of a Fairey 'Christina' boat to show around and soon found one from a boat sales website. He printed off a few copies to hand to his other staff. Leaving Anna to her searches, he told her that he was going over to Poole Harbour to try to get some information on the movements of this particular boat, should it have been seen. He drove over to Poole Harbour, found his way through the rather confusing sheds and stacks of containers and, after parking his car, located the main Harbour office. At the reception he asked for the Harbour Master and was directed to the Master's office on the second floor. Alex introduced himself and then outlined the reason for his visit and the nature of his enquiry, showing him the photograph. This was of the type of craft which had been suggested as the boat most likely to have been used in this incident and asked if this boat had been seen entering the harbour during the night of Monday August 30th, or the early hours of the 31st.
As there had been no reports of a craft matching this description, Alex changed his questions and asked where such a boat might have made for, given that it was dark and they may have had engine problems.
"Actually, unless there was a particular reason for a boat such as this to be reported to us, we would have no knowledge of its whereabouts. We would only become involved if there was any trouble or emergency."
"I understand that," said Alex.
The Harbour Master then suggested that the most likely place a craft would be found would be probably on an unoccupied buoy around 'Evening Hill' as that is where there would probably be a number of vacant, small mooring buoys on the 'Trots'.
"I'm sorry; I'm not very nautical - what are the 'Trots'?"
"They're heavy chains on the sea bed with mooring buoys attached at intervals so that a number of boats can be kept in line and

separated so that as the tide turns and the currents change, they do not get damaged by colliding with each other."
"And a boat such as this one could come in and tie up to one of these?"
"Yes, that would be fairly easy."
"Ok, thanks," said Alex. "I'll head on over to Evening Hill. Can you suggest anyone over there who I can talk to who might have seen something?"
"There are a few boatyards over there but I'd say your best bet would be one of the smaller yards. They would have a pontoon or jetty and slipway for tenders, but most of the moorings would be out on the 'Trots'."
"Can you give me any names?" Asked Alex as he opened up his notebook
"Well there is one that springs to mind, that's Brizey's boatyard. He lives there on the top floor and I know he has big windows which look out over the harbour. He's an ancient old guy and been there for donkeys years, but doesn't miss much."
Alex thanked the Harbour Master for this information and set about looking for this boatyard.
As he drove towards Sandbanks, he came to 'Evening Hill' and looked out across Poole Harbour. Stopping the car, he realised that at this point, he was looking at quite a long distance across the water to where the main shipping channel was. With the fantastic view towards Brownsea Island, he presumed that 'Evening Hill' was so-called due to the beautiful and well-known evening sunsets across the harbour. This part of Poole Harbour had an almost 'magical' quality about it and he never tired of the views from here. During the summer in this part of the harbour where the water was relatively shallow away from the main channel, there were usually hundreds of people out on the water enjoying various water sports such as windsurfing, sailing and fairly recently, kite-surfing but thankfully, jet-skis were banned from this section as they were considered too dangerous when there were so many people using the harbour for pleasure. There were a great many craft either at anchor or moored further out towards the main channel but it was very hard to actually distinguish any particular boat even though there was good visibility. He came to the realisation that at night, or even in late evening, it would be almost impossible to see a boat of the type they were looking for, as it wouldn't be very visible at that distance and even more so if the boat was not showing any navigation lights.
'This is making things even more difficult', he thought, 'but we have to get some clear understanding of how things had transpired'.
Realising that he had perhaps travelled too far and he was getting closer to Sandbanks, there were no obvious boatyards to be seen, so he turned round and went back the way he had come, stopping at a newsagents to ask the staff for directions.

"Good morning. I wonder if you can help me. I'm looking for a boatyard called 'Brizey's Yard'."
The two young female assistants looked at each other. Saying nothing, they both broke into giggles.
"Why do you find this funny?" he asked.
"No, he's a funny old codger but 'e's got a wicked tongue on 'im. You don't want to get on the wrong side of old Brizey."
"So you know him then?"
"Oh yes, we know him; dirty old sod." They looked at each other and giggled again.
He thought he'd leave out any questions in that direction. He didn't want any distractions of that nature. "Can you tell me how to find his boatyard then please?"
"Of course, which way are you going?"
"I'm heading towards Poole at the moment."
"Then you've missed it. Go back towards Sandbanks and you'll come to a little patch of trees on a sort of 'island' in the road. Just there, you'll see a white gate and this is the entrance to ol' Brizey's boatyard." They looked at each other again and began giggling again. "Best of luck."
"Thanks," Alex said, wondering what he might find, although all he wanted was firm information.
Following their directions, he travelled back along Sandbanks road until he came to the place which had been described. He saw the gate and turned into the narrow entrance to the boatyard.
The road down to the slipway was not quite straight and as he looked for somewhere to park, he heard a loud rasping voice from above him shouting "Oi, don't you be tryin' to park your car down there, you be blocking the slip!" Craning his neck, he looked up and there was a rather strange bush of white hair looking down from an upstairs window.
'That could be the man I'm looking for', thought Alex and, suitably warned, he reversed with considerable difficulty back up the narrow road. After some time he managed to find a place to park, quite a distance from the yard.
Muttering about the difficulty in finding a parking space with all the double yellow lines around, he walked back to the boatyard. As he went down the slipway access road, he looked out over the short jetty where several small boats were berthed and saw a number of cruisers and yachts obviously moored to small buoys at quite a distance across the harbour.
'Ah ha, they could be the 'Trots',' thought Alex.
He knocked on what he took to be the residential door of the boatyard and after quite a while, a man in his 'later years' (although Alex placed him at about 150 years old), opened the door. He was dressed in very well-worn, 'comfortable' clothes of the 'nautical' variety in varying colours and condition, sporting an enormous white beard. He said very gruffly, "What do you want?"

"I am Detective Inspector Alex Vail from Bournemouth Police and I'm making enquiries linked to a body found in Christchurch Harbour recently. We are trying to locate a witness who might have seen or noticed a blue and white cabin cruiser of about 25 to 30 feet in length, in this area on Monday late evening the 30th of August." He showed the old man the picture. "One like this, Sir?"
"Didn't see no boat like that on Monday evenin', no."
"Would you have noticed a boat like that coming into the harbour, as it was quite dark?"
"'Tis probable that I might have seen it as I live right at the top on the third floor and I can see right over the harbour but like I said, I didn't see it."
"Okay sir, that's fine. Could I just ask your name so that I can keep my records straight?"
"Brizey."
"Thank you Mr. Brizey and your first name is?"
"Just Brizey."
"Very well, and many thanks for your time."
With that Alex turned to walk back up the slipway road. He had walked about five yards when he heard the loud "Oi," again.
He turned and looked back. Brizey was standing with his hands on his hips. It was hard to read his expression due to the great bush of white hair which encompassed his face.
Brizey said, "I said I didn't see a boat such as this on Monday night but I did see 'um on Tuesday morning 'cos she were tied up to one of my pontoons. T'was one like the one you did show me in the picture."
"That's great. This confirms where this boat went from Christchurch as it was misty there and it wasn't seen again after leaving the harbour."
"Mr. Brizey, did you notice anything about this boat, such as how many people were on board or what they were doing?"
"'I told you, just 'Brizey', don't you people listen? Anyways, I did see one man - he was on the stern. I think he must have been fiddling with the prop as his head was nearly in the water."
"I don't know much about boats but surely, if he was 'fiddling with the prop', he couldn't have reached it unless he was under the boat?"
"You certainly don't know much do 'e?" See, this one had a stern drive where the prop is attached to a leg which can be raised or lowered so as to make it easy to get at such as the propeller."
"Oh, I see," said Alex.
"Well, 'e don't see much do 'ee?"
"What time was this?"
"Must've been 'bout nine or 'alf past."
"Did you see what he did after 'fiddling about on the stern'?"
"Aye, t'other man did get into his little inflatable what was hangin' on davits and he rowed like the devil to shore."
"But you just said you only saw one man."

“I said I only saw one man fiddling with the prop. There was another man.”
“So there was a second man."
"Didn't I just say that or are you deaf?"
"Did you see him come ashore or where he went?”
Alex was in considerable danger of losing his cool somewhat.
“No, damn him - he must’ve come ashore somewhere along the beach. I wanted to catch him for mooring fees. See, they be my ‘trots’ out there and there be mooring charges to pay.”
Alex could understand that he wanted his mooring fees. 'I'll bet no-one gets away without paying, usually', he thought. “So he came ashore but you don’t know where he might have gone after that?”
“I just said that didn’t I?”
‘Cantankerous old bugger’ thought Alex – ‘I bet he’s popular with customers’.
“Okay then. So, we can only assume that he made his way to the road. Could he get a bus from around here?”
“If he do wait long enough.”
“Perhaps he could have got a lift from a passing car.” Alex said to himself, 'this is like getting blood out of a stone...'
"Tis possible I suppose but if’n he were in a hurry, ‘appen he’d not want to walk with a damn great big prop to carry.”
"So he was carrying a propeller?"
"How the hell would I know, I didn't see him."
"Then, how do you know he was carrying a prop?"
"You’re the detective, so I imagine that you'd realise that if'n one man were takin' off a prop, then t'other man would take it with him in the tender. Or is that too difficult for the police to understand?"
Alex was having a little trouble restraining himself. He had a mental picture forming which included ‘hands round throat’. “But you didn’t see anyone else on the boat?”
“Didn’t I say I saw t’other man?”
“He’s the one you saw leaning over the stern?”
“That's what I said!”
'Give me strength', thought Alex. “So to be sure, there were two men. One who apparently took off the propeller and one who got into the small inflatable boat?”
“I can see why you be an Inspector then,” said Brizey.
Alex asked carefully, expecting another oblique answer. “When did you last see the boat?’
“Well, I did have to go to Dorchester t’other day, see, an’ I didn’t get back ‘til last night and she were gone by then.”
“So, with today being Friday, that would mean that he was gone by Thursday evening?”
“You be right quick you young fellas, ‘an no mistake", chuckled Brizey.
‘I bet he calls anyone under 80 ‘young fella,’ thought Alex, containing the desire to hit him.

"By the time I were back from Dorchester, I looked for the inflatable but it'd gone or I would have taken it to the store until he came for it so I could charge him - but I missed him, dammit."
Alex handed Brizey his card. "Perhaps if you hear of anything that might help our investigation or to trace this man from the boat, could you give me a ring on this number?"
"Mebbe," said Brizey.
"Before I go, can you tell me where there might be a place to get a propeller repaired?"
"E want nothin' but information, don't 'e? Anyways, there be a repair workshop on West Quay Road, just by the RNLI College. That'll be the best place to try as there b'aint many places able to do that sort of repair now that the big powerboat place has almost taken over most of Poole."
"Well, thanks for your valuable information and if we need a statement from you, we'll be in touch."
"Aye, well just don't go tryin' to park your squad cars down my slipway and blockin' it."
"We'll try not to, and thanks again Sir."
Alex couldn't wait to get away from the curmudgeonly old bugger.

CHAPTER 21

Back at the station, Alex gave instructions to the DC's to take copies of the photograph and show them to any boat owners they could find in the area of Brizey's boatyard to see if anyone saw anything relating to that boat. This could take some time and there were other more pressing enquiries to be made by Anna.
She was on the phone when he went in to their office. After finishing the call, she turned to Alex and said, "I think there might be a lead on the fingerprints, but they have to do some more checks to be certain of a match. They think there might be a mistake with the name as it is unusual and they think there may have been a typo. She seems to have a conviction in Durham some years ago. It is a long way north, but you never know. There may well be a connection. We'll have to wait and see when the PNC boys get back to me; at least we may have a name."
"Have you had any joy with the 'T' shirt design?"
"No, but I've been trawling through design pictures until my eyes are hurting, but nothing like this one. I think it must be a really special 'one-off' and maybe hand-printed. This is going to take a lot of finding. "How about the places that hand-print garments? There must be a way of contacting them, but I've no idea how many there might be. I'll draw up a list of possible places starting with this area and email photos of the 'T'shirt design. We might get lucky."
"Go ahead, and get any spare DC to help you until we have something more definite to go on."
"Okay Anna, what have we got so far? We have the body of a woman who was beaten and murdered, then taken to be dumped. My feeling is that it was dumped in a little-used area of water which enabled the boat which carried her, to make a quick escape virtually unnoticed. Unfortunately for the perpetrators, there was a particularly low tide which exposed the body.'
"But why dump the body where it was so shallow sir?"
"Do you know, I'll bet they had no idea it was that shallow there. Even If they had known the harbour, it would have been unlikely that they knew about the shallow part unless they had been around during a low tide event and I very much doubt that they were that thorough. Anyway, didn't Zak and Daniel say that it was called 'Blue Moon Island' because it only becomes visible 'once in a Blue Moon'?"
As he was saying this, Alex had a thought and opened 'Google' searching 'Blue Moon'. The Wikipedia answer gave him the information that a 'Blue Moon' only occurred once in perhaps two or even three years, when the position of the moon coincided with the low spring tides, causing exceptionally low water.
"There you have it Anna, that's the reason why the island was exposed I reckon."
"That seems to fit sir."

"There has to be a very good reason why they or someone, beat a woman and murdered her. Our questions are; who is she, what is her connection to these two men; why was she beaten and killed? And, where did she or they come from? Are they local? Are they the killers or just the ones who got rid of the body?"
Anna said, "We also need to know where they came from, because although we know the boat came from a local boatyard, the men could be from anywhere."
"Which makes it all the more difficult? Where are we up to with the body?"
"Well," said Anna, holding up the fingerprint report, "we have a fingerprint lead, and we'll keep at the 'T' shirt design. The tattoo must have some meaning."
Alex looked puzzled. "One thing that does really puzzle me is how and why did she get from South London down to Christchurch? Who took the body?"
"That is a big mystery at the moment but I'm sure there is a simple reason that we just haven't found at the moment."
"I'll be a lot happier when we have found that 'simple reason', that's for sure. What are your thoughts on that tattoo?"
"I found that it's actually Persian script. It is not a normal phrase that would be tattooed. The best I can find is that is means something like 'Unknowable Me'. That says to me that it could mean something like 'mystical me' or maybe 'you can't really know me'.
"Blimey, Anna, that's a bit deep isn't it?"
"Well, it has to have some sort of deeper significance; it isn't just a meaningless phrase. I was just hypothesising."
"I guess that you have a different way of looking at these things, so keep at it Anna."
"What else do we have sir?"
"At last we have definite sighting. We have a witness to this boat which I am certain is the one which brought the body and dumped it. We now know that the same boat went to Poole harbour and moored up during Monday night or early Tuesday. How they managed to get into the harbour in the dark, I don't know but they did and tied up to a buoy in the harbour at Evening Hill. I went over and in a boatyard there I found the yard owner, grouchy old bugger, but he said he did see this boat and gave me some useful information. He spotted a man doing something on the stern which looked like he was taking off the propeller. If that's the case, then this ties in with what we were told by the two fishermen, Zak and Daniel. They said they thought the boat had damaged the prop as they were going out of the harbour. This could have meant that they had to change their plans and get some repairs done before continuing to their intended landing place. This means that I have to go over to Poole to see if I can locate the workshop which would have repaired the propeller."

"Right, so I'll go back to trying to trace this woman then. We should have the final results and hopefully confirmation from the fingerprints soon."
Following the instructions that Brizey gave him, Alex drove into Poole and soon found the marine repair specialist which was very near to the RNLI Headquarters. He walked down a small lane past the rear of a huge building which now housed part of the Sunseeker power boat building complex. Sunseeker Powerboats had virtually taken over Poole as they were one of the major super-yacht builders in Europe and made the most expensive craft for the super-rich.
Asking a chap working just inside the RNLI HQ compound where he might find the repair workshop, he was directed to the small lane which seemed to finish at the upper harbour-side. Spotting the sign which confirmed he had found the right place, he walked into the small workshop which specialised in propeller repairs and introducing himself he asked to speak to the owner.
"Hello, I am Detective Inspector Vail from Bournemouth Police. I am making enquiries relating to an ongoing investigation into a crime which occurred around August 30th in Christchurch Harbour. We are sure that someone brought a propeller to Poole to be repaired and you were indicated as the most likely people to make such a repair. Would that be the case?"
'Well that's most likely, as we are probably the last remaining specialist repairers in the whole of this region."
"So, do you remember anyone calling here with a propeller for repair recently?"
"Actually, yes. There was a chap who came in last Tuesday morning, early."
"And he had a propeller for repair?"
"Oh yes, and it was in a pretty bad condition. I asked him how it happened and he was a bit cagey, to say the least. In fact he seemed a little surly to me but he said he thinks he hit a sandbar or something, maybe a mudbank, as it didn't make a 'bang' from hitting something solid, so to speak."
"Are you sure about the date?"
"Yes, I always log in repairs."
"Can you describe him?"
"He was about 50 yrs old, just under six foot. Dark brown hair and was dressed in casual clothes. He gave a name of David Smith. When I asked him what boat it came from and what engine size it was, this man said he didn't know."
"Didn't you find that strange, you know, him not knowing what boat it came from and so on?"
"Now you mention it yes, but he seemed in such a hurry and not inclined to chat, if you know what I mean. Usually 'boaty' blokes like to have a natter about things, but I would have imagined that he would have at least known something about it as he said that they had hit a sandbar or mudbank; and then to say that he didn't know

what boat it was, must have been a little strange I suppose, which is probably why I remember him."
"What opinion did you have about this man, anything unusual?"
"Well, I was a little unsure of him as he didn't look like someone who knew about boats and he was not dressed like a 'boaty' person. He said it came from a '25ft cabin cruiser'. Well, this size of prop doesn't come from a normal 25 foot 'cabin cruiser'. Anyway, that description is usually given to a river or canal type craft.
"Someone has called this boat a 'Christina', does that mean anything?"
"Yes, a Fairey 'Christina', similar to a Fairey 'Huntsman', a beautiful boat. The 'Christina' was designed by Bruce Campbell of Hamble, in around 1960 and built of triple skinned mahogany and weighed about 3 tons."
"You seem to know a lost about boats."
"I suppose when you have been around boats and their power units for so many years, some of it rubs of," he said with just a hint of irony.
"Of course, I'm sorry. It's just that I am not in any way nautical and I appreciate your knowledge. In fact it is very useful to know exactly what sort of craft it would be and it helps our investigations. Would it be a fast boat?"
"Not particularly by today's standards, but this propeller was about 40 cm diameter, and at that size, it had to come from a craft with a large engine and it appeared to have been 'tuned for performance'. You can tell this from the way the blades were shaped for a special purpose and I would say that the engine would have to be something like a big modern diesel, to drive a prop that big. If it was a 'Christina', then I would suggest that the craft had been re-engined, probably by a boatyard who was using an old boat to try different engine and prop configurations. With a big diesel she could be up to about 30-35 knots.'
"Why do you say that it had been re-engined?"
"Because I happen to know that virtually the same boat won the Cowes-Torquay race crewed by Tommy Sopwith in 1961. In those days the power boats weren't so fast. Back then the engine was much less powerful than the diesels of today, although the hull would have been strong enough to handle the increased stresses that the extra speed would cause. Another thing is that this prop is from a 'Stern-Drive' unit."
"And how do you know that?"
"It is too big for an 'underslung' propeller."
"What is an underslung propeller?"
"It's what it sounds like. It is under the stern section of the boat through a propeller shaft to the engine. There wouldn't be enough clearance to spin a prop of this size. This one has to have come from a rear-mounted drive unit, hence the name 'Stern-Drive'."

"Right, now I understand a little more. If it had hit a sandbar, say in Christchurch harbour, would that have caused the damage this prop had suffered, the one that this 'David Smith' brought in."
"Absolutely, but in the harbour they would have been going slowly and if they'd hit perhaps a sandbar, that would seem about right given the damage that I saw. If they'd been going at speed the prop would have been completely smashed and they would still be wherever they hit!"
"There is another reason I say that he didn't know much about boats. As I say, this boat has a stern drive and in shallow water, this can be raised slightly to give some more clearance to the draught. I think this might be another reason why I remembered him and able to describe him."
"I see what you mean; that sounds reasonable. Did he say where he was going?"
"No, but he did say that they would get going as quickly as possible and could I do anything to the propeller to improve the performance. I said that I could 'cup it', to give a little more thrust. He asked what cupping was. I told him that it was putting a small extra 'curl' to the top of each blade, to give more drive, but it may not be the best idea as it may overburden the engine, as it is rather like adding a higher gear to a car. He said that it had a big engine and there was plenty of power to spare, so I made the alteration."
"How long did it take to make the repair?"
"Well, this chap said it had to be quick as they wanted to make a trip as soon as possible and this had already caused a delay, so no matter what it cost, would I do it quickly? I said yes, Thursday, and that's when came."
"Did he leave any contact details?"
"No, I told him that it would be ready on the third of July which was the Thursday morning. He came around ten a.m., paid the full price in cash and went."
"Is that the last you saw of him?"
"Yes."
"Did he have an accent?"
"Yes, I'd say a London accent; I'm not from there but that's what it sounded like to me, although to be honest, he didn't say much at all."
"Thank you for your help. It's been most informative. I'll leave you to your work now."
Alex left the workshop knowing a great deal more about the reasons and need for the propeller repair and how that might have affected the actions which had occurred so far.

CHAPTER 22

Returning to the station, he met with Anna who was researching the 'T' shirt patterns, but with little success.
"Hi Anna, have you had any luck with the 'T' shirt?"
"No, nothing of any real interest and quite honestly I don't think it would help much anyway. What did you get over at Poole?'
'Well, I've spoken to the chap who repaired the propeller and he said that this was collected on Thursday morning and the chap who came was about 50 yrs old, nearly six foot and had dark brown hair. He said he was casually dressed but did not look 'nautical'. He said his name was 'David Smith', but I don't believe that for one minute."
"Well, at least that's getting somewhere," said Anna, "so what do you think happened then, did he go back to the boat?"
"I think that's the most likely thing as it's gone, so they must have replaced the propeller and no one has seen it since. Finding that boat is vital, so that we can try to trace these two men, and try to find out who they are. Anna, can you go to the harbour master over at Poole, to see if he can give you any idea as to the movements of craft out of Poole harbour. I don't really know if he would have seen this, but perhaps he's got some way of finding out about the movements of boats. Anyway, see what you can discover."
"Should I actually go there or should I simply phone him?"
"I think if you go over there, it's not far, you can also ask around the likely places to see if anyone actually remembers seeing this boat moving. I think it's worth a try although it might be a long shot."
"Okay Sir, a little trip it is."
"Good girl Anna."
Being referred to like this she found very patronising, but let it pass. For now.
"Meanwhile, I'm going to the auction place up at Tuckton," said Alex, "to see what I can find out about the boat and who owned it. Maybe they know who these men are. Oh, and when you've been over to the harbour at Poole, can you get Alice and Tom on to all the likely places that boat could have gone to. I can't think that they would have gone too far as they can be followed along the coast. There's always someone watching somewhere."
"Right," said Anna, "I'll tell them to get 'Googling' and see what they can turn up. I don't know these places but we'll find someone who does."

Alex drove to Christchurch, located the building he was seeking and went into the Marine Auctions site at Tuckton,
He parked his car on Willow Way which was just behind the boat sheds, and walked down to the buildings. They were timber and corrugated steel buildings with large doors as would be expected, to allow boats to be brought inside. He walked around briefly outside just to take a look at the situation of the buildings to give himself an

idea of the layout. He noticed that at the far end of the largest building he could see some pontoons where there were a number of larger craft moored. Walking back into the main shed he saw a man who was working on a boat.
"Good morning sir. Are you one of the staff here?"
"No, I'm just tarting up my boat, ready for the auction. Go over there, you'll find Keith. He's the yard foreman."
"Thanks." Walking over the large shed, he found Keith. Introducing himself, he said, "Can you take a look at this photograph and tell me if you recognise this boat or one like it?"
"Yes, although it's not exactly the one but we had a boat very much like that. It was stolen recently. We don't know exactly when it was taken, but it was discovered this morning. I suppose you are here about the theft?"
Alex passed over that question, not wanting to alert anyone to his real enquiry at this time. He needed to get far more information.
"How come it was not noticed until now?" asked Alex. "A very similar boat was seen on Monday in Christchurch Harbour and we know it was also in Poole harbour last night. As it is now Friday morning, it seems very strange that it was not noted as missing before this. Has the theft been reported to the police?"
"That was done earlier this morning. The reason it was not noticed is that the owner lives in London and he told us he wouldn't be down to move the boat until this coming weekend."
I'll check on that, thought Alex. His detective mind was ringing some 'bells'. "But someone surely would have noticed it was missing from the mooring?"
"Not necessarily," said Keith, "it was moored in a small basin out of sight from our offices and as we only have a couple of staff, we rarely go round there unless we have to. There's enough to do with logging and cataloguing all the small items ready for auction. Once we have logged in for sale a craft like that, we tend to get on with all the other things."
"I see. So you're saying that no-one missed the boat until this morning. And how long would the boat 'not have been checked'?"
"Dunno really," said Keith "could have been up to a week. Just depends on the work load for all the other things, especially close to an auction."
"Do you have the name of the owner from London and his contact details and just for the record, the name of the boss here?"
"Of course, just hold on a mo' and I'll get them."
He came back with the boat owners' name which was Michael Fortune and the proprietor of the Boatyard was Frank Jordan.
"Thanks for your help Keith."
Alex made his way back to headquarters. While he was driving, he was musing over what information was to hand at the moment and he was not best pleased as so many points were not linking up. Who was she? Why was she killed? Who killed her? Why beat her up? Who brought her from London to Christchurch?

Back at the office, he saw Anna. "Are we making progress?"
"Well sir, I saw the harbourmaster and he says that it was very likely that this boat exited the harbour at night or late evening, but it was not actually seen. He did say that although it was not a moonless night, if this boat didn't show running lights it would have been very difficult to see."
"But surely someone would have seen this going past the chain ferry at Sandbanks, from the Haven Hotel; it would have been very close."
"I'm sure someone might have seen a boat passing, but finding them is going to be like a needle in a haystack. I'd imagine that most people are either in the bar or asleep in their rooms, certainly not looking out at a very dark seascape where nothing much is happening. The harbourmaster thinks that they'd be heading along towards Southampton as anywhere else is a lot further."
"Yes, I suppose you're right. Have you had any results in finding where they might have gone?"
"I've got a couple of suggestions sir, but probably, from what information I've been able to gather, Lymington might have been their best bet, as we know that they are fugitives and need to get away as soon as possible."
"Why Lymington," Alex said, "you don't think they could have gone up the Beaulieu River as it is quite quiet there?"
"I don't think they would as I understand that it's very shallow and would be extremely difficult to navigate at night, whereas Lymington is very well indicated with plenty of depth of water at all states of the tides. Another thing would be that with so few people around Beaulieu, they would probably be more noticed."
"Yes, good point, but they would have been noticed at Lymington, surely?"
"Actually sir, I don't think they would have been, as with so many boats moored up there, I don't suppose most people would give a second glance to a boat moving around as it is always so busy; maybe I'm wrong."
"No," said Alex, "I don't think you are. Go for that option and get the DC's to make some enquiries further along the coast anyway, there might be someone who can give us something. We need to know where they have gone as they obviously won't stay on the boat."
"Okay sir, I'll check the boat yards over at Lymington and see what I can find. But before I do, we have a name for the woman."
"At last," said Alex, "you've been saving that little gem for me then?" he said with a grin, "just a name or anything better?"
"Not just a name but an address, or actually her 'last known address'."
"And that is?"
"Her name is, or was, 'Yaren Ganim'. We got her name from her fingerprints on the police national computer."
"I do know what the PNC is Anna."

"Sorry guv, I'm just excited. She was arrested and convicted of shoplifting in Durham, of all places but that was back in 2002. Her last known address was in South East London, South Norwood, to be exact."
"That's near Croydon," said Alex, "quite a coincidence, as I was born in Croydon, and moved down here about ten years ago, but I know the area quite well as I lived there for many years. Perhaps you could try looking a little more closely at that area for either the tattoo parlour or the 'T' shirt printing shop that might have done it."
"I think that might be worth a try sir. It might narrow our search area with any luck. It would follow that she had this printed or been tattooed somewhere closer to where she lived."

CHAPTER 23

Alex took a phone call from George Matthews, the pathologist who had conducted the Post Mortem.
He told Alex that the toxicology tests revealed that she was given or took cocaine prior to being beaten. Other than that, it was just the injuries sustained from the beatings which would have been very painful but she probably wouldn't have felt much after the cocaine.
"It was most certainly the one gunshot to the head which killed her."
Alex asked, "Was she a drug user, you know, did she have needle marks?"
"I couldn't find any other marks or indications that she was, although she could have been a small-time user of coke."
"Thanks George. Why do you think they might have given her cocaine and then beat her?"
"I don't think she would have been given it, I rather tend towards the premise that she was a small user although perhaps someone had a little remorse and wanted to 'ease the suffering' once they had the information but in my experience, that would be very doubtful. My thoughts are that she simply took some cocaine before all this happened. There is often a 'blurred timeline' to the things that people do when there is violence. This usually shows only after the culprits have either confessed or the full events have come out at trial or inquest."
"You're right George; I'll never understand what goes on with these sorts of animals."
Alex added, "By the way, is there any more information that you could get from the tattoo?"
"The only thing we could find was that this was done some time ago. I'd say about eight or ten years, but perhaps that is not much use."
"That's okay; it just gives us more of a picture build-up of who she was. We just need to know what she has been doing and who she's connected with. I don't suppose you got anything from the strapping or the clothes, such as where they might have come from?" said Alex.
"Nothing, as the strapping, as I told Anna, was very common. There were virtually no identifiable clues from the clothing except that once again they were obtainable in almost any clothing shop. All I can say is that they were not really supermarket standard, but probably somewhere like 'Gap' or that sort of quality. Not that I know much about female attire you understand."
Alex smiled inwardly at George's choice of 'female attire'."
"Thanks George, you've been very helpful."
One of the DC's, Alice Compton, came in to Alex's office. She said that she'd contacted three more possible mooring places which the boat could have gone to, but there was no sighting of it at any of them.

"Right Alice, thanks," said Alex, "keep on checking. I know you are a whiz with 'IT' so can you do some research on the boss of the Marine Auctions up at Tuckton? His name is Frank Jordan. I've not met him but there is something nagging at the back of my mind which doesn't add up for me. I still can't quite take in that the boat theft was not reported sooner. Please get back to me as soon as you have some information."
"Right sir, I'll get on to this as well," said Alice, thinking 'I might as well sweep the floor as well while I'm at it.'

CHAPTER 24

Anna had been using the internet to search for likely landing places along the south coast towards Southampton. From the advice she had received from the Harbour Master at Poole, she assumed that they would have headed east along the coast because, to have gone west, the nearest likely place would have been Weymouth and that was quite a fair distance. Going east, she had discounted Beaulieu as this was described as very shallow beyond a certain point and had many turns along the Beaulieu River or River Exe, as it was formerly known. She also looked at the possibility of Chichester Harbour and found that the access was also difficult because of the possibility of low tides. Another candidate was Swanwick Marina but that would have meant going up the Solent. Once again, the difficulties of navigating through a large number of boats would have meant that there would be more chance of being seen, noticed and possibly reported if it were late at night, so she felt that was a non-starter also. The best looking opportunity, it seemed to Anna, was Lymington. She found out that it was well marked and had good access at all states of the tides. It was also where the Isle of Wight ferry docked on the mainland, so another boat would not cause any excitement. However, Anna sent emails to all the likely places, including a picture of a similar boat.
The following morning, she received a call from a Mark Mullies, the Harbour Master at Lymington Yacht Haven, saying that a boat which was very likely the one they were looking for had been found, moored to the far end of the pontoons at the marina. He further told her that it would have come in quite late at night as no-one had reported seeing it arrive.
Anna thanked Mullies for this information and went straight to Alex's office and knocked on the door, eager to pass on her news.
"Come in Anna, you look excited - what do you have for me?"
"We've only found it!" she said.
"Great stuff - at last! Well done you!"
A phrase that she disliked intensely.
"So where is this bloody thing then? Don't keep me waiting Anna."
"It was 'dumped' at Lymington Yacht Haven. They've just called to say they found it at the end of one of their pontoons but there was nobody there – no surprise there sir."
"Right, get over there right now and find out all you can about it and what happened to the blokes on board."
Anna told him what Mullies had said about it not being seen arriving by anyone.
She quickly drove over to Lymington and arrived at the yacht haven where the missing boat which they were looking for had been reported found. She went to the marina office and introduced herself to the Haven Master, Matthew Addison.
"I am Detective Sergeant Anna Jenkins of Bournemouth Police. We are looking for a boat which may have been involved in a serious

incident that we are investigating. I understand that the boat we are looking for might be the one you reported to us in response to our email which included a picture of one which fits our parameters."
"That's correct," he said.
"You said that there was no report of the boat in this picture actually arriving."
"That's correct," he said again.
"Was anyone reported being seen leaving this boat?"
"No-one was seen leaving the boat but that a man was seen running up the pontoons late last evening. That's all that I can tell you."
"And nothing else?"
"That's correct."
'Christ, this guy's beginning to annoy me – 'that's correct, that's correct' – that's all he's said', she moaned in her head.
"Can you show me this boat please?'"
"Of course, I'll get one of my staff to take you down to it. It's quite a way down to the end of the pontoons."
He telephoned to find a staff member who would take her to the boat.
A man with short fair hair who seemed to be in his early thirties and dressed in working clothes came in, and Addison said, "John, would you take this Police Sergeant down to the 'Christina' which evidently came in late last night? It's the one at the far end of the pontoons."
"Yes, Mr Addison. Turning to Anna and looking at her a little too carefully for her liking, John said "If you'd like to follow me. Please be careful, there are a lot of ropes and stuff that could trip you up and I don't want you to end up as a soggy cop!"
"I'll try to look where I'm going then," thinking that she'd better be on her guard as she felt he was a little too 'forward'.
It was quite a way down to the boat as the marina at Lymington is very big. John turned toward Anna, saying "The people bringing this boat in must have been lucky in finding a free berth; we don't get many spaces as this is a very popular harbour."
Anna said, "Have you looked inside the boat?"
"We've not looked inside and once we realised it a bit unusual and might be a police matter, we reported it to you and kept away until you came."
"That's good and sensible,"
After what seemed like a half mile walk, they came to the boat. Sure enough, it was the blue and white craft of the proportions they were looking for, closely matching their picture.
"Did anyone see this boat arrive?"
"No, it just sort of 'appeared' but the person who berthed the boat must have left very quickly as they didn't register the arrival or pay the mooring fees as they should have been done but simply 'rushed off'."

"Apparently a man was seen. Do you have a description of this man?" asked Anna.
"All I know is that a man was seen running up the pontoons, so I don't but you could ask around as he would have been noticed by someone, I'm sure.
"Is there anything unusual that you have noticed about this boat? I guess you are used to all these different types of craft and I'm sure, with your expertise, you would spot something 'out of the ordinary'?" 'Flattering him might get a bit more out of him and perhaps he will be a bit more respectful of me'. She thought.
He seemed to grow a little taller at this remark and Anna thought he must have taken it as a compliment. Perhaps he didn't get much of those from the type of people who used this enormous marina. Money around here must be in incredible amounts judging by the variety of expensive-looking boats she had seen on her way along the pontoons; there were boats by the hundred!
"Well, as you ask, the only thing I would say is that the bloke who tied her up was not much of a sailor as the berthing ropes are tied all wrong."
"How do you mean, 'all wrong'?"
"Well, he should have used at least clove hitches on the bollards and as it is so close to the entrance, springs would have been a good idea too, but I guess he was in a hurry."
"Clove hitches and springs? Sorry - but you've lost me," said Anna.
"A clove hitch is a simple knot for mooring to a bollard. He hadn't used that and what he had tied would jam, as the boat was pulled with currents and wind and that would cause problems. Springs are ropes running from the bow to the stern bollard and vice versa. They hold the boat steady against a running current."
"Sorry, but I don't have sea legs, so this is all above me."
"You may not have sea legs as they are usually big and hairy but the ones you've got look pretty good to me."
"Any more of that and I'll have you in handcuffs," said Anna, hiding a smirk as best she could.
He just looked at her and held out his arms as though she could handcuff him. "I was hoping you had some."
With that, Anna said, "Enough! I'd better take a look inside to see if there is anything which can give me a clue as to who the missing man is."
Anna was thinking that earlier information told of two men but only one had been seen running away. 'Perhaps the other one wasn't actually seen by anyone'. She thought.
"If you can stay outside, there may be something that needs protecting, some evidence we don't know of yet."
"Right you are Constable."
Anna gave him a withering look saying, "Detective Sergeant actually."
"Sorry Sergeant," and gave her a salute.

"Just you watch it, sunshine - you're getting this close...' she said holding up two 'pinched fingers'.
Anna boarded the motorboat and looked around the open cockpit where there were the engine controls and wheel, together with the instruments such as compass, fuel gauges and other dials. At the stern, there were two metal poles with fittings hanging down.
She called to John and asked, "What are these poles for John?"
"Those aren't poles, they're davits."
"Davits then," she said, thinking, 'smart-arse'. "What are these davits for?"
"They're to hang a tender on."
"A tender what, piece of beef?" She said with a stony face. 'I'm not giving in to him,' she thought.
"No, you 'wally', a tender is a small boat used to get crew or passengers to a dock or pontoon when the main boat is moored away from the dock."
"I am not a 'wally'. I've just told you that I am a Police Detective Sergeant and you'd best remember that or we'll fall out!"
"Oops, sorry. I'm just not used to dealing with people who don't know boats and boating. I spend my life around these people and I guess I just expect everyone to know these things. Around here, even the girls know about boats. You're an exception or should I say, exceptional?"
The compliment was accepted inwardly but evoked another hard stare from Anna. "Okay, let's leave it at that. Did you see a 'tender' on this boat or was it like this when you first saw it?"
"I can only say that I doubt that it had a tender on as it would be left here somewhere when the man ran off – there's nowhere to put one at this end of the pontoons."
"Right, so we can assume that there was no tender then?"
"I reckon that's right and if you think about it, if there was only one person who got off this boat, then there won't be a tender to think about."
She realised that there was nothing else that she could see here but then thought that perhaps there might be a locker or somewhere where things could be hidden. Apart from a large box at the rear of the cockpit, there was nothing else evident.
She called to John, asking "Do you know what is under this big box?"
"That 'big box' as you call it, is the engine housing and underneath, you'll find a 'gert big engine' I reckon," he said with a smirk.
"Clever dick," said Anna.
"That's been said before," said John with a cheeky grin.
She ignored this.
"Okay, maybe we can take this off later, when I've had a chance to look in the cabin."
"If that's all you want to take off, then yes."
Anna turned to him and with a steely look, said, "That's it. I've warned you twice and won't do so again, do you understand?

"Sorry Sarge. It's not original though."
"What; what did you say?"
"I said it's not original - the engine I mean."
"Why do you say that?"
"Because I know the Fairey 'Christina' and it used to have the engine below deck. This engine must be a different type, probably bigger than the original and... I can see this has now got a stern drive."
"What's a 'Stern-Drive' then?"
"Normally, this boat would have a propeller on a shaft underneath the hull but, if you look over the stern, you'll see the unit that has the propeller on it, sticking out – do you see what I mean?"
Anna just nodded as she focused on the 'thing sticking out'.
He continued; "This can be hydraulically lifted, so the prop can be lifted clear of the seabed when the draught is too shallow and you can also get access to the propeller."
"Thanks for the technical lesson; something I've always wanted to know."
"I've lots of things I know that I can show you if you like."
"That's it! This is serious John and stay off the boat please. It might have to be examined by our forensic person which means it might be treated as a 'Crime Scene'."
"Oh, so it's like CSI then?"
"You should watch less telly and get out more."
With that, she pulled on latex gloves, then ducked down and entered the cabin. On one side there was a small, what she supposed was called, a galley with a stove and other cooking equipment. There was a small fridge which contained nothing but fresh air and a cupboard overhead was also empty. There seemed to be nothing on board in the way of food or drink. This suggested to her that this indeed was the boat which had been used to dump the body on to a small island in Christchurch Harbour and not for pleasure.
On the other side of the cabin were small cubbyholes and in one of these were a number of tins of beer, all unopened. 'So,' she thought, 'they did have something to drink so maybe there could be empties. If there are, they may have fingerprints on them and DNA from saliva as well'.
Suddenly, she remembered that there were two men being seen on this boat on the night the body was apparently dumped but since then, only one person has been seen. 'Where is the other one; where's he gone'?
Moving to the front of the cabin, she saw two seats which must have been in the very front of the boat, 'or is that called the bow', she thought. It occurred to her that these seats would have been made into a sleeping area and to do that, they would have removable mattresses. 'Aha', she thought, 'more hiding places...'
With that, she lifted one of the seat pads, saying to herself, 'you can't call these thin things mattresses' and then saw that there was

space underneath which contained an anchor, rope and chain together with two or three buoys. 'Just the usual 'stuff' for boating', she thought.
She lifted the other seat pad and stood up so quickly that she banged her head on the low ceiling.
"OH SHIT!" she exclaimed. "Not another one!"
Underneath this seat pad was a tightly folded naked body - male...
John had heard her exclamation and called out, "Are you alright?"
Anna shouted to him, "Yes, but do 'NOT' come on board. This 'IS' now a crime scene and this boat must now be sealed off and *no-one*, she said very firmly, must be allowed on board until Crime Scene Officers arrive. Do you understand?"
"Why, what's the problem? Why do you need them here?" said John.
"Nothing for you to worry your head about, just do as I say and make sure that no-one, I repeat no-one is allowed on this boat for whatever reason. Do you understand?"
John had seen too many CSI programmes not to realise that something serious had happened. He said to Anna, "This is a turn-up; we don't get many crimes around here, well nothing that needs CSI's."
"There are times when things get serious and this is one of them, so do as I ask and guard this boat until our team show up. I'll report this to Bournemouth HQ and I'll go back and tell your boss what is going on so that you won't get a bollocking for being away so long."
Anna thought, 'that's taken him down a peg or two but I'll bet he'll be in the pub tonight bragging to his mates about how he was involved in a 'Police Incident'.
Before making that call to HQ, she went back into the cabin to take a closer look at the body folded up into the small space under the seat or the 'bunk' she supposed was the correct boating terminology.
She didn't touch the body and anyway, it was too dark under the bunk to see anything more detailed, so she took out her mobile phone which acted as a torch and then she could see that the man was reasonably young. Looking more closely at him to see what colour his hair was, she could see that there was a small red dot on his forehead, with a dark ring around it. Although Anna was not trained in forensics, she knew that the ring was known as 'tattooing' and was the result of a very close range shot causing the unburned grains of gunpowder from the propellant of the bullet to be impacted onto the skin.
"Oh God!" she said, realising that he'd been shot in the same way as the woman's body. Immediately, she had the thought that the same person could have killed both victims.
With slightly shaking hands, Anna dialled Alex on her mobile.
"Alex," she said excitedly, normally calling him 'Sir', "We've found it – the boat I mean! It was moored at Lymington, just as I – sorry - we thought."

Alex smiled inwardly at her addressing him as 'Alex'. It somehow gave him a warm feeling.
"Is it the one we were looking for?" he asked.
"Yes sir," said Anna, "and there's something else - There's another body Sir!"
"What!"
"Male. Naked."
"Oh Christ, I hope you are joking. No you're not are you? Bloody hell Anna, this is becoming serious. What are the circumstances?"
"I was taken to the boat and it's the one we were looking for. I went on board to have a look around and then I discovered him hidden under one of the forward bunks in the cabin. He had been shot in the head, the same way the woman was. He seems to be around 25-30 years old. He has light brown hair and he was clean shaven.'
"Did anyone see the other man leaving the boat?"
"There has been a report of a man seen running away from where the boat was found."
"I don't know any more about that part sir." I called this in as soon as I could. I'll do some asking around but it's getting late, so we'll have to come back tomorrow to do some more checking."
'Okay Anna, we'll all meet up at 8 a.m. for a briefing. Just make sure that the CSI get straight on to this and get that boat guarded so that no-one interferes with it or disturbs whatever evidence there might be."
Anna thought, 'he must think I'm new to this game...' "Yes sir, all in hand."
"Well done and thanks Anna. See you first thing and Anna, are you okay?"
"Goodnight ir." She was so caught up in what had just happened that she didn't even respond to his last question.

CHAPTER 25

The next morning, Alex called a briefing to recap on what they knew so far.
Present were DS Anna, as well as DCs Alice Compton and Tom Peterson.
"Okay everyone, this much we know. The body of a woman who had been tortured and then shot had been dumped, probably from the inflatable boat which was on the back of the cruiser which was purportedly stolen from the boatyard at the Marine Auctions in Tuckton. This theft was only reported by Marine Auctions yesterday. Their story is that as the boats for sale are only checked occasionally, the theft was not noticed until yesterday."
"We understand that it was taken through Christchurch Harbour on Monday 30th of August, quite late in the evening. It was misty and the body was thrown overboard, probably in the hope that it would go to the bottom and never be found. Unfortunately for the two men who were seen on the boat, the body, which was weighted down by being strapped to a concrete beam or post, settled on a small patch of sand which turned out to be a small island. The water was not deep enough and we think that they did not know this."
"This island was something that only few locals know about as it was so rarely uncovered and, only at extreme low tides, such as the one on that night. In fact, it is known locally as 'Blue Moon Island' It appears that the boat, in making its escape, and due to the lack of water depth, struck a sand bar just before the harbour exit through the 'Run'. This most probably damaged the propeller which meant that the speed of the boat was severely limited and repairs were immediately necessary. Because of this the boat then made its way, probably at a much reduced speed, to Poole Harbour where it was tied up to a mooring buoy some way off the shore."
"According to the owner of a local boatyard, a man was seen probably taking off the prop, and then making his way to the shore in a small inflatable. We also know that he went to a workshop where the propeller was repaired and this was collected on Thursday morning. No one saw the man return to the boat, or at least we cannot find anyone who saw him, but we know that it must have been repaired and refitted as the boat, we have to assume, left Poole sometime late on Thursday evening. Again, it was not noticed, probably because it was running without navigation lights."
"Does anyone have anything to add at this stage?" asked Alex.
There were no replies.
Alex continued, "The boatyard owner, who lives above the slipway with good views of where the boat was moored, was away in Dorchester until Friday morning, so saw nothing, although he was

trying, unsuccessfully, to catch the man who he'd seen to get some mooring fees from him."

"We now have proof that this boat was taken to Lymington where it was found last evening with a man's naked body hidden under a bunk in the cabin. He had been shot in the head in the same way as the woman. A man was seen hurrying away from the boat but we have no idea yet of who he is or where he has gone. Hopefully, we can get some clues from CSI although as the dead man was naked, any DNA is going to be sketchy, to say the least. There was very little in the way of food, on the boat but there were some cans of beer so maybe we can get some prints or DNA from them."

"By the way, in case you didn't know this, Anna has discovered that the woman's name was Yaren Ganim and she was Turkish. We now know her address in South London, near Croydon. Although we still have no idea where the missing boat man has gone, we suspect that it maybe to London, but that is just a wild guess at the moment. Again, does anyone have any questions?"

They all shook their heads but Tom said, "Well, at least we are making some progress. Let's just hope we don't find any more bodies!"

"Indeed Tom. As I see it at the moment, it is most imperative that we find this killer. Two murders are two too many, so let's get busy in tracing the..., I was going to say 'them', but I'm certain it's 'him' now." Finally, Alex posed the question, "Where did he go after the marina?"

Alice said, "Won't the marina have CCTV Sir? Perhaps that will give us something to start with."

"Good idea Alice. Can you give them a call and see what they can give us?"

"No problem sir."

"Okay. We all have work to do and enquiries to make, so let's get to it. Alice, Tom, you know what you have to do?"

"Yes Sir." They said in unison.

CHAPTER 26

That evening, Alex was thinking of going down to a restaurant in Northbourne which he rather liked, for a meal. 'It would be rather nice to have some company', he thought. He had frequently considered asking Anna out as he really liked her and she was unattached, or so he thought. The problem was that when you are working closely with someone, and that someone is your subordinate, it can quite easily become very difficult to keep that distance if you develop a close relationship outside work. 'Oh well, I'll just have to have another solitary meal', he decided. In fact, if only he'd known Anna was rather hoping that he would ask her out. She had always not only respected him, even though he could be a bit patronising at times, she also found him quite attractive. However, her thoughts were very similar to his in that working with your boss was probably not a good idea. 'I wonder if he has a girl friend or someone close to him,' she thought. He had never mentioned anyone but perhaps there is a special someone.
Alex had a good relationship some time ago but it had ended badly...
He went to the restaurant and enjoyed his meal alone with his thoughts but the image of Anna was never far from his mind except, however, when he began to think through the case with the two bodies and how and why did they meet their end; what were the reasons and, therefore, the ramifications of what had happened. With those thoughts uppermost, his more private thoughts took a back seat.
The next morning, he asked Alice to find out more details on Yaren Ganim such as the area in Turkey where she came from. Also, whether she still has family over there and to continue looking into the tattoo parlours near where she lived in south London. "Have you tried Googling them to see if anything useful came up like tattooists that specialise in foreign scripts? Also see if you can get more information on where she lived."
Alice mused, 'I never thought of 'Googling', I'm only an IT specialist...'
"I'm on it sir and I'll report back as soon as anything new comes up." Alice liked her boss but sometimes...
Alex had given some thought to the auction premises since his visit. He checked that this particular boat had been 'reported stolen' only the previous morning and although this was a fact, there was something which seemed to be a little 'out of kilter' with their story that the boat was not missed for a considerable time. He was sure that all the boats in their care would have been checked on a more regular basis, if only to make sure that they were still floating! Also, an owner from London who was not coming down 'until the weekend', although seemingly innocuous, was somehow ringing gentle alarm bells with Alex - he thought the reply was too 'off pat' for his liking. Maybe he was just looking for trouble where there

was none but he had always taken notice of that 'gut feeling' which is what he felt right now. 'Hmm, worth a little punt', he thought. 'You never know what comes out of the woodwork; we'll need to do a little more checking'.
Alex, looking out of his door, asked around the general office if anyone had seen Tom. Apparently, he'd not been seen recently, so Alex shouted, "Tom!" Still nothing, so he asked Alice if she'd seen Tom recently. She said she'd seen him chatting to Anna just now. He was not best pleased to be told this and asked Alice to find Tom and to, "get his arse in here ASAP."
Tom was DC Tom Peterson, a 38 year old local man who was very pleasant and hard-working but a little shy. He had transferred from the normal day-to-day police work a little over two years ago and found that he liked being a detective and was hoping for promotion in the not too distant future. Although he was conscientious, he didn't have the drive and push that Alex would have liked but maybe that would come with more experience. Tom had a shock of floppy blonde hair and he seemed to have more than a passing interest in Anna. This gave Alex cause for a little feeling of, not jealousy but possibly envy.
Tom came in and Alex said, "You're here to work, not chat up the higher ranks. I want you to go over to Tuckton and have a little 'snoop' around the Marine Auctions there. They don't know you, so you can just have a wander around as if you're looking at the boats as a possible buyer. Just see what comes to mind when you think as a detective - there might be something which doesn't quite look or feel right. I'm not saying that there is, but there is certainly a background to this murder which tells me that all is not what it might seem at first glance."
"Right Sir, I'll see what I can find out and I'll let you know how I feel about the place." Tom was keen to be seen to be competent.
"Fine, but just don't come back with a boat!"
There was a knock on Alex's door. "Come in." Alice walked in wearing a grin. "You look like you've just found a cream bun. What do you have Alice?"
"Sir, the name Yaren Ganim is definitely of Turkish derivation but more than that I can't say at the moment; I found out that it's a common name from that part of the world, so I expect it's going to take some time to trace any family she may have over there. Perhaps there will be information about her family at her home, once we have gained access to that. I'm still working on the details of the owner of the Tuckton Auctions; I hope to have them very soon, or as soon as those minions up at Companies House have got their skates on. I'm also waiting for a reply from our boys regarding any 'previous' for Mr Jordan or anyone working at the boatyard."
"Ok, great stuff Alice. Keep on to them and tell them to take their thumbs out!"
After lunch Anna came back with her findings about the man who left the boat at Lymington with the murdered body on board.

“Have SOCO been over the boat yet Anna?”
“Yes Sir, they say that the preliminary findings are that he was simply shot in the forehead from very close range, in exactly the same way that Yaren Ganim was murdered – it’s a definite link between to two deaths. In fact, their head of section said he was ‘executed’. I asked him how he was so definite, and he said it couldn't have been suicide, not unless he could shoot himself in the head, folded himself into that position and then threw the gun overboard."
“What position was that then?” He’d not received much information at this stage so he was keen to fill in some of the gaps until the full forensics report came through. Anna had only told him the basics when she called him from the boat but now she had the opportunity to give a more detailed description of the crime scene and the situation of the body.
“He was under a bunk which had a mattress on top and he was curled, or folded up if you like, with his knees tucked under chin. These bunks are not king-sized you know."
“Hmm, I would think that would be tricky and whoever did that would need to be quite strong to manoeuvre a body in a confined space. I just wonder why he was shot? Earlier reports suggest that there seemed to be two men involved in the original victim being dumped where she was, so I guess that this one will be one or the other, don't you think Anna?"
“Quite likely sir. Perhaps they either argued about something or he was simply ‘in the way’ and was disposed of. The killer must be a particularly vicious bastard to kill that way ‘in cold blood’ as SOCO say there is no evidence of a scuffle or fight on board, except that he had both his arms broken.”
“That sounds more than a ‘scuffle’ to me, so if I read this right, this murderer has not only killed the woman but for some reason goes on to dump her body many miles from where he killed her and, not only that, but he kills again - just like before - at point blank range apparently and a display of brutality or torture. It’s a nasty one Anna.”
“Yes sir, and he must have made him take all his clothes off before he shot him, and there seems to have been some sort of fight, don’t you think, with his arms broken, as thought trying to defend himself. And his clothes are missing."
"But hang on a minute; why did he make him take all his clothes off? Is he some kind of pervert, or is there another reason. I would have thought that just chucking the body over the side would be enough. Why leave the body on the boat?"
"That does seem very strange, but there must be a reason."
"I can't think what the hell that might be. It's weird Anna, to say the least."
"By the way, will the autopsy provide a report for us tomorrow?”
“Yes sir but they did say that there would be no point in doing all the toxicology tests as it was obvious as to how he had died.”

Alex was obviously not content with that and he said quite harshly, "They're just pulling a fast one Anna. They must know that with a firearms death, they have to do a 'forensic autopsy' which includes full toxicology. They're a lazy bunch. If there's any trace of drugs in him, it could mean that we have a connection of some sort.'
Anna was not too happy about her friend George Matthews, the pathologist, being called 'lazy'. That was the last thing he was. "I think that perhaps George meant an interim report as full toxicology takes a long time and he knows that we are in a hurry to get results, sir," she added, being 'conciliatory'.
"I understand what you're saying Anna, but my point is that if there is a drugs connection and we have boats in the picture, isn't that where a lot of cross-channel drugs-running is done, you know, in small boats?"
"So you think there is a drugs connection then."
"Yes, I think that there's a bloody strong a possibility and that's why we can't leave any avenue unchecked at this stage. We have two people murdered in very strange and similar circumstances, so we need all the information and leads we can get, as quickly as we can. Every aspect has to be investigated – everything; is that clear?"
"Yes sir, of course," thinking, 'As if I couldn't work that one out for myself'!
"Right, what information do you have regarding the man who has obviously escaped?"
"I found out that he was seen and the description I got was roughly the same as the man who you were told went to the propeller workshop - 50'ish, about 6 feet tall with dark hair. That's all we've got so far sir."
"So where the hell did he go after leaving the boat yard, that's what I want to know?"
"If he's trying to get away from the area, I would assume that he'd go by train from the nearest stations which are either Poole or Bournemouth," offered Anna.
"So what do you think - why Bournemouth and not Christchurch station?"
"I reckon he would have got the mainline train direct to London or wherever because Christchurch is only a local line."
"Damn! You're right. We'll have a heck of a job to trace him now as he's been gone for some time and the trains are quite frequent to London. We could try the ticket office but these days you can buy a ticket from your phone can't you?"
"That's right, and anyway, I would think that he bought a ticket for cash rather than risk his credit card details being logged. I tried to trace mobile calls from that area but the ones we could verify were all legitimate and traceable. He must be using a Pay As You Go phone so he'll be untraceable if he is."
"Damn again! Okay Anna, keep on digging and by the way, can you get on to the pathology boys to see what they get on the naked body? I don't suppose there's much in the way of DNA from the

killer for them to go on. That's probably why body was naked, although I dare say they can eventually trace him somehow."
"Will do sir and I agree with your theory."
After this and feeling just a little bit riled by Alex's attitude after all her thorough work, she put the call in to the pathology boys who said they would call back later, Anna went back to her task of helping Alice to trace the tattoo or the T-shirt pattern, but by now she was thinking that this was possibly a complete waste of time as the T-shirt did not really offer any clues as to why she was beaten and murdered. But she was nothing if not determined and got on with trying to find any links which might form some sort of connection later on.
Then, a little later, she actually found some worthwhile information and couldn't wait to tell Alex.

CHAPTER 27

Except that Tom arrived back from his enquiries at the boatyard and had gone straight in to see Alex, getting into his office before she had a chance. 'Damn!' She thought.
"Tom, how did you get on at the boatyard, anything that seems a little 'out of sync?"
"Well, yes and no sir. I know they said that the boats weren't checked often but I would have thought that from the layout of the yard, it would be very easy to just look 'round a corner' - a quick glance would be very simple and it would have been quite obvious if a boat was missing or possibly even sunk."
"That's precisely what I suspected. When I went over there, I could see some of the boats on the pontoon myself quite easily. What other conclusions did you come to?"
"Then I thought, if the boat had been noticed as missing and yet they knew the owner was due to come down at the weekend, why didn't they report it sooner? Perhaps they knew the boat had gone and they were, in fact, completely aware of that because it had actually been taken *with* their knowledge."
"Now you're thinking like a detective Tom. In that case, it could mean that somehow, they were linked to either the use of the boat for some 'dodgy' reason, or that they were 'turning a blind eye' to whatever else was going on. Now, if that were the case, then perhaps there is also more to the 'use of' the boats at their disposal and they would obviously have easy access to boats left in their hands ready for auction."
"Yes sir. I got talking to one of the yard staff, you know, just pretending to be interested in selling my boat through the auction house, and he gave me a few details on how they operate."
"Go on."
"Well, it seems that if you have a boat to sell and don't live locally, they'll berth the it for you and look after it, so that prospective buyers can look around it and maybe be taken out in the boat for a short sea trial if they're interested. All with the owners' consent of course. I would imagine there would be a charge for this 'service', but I don't know."
"And do some of these boats look as though they could cross the channel?"
"Oh yes, they've got some real beauties there, both yachts and powered craft. Some of them almost 'gin palaces'. I wouldn't mind a spin out in one of them and yes, they'd certainly cross the channel. Why are you interested in them crossing the channel though sir?"
"Excuse me for having a suspicious mind but what better way of getting 'stuff' either out of or into the country without arousing the suspicion Customs, as they can't be at all the ports along this coastline, to check every boat that comes and goes across the Channel."

"I see what you mean sir. I know that even at Poole Ferry Terminal, they only have Customs Officers on an 'ad hoc' basis." Tom observed.
"So you can see now Tom, how easy it would be to take a boat out on a 'demonstration trip' and just nip over to France to some 'out of the way' mooring for some 'naughties' I suppose drugs spring to mind but it could be something else – anything that could be construed as illegal, maybe even 'people trafficking."
"But wouldn't the owners know if their boat had been taken out?"
"There are two things Tom: Firstly, my understanding is that these boats don't have speedometers with mileage showing like cars do and secondly, all the boatyard office have to do is either say that there was a punter, interested in a demonstration run or, simply replace the fuel so that nothing would be different; and... don't forget, they have the owners' consent so, in effect, they're untouchable. Mind you," Alex then said, if it were 'trafficking', it would be a damn sight more difficult to bring people back without it being noticed in such a built-up area and very risky."
"Yeah, I see what you mean sir," agreed Tom.
By this time Alex had calmed down a little and his earlier displeasure towards Tom had somewhat dissipated. "Anyway, well done Tom. I think we have some very interesting and complicated avenues of approach to be wary of. Let's see what other links we might get, that tie up with this possibility."

CHAPTER 28

After Tom had gone, Anna knocked on Alex's door and he called out 'yes?'
Anna walked in and Alex said, "Ah, Anna, I was wondering if you'd found out anything else yet."
She thought, 'Cheeky sod, he's been swanning off all over the place and I've been stuck here turning my eyeballs to jelly on the computer while he's been enjoying the views.'
She was controlling her desire to make a caustic remark, aware of the fact that he was her superior. Even though she did quite fancy him, she simply said, "Sir, I think I have something interesting about Yaren." She was excited that she now had some concrete information to give to the investigation. "I've found a tattoo parlour in an area called Woodside Green that did this tattoo. We know that she moved down to South East London sir so, most likely it's close to where she lived!"
Alex started at this information and looked up at Anna. "Woodside Green, I know that place very well, and it's in South East London. It's almost like a village although it's just outside Croydon and in the middle of a very built-up area. I don't think it's changed much since the war, at least I do hope it hasn't except for now having a tattoo parlour. It never used to be a 'tattoo parlour' sort of place - sorry, carry on Anna."
"Well, I contacted this place and they said that they had actually tattooed this design for a dark-haired lady with a description which matches Yaren. When I asked them when it was done, they told me that they had done the tattoo quite recently. They didn't have an address for her but they did say that she looked 'Eastern European'. Apparently, she spoke good English with a distinctive accent but that she seemed quite 'posh' and 'intellectual'. I think finding this place was a stroke of luck. It was only after trawling through loads of parlours on Google. I must have sent out hundreds of emails, together with a picture to these places. We're lucky a registered parlour responded as if it was done by an unregistered one, we may never have found out where it was done, still, a good result."
"Good job Anna but, does it have any significance?"
Anna showed him the email which George Matthews the pathologist had sent her and the tattooed inscription.
ناشناختنی من
Anna thought, 'How the hell do I know? It's taken me hours of work to get this far and now he wants to know if it has 'significance'."
Instead she said, "Do you know what sir, I haven't a clue. I put it into 'Google translate' and tried a few different languages. It wasn't Turkish, although I thought it might be but eventually, I found that it was 'Persian'. I only know that it means *'unknowable me'*, but what

that means is beyond me. It'll take someone better than me to work that out, someone like you sir." 'A bit patronising', she thought, 'but hey...'
"And there's me thinking that you were the deeper thinking person Anna."
"Flattery won't help sir, I haven't a clue about this sort of thing, sorry. I just know that it looks very artistic and beautiful in that Persian script."
"Actually, I've been thinking about this and I'm not sure that it really does have much of a bearing on the case but we'll keep it to one side just in case it changes relevance? What do you think?"
"I did wonder if it had some sort of sexual meaning. I couldn't suggest quite what, but where it was positioned, at the top inside of her thigh, it may have had some sort of meaning or message."
"MMmm..." said Alex. You could be right, but once again, we'll probably never know, unless we find someone who knew her very well."
"Well, I did wonder if it was linked in some way to the T-shirt design. Actually sir, it does have some bearing on the case – it's backed up the information that she came from the South East London area."
Ignoring her remark regarding the tattoo parlour location, Alex said, "Yes, that's a thought about the T-shirt design. Perhaps you could get a DC to do the same with this as you've done, and get them to send out loads of emails with photos of it to T-shirt printers, particularly in the surrounding area. I know it's probably a long shot and in the end, not worth a lot but who knows, we might come up with something worthwhile."
Anna thought, 'After all this work, now he says it's insignificant and he's totally ignored my comment about the tattoo parlour link to her possible home location. Well, I'll just let some of the 'lower ranks' waste their time on this - there are bigger fish to fry'.
"I'll get Alice to carry on with it - it'll make her day – not! Oh and by the way, I was thinking that there won't be much DNA from the naked man in the boat, unless we get a match from the PNC. I know forensics will be checking dental records but that's going to take ages, but I'll ask them to make sure. It will certainly help if they can get a match; that would give us something to go on."
"I think you're right again Anna. The problem is that we just don't have much else at the moment, especially on the bloke who got away. He must be our killer.
"No sir, he'll be long gone by now but if we go back to the auctions boatyard, maybe there will be a link to the boat somewhere. I thought you said you had doubts about the owner and maybe some of the staff there."
"Indeed I do Anna. Let's do some more digging on this Frank Jordan, the boss, and maybe his son Mark. There could be some nefarious connections there."

Alex then said, “We also know that Yaren has a record for shoplifting and that her last known address was somewhere in South Norwood. That’s actually not far from Woodside Green which is an area I know very well. I think we should go there and do some digging, so can you get me the full address please. Who knows, we might just find something worthwhile.”

CHAPTER 29

Alex had decided to take Anna with him to look at the address where Yaren had come from and he was actually looking forward to spending some private time with her away from the office.
They left the backroom staff to the task of finding more details about Frank Jordan, the owner of the Marine Auctions at Tuckton. Alex had some 'feelings' about the place and he wanted to find out where possible links might lead.
The journey to London in a pool car was fairly uneventful, which was quite unusual as the M3 was very often either choked with traffic or maybe an accident had caused a jam, but today it was smooth going and gave Anna and Alex time to relax just a little. Their conversation drifted from the current investigation to a more personal level.
Anna said, "Please don't think I'm prying sir, but I know virtually nothing about you. You are a very private person and I think it helps to know just a little about the people you work with. It gives a better understanding of the person and could explain things. You know, sometimes, something is said and you ask yourself whether there is a reason behind what they've said."
"Anna, first of all, let's cut the 'Sir' bit, at least when we are out of the office. I don't really like the title except that it does give me a little 'clout' when needed. I much prefer to have a rapport with my staff and I think it leads to a better working relationship. I know I can get a little heavy at times, but that is just because I want to do my job effectively and sometimes there are occasions when it's necessary to crack the whip."
"But if I call you Alex, it does seem rather familiar. Is that alright? It seems strange and very personal and I don't want to spoil our working relationship as I think you are a very good boss sir; I mean Alex," she said laughing.
"Thank you for your compliment Anna, and yes, it is alright. I feel that you and I have a good working bond. You are very competent and thorough with good attention to detail, something that some of the lads seem to gloss over with their kind of 'gung-ho' attitude. This is when I get a little heavy. On a personal level I think you are very attractive and I would like to know you better - but as we all know, it's difficult when we work together and I rank above you but I really don't think that should be a problem, do you? I hope you don't mind me saying this and perhaps I shouldn't have put it into words, but the deed is done."
She looked at him with a gentle expression and she was getting good vibes. "I don't mind at all, because I've had the same thoughts for some time, to be honest, but obviously, I couldn't say too much in case you took it wrongly."
"That's a relief, there's me been trying to say this and finding the right time, which has been difficult. Perhaps we can move forward,

carefully and privately, without it becoming general knowledge as it could well jeopardise things in the office."
"I'll be very careful as I know the lads would latch onto things if there was just a sniff of intrigue."
Their journey continued from the urban sprawl that seemed to continue for miles and finally gave way to the countryside of Hampshire. The green of the fields and trees with the rolling countryside was a welcome break from the seemingly endless houses of their normal working area. Very attractive though it was, Bournemouth had become, of late, very crowded with an extremely mixed population of holidaymakers, language students, not to mention the great many residents of 'a certain age' for which the area had become synonymous.
They enjoyed the change of scenery and Alex continued, "Well, that's out of the way and I feel a lot more relaxed now that I've got that into the open. You know, I was very worried that you would take it the wrong way as I don't even know if you have a boyfriend or even a girlfriend, come to that. You see I don't know you at all really."
"Do I look as though I might have a girlfriend then?" she said laughing.
"I'll tell you straight, I'm bloody glad that you don't as it would've made me look a complete idiot, wouldn't it?"
"I am as 'normal' as they come, I think, and happily so. I just hope you don't play for the same team as well."
"What do you think?" he said, with a meaningful glance.
"That's good, so maybe now I can ask you some questions. Are you ready for interrogation?"
"Go ahead. Ask away. If it gets too personal, you'll know."
"Right, do you have a current girlfriend?"
"No."
"Do you have a recent girl-friend?"
"What do you mean by recent?"
"Let's say within the past year, someone who might still be on the sidelines."
"No"
"Have you had many girlfriends?"
"I had a relationship a few years ago but that ended rather badly."
"Did you end it or did she?"
"She was killed in a car crash; by a drunken driver who went through a red light."
"Oh, my God, I'm so sorry Alex. I wish I hadn't asked that question now."
"Don't worry; I've managed to get over it now. With some of the things which we see and which we encounter in our work, it has seemed to pale into somewhat of an insignificance, to be honest. I only wish the driver had been killed as well, but as he hit her car head-on, he survived when the airbag saved him. Jane, that was her name, took the full force of the impact side-on. She was killed

instantly. This was the only saving grace, to be honest because I think if she had survived, she would have been so seriously injured that her life would have been completely devastated. Unfortunately, the bastard that killed her only got an 8-year sentence and we know that means he could be out in about 3 years now."

"But that sort of offence carries a 14-year sentence I believe," said Anna.

"Yes but he said in mitigation that he was not used to driving in the UK as he was an immigrant from Slovakia and hadn't been driving over here for long. So much for justice!"

"I can understand that not being used to driving over here could be difficult, but don't they have red lights in Slovakia? I'll bet being drunk was the main cause".

"I know it was and to be honest, I still feel that if I should see him again, I'll be very hard pushed not to do him some serious harm."

"No," said Anna. "Don't even think like that! You could lose everything. I know it must still be hurting, but you must try to move on."

"I only wish that she'd been driving a car like an Audi for instance."

"Why do you say that? What's different about a car like that?"

"Well, I know that that type of car has an airbag in both drivers' seat and the passengers, so a side impact is much more protected. Hers didn't have that."

Do you still think of her after all this time?"

"Sometimes, but I can live with it now and I know she would have wanted me to have some happiness again."

"I won't mention it again and I'm sorry to have raised the memories."

"As I said, things are better and you must realise after what I've said, that you are right there in my mind and I don't feel any guilt whatever, so please don't apologise."

Anna changed tack and asked, "What is your taste in music? Do you have any pet hates or particular favourites?"

"My only real dislike is opera and I prefer instrumental music to lyrical. Probably because I can never remember the words even though I might feel like singing along sometimes; when I'm on my own," he added hastily.

"I would have thought you'd have no problem with remembering the words, given the job you do."

"P'raps it's that there's so much going on most of the time that we have no room for non-essential stuff. That's my excuse anyway and as I say, instrumental music which has clear tones and the good melody is always 'listenable'. I also like some classical, but not the heavy, full orchestra stuff, more gentle Bach or Chopin, usually piano. Mind you, I really don't go for traditional jazz but sometimes 'smooth jazz' does soothe the soul, or so they say. How about you?"

Anna said, "Strangely I don't like opera either so at least we won't have the problem of having to turn down a visit to the Opera House - should I be asked of course."
"And I won't have to ask you, thankfully, but I would like to ask you to dinner one evening if you would accept."
"I would, kind sir, that would be really nice," said Anna.
"Now, I've told you, don't call me sir," said Alex.
Laughing, she said, "Okay, how about 'Guv'?"
"I'll accept that, but only when we are working."
"It's a done deal Guv."
"Anyway," said Alex, "how about your taste in music and stuff? I need to know so that I don't make a complete pillock of myself."
"I like good rhythm and good musical ability from the performers, not just noise. Maybe that makes me 'old fashioned' as most people of my age seem to like clubs and noise, although perhaps they are growing out of it by now if they're not deaf."
"I know what you mean. I'm quite a bit older than you and my clubbing days were very short lived I have to say. I could never stand the noise and simply the fact that it was usually impossible to have any sort of conversation in a club. I'm just a grumpy old bugger now but that's me, I'm afraid."
"No, you're not. Just because you might sometimes have a good old moan, doesn't mean you are grumpy, perhaps just because you can see another way of doing something or maybe someone could have done a better job or in a better way."
Alex pulled up at traffic lights and turned to look at Anna. "You're too kind Anna. I know my faults, I think, but that doesn't make me easy to cope with. We'll have to see how our 'friendship' progresses, won't we? Oh, and by the way, you never told me if you have a boyfriend."
"I've had a few relationships but never the one which seemed to tick the right boxes and of course, no-one at the moment but I'm hoping that someone will come along soon."
Alex looked at her directly for many seconds without saying anything and then said quietly, "Will I do until then?"
She looked back with a warm smile and said, "I think that might be worth a try, but maybe you should move on or the bloke behind is going to be a 'tad' upset.
He gave her a nod and they continued to enjoy their small talk on the drive to London to find the flat which had been occupied by Yaren Ganim.

CHAPTER 30

Frank Jordan was the boss of the Marine Auction Business in Tuckton. His money came from his being a scrap metal dealer in London many years ago and as often seems to be the case the money is made from 'questionable' deals and usually in cash. In the case of Frank Jordan, this was indeed the way that his money was obtained. Sometimes legally, sometimes not. He was certainly charged and convicted of fencing stolen goods in previous years and had served a number of years in prison. The stolen goods were most often metals which came in from various sources in the early days, such as church roofs; copper wiring from old buildings and sometimes from railway lines. Taking this from railway lines, often led to train delays and sometimes even worse. Sometimes it was aluminium but it does seem as though there were other 'items' that were fenced and this information would no doubt come to light as further investigations took place through the CID rooms at Bournemouth Police Station.
Alex had some doubts about Frank Jordan and he had asked Alice and Tom to do some investigation of the Auction house to see what turned up.
Alice had managed to get company records going back some 8 years and all seemed to be above board with no untoward entries or tax problems. He was listed as the Managing Director and his son Mark Jordan was also listed as a director. The staff numbered only three and they ran the day to day intake of lots for the auction. These had to be listed and itemised together with the description ready for the auction day. This took quite a good deal of time and paperwork.
Tom said that he would go to the Auction house to get some more background on what the day to day routine would be, but Alice reminded him that he had already been there under the pretext of a prospective buyer, so she said that she would go.
Tom asked, "How will you get this information, you can hardly go as a possible buyer and ask those sort of questions, and you can't really go as a police officer as that would put them on their guard if they've something to hide."
"You're right Tom, maybe I should say that I am a local journalist and looking to do a piece on the Auctions. Do you think they'll buy that?"
"Yeah, I don't see why not. You can say you're from the Echo, but then again they might know people from that paper so maybe you should use another magazine to work for."
"Which magazine do you think would do an article on the Auction?"
"I'd think a boating mag would be your best bet, something like 'Boating World' as they would probably cater for all types of boating. You can't use a magazine like 'Boat' as they deal with top-

end gin palaces and you don't want specialist mags because the Auction deals with all sorts of equipment for sail as well as powered boats. Yes, I'd say that 'Boating World' would do an article like that and they'd probably think an article would be good for them."
"Okay then," said Alice, "I'm a journalist from 'Boating World' and would like to do a piece on how they operate and who does the work and what sort of things do they handle."
"Sounds plausible, so give it a try; it can't do any harm to get an insight into the way they are set up."
Alice was eager to get some time away from the computer screen and she needed no encouragement, so she made the fairly short journey to Tuckton and the Marine Auction premises. On the way, she was thinking of the questions she would ask of the staff there and by the time she arrived, she was quite settled in the sort of information she would be seeking.
She made her way across town to the address she had for the Marine Auctions. As she'd not been there before, she was very impressed with the charm of the river Stour at Tuckton. She noticed a number of boats on their private moorings on the riverside with the houses behind. She thought to herself that those houses must have cost a fortune given the position they were in and the beauty of the area. The view from Tuckton Bridge down past Wick Ferry was really quite beautiful in the afternoon sun and as there was very little wind, the river was very calm and the reflections added to the incredible view. Looking for a place to park, she caught sight of the 'Riverside Inn'. This was a very well-known local pub restaurant close to the Auctions and as Alice was rather fond of her cream cakes, she couldn't resist a peek at the menu, just to see what was on offer.
Parking the car in the restaurant car park she spotted the menu on the wall, close to the entrance.
She spotted on the menu 'chocolate fudge cake – A delicious wedge of chocolate fudge cake served with Belgian chocolate sauce, ice cream, honeycomb & fudge pieces'. That was it, hooked. She thought, 'Well, it's vegetarian, so that's allowed and anyway, it won't take long so they won't know anything about it. I'll just say that it's taken a little longer to talk to them at the Auction'.
With that, Alice took a little detour and after about 15 minutes, completely unaware of the CCTV camera on the side of the restaurant, she happily strode over to the Auction house and saw a man in working gear. Making her way across the yard towards him, she gave him a big smile. "Hello, are you the person in charge here?"
"No, I just work here. The man you want is over that in that office at the far end of this shed." He was pointing through the large double doors through the huge shed which contained heaps and mounds of completely indescribable things. They all meant absolutely nothing to her and she recognised only things like nets and ropes. All the other items she was sure, were as if from a different planet.

Knocking at the door of the office, she heard a gruff voice saying in a harsh tone, "Yes, what do you want now?"
She entered the office and was rather taken aback at the man sitting at the desk. After the harsh greeting, she was expecting someone different. He was dressed in a suit that obviously wasn't from the local shops. The office was tidy with shelves and files arranged in a way that were very ordered. She found this surprising, as the impression she'd gained from the information she'd already received, was that he was a scrap dealer. She thought to herself, 'scrap dealers are usually dirty, smelly, grease stained blokes with greasy hair, aren't they'? but this man was immaculately dressed. This threw her if she were honest. 'So much for preconceptions'.
She introduced herself. "My name is April, and I am from 'Boating World' magazine. You may have heard of it."
He stood up and offered her his hand. "Frank Jordan. Please forgive me for being rude just now, I thought it was one of my staff and they always want something or other. "How do I do this, or what's this for?"
The hand he offered was warm and dry. Very clean and nails clean and manicured, which went perfectly with the sparse, but carefully managed hair?
"April, a nice name for a nice lady," he said, putting April at her ease.
'This is not what I expected', she thought, but let's get on with what I came here for. Deception.
"Thank you, Mr Jordan. As I said, I am from Boating World and we are looking to do an article on boat auctions; how they operate and what do they give to the ordinary boating man or woman. Do you think it would be possible to talk to your staff to get an idea of what you do and how the auctions operate? I am sure an article would do no harm and may even bring in more business." Alice was hoping that she sounded convincing and that Jordan would not call Boating World to check up on her.
"Well now April, I do know Boating World and yes an article would be rather welcome, although we are very well known in the area. I'm sure there will be people from further afield who would benefit from knowing we exist and what we cover, so please feel free to talk to my guys. They'll help you to understand some of the things you will see in the shed, and the boats we have on offer and how we organise the auction."
Alice was a little nervous now because Frank Jordan was not at all what she expected. In her working life she encountered all types of men, most of whom were not too savoury, but in this case, Frank Jordan was altogether a 'gentleman', she thought and actually quite suave. It was quite hard to believe that his money had come from scrap dealing, but then she thought that it was many years ago, things have changed and he with it perhaps, although she was sure that the accent was not the original one but something he had 'worked on'.

"Do you live locally Mr Jordan?" she asked.
"Yes, I have a house on Panorama Road, that's on Sandbanks actually," he said. "I moved here many years ago when business allowed and I became interested in Powerboat Racing."
"Wow," said Alice, "that must be exciting. I've never been on a fast boat, but then again, I do get seasick, so that's not surprising."
She was thinking, this man must have an enormous amount of money as she knew that powerboat racing was an extremely expensive sport. At least he would be worth a shed-load of money if the house were his and not on some sort of mortgage. But then, who could afford a mortgage on a place with that sort of value? It must be worth millions! A thought then occurred to Alice which had more to do with her being a police officer. The sort of money that he must have had or has, must have come from more than scrap. Don't those sort of people usually get mixed up in much more nefarious things such as money laundering or drug dealing? I must get back on track, she thought, I'm getting distracted.
Jordan said, smiling, "actually, one doesn't usually get seasick except when one is waiting for the race to start and the boat is wallowing about. Once the power kicks in you don't have time to think, never mind get seasick."
"I'll have to take your word for that as I'm not really the 'boaty' kind. I'm just a journalist." She thought the use of 'one doesn't' did not seem to sit with the image she had but that was fast disappearing. She just wanted to get out to the shed and talk to the men she was more accustomed to dealing with.
"If I may, I'll go and talk to the chaps outside. Is there anywhere I shouldn't go?"
"Not at all, just be careful if you go out to the pontoons where the boats are moored. There are a few ropes and for 'non-boaty' people they can be a hazard."
"Thank you, I'll be very careful," she said ignoring the slight jibe and went back into the large shed with all the nautical paraphernalia. There she met Keith. He was the man who Tom had talked to on his previous visit. She said, 'I am a journalist with 'Boating World' and I'm going to write a piece about auctioning marine equipment and stuff. Your boss has given me permission to talk with you and I was wondering if you can help by explaining how the auction works?
"Sure, where do you want to begin?"
Taking out a notebook and pen, she began to take notes. "Can you explain what all these heaps of 'things' are?"
Sure, "they're all the various items of boat and marine chandlery which will go into the auction. We sort them out into different categories and then list them with a description and a 'lot' number and all this information goes into a catalogue ready for auction day."
"It must be a lot of work," said Alice.
"It certainly is and as you can see there is a great variation of items. Anything from ropes and buoys to nets for fishing boats, sails for

the 'stick and string' brigade, you know, 'yachties', propellers and outboard motors, blocks, pulleys, ships wheels, binnacles, compasses, navigation lights....."
"Stop!" said Alice. "You've lost me, but I get the idea. So you list everything, catalogue it and then how about the auction itself. What happens then?"
"On the auction day, there is a period in the morning when prospective buyers or bidders can look over the items for auction and in the afternoon, the auction itself gets underway. The items are brought out like any other auction and either shown or indicated and the bids made. Sometimes, a whole load of stuff can be bid for at one time. This is usually the local lads or fishermen who want to buy a load of rope or fenders and the like. The auctioneer signals the final and winning bids and, Robert is your mother's brother, as they say."
"I'll bet that it could be a lot of fun, with all the various items which you handle. You must know an awful lot about boats and boating."
"I'll tell you what, when I first started, I knew almost nothing about all this stuff, but I learned a heck of a lot by asking the punters who used to look over the bits and pieces before the auction, just what 'this' or 'that' was. They were very happy to tell me all about some of the less obvious things and I built up quite knowledge. This comes in very handy when someone comes in and asks for a certain item and they don't know either what or where it is, and I can give them some information."
Alice said, "This will look very good in the article; you know, the fact that you can help people find something they are looking for."
"I suppose it could, yes. It all helps to bring in custom."
"Do you sell the boats the same way; you know the ones that are outside floating by the dock? I saw some lovely looking boats out there just now."
"We call it the pontoon but yes, sometimes. We do get some powerful craft but they come and go quite often. Depends on the boat and how the owners want to make the sale. Usually, it's the smaller boats or dinghies which come into the auction shed."
"You say they come and go, do you mean the bigger boats, do they go away and then come back again, or just from the selling point of view?"
"Sometimes, yes, they can go for a couple of days and then back. I suppose they are taken for a demonstration run, or maybe the owner just wants to go out in her for a spin while they still have possession."
This snippet of information gave Alice pause. Then she said, "Do you ever have boats stolen, because they seem to be only tied up with ropes."
"That's very rare but we did actually have one stolen a few days ago. A nice boat she was, fast too. Didn't notice it straight off, but we've heard nothing more yet although we did report this to the police."

"Yeah, well we all know how useless they are don't we?" said Alice, with a little chuckle.
"That's about right, but a shame, though, all the same. Probably taken by some low-life and maybe sunk now. Just like joy riders, run out of fuel. 'Tidn't right," said Keith.
"So who does the cataloguing, you?"
"No," said Keith," that's done by Ben. He's off today, but he does all the paperwork; keeps him out of mischief for days sometimes."
Alice had seen enough to make some impressions and thoughts regarding the owner Frank Jordan and the fact that some boats can come and go 'at will'. This seemed to fit in with Alex's comments regarding the cross-channel possibilities.
Alice said to Keith, "Thanks for everything, I'll get back to the office now and make a start on what I do best. Bye then, and keep an eye out, you never know, you might appear in print." She was thinking to herself, "What I do best, mate, has nothing to do with boats, believe me," and went back to her car. On the way, she stopped and looked over the bridge at the view down the river. 'What fantastic place', she thought. 'I'd love to live here with the river to look at. Not my place with 360 degree views of other houses'. She drove back to her real world and the office.
On the way back, she thought more about Frank Jordan. He lived in Sandbanks, probably one of the most expensive places to live, certainly in England; probably in Europe and he has access to boats 'at will'. 'What does that give you', she thought. 'Connections, connections possibly across the channel from where he was placed. Let's do some more checking on his background and who he might know. He was well suited and booted obviously, and has come up in the world more than likely through some expensive tuition. He would move in quite high places, with some very influential and well-heeled contacts. Her 'investigative' mind was now working at full capacity and she was making some connections which would no doubt intrigue Alex.
'And, how about the elusive son, Mark Jordan'?

CHAPTER 31

Back in the office, Alice was waiting to see Alex with her report on the Auction House.
"Hi Alice," said Alex. "How did you get on with your impersonation of a 'hack'?"
"I think it went well sir," said Alice. "I got to see the boss, Frank Jordan. He was not at all what I expected."
"How do you mean. What did you expect?"
"Well, for one thing, I didn't expect the boss to actually be there. What I meant was that he was not what I expected an ex-scrap dealer to be like."
"What, he wasn't dressed in a greasy boiler suit with tattoos and shaven head?"
"You know what I mean. We all have a preconceived idea of a scrap dealer don't we? Well, this guy was nothing like I expected. He was dressed in what I would describe as a 'Savile Row' suit, very expensive watch, manicured hands and overall extremely up-market. Suavity personified, with an obviously 'worked-on' accent. Not posh, but not from the scrap-yards by any means."
"I see what you mean. Must have come as a shock then?"
"Well, it was when I realised that he was the ex-scrap man. I nearly blew it there and then, I can tell you."
"But he didn't rumble you then, obviously."
"No, in fact he was most helpful and courteous. He told me he lived in Sandbanks and was into Powerboat Racing now."
"I don't know much about that except that it takes a shed load of money. Did he say how much he made at the auctions?"
"I didn't ask him and anyway, I really don't think he would have told me and also, that may have made him suspicious. Mind you, I 'm pretty sure it can't make the sort of money that you'd need to live in Sandbanks unless you were living in a tent there."
"So, do you think there are other funds involved with other 'interests'?"
"Well sir, I'd say it was pretty obvious that he's made the money from somewhere else as the auctions have not been going for that long and there can't be that much money in commissions from selling a load of boating crap and a few boats. I don't know anything about boats, but from what I saw of the auction, it's a bit 'hit and miss' when it comes to sales. The stuff they sell at the auction is usually to weekend sailors and local blokes or fishermen for their little trawlers. You know, 'odds and sods' and loads of little stuff that didn't look to make a lot of money. There were a few small boats inside up for sale, like dinghies and small sailing boats."
"Hmm, so you had a good look around then?"
"Yes sir, but one thing did make me think about what we have been speculating on. The bloke that Tom had seen before, you know 'Keith', said that boats quite often 'came and went' for a day or two at a time. That was quite usual and no questions were really asked,

apparently. It occurs to me that it wouldn't take long to cross the channel to France on one of those big cruisers would it? Perhaps they could be running drugs? He also mentioned the boat which had been stolen recently and said that he thought it would have been taken by some kids for some 'joy-riding', but that's a bit different from taking a car though, isn't it?"
"I think we can safely say that it wasn't for 'joy-riding' Alice. Not when it's possible that a body was dumped from this boat and another man was found murdered tucked up in the front of the boat. We still have no idea who the killer was as he's got clean away and so far we've no trace of him or where he went. That reminds me, how is Tom doing on that score? Has he come up with anything yet?"
"Not as far as I know at the moment, but I'm sure he'll let you know when he does."
"Did you get anywhere with your enquiries then? There must be something going on with Mark and his father. I mean, the link is too strong not to have connections. I want Frank Jordan's background dug into very deeply. I also want Mark Jordan to have the same treatment. I know you can get some very good information with your expertise in computers, so let's get digging. He also seems to go between the flat in London and his flat in Poole a lot. He is often away for two to three days at a time, but we don't know where he goes. We suspect back to Christchurch but we don't know why, yet."
"Well, perhaps he goes back there to go over to France with loads of drugs and stuff, and how about the boats which 'perhaps go out for a couple of days, with nothing being said'?"
"Let's not jump the gun yet Alice. You have a nasty mind, do you know that?" he said laughing.
"That's what comes of being a detective sir, makes you a nasty, suspicious person."
"Now, now, Alice, you are very far from being a nasty person."
"Thank you, kind sir."
"Okay then, off you go and start being suspicious over Messrs Jordan and Son."
"On my way guv."

CHAPTER 32

Alex and Anna finished their drive up to South London where Yaren Ganim occupied a flat.
They were going to look at the flat to see if there was anything that would give a clue as to why she should have been beaten and murdered, and possibly who did it. It was a very slim chance but at the moment, all they could do. The problem was that they didn't know that she shared the flat with Mark Jordan, the son of the auction house proprietor. They thought it was now unoccupied as Yaren was dead. What they also didn't know was how, and why, she was found in Christchurch Harbour.
On their way, they passed near to Crystal Palace. Alex said, "Do you know, my mum actually saw the Crystal Palace burn down in 1936."
"Wow," said Anna, "that must have been an amazing sight!"
"In those days she was very young and to her, I would imagine that the Crystal Palace must have been like a fairy tale with a building such as that. She said that she and a bunch of kids stood and watched the fire. She actually saw molten glass running down the roads like a river. From where they were looking it was totally terrifying but mesmerising at the same time."
"I would think it was something that you'd never forget."
"Umm," said Alex. "I used to know this area as I came from Croydon, umpteen years ago. It used to be quite reasonable but now it seems, from all you see in the press, that it's a good place to come away from."
He looked a little sheepish and said, "Anna, I hope you don't mind, but I'd just like to take a little detour. I was born near here and I'd like to visit 'Woodside Green', to see how it's changed. It's my old 'stomping ground' and when I was a kid, we used to play around the area and got up to all sorts of mischief."
"I can't believe you did bad things, with you being a copper and all that."
"You'd be surprised at some of the things we used to do, I can tell you."
"I'd like to see it, Alex, as it'll give me a little insight as to where you came from, so let's do it. Anyway, that's where the tattoo parlour is that did Yaren's tattoo."
"You're right. We could call in but, to be honest, I don't think they'll be able to tell us much except that they did it. She more than likely lived nearby."
"I think you're right, guv."
They drove down Portland Road, which was the main road from South Norwood towards Croydon. This was a busy road and almost the whole length was taken up with shops, building societies and 'emporiums' of all kinds. The shops were of many and varied nationalities. "My God," said Alex, "so many things have changed since I was here last. I really don't recognise the place." They took a long bend past a large church and came to Woodside Green. This

was indeed a 'Green'. There were not many such areas in the neighbourhood and Alex was pleasantly surprised that it was still there and not built on, like so many open green spaces. The whole area amounted to 3 acres and was surrounded by a low railing-type fence. There were a few trees and a lot of grassy areas which made it ideal for children playing and for games, such a cricket and football, for the lads. The houses around the perimeter were of fairly obvious 'Victorian' heritage as they were quite large and the gardens were mainly well-kept. Alex suspected that in such a built-up area as they were in, houses with a 'green aspect' were quite highly sought-after. At one end of the 'green' was a small cottage which was obviously not Victorian. "I know that cottage was built sometime around 1750, as I did some sort of historical project on the local area whilst I was at primary school just up the road from here. Lovely little place, that cottage, and I'm so glad that it's been looked after."

"I'm sure that will be a 'listed' building Alex."

"You bet - I seem to recall that this area was granted some sort of 'Ancient Charter' way back in history - I don't know when, but I do know that Croydon was called 'Croindene' in the Doomsday Book. At least the mediaeval charter made it 'untouchable' and it seems to have worked, thank goodness."

"I guess it was a nice place to grow up in," said Anna.

"It was Anna - many happy hours spent pretending to be Cowboys and Indians in the uncut grass and the trees."

As they drove past the war memorial at the end of the 'green', he saw the old 'Beehive' Pub.

"I can't believe it! It's still the same as I remember; it doesn't seem to have changed a bit. I expect it still smells of stale smoke and beer, but then again the smoke has probably gone, after the ban came into force and even the 'Joiners Arms' is still there. There used to be a massive brick-making factory not far from where I used to live; you could see the chimneys. They were huge and there were about ten of them I think. The brickworks would sound a very loud hooter at lunch time and then again when the workers had to go back to their jobs. I think the clay around this area was good for brick-making. And do you know, there even used to be horse racing here on Woodside Green up to the mid-nineteenth century and I believe it ranked second only to Aintree under National Hunt rules."

"Wow, fancy that," said Anna, desperately trying to appear interested.

"Yeah, amazing. I was looking up my old hometown a few weeks ago on Wikipedia and I found quite a bit of very interesting stuff. Well, it was to me anyway. Just up there is my old primary school. A cold Victorian building with many memories."

As they passed through the area he knew as a youngster, Alex was quite moved by the changes he saw. He said that when he was a boy, the changes had started happening even then. The old Victorian houses were being converted into flats and they'd lost

their character - the whole area had now become very run-down and shabby.
"Such a shame," he said, "it needs to have a make-over like places, such as Islington and Camden Lock in London, places that were once pretty bad and that have now become desirable."
"Who knows, it may happen here. It could certainly do with some tidying up."
"I know. I must be honest and say that Croydon has become a place that it's good to come from and not to go to. It's changed so much that I just don't know it and I don't like what it has become. – But enough of this," he said, "let's get to the flat where Yaren lived and see if we can get a look inside. I am sorry, have I been boring you, Anna?"
Anna gave him a sideways glance and said, "Not at all... I was, um, quite interested in your history lesson."
"Sorry."
"No, I said I was interested in knowing more about you and you've certainly given me more of an insight."
"Point taken. I'll just shut up then."
She gave him a little punch on the arm to show that she wasn't put out.
At the centre of Woodside Green, Alex turned up Birchanger Road, towards South Norwood. As they were approaching the road in which Yaren lived, they passed a turning and Alex pointed, saying, "Just up there, on the left is Selhurst Park, Crystal Palace's football ground."
Anna said, "And..." leaving the word hanging in the air.
"I guess you're not into football then?"
"No, are you?"
"I only ever went to one 'Palace' match, with my Dad. I remember I was so bloody cold and I spent most of the match dying for a pee and, I couldn't see much. I never went again."
"Sounds like a good choice to me. Now rugby, that's different."
"Oh, so you like the great hunky, hairy blokes, all macho?"
"Well, they're better than those fairies that prance about the pitch, hugging each other if one should actually score a goal and showing off their stupid haircuts and appalling tattoos. And besides, they all get paid an indecent amount of money; they certainly don't 'earn' it. It wouldn't be quite so bad if the teams were from the actual area of the club, but they're from all over the world. I think it's gone way beyond a game now, and with the corruption that's going on, I think it has become obscene."
"Wow, so I take it you really don't like football then?"
"I think you could say that."
Turning into Enmore Road, they found Yarens' flat. There were cars parked down both sides of the road and they had difficulty in finding a parking space.
"Okay guv, how do we play this? We don't have a key and we can't break in. What do you suggest?"

"I'd better phone the local boys and tell them that we just want to look around for clues in our double murder investigation. I really should have done this before but they might be agreeable."
He was about to call the local Metropolitan Police but stopped short. He turned to Anna and said, "Hang on. I don't think they know about her death yet. Has it been reported?"
"I've not had any reports, but that's no guarantee, although if she hadn't many friends, maybe nothing's been reported yet. I will make a quick check back to our HQ and see if there has been a reported death at this address. It won't take long."
"Okay, that's smart thinking Anna."
She made the call and they sat in the car until after a delay of about five minutes, the response came back. "Nothing reported, no death or any suspicion of one," so I think we're in the clear but we still don't have a key do we?"
"Don't you worry about that my girl; just turn the other way while the door opens as if by magic."
"Girl, mmm, I like that. Can I have that in writing? So you're going to pick the lock; I knew you had hidden talents."
"You might find that I have some other hidden talents, you never know."
"I might be keen to find out, Alex."
"Let's concentrate on the investigation shall we, DS Jenkins?"
"Yes, sir," said Anna with a wry smile. "What do I say to a nosy neighbour if they see us then?"
"Hopefully, most of them will be at work or if not, down at the benefits office getting their handouts, but we could say that we're from the Landlord's office. I don't suppose they know if it's owned or rented and probably don't care either – anyway, they're probably used to seeing police going in and out."
With that, Alex walked up to the door and, taking a small pouch from his jacket pocket, produced a small metal tool. "Just look the other way to check that no-one is snooping." He proceeded to unlock the door with very little effort.
"Abracadabra," he said with a smile, "let's hope that if anyone does see us, they don't think we're trying to break in."
As they entered the flat, it seemed that no-one had noticed them. Once inside, they were surprised that the flat initially appeared to be very clean and tidy.
Until they entered the main room.
They both stood silently, looking at each other for what seemed like minutes, and then looked slowly around.
It was still in the ransacked state as it was when she had been killed. The hideous blood spatter of red, containing flecks of grey marking the wall was still evident. So was the bloodstain on the floor where she had fallen. She had obviously been tied to a chair as there were the remnants of strong adhesive tape on the chair legs.
"This ties in with the post-mortem findings doesn't it - the tape I mean," said Anna.

Alex looked at Anna with a sombre gaze. "So now we know where she was killed."
"But how did she get to be dumped in Christchurch Harbour?"
"Someone has taken her. We must find out who that was and when, but before we do, we have to inform the local plod SOCO about this crime scene, so that they can do the forensic checks. They were obviously unaware of her death until now but I don't think anything has been touched since she was taken." They both put on latex gloves before carefully looking around the room, making sure that nothing was touched or moved. Anna then moved and looked at the paintings on the walls and said, "I don't know much about art, but these can't be originals, so they must be prints."
"Why can't they be originals?"
"Well, for a start, some are abstract impressionist and some are simply abstract but they are by artists who are well known and originals would be very highly priced and I doubt whether Yaren could afford maybe a hundred grand for one of these. I recognise some of the names."
"Something else I didn't know about you Anna, you're an art buff. I'm impressed."
"I wouldn't say I know that much about art but I know what I like and I have been to a few of the big London galleries like Tate Modern and the National Gallery. I do quite like art but I am not knowledgeable, I just know what appeals to me. I suppose that just by going to these galleries, one picks up some knowledge."
"Even so," said Alex, "you have hidden depths. I can see I shall have to do some more personal investigating."
"Investigate away guv, I've nothing to hide." She was back into her 'detective' mode.
'I'll bet you have...' he thought, 'but I'd like to find out. That will have to come later'.
They made their way around the flat, carefully looking in places where there might be information as to exactly who Yaren was and what she did for a living. After checking out some shelves and bookcases which contained many art books, they also found quite a number of brochures from an art gallery named 'The Arcadian Gallery'. These had an address in Wimbledon. It was on 'The Broadway'.
"'Arcadian', do you have any idea if that has a meaning Anna?"
"If my memory serves me right, it means something like, 'someone who prefers a simple, rural life, pastoral."
"Blimey, Anna! You're making me regret not doing my homework at school, but in our game, doing in-depth study of such things would be great, if we had the time."
"I'm just a mine of useless information Alex. These are things you just pick up 'on the way' and I suppose my liking of art gives me that sort of information without actually having to go looking for it. It just sort of 'comes along', if you know what I mean."

"With all these things that 'come along', I can see that there is far more to you than I'd realised and it makes me want to know you even more than I did." Anna gave Alex a long gentle look and then turned back to checking the flat.
"Guv, my guess is that with so many brochures, she might be connected with the gallery. You don't usually keep so many brochures of one place, so they might possibly be for giving out to interested people."
Alex said, "Anna, can you take photos of everything we touch so that we can put it all back in exactly the same place?"
"Great idea," and she took out her iPhone®, taking the necessary shots. Just then they noticed something else. There was a small filing cabinet which Alex noticed was locked. He said, "I'm going to have to become a 'Peterman' again I'm afraid," and with that he took out his little wallet with lock-picking tools.
"Hang on guv," said Anna. "I can do that." Alex looked at her with just a hint of disbelief.
"Go on then, 'miss clever clogs', let me see you open that without a key."
With a wry smile, she lifted the small cabinet up and turned it on its side. She reached underneath and inside the cabinet and felt around. There was a 'snick', and she put the cabinet back to the original position and said: *"et voilà!"*
"Bugger me!" said Alex, "do you know, I didn't realise you could do that. You really do have some talents that come in useful beyond looking gorgeous."
"Now you are just being patronising and that gets right up my nose, so be warned."
"Sorry Anna, warning received."
Alex opened the cabinet and inside they found some plastic folders which contained bank statements but they were not in Yarens' name. They bore the name Mark Jordan.
"Hell's teeth, this can't be the Mark Jordan, son of Frank Jordan of the Marine Auction House - that would be too much of a coincidence surely?"
"Let's get the account number and call the bank, they'll confirm the account holder's address."
"Yes, but if that address is this one here, it still won't tell us if it's the same person," said Alex.
"True, but it might refer to a different address somewhere else. It's worth a try isn't it?"
"Hold on Anna, we can't take these with us because the local plod will play merry hell if they know we've taken anything."
"Tell you what; I'll just take a couple of photos so that we can take a closer look later. It'll have various codes on the statement like IBAN and BIC numbers. That should help."
"Smart thinking again."

CHAPTER 33

Using her iPhone®, Anna phoned the NatWest bank contact number. The phone was answered with, "Good Day, this is the NatWest bank, Sydenham branch. How can I help you?"
"Yes, this is Detective Sergeant Jenkins of the Bournemouth Police acting on the authority of the Metropolitan Police. For the purposes of our investigation, I would like to discover the details of a customer of your branch. I have the account details to hand."
"I'm sorry, but in compliance with the rules of the Data Protection Act, we cannot give out details of our customers over the phone. You will have to put in an official request in writing to our Head Office."
"I understand your restrictions regarding disclosure of information but this is a matter of some urgency, so please will you transfer me to your manager?"
"Of course. One moment please."
Very shortly, the manager came on the line. Anna explained once again, who she was and the information she required.
Following the details being given, the manager replied in a voice which gave Anna a mental picture of exactly the type of person she imagined a bank manager to look like.
She guessed he was obviously not going to be very helpful when he said, "I am sorry, but as I'm sure my staff will have already told you, we cannot give out information of the type you require over the phone. Any information has to be authorised by Head Office."
With this, Anna had become more than a little aggravated by the 'stonewalling' of the staff, although she did understand that for security reasons, they would do this. She said, "You did not tell me your name, Sir."
In a very 'high-handed tone he replied, "I did not give you my name." This did not sit well with Anna.
"My name is James Anchor, as on a ship," was his reply.
Anchor the Banker. 'Now there's a name to conjure with; that says it all', she thought, barely stifling a smile.
"Mr. Anchor, do I really have to explain to your Head Office that you are being obstructive and this may delay our enquiries? I'm sure they will be quite displeased to hear that you are refusing to help, and perhaps in doing so, you are preventing us from obtaining further details relating to our enquiries concerning a very serious crime."
She heard several soft 'grunts' and 'chewing noises' as the manager was debating with himself as to whether or not he should divulge the information which he held. This gave Anna a further and quite repulsive picture of the man, for right or wrong. What he didn't know was that Anna was treading on 'very thin ice' over this matter and that she was taking a great chance in saying that she considered he was being obstructive. 'Still, worth a try', she thought.

After, a few moments more, he came back to the phone and said, "In this instance I think it will be acceptable to confirm that the account number you have quoted does indeed belong to a customer of ours. Further than that, I'm afraid, I cannot, and will not; divulge any further details without his knowledge and agreement. You will understand that this is not to go any further, if you know what I mean. I am taking quite a risk of internal personal discipline."
Trying hard to remain courteous, she said, "I do understand that Mr Anchor, and I am most grateful. It goes without saying that what you have told me will be retained only for our investigation and the source of this information will not be divulged."
Anna was about to tell him that this enquiry was linked to a double murder investigation, but she stopped abruptly. "For the purpose of our investigation, I would ask you to apply the same discretion in that you do not mention this enquiry to the account holder. This is just purely to obtain confirmation of some elements within our investigation."
"Of course, nothing will be said by me regarding this matter."
"Or by any of your staff either?"
"Of course not."
"Thank you for your help Mr Anchor." She ended the call and turned to Alex.
"The bank manager confirmed that the account holder with the number we gave is a customer at his branch. I was going to say that we were asking because of the murder investigation but I suddenly thought that if it's the same person who may be linked to the auctions and there is something dodgy going on there, then the bank manager might say something to this account holder. If it is actually the Mark Jordan we think it might be, it'll put him on his guard."
"Damn good thinking Anna," said Alex. "I can see that your detective mind is working well. If there is a link, the last thing we need is to alert anyone before we've had a chance to get some real information. If they find out that we are checking up, it will give them time to hide evidence or whatever."
"There might be some more documents which could give us a link. Let's keep looking."
They both continued to carefully check all the cabinets and other possible places where small papers or books would be kept. There was a bookshelf with a good number of art books and reference editions giving information on art generally. Alex found a small notebook with what looked like addresses and phone numbers. He saw that Anna was turned away and looking at something low down in the bookshelf. He quickly and surreptitiously put the book into his inside pocket.
"It seems as though Yaren was heavily into art, Anna. I wonder if she is connected with this 'Arcadian Gallery' in Wimbledon."

"One way to find out - let's give them a call." Anna checked on her iPhone® for the location of the gallery and found that it was not too far away from where they were.
Anna called the number on the brochure and a very cultured female voice answered.
"Good Morning. This is the Arcadian Gallery; may I help you in any way?"
"Yes, I am Detective Sergeant Jenkins from Bournemouth Police and we are making enquiries about a person whom you may know. She has a Turkish name. We have found some brochures of yours and we are wondering if you might know her."
"And this persons' name?"
"Yaren Ganim."
"Why yes, of course, Yaren is one of our assistants in the gallery; but she is not here at the moment because she is part-time and won't be back until next week."
"Does she live in South Norwood?"
"I believe so, although I have never been to that part of South London."
Anna thought, 'I'm not surprised, with that stuck-up accent; you wouldn't lower yourself to go to that area'.
"Can I ask your name please?"
"My name is Rebecca Connors."
"Would that be 'Miss' Connors?"
"It would indeed."
"Can I ask when you last saw Yaren?"
"Not since she was here at work on Thursday of last week. May I ask why you are enquiring after Yaren?"
"We have some bad news regarding Yaren. I am very sorry to tell you, Miss Connors that she will not be back next week. Very sadly, she was found dead earlier this week and we are investigating her death."
There was silence for many moments. Then, "Oh my God, no! That can't be true. She was one of my closest friends. There was a pause. "How did she die? Was it in a road accident or something?" Rebecca was sobbing now as tears welled in her eyes. "Tell me it's not true, please, please!" she cried.
Her accent had fallen somewhat and she seemed very distraught.
"I am afraid to have to tell you that Yaren was actually murdered. Her body was found in Christchurch."
"Murdered! Oh No! That's so awful. Murdered. But in Christchurch, that's in Dorset isn't it? What the hell was she doing in Christchurch? I think that's near where her boyfriend lives isn't it?"
'Boyfriend in Christchurch'. Anna realised that this could be more important than she realised at first. So she said, "Miss Connors, as a result of what you have just said, we will need to come to you now to ask you some more questions in person. As you will appreciate, we need to know more about Yaren, so please stay there until we arrive. It's only about 12 miles so we should be there quite soon. In

the meantime, I suggest you make yourself a drink and try to relax. This has obviously come as a shock and we are sorry to have to break the news to you this way but we don't have much information about Yaren and it is imperative that we have more details about her. Please do not and I repeat not, tell anyone about this until we have seen you. Do you understand?"
"Yes, alright. I will have to close the gallery and wait for you. I simply cannot believe this is happening."
While Anna was on the phone to Rebecca Connors, Alex had found some more documents which would later have a bearing on the investigation, but Anna quickly told him that Rebecca Connors had mentioned her 'boyfriend' who lived near Christchurch.
"Bingo! That could be the link we need," said Alex. "I was coming to the conclusion that this Mark Jordan could well be the 'lad' from Christchurch and if he was Yarens' boyfriend, that means that he was probably living here and he might come back at any time. We don't know where he is or what he is doing, so we'd better hop it right now, just in case he turns up."
They both made sure that everything was back in place by checking with the photos which Anna had taken, and that nothing was left to alert someone to the fact that they had been there. They just had to hope that no-one had seen them. If they were challenged by a neighbour, they'd have to say that they were from the landlord and just checking up on something.
After a final check round, they made a quick exit to their car which was parked a little way from the flat.
As it happened, they were not approached as they got into the car, but just as they drove off, there was a silver Porsche coming towards them which looked as though it was going to park.
"That doesn't look like it belongs around here Anna," said Alex. "What do you think?"
"I agree, it's a bit posh for this area. I wonder if it could be our boyfriend."
"I think it's a strong possibility, but we'd better not be seen, so let's get out of here pronto."
Anna turned round and took a quick photo of the registration number of the Porsche as they drove off towards Wimbledon.
"If it was him, I'd like to know why he's come back. We have to suppose that he knows Yaren is dead. Or maybe he doesn't?"
"We couldn't just stop him and ask what he was doing here, could we guv?"
"No, but just think, if he does know about her, why hasn't he reported it to the police? If he really doesn't know, then he's going to find out very soon, but because there is no body, it makes things even more inexplicable - if that was him of course. Either way, he should inform the police and we'll have some continuity or it will be very obvious that there is something really dodgy going on."
"We'll have to check with the local plod to see if a body has been reported, Alex."

"Just let's wait and see what happens. We don't want to spook him at this stage until we know what's going on."
"Let's suppose that he did find Yaren guv, and he actually took her body down to Christchurch for some reason, then wouldn't he come back here to clean the place up to hide any evidence?"
"I think that's taking things just a little far, but maybe you're right. If that's the case, why wouldn't he clean it up at the same time? But hell, who knows at this stage?"
They left the flat in South Norwood and headed toward the Gallery. As they were driving to Wimbledon, leaving behind the rather scruffy area of South Norwood, they passed Mitcham Common and continued on, as the area improved somewhat, although it still did not have the 'class' which would seem to be necessary for what they assumed to be a quality Art Gallery.
Anna said, "You know I said that the bank manager wouldn't give me any information? Well, I've occasionally used these websites that can check up on people. It shouldn't be too difficult. I could get Alice on to this as she's very good with IT. I think we could get most of what we need from them. We have enough information necessary for her to check it out.
"Good work Anna. I think we're making some progress at last and let's see what Miss Connors has to say."
After the relatively short drive to Wimbledon, they found the Broadway. They spotted the Arcadian Gallery which was along the one-way system so they had to navigate around that to find somewhere to park that was not too distant. They found a public car park just a little off the main road, and luckily with a few spare places. As its name suggested, the Broadway was a very wide road and was surprisingly very clean. There was a theatre and many high-quality shops of all types. The New Wimbledon Theatre looked to be Edwardian and seemingly very active judging by all the advertising for it. Anna did a quick check on her iPhone® and found out that it was indeed an Edwardian building, built about 100 years ago by a 'theatre lover', and entrepreneur, J. B. Mulholland. This was a listed building, which explained why it was in such a good state of repair. It was a very striking and had a completely different architectural style from the surrounding plethora of rather 'up-market' eateries and shops. There were all the usual high-end outlets that one found in the 'better' areas and Anna seemed to think that Rebecca would fit in rather well into this area with her accent, provided that it was 'real' of course.
They walked along the Broadway for some distance, taking in the affluence of the area which seemed to confirm that an art gallery would be of a standard that dealt with expensive paintings and ceramics, as is usual with a higher class of gallery.
On reaching the gallery, Alex said, "Okay Anna, let's see what this Rebecca Connors has to tell us. Do you think she was genuine when you said she sounded distraught?"

"Yes, I am sure she was. I think I would be if someone told me that my friend had just been murdered."

CHAPTER 34

Anna and Alex stood on the Broadway and looked at the gallery.
Alex looked at Anna with raised eyebrows, "Nice area," he said, "this is very classy. If Yaren worked here, she certainly worked in a better area than she lived." The door had a small notice saying 'Due to unforeseen circumstances, we regret that the Gallery is closed today. We do apologise for any inconvenience caused'.
They knocked, and an immaculately dressed woman came to the door. Alex held up his warrant card and the door was unlocked. "I am Rebecca Connors, please, come in."
Her eyes gave away the fact that she had been crying and she looked very sad.
Alex and Anna introduced themselves. "I am Detective Inspector Vail and this is Detective Sergeant Jenkins who spoke to you a little earlier. As she said, we are from Bournemouth Police investigating the murder of Yaren Ganim."
"Yes, of course. I closed the gallery, as you see; I just couldn't work after your devastating news. I am completely shocked."
Rebecca managed to keep her poise and she ushered them to a side room of the gallery. "May I offer you a drink?"
Anna adopted a gentle tone and said, "No thank you, Miss Connors, but please carry on if you need something. We completely understand how you must be feeling at this moment."
Anna would ask the questions, as they had discussed the best way to approach this interview on the way and decided that she was best placed for such a difficult interview. Anna had found that it was never pleasant to give this sort of news on the few occasions that she'd had this duty and once again she'd felt the same on passing on this news today.
Rebecca said, "I still cannot accept that she has been murdered, that she is gone. This is so terrible."
"We understand that you knew Yaren Ganim well?"
"Yes, as I said to you on the telephone, she was my friend." Anna remembered that she'd said 'my best friend', but just kept that to herself for the time being.
"Have you known Yaren for long?"
"Since she came to work at the gallery?"
"And when did she begin working here?"
"About two years ago."
"Do you know where Yaren came from, as she was not English?
"She was Turkish, but she has been here for many years. She came to England about thirty years ago I believe, which is why she spoke such good English I imagine."
"Are her parents still alive?"
"I really don't know. This was never mentioned. I think perhaps she had 'grown away' from her parents. I do know that she came from farming stock and that her parents were not well educated."
"And why do you think she had 'grown away' from her parents?"

"I think she wanted to improve herself and get a good education."
"And do you know how she did this? Did she tell you about her education?"
Alex suggested, "She must have been fairly well educated to work in a gallery like this. Knowledge of art would surely have been very important."
"Yes, of course. I do know that Yaren went to Durham University and gained a degree in Art History."
"Did she come to you directly after University?"
"No, she told me she'd had a number of jobs, all to do with art, in and around Newcastle for a while and then in London. She applied to this gallery and had an interview with the owner."
"So this is not your gallery then?" asked Anna.
"Oh, heavens no! - I am the curator and manager. I do the normal office work, keep accounts and arrange for shipping of pieces which have been sold or pieces coming in for exhibition. I also arrange for some pieces to be sent to other galleries and exhibitions as well as setting up exhibitions here, in the gallery. Oh, and I also sell works as well."
"I imagine that's the whole purpose of the gallery," said Alex, with a straight-faced look at Rebecca.
'Of course," she replied, with an equally benign look. "And I make the tea as well," she added with a quite pointed riposte.
"And what else do you do all day. There surely can't be that many people coming into or calling the gallery during a normal day?" asked Alex.
Rebecca bridled a little at this, regaining her 'haughtiness'. "It may surprise you to know that there are a great number of things to be done. Just because the paintings and sculptures are not moving around and there aren't hordes of people about, it could be a preconception that there is not much to do. One has to arrange for exhibitions and one also has to write announcements introducing, artists and works to be shown, together with pieces explaining the concept and inspiration which the artist had for that particular piece. Then there are critiques and promotional announcements of forthcoming exhibitions as well as the advertising of such events and their respective 'vernissages'. We also have to make applications for grants and other types of funding within the art community. One has a great deal to do on a daily basis."
"One is certainly surprised," said Alex, with just a trace of irony, which Anna thought was not missed, thinking Rebecca was beginning to rile Alex with her accent. Forgive my asking, what is 'vernissage'?"
Inwardly, Anna groaned. 'You've just made yourself look a prat'.
"Actually," Rebecca said with a very slight raise of her head, "the word is 'vernissages' in the plural. These are the 'openings' of an exhibition."
"Thank you," Alex said, in a slightly 'clipped' tone, suitably informed.

Continuing, Anna said, "And what did Yaren do as you said she was an 'assistant'?"
"Yes, she was but was also very knowledgeable was able to discuss the pieces with potential customers. As you can see by looking around, we not only have paintings and prints, we also have ceramics. Yaren had researched the artists on display and was able to talk about them with interesting and useful insights into their inspirations and methods, and techniques."
Alex then changed tack a little and said, "Did Yaren ever have contact with international artists or buyers?"
"Oh yes," said Rebecca, "she often had contacts and dealings with foreign buyers. In fact, she has been to Europe a couple of times to talk with buyers. She recently completed a sale to an Italian buyer, although she didn't actually go to Italy to meet the buyer."
"Was that on behalf of this gallery?"
"Well, yes of course, but I believe that she has been to France on business with her boyfriend a few times."
"We were coming to this," said Anna. "Do you have a name for this boyfriend?"
"His name was Mark."
"Do you know his surname then?"
"I think it was Jordan."
Anna and Alex exchanged glances... At last! Confirmation that it was almost certainly Mark Jordan who was Yaren's boyfriend and he absolutely *must* be the same one that was linked to their investigation.
Alex thought, 'this is becoming very 'drawn-out'';' he wished she were more forthcoming without having to drag each item from her. Anna was actually thinking along similar lines, but inwardly realised that by not pushing her, perhaps more information would be 'teased' out.
"So do you know anything about this 'Mark Jordan', for instance, like where he comes from or where he lives?"
"All I know is that he lives with Yaren." Here, she caught her breath and paused for a while with her hand to her face, as her tears welled up again. "Or, as I now have to say, 'lived' with Yaren. I still can't believe that she has gone. We would spend a lot of time together as Mark seemed to come and go a lot and was often away for days at a time."
At the mention of him living with Yaren, Alex and Anna exchanged quick but meaningful glances.
"So do you know where he was from or where he went on these 'days at a time'?"
"The only thing I know is that his father owns a Marine business in Christchurch in Dorset, but I don't know what Mark did for a living. I did not meet him often and I never asked Yaren as I don't like to enquire about someone's private life. All I know is that he had dealings of some sort in London and went down to Christchurch fairly often and I believe he also had contacts in France."

"Do you know what car he drove?"
"He drove a silver Porsche. It is such a beautiful car."
Another meaningful glance between the two detectives...
"Would you know the registration number?"
"Good heavens, no! Why on earth would I know that?"
"Just a possibility," said Alex.
Anna continued, "Is there anything else you can tell us about Mark; was he a nice person and were he and Yaren happy together?"
"As I said, I didn't know him really at all but he seemed to be a very nice man."
Anna definitely caught a very slight pause on the word 'seemed' and this made her senses quicken.
"So you have met him?"
"Yes, a couple of times but I had nothing to do with him really. It was only a passing meeting really when he would collect Yaren."
"And no other contact?"
"No."
"I'm sorry if all this sounds intrusive, it's just that we have to ask all these questions to build up a picture of Yaren's life and contacts so that we can find her killer. Sometimes, this can cause a great deal of distress as we have to ask many intrusive questions like these and they can cause undue hurt. Can you describe him for me?"
Rebecca was regaining her composure a little by now and she said, "All I can tell you is that Mark was nice looking and about six feet tall. He has medium brown hair which he wore quite short. He was clean shaven and Yaren said had a nice sense of humour. In fact, he actually looked quite dishy really. I'm not surprised Yaren went for him."
Anna again sensed the pronunciation of the word 'looked' was just slightly emphasised.
"Did Yaren mind that he was not around all the time as from what you say; he would go away for 'days at a time'?"
"Well, no, she understood that he had business interests in London and that he had to go back to Christchurch for the marine business."
Alex asked if she knew what the 'business interests' were.
Her reply was quite brusque, saying, "I would have no idea. As I've said, I don't make a point of venturing into other people's lives."
"But you must have had some idea from talking with Yaren about what sort of business he was involved in."
Her voice hardened slightly. "You are not listening to me. I said that I didn't interfere in her personal life. We were friends on a social level but it is not my nature to delve into a person's private life. If they want to tell me, that's fine, but I would not presume to be inquisitive."
"And Yaren did not tell you anything about Mark's business?" asked Alex.
"Oh, for goodness sake, how many times do I have to say this, no? The only thing she told me was that he sometimes met a client of

ours who is a collector. I presume that this man was a businessman who collected art."
Alex took that piece of information on board, thinking, 'now this could be a connection, we shall have to delve a little further when we finally get to meet this Mark Jordan'.
"Please, can you tell me the name of this client?"
"I am sorry, but that must stay confidential. We do not give out client names as they usually wish to stay private and in any case, I was not a party to that information. Yaren actually finalised the sale and everything is kept very confidential unless the buyer agrees to his details being divulged."
Anna said, "Rebecca, you must understand, that this information could be vital to our investigation. There may be links which you just do not understand, and to be honest, I don't think you have the right to withhold this information. We really don't want to get heavy, but we could if you don't co-operate now. Do you understand?"
Rebecca replied, "The owner of this gallery will not be best pleased if I gave you this information, In fact, it could jeopardise my job."
"Okay Rebecca, how about we talk to your owner and perhaps he will understand the situation and tell us this client's name. That will keep you in the clear."
"Maybe, but the owner is a woman. Her name is Olivia Harrington-Thorpe. I'll give you her telephone number but do please make it clear that I only gave you her number under duress."
Alex asked, "Does this Olivia Harrington-Thorpe live locally?"
"No, she lives in Surrey, Addington actually, in a place called 'Shirley Hills'."
'Aha', thought Alex, 'I know this place', and then said, "Shirley Hills, that's near Croydon, isn't it? A very expensive area."
"Oh please," said Rebecca, "not Croydon; it's very close to Addington Palace actually, not far from the John Ruskin College. I know Yaren lived in South Norwood. And that's a million miles from Shirley Hills," she said in a very deprecating tone.
"And where do you live Rebecca?" asked Anna.
"I have a flat in Wimbledon now but I used to live In Addington Village, which is the old part of Addington, not the new 'estate'; that's how I met Olivia Harrington-Thorpe. My parents have known her for years and through knowing her, I became interested in art. Things progressed from there."
'So, perhaps the accent was learned or acquired', thought Alex. 'No matter, she had a good job and it was understandable why she would be reluctant to put that at risk but I do wonder how or even 'if' her parents 'knew Mrs Olivia Harrington-Thorpe' for many years. That was not really important, but then again, you never know'. He kept that thought for possible further digging.
Anna said, "Thanks, Rebecca, you've given us some good information," and looking toward Alex for confirmation, said "I think that's all we can do for now." Alex nodded.

Rebecca had regained her composure and said, "Please call me "Beccy, that's what Yaren called me. I think it will keep her memory closer. I am really going to miss her terribly."
"I'm sure," said Anna. "Could you give me the phone number please? – I suppose she'll be at home, then we can finish here and let you get on, although I know it won't be easy for you."
Beccy said, "She is usually at home at this time of day," and then she added, thoughfully, "is it all right to tell people now, you know, about Yaren?"
Alex intervened. "Yes, you can, but if anyone that you don't know or anyone who sounds a little too intrusive, if you know what I mean, anyone making enquiries, can you please let us know as soon as you can? Here's my card; you can contact either me or Anna at any time. Any information you can give or that you remember could be more helpful than you may think."
"But of course," she said.
Alex and Anna said their goodbyes and were about to make their way back to the car when Rebecca came to the door. "Excuse me, there might be something." She waited until they walked back the short distance to the door. She was looking a little 'thoughtful'.
"Actually, there was a slightly strange occurrence the other day. A gentleman phoned asking for Yaren's address. I said that we couldn't give this information but he was insistent. He told me that Yaren had apparently concluded a sale recently to his 'boss' in Italy who wanted to possibly make another purchase and would only speak with Yaren. I told him again that I would not give out her address without her knowledge and that he couldn't speak to her as she was not in the gallery that day."
"And did you give him her address or phone number?"
"Absolutely not! We have a very strict code of confidentiality in the gallery because some of our clients are very private people, as I'm sure you can imagine."
"Yes, I can understand that," Anna agreed. "So what happened then?"
"He was very insistent and, although he was courteous enough, he made me feel quite uncomfortable. I thought he actually sounded a little 'threatening', if that's possible to hear in a voice. So I said that I would call Yaren so that she could contact this man but she was not answering her phone. After that, I called Mrs Harrington-Thorpe to explain the situation and she agreed that it would be okay, in this circumstance, to divulge Yaren's number. You understand that I didn't want to jeopardise my job."
"Of course, that's a 'given'; so you contacted your gallery boss?"
"Yes, and Mrs Harrington-Thorpe said that as there was the potential of another sale of a very high-priced work being made, that it would be acceptable for me to give this man her details. I have to say, Mrs Harrington-Thorpe likes 'big figure sales'."
"So you phoned him back with this information?"

"No, because he had said that he would be in a meeting and would call me back later, which he did."
"So you have no phone number for him?"
"I'm sorry, no. All I can say is that he told me his name was 'George' and I called him 'Mr George'."
'Damn', thought Alex, this would have been a very good link as it sounds as though this man could be a very strong lead.
Okay, Beccy, thank you for this information. Once again, we are really sorry to have given you such bad news.
Alex and Anna both made their goodbyes once again and made their way back to the car park.
"That could have been good Anna, if only there had been a phone number or contact details, but then again, if this 'George' isn't 'kosher', then he won't give anything away! " Life's a bummer sometimes, Alex."
Having concluded the interview, they made their way back to the car and returned to the Bournemouth Police Headquarters.
Later that day, Alex and Alice were talking in his office and he was telling her of his and Anna's meeting with Rebecca, especially the part about Mark Jordan being Yaren's boyfriend.
"Now that's what I call progress guv. That surely brings a new line of enquiry into the investigation. There must be something going on with Mark and his father. I mean, the link is too strong not to have connections."
"I'm sure you're right Alice. I want you to continue digging into Frank Jordan's background even more deeply now and I also want Mark Jordan to have the same treatment. I know you can get some very good information with your expertise in computers, so let's get digging. Oh, and by the way, we also know that Mark Jordan has two bank accounts with NatWest bank in one of their London branches. We have photos of a bank statement which give some bank coding, so maybe you can do a trace with that. Ask Anna, as she photographed them on her phone. He also seems to go between the flat in London and Christchurch a lot. He is often away for two to three days at a time, but we don't know where he goes. We suspect back to Christchurch but we don't know why or where, yet."
"Well, perhaps he goes back 'there' to go over to France with loads of drugs and stuff."
"Let's not jump the gun yet Alice. You have a nasty mind, do you know that?" he said laughing.
"That's what comes of being a detective sir – it makes you a nasty, suspicious person."
"Now, now, Alice, you are very far from being a nasty person and I actually think you have a valid possibility."
"Thanks guv."
"Okay then, off you go and start being suspicious over Messrs Jordan and Son."
"On my way."

CHAPTER 35

On their way back in the car, Alex had asked Anna what she had made of Rebecca.
Anna said, "I think she has made the best of herself and she obviously moves in higher circles than we do, but then I suppose that's natural when you deal with people with money to spend on paintings that fetch silly prices and not feel the pinch."
"Well, as it happens," said Alex, 'Little Miss Beccy' doesn't know it, but I know, or at least knew, the area that she has mentioned very well. I learned to play golf when I was about 9 years old at Shirley Park Golf Club and that borders Shirley Hills. I remember that I used to play past a house right in the middle of the Golf Club, which was very, very posh. At some point I was invited to go and play with the young son of the household. I now realise that he was, like me, an only child and I think his parents wanted another boy for him to play with. I think he must have been very lonely because, as I say, the house was in the middle of the golf course and there were no others close by. I remember that this great big place had its own tennis court and even back then, a television set which actually projected the picture on to a huge screen. We didn't even have a 'telly' in those days."
"So how did you come to know the family of this boy then Alex?"
"Do you know, I have absolutely no recollection of how I got to know them, except that I suppose I must have been invited through someone I met at the golf club or just being seen there as I played past? The club was full of really posh people who would say something like, 'We are off to the Bahamas, yet again, for another holiday. So boring, we should go somewhere else'. I mean, how the hell do you compete with that?"
"It sounds like you had fun though with just the two of you in smart golf club grounds to play in."
"It wasn't that much fun really and It didn't last that long. All I know is that this lad was such a drippy little git, that I was 'asked to leave' by the stuck-up mother one day."
"Oh dear, why was that? What did you do wrong then - disgrace yourself?"
"I remember it very well. We were sitting outside the kitchen door chucking acorns at each other, as you do when you're a kid. One hit 'drippy git' on the head and he yelled and started crying. An acorn - I ask you! Anyway, 'Mummy' came out and I remember her exact words, spoken in her plummy accent, 'Oh dear, I don't think this is the way we behave ourselves here, so perhaps you had better go home. Please don't come back'.
"Oops, and did you ever go back?"
"Never - but I do wish it'd been something bigger and harder than an acorn."
"That's your vicious streak coming out Alex."
"I know, I can be a right bastard sometimes."

"But not to me I hope."
He gave her a very gentle look.
"That is something I will never be, I promise."
"So what did you make of what 'Beccy' told us?"
"Well, as I said, I knew the area and she said 'Addington' instead of 'Addington Village'. There's a very big difference. Addington was a kind of overspill area from Croydon and the houses there were predominantly Council as I recall, and I'm sure that if you were from the village, you'd say so because Addington 'Village' was a different kettle of fish - chalk and cheese if you like - much higher class, but then she said 'Shirley Hills'. If this 'Olivia Trumpington-Whatsit' lives in somewhere like Bishops Walk or Oaks Road, which I know is a part of Shirley Hills, then she is extremely well-heeled or at least someone there is. The houses in that area would sell for anything up to three million quid."
"Bloody hell!" said Anna. "I can understand that she wouldn't want to blot her copybook in that direction. I expect that Olivia would be a little miffed if her own details were given out without her say-so."
"Beccy doesn't seem to have much of an impression of where Yaren lived but then I guess snobbery is inherent in the realms that she must move in now."
"It doesn't really matter though, does it? Yaren lived there and it looks like Mark Jordan is indeed our bloke from Christchurch who seems to be implicated in this double murder. We just don't know how far up the drainpipe he is at the moment," said Anna.
"Maybe we should contact 'Olivia thingy-thingy, and see what she has to say about Yaren. One always has to wonder where such money comes from. Probably the husband, who is most likely some sort of banker or other. Notice I said 'banker'," ventured Alex.
"Oh we don't have bad things to say about the people, who keep Britain afloat, or rather used to, do we?"
"Don't we? I do. Just take a look at how much money people have lost from their pensions and how much the government have given them of tax payer's money, just to keep the buggers afloat."
"Ouch! I guess we don't have much time for bankers do we?"
"No we don't Anna. Anyway, back to 'Harrington-whatsit'. We'll look into her or them if there is a 'him'. We also have to get a lot more information about the Jordans. I can't help thinking that the marine element has something to do with what might be going on. Who knows, there might be connections? Money seems to want money; they never seem to have enough, and we don't know what Mark does for a living either so I've got to talk to Alice to see what she can come up with. She did suggest that perhaps Mark might be involved in drug-running to France."
"Good thinking".
"I have to see what she came up with on her visit to the Auctions and didn't you say she'd gone there posing as a journalist?"
"Yep. I hope she didn't blow it and alert anyone. We'll see."

CHAPTER 36

Anna has been enquiring into Mark Jordan's bank accounts after information came to light when Yarens's death was being investigated. Statements were discovered at her flat and enquiries at his bank provided information of two accounts. She informed the bank that she was investigating a suspicious death and that Mark Jordan was in some way linked to police enquiries. The bank manager didn't want to divulge any information but he was reminded in no uncertain terms that as an ongoing police investigation, any and all information which he had regarding links with the relevant accounts would be subpoenaed should he choose to withhold them. This would not look good with his superiors, should it come to light that he had withheld vital information from a police investigation into such a serious matter.

Subsequently, after further phone calls and pressure, he gave her information which confirmed links between both Yaren's bank account and Mark Jordan's which showed both deposits and withdrawals of many thousands of pounds over a period of three years. There were also transfers to an account in the name of Olivia Harrington-Thorpe. She was known to be the ex-wife of Jonathan Harrington-Thorpe, whom she had divorced some three years previously. It now appears that there were serious amounts of money changing hands via deposits to accounts in the name of Mark Jordan and Olivia Harrington-Thorpe. What Mark did not know was that Olivia Harrington-Thorpe is actually his mother. When she and Frank Jordan were divorced many years previously, she wanted no more to do with Mark as she was too selfish and wanted a different life to the one she'd had with Frank, who was albeit, a successful scrap dealer. She wanted no more to do with that sort of life. She liked money but had her sights set on 'better' things. She consequently met and married Harrington-Thorpe who was a city trader in a merchant bank. The only thing she took from Frank was the house she now lived in. However, although she was under the impression that the house was hers, it was in fact still owned by Frank. Unknown to her, there was the document which gave her the right to live in the house with all disbursements paid for by herself but it was actually still owned wholly by Frank. She had signed papers giving him this right when there were so many documents to be signed that she had not looked carefully enough when putting her signature to that particular document.

Alex was working on the premise that both Frank Jordan and Olivia Harrington-Thorpe were involved in the fraudulent sale of copies of masterpieces, together with Mark Jordan who had definitely handled some of these. He had asked his staff to investigate the people who had bought artworks from the gallery and he would leave the further questions for a later interview when there were more details available.

CHAPTER 37

DC Tom Peterson had found some information which would help to trace the man who was seen running from the boat which was now moored in Lymington Yacht Haven and the where the body of a man was found in this boat under a forward bunk in the cabin.
This was, in all probability, the one which carried the body of Yaren Ganim which was subsequently found on 'Blue Moon Island' in Christchurch Harbour.
This boat was a fast cruiser with a large engine which was actually reported stolen from the Marine Auctions at Tuckton Bridge. The owners' name was Michael Fortune. He was not currently a suspect after he had been contacted and it was confirmed that he was in London at the time of the reported theft.
In summarising the information he'd gathered so far, the Detective Constable had established that the boat was seen leaving Christchurch Harbour during the evening of August 31st, where it had emerged from enquiries locally, that witnesses had seen what appeared to be this particular boat, suffering damage, probably to the propeller, as it approached the 'Run' at the exit from Christchurch Harbour. This had apparently affected the speed of the craft.
It was assumed to have made passage along the coast across Bournemouth Bay as it was subsequently seen in Poole Harbour where the propeller was apparently taken for repair. The boat then left, unseen, during the late evening of September 5th.
After enquiries at all the possible landing places along the coast towards Southampton, the boat then apparently continued along the coast and was eventually located and found moored in Lymington Yacht Haven. When investigations concerning it's' whereabouts were obtained by the police, the boat was searched, eventually revealing the naked body of a man which was found in the cabin. Again, witnesses said that two men were seen on the boat during the previous evening and the dead body was believed to be the second person. He had been shot and suffered a beating in a similar way to how Yaren Ganim had been killed.
A male, presumably the second man, was seen leaving the boat and walking to the street bordering the Haven. Since then, no traces of his whereabouts have been forthcoming.
DC Tom Peterson had been tasked to go to the Lymington Yacht Haven for yet more information.
He was in the Haven Master's office and looking around whilst he waited for the Haven Master to arrive, he noticed a great many official 'notices' on a large board on one wall. Presumably these were nautical instructions and information relating to the boatyard

and its' surroundings. There were also a large number of photographs of boats. Taking a closer look at these, he realised that they were photos of boats which were for sale here, at the Yacht Haven.
After a while, a man walked in, dressed in a dark blue sweater of the 'nautical' variety, with epaulettes on the shoulder. DC Peterson deduced that these would probably denote his rank in the hierarchy of the Yacht Haven. This man was quite tall and had a 'weathered' complexion. In fact, he really looked as though he was a 'seafaring' type of person who spent a good deal of time on the water and in the wind. 'I'll bet he's a sailor and not a 'motor' man', Tom thought.
"Good morning Sir. I am DC Tom Peterson from Bournemouth Police. We did telephone to make an appointment."
"Yes, that's correct; Matthew Addison." He held out his hand which Tom shook. It was a grip like steel! 'That's from pulling all those ropes', Tom guessed.
"As you know, a body was found on a craft which would have been moored here on or about September 5th or 6th. We also know that a man was seen walking from this boat along the pontoons and up to the main road just at the entrance of this yard. Our question is, do you have any CCTV coverage of this man leaving the boatyard?"
"Indeed we do. Because of the extremely high value of the craft around the Haven, our CCTV is comprehensive and of high quality."
"In that case would you have coverage of the evening that this boat came in?"
"We keep a good data base and we have tape recordings, although I suppose you don't call it 'tape' nowadays but anyway, we do have storage of the previous 15 days. We run our cameras on a 24 hour basis and we have large file storage capacity. One never knows when we might need corroboration for something which has happened and if there is a legal reason for an enquiry, this is extremely useful, as you may imagine. But you know all this of course."
"It's good to know that you have such a large storage system. Are your pictures of good quality as sometimes, the night-time shots are pretty useless for facial recognition, for instance?"
"I'm happy to say that our picture quality is first-rate. This sort of quality really impresses our customers who can rest assured that we are at the top of the scale when it comes to their security."
"Could you make a copy of the footage from the time in question as we would really like to get a look at 'chummy' who legged it off the dock and disappeared?"
"Of course. I'll just ask our office manager to locate the appropriate time and you can take a look. When you've found the piece you need, she'll make you a copy onto disc."
"Thanks, that'll be great."
"We're happy to do all we can to help as this nasty incident is not a good for our reputation so we hope you will soon be able to bring your investigation to a good conclusion."

"We'll do our best sir," said Tom.
Addison called the office and spoke with Jane Goodson the office manager. She said that the Harbour Master would check through the CCTV record and call him back when the appropriate section had been found and she'd make the copy.
After Addison had passed this on, Tom said, "That's great, thanks. I just wish that all our enquiries resulted in such good co-operation. This will please my boss as we don't have a clear picture of our suspect, so let's hope this gives us a good shot."
Tom realised that he probably shouldn't have used the term 'shot' but it was too late!
Addison said, "In the meantime, please pop down to the galley and help yourself to a coffee. I'm sure it won't take long."
"Very kind of you, I will," said Tom.
He was just enjoying a rather nice cup of cappuccino when Jane came into the galley and said, "Hi, I'm Jane Goodison. Our Harbour Master, Mark Mullies has the pictures of the time span that you want. Just come through to his office and we can get this copied to disc for you."
Tom was giving Jane a very 'appreciative' look and had to drag his attention back to the Harbour Master who shook hands with Tom and then said, "Do you know, this chap must have been very lucky."
"Why's that sir," asked Tom.
"Well, although from the information I have, luck is something I should not credit him with but he came storming in from the Solent and he had no choice but to find some space on the pontoons. He was going far too fast to be negotiating the channel at night and although it's wide and deep, there are buoys and various channel markings to be aware of, which are not at all easy to see, especially if you are new to the area.
"Oh, why was that then. I mean, why would he be in a hurry?"
"Well, the Isle of Wight ferry was still running at the time he would have come in and because of the density of boats, this is not the easiest of harbours to navigate. I'm presuming he didn't know this harbour or else we would probably know either him, or the boat. It would have been very easy to miss seeing the obstacles on the way in."
Tom said, "Perhaps he would have preferred to tie up somewhere and sneak ashore in his little inflatable dinghy."
"Even if he had one, there is virtually nowhere he could have 'tied up' apart from here in the Haven. There are no moorings out in the Solent. Anyway, if he had a dinghy or tender, it was not on the boat when he tied up to the pontoon and there would be nowhere to put one at that point. As I say, the way he probably charged up the channel, he was very lucky not to have damaged other boats coming in. I would say in many respects that he didn't know what he was doing. He certainly wasn't a qualified boat skipper or an experienced boat handler."
"Why do you say that?"

“You see, we have a CCTV camera at the far end of the pontoons and we can see him as he came into view; he was going far too fast for the conditions and light. An experienced boat-handler would keep the speed right down no matter how rushed they were, if only so that his wash wouldn’t cause damage to other boats. This guy was completely unconcerned with his actions.”
"Quite simply, he had no idea of how to tie up to a bollard or how to run ropes in the correct fashion."
"Do you think that he was in a hurry and too rushed?"
“Well yes, of course, as I said due to his speed and in my experience, anyone who knows boats will tie up a craft quickly and correctly without the need to rush - rushing would take longer anyway. This man had no idea."
"You do know that he had, apparently, killed a man and stuffed him under a bunk in the cabin."
“So I understand and if he wanted to draw attention to himself, he was going the right way about it. I would have thought being quiet and not attracting interest or questions from other boating people around at the time would have been a better bet. But then, I've never killed anyone so who am I to say? It's just a pity that there were so few people around who could have provided more information."
"Of course, what we have to do is to get a look at this man and get a good description and then, try to find out where the hell he went from here. We really need to catch this person, and quickly."
Just then, Jane came in holding an empty CD case.
Tom was quite taken with Jane and he was desperately thinking of some reason that he could use to possibly get back in touch with her again.
Jane had a quite low and 'dusky' voice. She said, "We've found the man you’re looking for. Would you like to take a look and then we can make sure we have the right copy for you?"
"This made Tom take even more interest in her, as he found her voice very sexy. She was quite tall and slim, with coppery hair and green eyes – and very attractive. Tom was almost rooted to the spot. He walked behind her to the computer screen where the CCTV 'footage' was being displayed, in the 'paused' state. As he walked, he had the greatest difficulty in keeping his mind on CCTV and not 'other things', such as her bottom, encased as it was, in tight jeans.
The CCTV was run and the images were very good even though it was dark. The light capturing capability of the camera was excellent.
"There we are Constable. You can see this man very clearly and I'm sure you'll be able to get some pictures from this which can be enhanced by your ‘boffins’. I hope it helps. If you'd like to hang on a 'mo, I'll just make a CD copy for you. It won't take long."
Standing beside Jane while she pressed the buttons to make the copy, Tom thought, 'she could press my buttons any time'. He sneaked a look at her and she sensed this, turned and gave him a

lovely smile. Tom's stomach looped and his knees almost turned to jelly as his mind went into overdrive.
Desperately trying to keep his voice normal he said, "It will be a great help and thanks to you all for your help. I'm going back to get these pictures made up so we can get on his trail. I don't suppose anyone actually saw him other than the people I spoke to earlier who said they only saw him walking out of the boatyard."
I'm afraid not, but if we do hear of anything which we think may be of some use, we'll call you of course."
"Thanks again for you time and help."
"You're welcome, 'bye."
Tom very reluctantly walked back to his car for the drive back to HQ. His mind was not completely on the investigation in hand...

CHAPTER 38

Frank Jordan had been invited to come to the station for an 'interview'. He had arrived that morning and was immaculately dressed as Alice had previously remarked upon, although this time, he was casual but not the common-or-garden variety of casual. He wore white Chinos with a pale pink shirt, open at the neck and showing a rather heavy-looking, gaudy gold chain. Alex supposed that this was the real thing which meant it was probably very expensive. He also wore a pair of moccasin-type loafers without socks and just simply looked expensively casual and perfectly at ease. This in itself was quite 'unusual' as, as far as Jordan was aware, there was no reason for his being asked for an interview. His calmness was actually causing Alex to be very cautious.
Alex and Anna were both present for the interview and Alex was especially interested in her view of Mr Jordan.
"I am Detective Inspector Vail and this is Detective Sergeant Jenkins. We would like to ask you some questions regarding recent events occurring at or concerning the Marine Auctions at Tuckton. You are Mr Frank Jordan and you are the owner of this business. Is that correct?"
"That is correct. How can I help you people?
"Actually, it is not really you that we are interested in Mr Jordan," Alex said, "at the moment that is," he added. "It's your son Mark we need to talk to but we cannot seem to trace his address or where he might be living. Perhaps you can give us his address or contact number so that we can ask him in for an interview. We have a number of important questions to put to him."
"Do you know, I really have no idea where he lives these days? We are not close and he lives his own life. I don't interfere with his and he doesn't with mine."
Now that did not seem feasible to Anna, given that Mark travelled to Christchurch and the Auctions fairly frequently.
Alex continued – "We think he has a flat in Poole but his details don't match with various official documents. Surely you must know where your son lives?"
"I'm afraid I don't. As I have just said, we don't have much contact - we lead quite separate lives."
'He might say this', thought Alex, 'although there seems to be evidence that they have met recently as Mark is known to have gone to France on a boat from the Auctions. Surely he can't have used a boat without Frank's knowledge? Perhaps we should ask one of the staff there if Frank actually knew of Mark's 'borrowing' the boat which belonged to someone else and did he have permission'?
Alex was about to move on to the possibility of drugs being taken to France by Mark and also the very real likelihood of his involvement in art fraud. He stopped himself as he thought that perhaps he

should not tell Frank that they had these suspicions about Mark because that would alert him which might affect the investigation, so, he let that line of questioning lie for the moment.
"Mr Jordan, the body of a female was discovered in Christchurch Harbour on August 30th. We know that this body was placed there by two persons, unknown at the moment, who were in a boat which had been taken from your business at the Marine Auctions. Not only that but a second body was found on this boat which was purported to have been stolen from its mooring at the Auctions, although it's not clear when this theft was noticed. We understand that the moorings are not checked on a daily basis for various reasons; is that correct?"
"Do you know, I really couldn't tell you because I don't involve myself in that side of the business? I leave that to my staff. In fact, I didn't know about it myself until you just told me. The staff check things like that as I tend to keep to the sales and promotion side of the business. Perhaps they have been a little lax but you will have to ask them about this."
"We have already Mr Jordan. When you say the 'sales and promotion side of the business', can you explain this a little more fully?"
"Whilst we run a marine auction business, perhaps a larger part of our operation is to find buyers for the boats which we sell or are put up for auction. There is more profit in selling a boat for perhaps £25,000 with a good commission rate than selling many small items in an auction, which give little in return. Therefore, I do spend a good deal of my time in connecting buyers and sellers for the movement and sale of craft, sort of 'networking' if you like."
"This is understandable. However, we believe that you are also connected with the movement of art paintings within the UK and also abroad."
"I'm sorry I don't understand what you mean. I don't deal in art or 'art paintings'."
"Oh, I think you do," said Anna in a soft voice. "We understand that you are connected with Olivia Harrington-Thorpe, who was formerly known as Olive, and who was, incidentally, your wife until your divorce. We think you are connected in the sale of paintings and possibly, copies."
Frank was actually taken aback by this. He did not realise that these facts were known as he had tried to keep his connection with Olive, as she was, totally secret. There was a palpable silence, which both Anna and Alex allowed to fester.
Jordan's facial expression had changed from relaxed to 'concerned' and now appeared quite 'hard'. "You have obviously been digging deep into my personal history," he said, "and I have to say that I am extremely disappointed that my privacy has been compromised in this way."
"Unfortunately Mr Jordan, we are investigating a double murder which means that we have to investigate and uncover all the

relevant details which we think fit and applicable to the investigation of the case. If that reveals some facts which are less than either relevant or public but which you find possibly embarrassing, you may rest assured that we will divulge nothing to the press at this stage."
Jordan looked a little perturbed at this point.
'That's ruffled his feathers a little', thought Alex. 'Nice one Anna'.
"I know that Mrs Olivia Harrington-Thorpe is the owner of an art gallery but I know virtually nothing about the sale of paintings or as you say 'copies'."
"Oh again, we think you do Mr Jordan but if you don't, then your son Mark certainly does. Can you please tell us why Mark is actually the son of Olive Jordan, and you are his father and were married to Olive Jordan as she was, but our researches have shown that he does not appear to be connected to her in any way that is officially listed? It would appear that, in fact, he probably doesn't even know that she is his mother, either that or he is in complete denial."
Again, Frank was totally amazed by this. He became aggressive, almost surly. "How the hell have you found this information?"
"We are the police Mr Jordan and it is our business to uncover facts."
He was severely discomfited by this, what he considered to be, very private fact. Frank was looking very uncomfortable but then seemed to reach a decision. After a long pause, he said, "Very well. That is something which goes right back to when we were married, but I must insist that this information is not made known to Mark as it is intensely personal."
"Perhaps you could explain the situation as it is very unusual, to say the least." Anna was curious to know why a mother would have nothing to do with her son.
"If I must explain, then the short story is that Olive was, and still is, a very self-centred woman and that she really didn't want children. She rather preferred to have her time to herself. When Mark was born, she simply 'gave him over' to a nanny who did virtually everything for him while she pursued only the things which interested her. Don't forget, at the time Mark was born, an abortion was not quite so easy and she actually went through the pregnancy rather than have, what she thought, was the pain and discomfort of an abortion, however right or wrong she was. The result was that after Mark was born, he was virtually and to all intents and purposes, 'motherless'. This probably sounds very strange to you."
"It certainly does Mr Jordan. I'm certain that this would have had a very deep impression on a young child, not to have known his mother."
"Well yes, actually, as the years have gone on, we have moved in different directions, to the point where we now have completely separate lives."
'Or so he says', thought Alex.

"When he was around two years old, he was told that his mother was killed in a car crash and I, together with a nanny', looked after him most of the time with a little help from other people and we have been very close ever since."
"Until recently it seems; as you now say that you have completely separate lives. I do understand more now, and I have to say that it is a most unusual situation but one that you must have found quite hurtful at the time, so I'll leave that subject, for now. However, the fact remains that you now seem to have renewed your contact with Mrs Harrington-Thorpe, or should we call her 'Olive'?"
"No, please don't. That brings back some rather bad memories so I'd prefer it if you would only refer to her as 'Olivia'."
Alex decided to take a chance. "We think that you are in fact in contact with Olivia and probably meeting her."
"Well, since you have obviously been snooping on me, I cannot deny this."
Anna came in with, "We have not been snooping Mr Jordan, we have simply been trying to trace the movements of Olivia through CCTV records and we've found that she has made numerous trips from her house but returning very soon after, so we are sure that as these trips were not for a holiday or weekend break, there must be another reason. Our investigations have thrown up a number of possibilities and we are seeking your explanations regarding this particular matter."
Frank was thinking hard. 'How had they found out about these trips? He realised that the police knew about his meeting Olivia on several occasions and had possibly been tapping his phone. Was this legal? It didn't matter how they had obtained this information but all they knew was that he had made the calls, not what was said. There was no point in him denying that calls took place, and with the knowledge that they had, traced her visits to him in Poole. He said, "Since you obviously know about her gallery, I can tell you that we did meet to discuss possible buyers for paintings through connections that both she and I have. The possibility of a sale of a high-priced artwork is always worth consideration. And, by the way, if you have been tapping my phone, I think I will inform my lawyers and they can take the necessary action."
Alex realised that this was completely plausible and he thought not to pursue this line any further as Frank Jordan was a slippery customer as his past had already proven and he was bound to have 'answers' to questions that he didn't want to answer, especially ones that might incriminate him. Alex wasn't worried about the threat of a lawyer as they'd not tapped his phone, but used CCTV data from the many cameras along the route she regularly took and correlated the time and dates of the journeys, but didn't mention this to him. 'Let him sweat a little', thought Alex.
"Very well Mr Jordan. That will be all for now but we will probably ask you to attend an interview in future as we are sure to have some more questions for you. Would that be acceptable?"

"Of course, just let me know."
"Oh, we will Mr Jordan. We will."
Jordan went out and Alex said to Anna, "What did you think of that then?"
"I can see what Alice meant - not the sort you would place in a scrap yard. A bit too suave for me, too 'oily' and I don't mean the greasy oil, just slippery, if you get my drift."
"I was on the same line as you. I think he's as slippery as an eel; far too smooth to be caught out. It was only when we mentioned Mark and his mother not recognising him as her son or even accepting him in any way, was he taken off guard."
"But he damn soon got back on track didn't he?"
"Yes, and that’s the bit that worries me. I think he'll squirm out of tricky questions, so we'll have to make sure we have the correct answers before we ask the questions. That way, we can spot the flaws and mistakes; he's bound to make some, don't you think?"
"Let's hope so."

CHAPTER 39

Tom got back to the station with his CD and went straight to DI Vail. "Boss, we've got some great images of chummy who ran off the boat at Lymington and legged it out of the boatyard. Trouble is, nobody saw where he went after that."
"What time does the CCTV show?"
"10.22 guv."
"So we know that he left the boat haven at 10.22 p.m. At least we have some definite time-frame now. Can we get some blow-ups done so that we can do a house to house?"
"Already being done boss."
"Good. How about any CCTV from the private houses near the boatyard?"
"I didn't call at any private houses."
"Oh, for Christ's sake Tom, you're not thinking. Didn't it occur to you to take a look at some of the houses there? In that area there are some very expensive houses and some are sure to have some cameras on 24 hour watch. What sort of houses did you see there?"
"There were some big houses but I was in such a hurry to get back that I didn't think about them maybe having cameras."
"And yet you've just been looking at images taken by CCTV cameras at the boatyard and that was the only place you thought about? I gave you more credit than that Tom. Go back there now and look at all the houses which have cameras in the area where this guy would have gone looking for a way to get wherever he's gone."
"Yes boss," said a rather crestfallen Detective Constable. Tom had not been in CID for too long as he had joined the police force some six years before serving time as a normal Constable before applying to join the CID. He had become a Detective around 2 years previously and was considered something of a 'rookie' by other members of the team.
He was about to leave to return to Lymington, when Alex asked him, "Tom, how do you think he got to wherever he was going?"
"My guess is that he must have got a lift or perhaps a taxi. We have no idea of who he is or where he was headed, so we have to get some idea of where he might go after committing murder. If he got a taxi, which I find rather unlikely, we could trace him very quickly. I'll check on my way there to see if that's what he did, but if he did get a lift then perhaps one of the private CCTV cameras could verify that."
"Now you're thinking. Now get your arse into gear and find those private cameras. Don't give anything away about the body found on the boat. We must keep this under wraps as much as possible until we have more information. The press will find out soon enough and we'll have every hack in the area molesting us."

"You did tell the people at the boatyard not to divulge that a body was found, didn't you?"
"Yes boss, I think so."
"You think so!" Alex was really annoyed that this vital request had been overlooked. "Get back on to them immediately and make sure that they do NOT release this information to anyone until we give the 'all-clear', unless it is too late, which I hope to hell it's not!"
"Yes guv."
"Oh, and one other thing Tom, which we seem to have overlooked, is that this bloke may well be still armed. I'd like to think he dumped the gun into the water before he got away. Perhaps we should get the underwater bods to have a look."
"And do you think that would give us any help, boss?"
"It would prove that both people were probably killed by the same gun, although I think they can tell from the recovered bullets, but Forensics might come up with something that we wouldn't think of, they're pretty canny at finding links."
"Shall I get a call through to the Under Water Search Unit boss?"
"No, you get off and I'll do that. We know roughly where to start looking as the CCTV stuff will tell us which pontoon he came up on."
A rather chastened Tom went to his car for the trip back to Lymington, while Alex called the Underwater Search Team. Reaching their office, he spoke with their Team Leader.
"Hi Jim, I've got a little job for your guys if you can fit it in? We have a murder victim over at the Lymington Yacht Haven and we think that the murderer may have dumped the gun overboard. I know it's probably a long shot as he could have thrown it overboard almost anywhere between Poole and Lymington, but perhaps it's worth a try."
"Oh, shouldn't take us long then" said Jim with heavy irony,"to search about 30 kilometres of sea-bed? Perhaps he tied it on with a bit of string in case it sank.....?"
Alex and Jim knew each other and it was quite usual for them to mercilessly goad each other in a friendly way. Sarcasm was their normal repartee.
"No, you muppet, I should think he'd have kept it until he finished messing about with the boat, but who knows?"
"Okay Alex, we can take that. Where would the possible dump site be?"
"It'll be at the far end of the mooring pontoons possibly. I would think the water is fairly deep there but really I've no idea. I'll tell the Haven Master, a chap called Matthew Addison, to expect you, or perhaps it's better that I give you his number and you can arrange times with him and he'll tell you where the boat is."
"That's probably better and I can schedule our search, as if the gun is there, it's not going anywhere is it?" Another piece of their banter.
"Right." Alex gave Jim the necessary information and left him to get a search underway for a possible weapon.

Tom was on his way back to the yacht haven and feeling a little 'bruised' after the encounter with Alex. He was thinking rather guiltily, 'I should have thought of telling them not to let the information out'. The truth is that he was too enraptured by Jane to think ahead.
He put a call through to the local taxi service. He knew which ones would be likely for that area as not long ago he'd had put a similar request to various taxi services and thanks to that he had a good idea of the most probable ones. He didn't hold out much hope for this, and he thought to himself, 'I wonder how I would get away? At that time of night I'd probably thumb a lift as there would be quite a few people going home or even going to the local pubs'.
There was no luck with any of the taxi services which he tried. No-one had been called to the Lymington area in the time frame that Tom had given.
When he got back to the Yacht Haven he left the car and walked up to the main road where he thought that this man would have gone. Opposite the entrance to the Haven was a choice of two roads, Kings Saltern Road or Westfield Road.
Just as he was about to look along Kings Saltern Road, he had a thought. 'Oh SHIT!' I did forget to tell them not to mention this to anyone. He ran down to the office again and was about to ask for Jane but stopped himself. 'I'd better just tell Addison'. Asking at reception for Matthew Addison, he only had to wait a few moments before he appeared.
"Back so soon Detective?"
"Yes, I'm sorry, I should have asked you specifically not to mention the body found on the boat to anyone outside this office or at least anyone who knows about it. Just keep it very much to yourselves for the time being please."
"That goes without saying Constable. It will be kept very much 'under wraps', you can be sure of that."
"Thanks, I should have mentioned this before."
"No problem."
"Thanks again." He left to go back to the main road. He walked up Kings Saltern Road as there were big houses on one side and just scrubland and trees to the other with no buildings. He walked along until he found the first building with cameras at the front. His enquiries at this building, which was a commercial office complex, proved worthless as the cameras were only covering the parking and entrance areas.
He tried another couple of large houses, but again the cameras only showed the gardens and entrances to the houses.
This is a waste of time, thought Tom, so he went back to the Haven entrance and as he was going to try up Westfield Road when he saw a sign for the 'Bistro and Restaurant at the Haven'.
'Hmm, I wonder if this guy asked for a lift from a customer the other night', thought Tom. 'Worth a try', so he went in to the Bistro. He looked around at the very obviously 'themed' decor. 'Nautical, to

say the least', thought Tom. On the walls were numerous pictures of yachts under full sail and also many of what were obviously racing yachts, with large crews hanging over the deck as ballast. There were also many yachting 'artefacts' and memorabilia. There were only a few customers and he smelt the waft of cooking and was very tempted to get himself a snack but then realised that if he was late back he might get another bollocking from his boss, so he put the thought out of his head and tried to feel tempted by the food at the station canteen - without success. He walked over to the bar. "Good evening Sir," the barman said. "What can I get you?"
"Nothing thanks," said Tom. "Can I ask who was on duty the night of the 5th of September?"
"Let me think. That would have been either Janice or Peter, and me."
"Are either Janice or Peter here now?" asked Tom.
"Peter is."
"Can you call him over then please?"
"He's very busy Sir, I don't think he'll have time to talk to you. What is it you want anyway?"
"Sorry, I should have said. Taking out his warrant card and holding this up for the barman to see, he said, "I'm DC Peterson from Bournemouth Police" and we're making enquiries about a man who was seen either walking quickly or running from the Haven during the late evening of September 5th."
"I don't think we'd have seen anyone running as we rarely look out of the windows because we're too busy. Anyway, if you notice, our windows only face out onto the main road. He would have come up beside the restaurant and it's doubtful that we would have seen him anyway."
Realising that what the barman had pointed out was correct, he said, "No, I don't suppose you would have noticed him, but he perhaps he came in. We know that he did not have any transport and it's just possible that he got a lift."
By this time, Peter had joined them and heard the last part of the conversation.
He said, "It's funny you should say that because there was a chap who came in late on and asked me if I knew anyone who was going towards Bournemouth and might be able to give him a lift."
Tom brightened a little as this information could be what he was looking for. "Did he say much, this chap?"
"Not a lot but he did say that he was embarrassed to have to ask but he'd been out on the Solent with a friend and they'd had some engine trouble and had to come in to the Yacht Haven while he went back to Bournemouth. He had no money with him as they had been out on a 'fun' trip and left their money behind."
"What did this man look like, can you describe him?"
"As far as I remember, he was about 6 foot or a bit under, dark hair."
"What clothes was he wearing?

"Oh, casual, but thinking about it, although he'd said he had been out on the Solent on a 'fun trip', he didn't say what sort of craft they were in but he wasn't in 'sailing' clothes. It did occur to me that he was not exactly dressed like someone who would be out on the water in those sorts of clothes. I mean we get all types in here, but they're mainly boating people and one gets a sense of 'boating people' and this guy just didn't seem to fit somehow. I didn't give it much thought to be honest, but I did notice that he didn't have the right shoes for being on a boat."
"How do you mean, 'Not the right shoes'?"
"Well, you should have at least trainers or proper boating 'non-slip' shoes, but his were ordinary leather type, you know, 'city shoes'."
"I see." Tom felt he was on to something here, so he said, "And did this man get lucky for a lift then?"
"Well, actually, yes. There was one of our regular chaps who said he was going over to Ridge Wharf to see a mate and probably stay the night with him."
"And where's 'Ridge Wharf?'
"I would have thought that you would know that coming from Bournemouth. That's over towards Wareham. I suppose he would go through Bournemouth to get there. Anyway, they were at the bar and I was serving so I couldn't help but overhear."
"Do you know this regular customer's name?"
"Yes," said Peter. "His name is Bob Parsons and he has a boat here at the Haven."
Fantastic, thought Tom. "I know it's a long shot but I don't suppose you have a number for him by any chance."
"Don't be daft, we only serve food and drink here, we don't collect customer's details, but if you ask in the Marine Office at the Haven, I'm sure they'll be able to help."
"Thanks Peter, you've been a great help. I know the Marine Office and I've met the rather lovely Jane. Very fanciable."
"Oh, I don't think her partner Janice would be too pleased to hear that."
Tom's heart sank like a stone. "Don't tell me she plays for the other team."
"That's one way of putting it I suppose. Let's just say that she rows in the 'coxless fours'."
"Oops," said Tom."
"Don't worry, it's no secret."
"Right, well thanks again," and he went back to seek Jane at the Haven Office, now feeling very dejected at his chances of a date had sunk like a stone. 'My day's really turned to shit', he thought.

CHAPTER 40

Tom went, rather disconsolately, back to the office and found Jane again. This time without the distracting thoughts.
Jane was at the reception desk and she said, “Back yet again constable. This is getting to be a habit,” she said with another beguiling smile.
"Hello again Jane, I understand that you have a chap called Bob Parsons, who has a boat here. I wonder could you give me a contact number for him as we need to get in touch with him rather urgently.
"Yes, we know Bob. He’s a lovely man, always very helpful. I hope he's not in any sort of trouble."
"No, not at all, we just need him to confirm a few details, that's all.”
"Oh, that's good then. I'd hate to think there were any problems."
Jane said this with a lovely smile. Tom thought; 'what a waste.'
Armed with Bob Parsons' phone number, he called into Alex's office to update him on his find. He'd tried to phone the number he'd been given, but got no reply. He asked Alice to keep trying for him while he attended to other jobs he had ongoing.
"At last we seem to be getting somewhere Tom. Good. Keep trying to get onto this Bob Parsons. We've got to find out where this mysterious murderer went to ground."
"How did the pictures come out boss? You know the one's from the CCTV."
"Not bad actually. Just as the descriptions we had show us, although they're not in colour. Shame, but we can see that he is clean shaven, has short dark hair and he has a 'stocky' build, at least not fat but in good physical shape. Can't see much of an expression but he's obviously in a hurry, but then again, that's not surprising really, given what we suspect he's just done, so let's get this picture over to the local papers and have them put out a request to find this man as he is required to 'help the police with their enquiries'."
"But shouldn't we wait until we've spoken to this Bob Parsons who gave him a lift?"
"No, the sooner we find this man, the sooner we can get this case moved on. I'm pretty sure he's the same one who killed Yaren."
"I'll get onto this right now, both the Bournemouth Echo and Dorset Echo."
"Don't forget the smaller locals cover Wareham, Lyme Regis and so on Tom. Get the whole area covered. This man's a double murderer."
"Okay boss."
Alex called Alice into his office.
"Did you have any joy with Jordan and Son Alice?"
"Yes sir, quite a bit of information to be honest."
"Come on then sleuth, cough up."

"Right, firstly, they have both been bad boys in the past. Frank, the father was convicted of 'fencing' back in 1994 and served three years for his part in handling stolen metals. It seems that the actual thieves were cutting copper wiring from alongside railway tracks and this disrupted signalling and caused all sorts of mayhem at the time. There were other things taken as part of the crime but he seems to have had a clean sheet since then. Perhaps his time in prison did the right thing and he reformed."
"And how about the son Mark?" said Alex.
"Now then," said Alice, "Mark is a different case altogether. He was arrested and convicted for fraud back in 1995. Something to do with property fraud. Buying and selling in what is euphemistically called the SRB market."
"I've never heard of that," said Alex.
"Neither had I until I did some research," said Alice. "It's the 'Sale and Rent Back' market. This is where unscrupulous buyers look for people who are in financial trouble and offer to buy their property at a much-reduced price and then rent it back to them for an exorbitant fee. It is apparently quite legal but can cause untold financial difficulties. An added problem seems to be when the property is put on to the market again for a much higher price, after it's been 'valued' by a dodgy assessor who puts a high value on the property and then the fraudster gets someone to apply for a mortgage based on this valuation. The valuer must be in league with the seller. If the mortgage application is granted, this person gets the mortgage money, which is then shared out with the people who organised these deals, some given to the new mortgage holders who think they have made a handsome profit. Then the house is sold on again but without the mortgage debt being repaid."
"Sounds complicated," said Alex.
"It is, but as I understand it, the person who raised the mortgage is then saddled with a huge debt which they can't afford so the house has to be repossessed and then sold on and they can lose many thousands. This is very complex and I don't really think I understand it completely. I'm sure I've got some of this wrong but the outcome is that Mark was convicted of this fraud and he served his sentence of 5 years. It seems as though Mark had accomplices in all of this but there is no mention of them that I can dig out."
"You've done well Alice. It does sound as though our friend Mark is a bit of a dodgy character and I wonder if he has cleaned up his act as well as his dad appears to have done."
“Do you know, I had a word with a lawyer friend of mine and he said that 5 years seems to be a little lenient given the seriousness of the fraud, and he suggested that the courts take a very dim view of ‘wire fraud’ as they call it? He also said that there could be some ‘extenuating circumstances’, although he didn’t know what they might have been.”
“Hmm, very interesting that.”

"I understand that we think that Mark Jordan was living with Yaren in London. Do we know what his business was up there?"
"No, and that's what we have to find out as soon as we can because there is a link somewhere and with two people murdered, it is a matter of extreme urgency that we get some progress."
Alex went to see Anna who was doing something on her computer.
"We've got a good picture of the bloke from the boat in Lymington Anna. I've asked Tom to get it into all the papers in the area. We might get a sighting. But even better at the moment - Tom has found a customer at the Bistro in Lymington next to the yacht haven who has a boat there and who gave this man a lift on the night in question. We've not been able to contact him yet but we will soon and then we can find out where he went. It may just narrow our search down a little."
"Do you think he's from this area then guv?"
"Dunno, could be. Let's hope so. He has a boat at Lymington but that doesn't mean that he lives here. A lot of people have boats here and live miles away but come down now and then for some R and R. It would make things a little bit easier if he was local. I do have serious doubts about this Mark who seems to live a double life. I wonder if that really was his car we saw when we were at the flat."
"Bloody hell, sorry guv, I've just realised, I took a sneaky pic of the car as we were going away. I don't think you saw me take it as you were turning into the main road at the time. It's still on my phone and I've not given it a second thought until now, what with the pace of all that's going on."
"All right, so come on then 'Linda McCartney', let's see this photo and get a number for the Porsche, perhaps it may even show his face. That would be a bonus."
"Linda McCartney guv?"
"She was a well-known female photographer wasn't she?"
"So she was but I'm surprised you knew that."
"I'm not a complete plod Anna"
"The thought never entered my head ... sir - she added after a very brief pause."
"So you say." He'd not missed the riposte and he gave a little smile. "But never mind that, where's this bloody photograph?"
Anna found the photo on her iPhone and sure enough, the registration number was clear enough. "I'll get on to the DVLA right away and we'll find out if Mister Porsche driver is who we think he is."
Very quickly, the cars registration number was confirmed that the car was *not* registered to a Mr Mark Jordan of Poole.
"He lives in Poole doesn't he and we know he drives a silver Porsche, so perhaps we could go and see him? What do you think Anna?"
"Well, we think he lives in Poole, but we don't have an address. I suspect he has a place using a different name, so we are looking for

the proverbial 'needle'. Mind you, I suppose we could check on all the silver Porsches in this area and look for them and where they're registered; but supposing he uses another car, we'd be chasing our tails I reckon."
"Yep, too much of a long shot but perhaps we could get Tom or Alice onto that, it's a possibility."
"Okay, I'll get them tasked."
Alex then came back with, "I think we need some more information about Yaren and her link with Rebecca. You know, such as 'what was her working relationship like with this Olivia Harrington-Thorpe lady'? 'The one with the money'. I am always a little wary when it comes to art. Some of these paintings are so valuable and so small that there must always be a temptation along the line. They have to be easy to move and I keep having little thoughts about the connections between art, boats, channel, drugs, France, and I'm finding there are things that are linking together slowly."
Anna looked thoughtful, and then said, "I agree. I think that Yaren must have had other friends apart from miss, 'she was my best friend' Rebecca. Perhaps we should go back to the gallery and get her to open up more about her 'out of work' habits and likes."
"Excuse me for having such a suspicious mind," said Alex, "but there are so many unanswered questions that we have to look at all possibilities. Yaren was killed for a reason and this must have been a very good reason to someone and that usually means money, and lots of it, at stake."
Anna said, "I did wonder at the lack of a mention of Yarens' life outside of work. I mean, when you work with someone, you usually find out a little of what goes on outside of work, but in this case, she didn't offer anything, did she?"
"No," said Alex, "how do you feel about taking a trip back to Wimbledon on your own and seeing what one girl to another can uncover?"
"Okay, but it won't be quite the same as our trip before. It'll be a little lonely."
"In that case, how about we have a little private time tomorrow night? Do you like Thai food?"
"Yummy."
"How do you fancy dinner together at that Thai restaurant in St. Michaels Road in Bournemouth?"
"That sounds great to me."
"Okay, it's a deal."
Alex carried on with a very satisfied little smile on his face.

CHAPTER 41

Anna had made an appointment to see Rebecca once again, saying that just wanted to talk over her knowledge of Yaren a little more to get some background on what sort of person she was like.
When she arrived, Anna strolled past and had a better look at the building and the façade before walking back to the gallery.
The name 'Arcadian Gallery' was on the windows in gold lettering and the appearance of the gallery itself was of very high class. The simplicity was deceptive and showed extreme quality in the design understatement. The overall effect was superbly stylish and composed.
Anna approached the gallery and as she entered, she saw that Rebecca was once again immaculately dressed.
Her makeup was faultless and this actually made Anna feel a little under-dressed. But then, she thought to herself, I am in working clothes and Police Detectives don't go around looking quite so well-dressed, especially doing some of the things we have to do on a day-to-day basis.
Rebecca came over to her and said, "I am pleased to see you again. I was quite overcome when I learned of Yarens' death, as you may imagine. You were so pleasant to me."
Rebecca had much more composure today and it was easy to see why she would be in charge of such a gallery, when the sort of people she had to deal with would expect nothing less than the top class attention and poise.
She said, "Please call me 'Becca', that's what Yaren called me and we were very good friends."
"So were you good friends outside work as well?
Just then, there was a phone call and Becca said, "Do you mind awfully if I answer that. I really don't like to keep anyone waiting as It does give a rather negative impression of the gallery."
"Not at all, I quite understand," said Anna.
This gave her time to have a closer look around the gallery.
There were various schools of art from post-impressionist to abstract, realism to expressionist, represented on display. There were, of course, no prices on display but Anna could see that they were all of high value. She supposed that in such galleries, prices would not be on show, but to be 'negotiated' later. She also supposed that the old adage of 'if you have to ask the price, you probably can't afford it', was paramount here.
Becca came back from her call. "Please excuse the interruption. You were asking if we were friends outside work."
"Yes," said Anna," I was just wondering how you, as a person from your class would get on with someone who was not from a similar background."
"Well, as far as people from different worlds can be I suppose," said Becca "but we did spend some evenings together after work, until around eight or so I would think, then she had to get home. It

wasn't a close friendship but she was a very intelligent person and she did have a degree in Art History from Durham University. They don't grow on trees you know. We could discuss our shared interest away from the rather busy life in the gallery, despite what some people may think."
"Did her boyfriend Mark come to pick her up sometimes?"
"Yes, but only occasionally. He came in his pride and joy, the Porsche sports car. Yaren used to like driving around in it with the top down."
"So what was your impression of Mark?" Anna was thinking back to the slight 'hesitation' when Becca was answering questions about Mark previously.
"On the face of it, he was very charming and personable. He was good looking and had a great sense of humour. He came with Yaren once or twice and he was very good company. But having said that, there was something about him that I couldn't quite place. Call it feminine intuition but there seemed to be an undertone. Nothing one could put a name to but there was just a 'frisson' of something much deeper in him. I'm sure that Yaren was unaware of this, but then she was close to him and I was not. She did say once that he had quite a temper on him and on one occasion when she'd asked him about his work, he was very aggressive and told her not to ask questions."
"Does that sound out of character?"
"I really cannot comment as I don't know him but I do know that Yaren was not happy about his attitude. I suppose some would call him quite 'dishy' but in fact, he is not really my type of man."
"And what is your type of man, Becca?" Anna said, with no hint of intrusion.
"Perhaps a little more intellectual and less showy, someone with a little more polish and less brashness."
"And do you know where they went when they were out together?"
"All I know is that they went up to some part of London occasionally, but Mark seemed to go there much more, on his own. Yaren said he would be away for two or three days at a time. I had no idea where he went and I don't think Yaren knew much either."
"Did Yaren have any other friends that you know of?"
Becca had a thoughtful pause and said, "Apart from Mark, I think she only had one other particular friend that I know of and that is...."Becca paused and swallowed hard, "was Katya. I know she saw a lot of Katya, but I don't know where she lives. I suppose she would have lived near Yaren as she came from the same part of Turkey.
"Did you meet Katya?"
"No, I never met her and I only know of her as Katya, not her full name."
"Is Katya an artist?"
"Yes, she is very accomplished; she sometimes undertakes restoration work for the gallery."

Anna was looking at Rebeccas' eyes and she detected a subtle change in her gaze. 'There's something she's not telling me', thought Anna. 'Did she know Katya a little more'? What about 'restoration' and how did they come into the equation. I need to know more'.
"You say you never met her and yet she carries out restoration work for the gallery?"
"Yes, she does work for the gallery, but any pieces for her to restore are taken to her studio, so we do not see her."
"I see," said Anna, although this did seem a little 'odd', but she let ride for now.
"So what did you and Yaren talk about when you were together in the evenings?"
"Art, as that was her passion, painting styles and the inspirations for various pieces, in fact mostly centred on art subjects. She was as I've said, very knowledgeable and interesting. This gave her the ability to talk to clients and discuss values."
That gave Anna a little pause. 'The value of paintings' - There was some talk back at the office regarding the value of paintings and the possibility of shipment of these to France via the boats at the disposal of Mark, but nothing had 'gelled' so far. Anyway, thought Anna, this does give some credence to the theory and it gave her a line of enquiry to be followed up. Perhaps Yarens' diary or address book would give them a clue.
Anna made a note to check if any diary or notebook was found in her flat. She seemed to remember that Alex had found some other things during their search which had been curtailed due to the possibility that boyfriend Mark could turn up at any time.
"You say that Yaren's knowledge of art was very good?" said Anna.
"Actually, she had a very good in-depth knowledge, especially of art history. I suppose this comes from her time at Durham University where she got her degree."
"And this knowledge would be useful within the gallery?"
"Most certainly," said Becca, "she was able to talk to the potential buyers with authority and she was able to assess potential value based on that history and her knowledge of the artist. This was most useful as the buyers were often impressed by her comments and her information. The truth is that most people had no idea of the artist or their worth, in fact, they knew almost nothing, but liked to think that we thought they knew, if that makes sense."
"Yes, that does make sense. I would imagine that the buyer could then pass on this information to impress their friends as though they were knowledgeable when in fact most of them don't have a clue."
"I could not possibly comment," said Becca, with the merest hint of a smile.
"By the way," said Anna, "can you tell me a little more about Olivia Harrington-Thorpe, the owner of this gallery?"

"Only that she lives in Shirley Hills, on Bishops Walk. A very beautiful house. Big, with an immaculate garden. I would imagine she has a gardener and other servants; if one is allowed to call them 'servants' these days, but I'm sure she will have some help to keep the house and garden in that sort of state."
"Why do you say that Becca, does she not do some gardening or housework herself?"
"I don't think she would lower herself to get her hands dirty and anyway I don't think she'd have the time. She always seems to be either attending a soirée or an event somewhere or holding dinner parties for her 'important' friends."
"And what sort of friends are these, do you know?"
"I don't know exactly as I don't move in those circles, but one picks up little hints and snippets during our conversations about the gallery when she deigns to come in, which is not very often - usually to ask how much money the gallery is making."
"So what sort of friends do you think they might be?"
"Oh well, they are obviously very well off and I do know that she says she has many 'influential' contacts and this must be the case, as we have made sales to various celebrities and politicians and some overseas clients in France and Italy. Who knows who these people are, except that they must have plenty of money to pay some of the prices which we ask? - and one thing I do know is that Olivia does like money."
Once again, little bells began to ring in Anna's head; someone who likes money usually likes more money, she thought. Another person to take a closer look at, perhaps.
"Well, thanks Becca, you have been most helpful and I am very sorry that you have lost a friend. I hope that you can move on from this and remember her for the good times."
"Thank you, it will be hard but as you say, I will have to move on but she will be very hard to replace."
"If you should think of anything else that comes to mind that might help us to find her killer, please just give me a call on this number," handing her a contact card.
Becca shuddered as Anna said the word 'killer'.
She replied with a very sad expression, "Of course."
"Oh, just one other thing; do you know Frank Jordan, Marks father?"
"I don't 'know' him, but I have met him once or twice when he has been here. He is a very stylish man, quite handsome for someone his age."
"And do you know why he came here?"
"Only that he had introduced a couple of his friends or acquaintances."
"And did these friends subsequently buy paintings?"
"I think so, yes, although I don't know offhand which ones, but I could find out."

"That won't be necessary at this time, but thank you for the information. Did he meet Olivia Harrington-Thorpe here?"
"Not to my knowledge, no."
"Right, thank you Becca. Again, you've been most helpful."
Anna left the gallery and on the way back to Bournemouth, the thought occurred to her that although Rebecca had said that' Yaren had a friend called Katya who came from the same part of Turkey as her', she said nothing more about her and said that she 'knew of her, but not met her'. But didn't Katya actually restore paintings for the gallery? If that were the case, then Rebecca would most probably know her quite well, if only from a professional standpoint; 'something is not quite adding up here. If she were good enough to restore, then maybe she is good enough to copy'?

CHAPTER 42

Finally, a phone call to Bob Parsons was answered. He was questioned by Tom about the lift he gave to the 'mystery man' from the Lymington Boat Haven on August 15th.
"Is that Mr Parsons?"
"Yes. Who wants to know?"
"This is DC Tom Peterson from Bournemouth Police, sir. I understand that you gave a lift to a man last Friday from the boatyard at Lymington."
"Would that be the early days of September?"
"Yes sir. I believe you offered him a lift from the Bistro at the Haven."
"That's right. I remember him. He was standing at the bar and I think he'd just asked the barman if anyone was going towards Bournemouth. I overheard the conversation and I said that I was going to Ridge Wharf in Wareham to see a friend and that he was welcome to come."
"Can you describe this man for me?"
"What is your interest in this man?"
"All I can say is that we know that he came into the Haven quite late at night. We found a body on the boat he left on the far pontoon that evening, and we think he is responsible. We need to know who he is and where he has gone."
"A body? You mean a dead body?"
"When we say 'body' we usually mean a dead body, sir."
"And you think he is responsible for killing somebody?"
"This body, yes sir."
"Oh Jesus, do you mean I gave a lift to a murderer?"
"That is very likely sir. Perhaps you can describe him for me and tell me where you took him?"
"If he'd killed someone, and I've got him in my car, did he shoot someone?"
"I have to say 'yes' to that"
"Bloody Hell, you mean that he could still have had a gun on him?"
"That is a distinct possibility sir."
"Good God. I suppose I should count myself lucky in that case."
"Quite honestly, I think he was more concerned with getting to wherever he wanted to go than to get into more bother by killing you. To have done that would mean that he no longer had a 'lift'.
"Yes, but he could have killed me and taken my car, couldn't he?"
This guy was writing a mental script for a film, thought Tom.
"Let's just say that you were lucky sir, that it was only a lift and it was be much easier to just keep quiet and tell you nothing. Perhaps we could concentrate on his description please."
"Of course; he was, I would guess, about 45 to 50 years old and had dark brown hair."
"And how tall would you say he was?"

"At a rough guess, because I didn't see him standing up very much, I'd say around six foot but we got into my car pretty smartly as I was late anyway and he did seem to be in a hurry."
"And where did you drop him off?"
"He asked me where I was going and I said to Ridge Wharf but he didn't know where that was and he asked if I was going anywhere near Bournemouth or Poole. I told him I would pass both and where did he want dropping off."
'This is like pulling teeth', thought Tom.....
"And he said?"
"He said anywhere near Poole would be good. I asked him why he didn't have transport of his own and he gave me a bit of a hard look which I did find a bit aggressive at the time. He said that he'd been out on the Solent and had engine trouble and had to get back to arrange repairs. I guessed he meant to get back to Poole."
"Was there anything about him which you found a little strange?"
Parsons thought about this for a moment. "Now you mention it, yes. I did think that he was dressed in the wrong sort of gear for messing about in the Solent. That is not the sort of place you want to be at night unless you are pretty clued up on navigation and are fairly competent. I didn't think he looked as though he had a Yacht-Master Certificate or even a Day Skipper qualification as he was just dressed in casual clothes, not even any waterproof or windproof jacket. He did'nt even have the right sort of shoes on."
"And what sort of shoes would they be?"
"Well, if you are on a boat you should at least have good trainers or better still, non-slip boating shoes because to slip when you hit a wave and you are either steering or even moving about on a boat in a swell, could easily have you overboard or injured. He only had ordinary leather shoes on. I did notice that but didn't say anything as it was none of my business and after the look he'd just given me, I kept things to myself."
"So where did you eventually drop him?"
"Well, I went via the A338 and into Bournemouth and I said to him that I could drop into Poole and then pick up the A350 and go on via Lytchett Minster and Holton Heath to Wareham that way without it being too much out of my way."
'I will get the answer if I have to drag it out of him by his tonsils', thought Tom.
"And whereabouts in Poole did you actually drop him?"
"I dropped him at Poole Station."
"And what time was this, do you know?"
"Not really, but it must have been well after ten."
"Did he say anything about where he was actually going, catching a train perhaps?"
"No, but my guess is that if he was going to get repairs to the boat organised, he would go into Poole where there were facilities."
Tom thought, if I'd just killed someone, I would get away as far and as fast as possible.

"Okay, thanks Mr Parsons. You say there was not much conversation. Did he have an accent perhaps or something which stood out?"
"He spoke good English but I don't think he was. Maybe somewhere in Europe, but I don't know where. But then it could have been an English accent from up country somewhere, I've only ever lived here so I wouldn't be able to accurately place a different accent."
"Fine, I understand. You've been most helpful and thank you for your time. If you do think of anything else which you think might be helpful, please give us a ring. Here's my card."
"Of course."
"Oh, and one other thing. I would really like you to keep this information we've been discussing, to yourself for the time being. I would have not mentioned that he had killed someone, but I'm sure that this would be well-known at the Yacht Haven by now. You will understand that we would really like to find this man but we don't want to scare him off with newspaper speculation just now."
"I understand. I'll keep it to myself, although I have to say it'll be hard. You don't get something like this happening to you every day, do you?"
"Thankfully, no sir. Thanks again."
Tom made his way back to the station at Bournemouth with some good news for his boss, which made him feel a little better.

CHAPTER 43

Back in the office, Alex has been checking through the notebooks that he and Anna found in Yarens' flat. He had found an address for 'Katya' and a phone number.
I wonder if she knows about Yaren yet, thought Alex but then, how would she know?
Alex called over to Alice. "Alice, can you get some information for me on Olivia Harrington-Thorpe. She lives in Bishops Walk on Shirley Hills in Surrey. I need all the guff you can get on her and her way of life. She has a lot of money and so far we have no mention of a husband. Just find out all you can about her lifestyle. We know she likes money and does a lot of entertaining and lots of being entertained apparently. I need to know what makes her 'tick'. She seems to move in quite high places with lots of interesting contacts."
"Okay boss," said Alice," I'll see what I can get."
Anna had returned from her meeting with Rebecca Connors, the curator of the gallery.
"Hi Anna, how did you get on? What do you think, is she 'on the level'?"
"I think she is boss, although I'm not 100%. She does seem to be very competent and although she has a plummy accent, I don't think she is quite as high-classed as she seems to be at first. But then, that's not a bad thing I suppose, being in the sort of business she's in and the sort of people she meets and does business with. You wouldn't want some sort of 'gorblimey' type in that sort of business, however much that person might know. Stuck-up people who are the top, or at least think they are, need a special sort of person to deal with them I think."
"You don't like snobs then, I take it?"
"Nope."
"Anything else that's of use to us?"
"Only that Olivia whatsit-whatsit has a lot of contacts. Some politicians and a few so-called 'celebrities', so I suppose that might link to people who would buy art pieces and maybe they wouldn't know an original if they had one. Unless they had an 'Authentication Certificate', of course," she added.
"Now there's a point," said Alex. That may be another link. Let's hypothesise for a moment and say that chummy bought a painting and he was convinced that it was genuine, but in fact it was a fake, wouldn't he have it authenticated? I don't know much about art, but I do know that this would be a 'given' for anything which has a big value."
"But why would he think it was a fake?"
"Perhaps someone who knew a lot about these things spotted something and it aroused suspicions? Wouldn't they say something to the owner and then he or she would have it checked out more thoroughly?"

"Sure, that could well be something, but it could take a while before a person who knew that much came along. It could be ages before a fake was spotted. And they have a certificate, so maybe they're not in a hurry but just wait until 'someone comes along'."
"But I don't think the people who authenticate this level of art would risk their reputation by giving false documents. But what I'm getting at," said Alex, "is that perhaps somewhere along the line, a painting is switched, you know, a real one for a forgery, together with an authentication document, which would be kosher, then the buyer wouldn't be aware of the fake and they would carry on, blissfully unaware."
"When 'this person' came along and spotted something, that would make the buyer pretty pissed off, that's for sure, but it would be very difficult to pull off surely?"
"It would, but let's try to figure out how it could be done. There's always a way when big money is around, so let's pursue this direction for a while and see what comes up Anna. There might be a connection somewhere. We don't know about this 'Katya' for one, which reminds me, I must give her a call, and at the moment we know virtually nothing about this Olivia 'whatshername'. I do know that people who have money don't like to let it go and like to make as much more as they can."
"While we're on the subject of fraud," said Anna, "how about Mark Jordan? He's served time for fraud hasn't he?"
"That's true but I believe this was for some mortgage and rental fraud. I don't understand quite how it worked, but he did get a 5 stretch for it."
"Fraud is fraud, however you describe it. Its deception and I don't see that art fraud is much different. Maybe a little more difficult to achieve, but I would think it leaves less of a 'paper trail' than loads of bank details, mortgage lending and other financial papers."
"I see where you're coming from," said Alex "and I think there could be some mileage in this direction. I know that Rebecca said that she thought Mark was a little 'deep' and there was something "she couldn't quite place."
"Do you think this might be jumping the gun a little? What I mean is that if Becca is in some way involved in this, she could alert someone. I know there is no mention of this at the moment but there are so many things that we still don't know and we're just flying kites at the moment, aren't we? I mean, Becca said that she didn't know Katya, but Katya restores and maybe copies paintings for the gallery. I can't believe that she doesn't know Katya when she carries out work for the gallery, unless it is Olivia who organises this, although that seems highly unlikely.
"Again, you might be right Anna. Yes, let's keep things close to our chests for now."
As soon as he'd said this, his thoughts turned to 'keeping things close to chests'. He was thinking about their dinner date........'The others mustn't get to know of this'.

"HMM, I think I'll have to phone this 'Katya' person," he said again, "and see what she can tell us about Yaren."
"Would you rather I did this?" said Anna, "maybe it will be better coming from a woman and I can use Becca as a link to share the bad news perhaps."
"Not a bad idea. Okay and meanwhile, I'll get on to trying to find our killer who was dropped off at Poole station. Heaven knows where he went, although I do have a sneaking suspicion that he went back to the boat auctions. There seems to be links that all point to that place. I have strong feelings that there are connections and I think they may lead to much more than we know at the moment. If this bloke had taken a train, probably to London, we may never know who he is. If he used cash to buy a ticket there will be no way of tracing him."
"Ah, but we do have CCTV at stations don't we? We have a description and the picture quality is much better than they used to be, so maybe we can get a lucky break. Also, did we ever find out if the boat auctions had CCTV? I would have thought that they would, with expensive boats all over the place."
"Shit" exclaimed Alex, smacking his head, "I should've thought of that. I'll get Tom to check it out and see what they have from the date all this started."
"Tom!" Alex yelled.
Startled by the loud voice, Tom almost ran into Alex's room. "Tom, did you ask the boat auction place if they had CCTV when you were there?"
"No boss," said Tom."
"Tom, I should probably have asked you to check that out, but surely you could have thought about that yourself? You are supposed to be a detective for pity's sake"
For all of Tom's 38 years, he flushed slightly at being given another bollocking. But, he thought, 'you're the boss, why didn't you think of it'?
Anna did think that perhaps Alex shouldn't have told Tom quite like that, and he was being unfair, but then again he was right; Tom should have thought of it for himself whilst he was there.
"Right you are boss. Is this to try to locate this mystery bloke?"
"Yes, and anything else that might show up, like who stole the boat that night. When you get any footage, go through it with a fine tooth comb and get detecting, Okay? And while you're at it, get the CCTV from Poole Station for Friday evening from around 7pm to midnight. We are looking for a man around five eleven to six foot or so, with dark brown hair and wearing casual clothes. And leather shoes, not trainers."
"Leather shoes, boss? That's a bit strange, why leather shoes in particular?"
"Because the chap who gave him a lift noticed this as not being the sort of shoes someone who had been out on a boat should have been wearing."

"Got it," said Tom. "Let's hope that their CCTV is in colour."
"Indeed; now hop it; I've got to get some gen on this 'Katya' friend of Yarens'.
"Anna, can you give this Katya a call and break the news? As soon as it seems to be the right time, maybe you can pass her on to me and I can get a bit 'heavy' with her but only if you think it necessary. She must know more about Yarens' movements than we know at the moment. I need to know who she is and what she does and where she goes and where they both went when they were together."
"Right'o guv, I'll get on to 'Becca' and get her number."
"It's okay Anna; I got her number from one of the books I found at her flat." He gave her Katya's number and Anna went to her desk.

CHAPTER 44

Alex had wanted to make sure that his first date with Anna would be something special. He had considered going to a small bistro type place but maybe that would come later, as this night would be a tad expensive, but he thought making a good start was a good move.
Alex called for Anna at her flat in Boscombe. When she opened the door, he was bowled over.
She wore a long skirt which was a dark purple with a very subtle design in black with some crimson detail. Her top was a simple black camisole in a silky material, and a soft neck wrap with a smoky pattern in a gentle ochre colour. Everything accentuated her slim figure and the overall effect was to make Alex simply stare at her.
"Will I do?" she said.
"All I can say is, Wow! You look stunning Anna."
"Thank you," she said with a very warm smile.
I've made a reservation for two for 7.30, if that's Okay with you."
"That was a good idea Alex; I would prefer just the two of us..." She said deadpan. "I didn't really want a party."
Alex thought her sense of humour would take some working out...
"You know what I mean; I hope you don't mind that I chose a place without asking you. I don't even know what sort of food you like."
"I thought you said we would go to that Thai restaurant in St. Michaels' Road."
"Oh, I know but I thought about it and I wanted something a little different. Do you mind?"
"Of course not and as long as it's food, tasty and well cooked, I'm sure it will be fine, don't worry. Anyway, where is this place?"
"It's over in Canford Cliffs. I hope you like it Anna."
"Hey Alex, that's a bit posh isn't it?"
"I think you're worth it. I've been looking forward to this for quite some time; I'll have you know madam."
"So have I," said Anna, I'm really looking forward to spending some private time away from the office although I do have to say that I really like working with you. We seem to be getting somewhere don't we?"
He supposed that she meant with the case.
"I think things are coming together a little now. There are links that seem to be closing together but we have a long way to go to getting a result."
"I meant you and me but yes, I think we are although I hope we can keep away from work for a little while."
"You're right, so we'll leave things back at the office for tonight." He was inwardly pleased at her thinking that he'd referred to their private time.
They kept up a thread of small talk on the way to the restaurant and when they pulled into the forecourt, Anna looked at the restaurant

and the buildings. Looking at him she said, "Wow, Alex, this is going to cost an arm and a leg. Are you sure?"
"To hell with the cost Anna, that is not the important thing. What is important is that you have a good night and we can get to know each other a little more."
"Right you are Sir," said Anna with a wry smile.
"Enough of that young lady."
"Oo-er, 'young lady' is it - can I have that in writing?"
"Come on, let's get in and stop this nonsense...."
Entering the foyer, they were greeted by a very smartly dressed young woman who was extremely courteous and spoke with a quite 'cultured' accent. She quietly enquired if there was a booking and Alex said that he had booked for two in the name of Vail. Alex also discreetly asked if they could have a table in a 'quiet corner' if that were possible.
"Of course Sir, if you'd like to follow me."
She led the way to a suitably private table for two overlooking the garden of the building.
"This is really nice Alex. What a lovely place."
He was thinking that he really appreciated Anna's slightly 'wacky' sense of humour. He remembered his previous girlfriend who was so tragically killed in the accident, was quite 'subdued' in the humour department and he really did like a light-hearted approach when appropriate.
Anna thought the restaurant was really superb and the décor was sharp and modern. The night was pleasantly warm and it was really quite romantic to sit in the open conservatory style dining area surrounded by trees and shrubs. The lighting was subdued and quite romantic.
"What would you like to drink?"
I'd love a Gin and Tonic please, but please ask them to let me pour the tonic as they sometimes drown the Gin."
"Of course. You must be a 'connossor' then?"
"But ‘corse - must have me Gin dearie."
"I think I'll stick with a beer for now."
"How boring."
"Maybe the hard stuff will come later."
"Oo-er! That’s enough of that now."
"Oops, sorry. Didn't mean nuffink by it Miss."
That little exchange made them both laugh which really made them relax a little, as they were both on 'tenterhooks' given that it was their first date.
A waitress appeared, equally smartly dressed, giving them a menu each. She asked, "Would you like an aperitif?"
"Yes, please. A Gin and Tonic for my partner here and I'll have a beer, oh, and please can you just bring the tonic separately?"
"But of course sir."
"Do you know Alex, isn't it nice to have courtesy and decent manners like this, when you go to a restaurant? I mean when you

compare this degree of service and the surroundings, don't you wonder why some places have such unpleasant service and the surroundings so depressing. I know that all this costs money, but surely courtesy and care over the way you run a restaurant or business, can't cost much?"
Alex was beginning to realise that Anna had some high standards over a number of things and was very critical of certain types of people or activities.
"I have to agree with you about courtesy Anna, although with some of the low-life we have to deal with from time to time, I do really appreciate what you are saying."
The waitress came back and stood just a little way from the table, obviously waiting for their order. Alex looked at her and without having to say anything, she said, "I'll just give you a little longer to choose from our quite extensive menu," and walked away after given them both a smile.
"Do you see what I mean," said Anna.
"I do."
After looking over the menu, Anna chose the English charcuterie board with pickled onions, chutney & crackers as a starter. She said, "I hope you don't mind the pickled onions, but I love them."
"If I get close enough, I'll let you know," said Alex, with a meaningful glance.
"Hmm," said Anna.
Alex chose his starter. 'Soup of the day and crusty bread'. "That'll do me, bread and soup, just about what we men are worth, isn't that what you women think?"
"That's about right. Know your place you men. Let us women get on with the important things in life, like cooking, looking after the house, doing the washing, shopping, having kids, cleaning up after the men, while you do all the other stuff like watching football or playing squash or tennis or cricket or golf and other important 'men stuff'."
"I think you've been indoctrinated," said Alex, "you sound embittered."
"Not really, but it seems to be the way that we are all portrayed these days."
"What have you chosen for your main course then, embittered lady?"
"If it's okay, I'd like," and she quoted from the menu, 'The Rabbit leg stuffed with black pudding and pear, mash, choucroute, carrot & cider cream', it sounds scrummy."
"Absolutely, that sounds pretty good. I was going to go for the glazed ox cheek with smoked mashed potato, star anise and black pudding crumble, but it does sound a bit heavy so I'll go for the pork loin, honey belly, apple, smoked elderflower dressing & lard cooked potatoes. I don't quite know what 'honey belly' is, but I'm sure the chef knows his job. I just hope the potatoes are roasted with crispy edges."

Anna had a surreptitious thought...'Honey Belly', how's that for a nickname....but perhaps not....
"Not that you're picky then?" She said.
"Not really, I'm pretty plain when it comes to food. I just have certain preferences, that's all. Mind you, I would like to know what 'choucroute' is."
"As far as I know it's a kind of Sauerkraut. I don't know if this is a spelling mistake as it is spelled 'chouroute' on the menu but as it is French it's usually spelt 'choucroute' but I believe it's really tasty."
"Well, there you go, miss clever clogs, so what's 'honey belly' then?"
"I think it's just the cut of Pork, but cooked with honey. Quite why they should have pork loin and pork belly together beats me, but I'm sure it will be really fine. Mind, you I didn't know you could smoke elderflowers. I do know that they're not on the 'class' drugs list."
"Now you're taking the 'you know what' Anna."
"Yes," she said with a chuckle.
The waitress was a little way from the table and she had seen that Alex had closed the menu and she had correctly taken this as a sign that he was ready to order.
She approached the table and said, "And what would you like to order sir?"
He gave the order for them and then asked for the wine list which she was holding. He cast his eye down the list and recognised some really classic wines, from Bordeaux to Pouilly Fumé, from Alsace wine to those from the very dark wines from South-West France. The wine was ordered and they were both in a relaxed mood with Anna having chosen a mildly sweet white Gewurztraminer and Alex with a full-bodied Cabernet Sauvignon, the talk flowed as smoothly when the wine arrived fairly quickly. They talked about their childhoods, their past work life, their respective likes and dislikes until their orders arrived and the conversation was interspersed by taste.
"How is your starter Anna?"
"Really nice, the meats are good and the bread nice and fresh." She was surrounded by cracker crumbs. "Oop's, sorry about this," she said.
"I don't think the staff will find it too difficult to cope with a few crumbs... My soup was really tasty. I'm looking forward to my 'honey belly'. This caused Anna to have a smile at that name again.
“And what are you smiling at, may I ask?”
“Oh, nothing really, I’m just happy to be here wlth you.”
‘Another ‘brownie point’, thought Alex.
They finished their starters and after only a couple of minutes, the waitress 'appeared' and quietly removed their plates.
'You don't find this sort of attention to detail usually, do you?" said Anna. "Normally, the plates are left for ages or until your main course arrives, but you see here, the staff are probably trained to keep looking for finished plates and watch what the diners are

doing. It's the attention to detail which gives a restaurant the ambience and quality which enhances the dining experience."
"I quite agree with you Anna. I can easily see why you are so good at your job. You look at the situation and consider not just the immediate things, but the peripheral things which can have an effect which may not be obvious immediately."
Anna was pleased by his compliments and she felt it was really nice to be appreciated. Not only appreciated but to be told so as well.
A few minutes later, their main courses arrived and they were enjoying every mouthful when Anna said, "This is a really nice place. Have you been here before?"
"No, but I've heard about it a few times and I thought that anywhere in this area is going to be a bit above the usual eating places. There are so many to choose from, but I thought I could impress you."
"You certainly have and I do appreciate it, really, but it's not necessary to spend all this much to impress me. It is the company which impresses me."
"Thanks Anna, I'll take that as a compliment and can I say now that you are so nice to be with, you have a great sense of humour and you look stunning tonight. Out of working clothes, you are so different." He realised that he was digging a hole for himself. "I mean, not that you are not good looking in working clothes, but now you look drop dead gorgeous." He hoped that maybe he had stopped digging the hole.
"If I didn't know you better, I'd think that you are harbouring improper thoughts Alex."
"And if I were?"
"I don't know about that, perhaps we'd better take things 'as they come' shall we?"
He detected what he thought was a very slight frisson of something 'not quite right' at that moment.
His hopes took a little dive at that, but he said, "Of course, I'm sorry. I just meant that you do look so good that I'd be a complete idiot not to tell you how I felt. I'm not going to spoil things by rushing into anything or pushing you. Please don't think that. I really like you a lot and I think we have a lot going for us as we get along so well. Don't you think so?"
"Let's just see what happens naturally."
Her expression changed slightly and she looked at him a little 'sideways' and said, "I suppose you didn't notice that this place had 'rooms'. I saw that on the menu. Did you have an ulterior motive when you booked here?"
He was taken aback at this. "Absolutely not Anna. I promise you I had no idea that they had any rooms. I was just told that this place was a restaurant. I believe it used to be called 'The Beehive' some years ago and I heard that it had been refurbished recently and thought, well it's a nice area, so let's give it a try. I do hope you believe me Anna."

"I'll have to give you a proper interrogation on this one to make sure you're not lying to me," she said with a twinkle in her eye and a smile on her lips.
"I'll come quietly officer," said Alex.
"So you say, but how do I know?" she said, with another very cheeky smile to accompany the innuendo...
These comments were having a definite effect on Alex.
Finishing their meals with Clementine custard tart, burnt limes, passion fruit and coconut sorbet, they ordered coffee.
They both felt very relaxed and had thoroughly enjoyed the meal. They had coffee to finish off the evening. Maybe this was the beginning of a relationship that could go far, thought Alex. Similar thoughts were going through Anna's head too.
"If you're ready, perhaps we should go, as we both have to be in work early tomorrow and I don't want to keep you up."
"I suppose you're right Alex, although it does seem a shame to end the evening too early, but yes, we do have an early start and I need my sleep or I'll get a rocket from the boss for being slow."
"Okay then spoilsport. I'll take you back so you don't get into any sort of trouble tonight. I'll be your boss is a grouchy old bugger."
"It's been said but I don't think so. It's a shame we have to go but perhaps it's for the best."
Alex drove them back to Anna's flat and as the car drew up, there was a little hesitation between them; not quite knowing what came next. They looked at each other for a few moments without saying anything. The looks said everything, and nothing. Then they both broke out laughing.
"I suppose this is where I ask you if you'd like to come in for a coffee Alex, but we've had some and I think it may be too soon to take things further right now, but thank you so much for such a lovely evening and I hope we can see each other, outside work, a lot more."
"I'd like that very much Anna, and I understand completely, I don't want to do anything to spoil what I think could become very special, so I'll say goodnight and, 'see you in the morning'."
With that, Anna leaned her head towards him and paused until Alex turned to her. They kissed, and it was not just a 'goodnight' kiss. It was a tender and meaningful expression of what was to be both their feelings.
"M'mm, nice," said Anna, "thank you again and, goodnight."
"Goodnight Anna. I'll be thinking of you all night."
"You'd better get some sleep or you'll be dropping off at your desk and we have a lot to do."
"Party pooper, but you're right, as always Anna. Sleep well."
"You too Alex. G'night".
Somewhat reluctantly, Alex drove off. As he looked back in his mirror, he was very pleased to see that she was standing at her door and looking back at his car as it turned the corner.

CHAPTER 45

Back in the office the next morning, Alex asked to see Alice.
"Mornin' Alice," said Alex in a cheery voice. Alice picked up on the bright tone. 'I think he had a good night with someone. I wonder who that might be. Could be someone we know but I've absolutely no idea. I shall have to keep an eye open for some clues. After all, I am a detective', she thought.
"Alice, have you had any joy with this Olivia something hyphen something?"
"As it happens, yes, and I think this will get your hairs standing up."
"Go on then, don't keep me in suspense."
"Well, for a start I looked at her details in the electoral register and other places where all the private details are stored, and found out that she was married to a merchant banker."
"Careful how you spell that Alice," said Alex with a smile.
"I use the term advisedly, guv. He was a dealer at a merchant bank for some time and then he was something else in the bank but higher up. Anyway, he made, and I won't say 'earned' a shed load of money. Probably enough to buy that bloody great house in Shirley."
"How much do you reckon that's worth then?"
"I checked it out on Google Earth and the only picture I could get was a long-distance shot from the front gates and an aerial shot. It's got a damn great drive, but from what I could see, it has to be around the one and a half million mark if not a lot more, but I'm not an estate agent. I got on to some agents in that area who handled those sorts of properties and I was told that they can go from a million up to three million."
"That's not making my hairs stand up Alice."
"To continue, she and Mr Banker bloke separated and subsequently divorced around three years ago and she is now the sole occupier, or to the best of my investigations she is. I don't know if the house is hers or what the divorce settlement arrangements are, but if she does own the house, then with that and the art gallery, she must be absolutely rolling in it."
"Still not standing up Alice."
"Now how about this? The first name on her marriage certificate is not Olivia but Olive."
"I can see how you'd want to change that; it's very old-fashioned isn't it?"
"Yes, but you'll never guess what her first married name was."
"For heaven's sake Alice, you're dying to tell me. Go on, get it out."
"Jordan".
"Bloody Hell! You must be joking Alice. No, that can't be the Jordan as in Frank Jordan surely to Christ?"
"I'll have to do a little more checking to confirm, but it looks that way."
"Hell's teeth, if that's the case then we have something concrete to form a link. We have art, artists, art historians, means of transport

across the channel, access to boats whenever. Maybe I'm making wrong connections but this does look as though it could form some sort of devious course. We'll have to do some suppositions to see how these links could actually work."
"I think there are too many coincidences to ignore boss. Shall I do some more research bearing these views in mind?"
"Abso-bloody-lutely Alice. Great work. I really think we're on to something here."
He didn't have the heart to tell Alice that they already had most of this information, so he carried on with a little subterfuge to keep her spirits up, although he did want to know who the house actually belonged to.
"Can you give Tom a boot up the arse and get him in here please with the CCTV stuff from Poole?"
Alice went out to continue her research and told Tom that his boss wanted him.
Tom strolled in to Alex's office.
"So Tom, come on, amaze me with astounding news from the CCTV stuff, what have you got?"
"I think we have some pictures of the bloke we are looking for. It does show a man about the right height, dressed in what appears to be casual clothes. The pictures are in colour but they are not really that good enough to see the proper colour of the hair but it is obvious that it's not blond."
"When you say he appears to be in casual clothes, what exactly?"
"Well, not 'jacket and trousers', if you see what I mean. It could be a bomber style jacket but it's certainly not a suit jacket."
"Okay but how about his shoes?"
"Well now, that is obvious. They are not trainers and they look as though they are normal leather type shoes and not the heavier 'walking' variety either. They are quite thin looking whereas the walking varieties have a thicker section altogether."
"Good. Good work Tom. So it does look as though this is him. How about the time frame, does it fit?"
"Absolutely, and he is on CCTV at 9.45 p.m. in Lymington. He got a lift shortly after that. It takes about an hour depending on the route you take from Lymington to Poole, and the CCTV at Poole station shows him at 10.35 p.m."
"Hang on, that might be too early. You say it takes an hour for the trip and yet this is 10 minutes earlier. Could we have the wrong bloke?"
"From the pictures I got off the CCTV at Lymington, it's the same bloke guv, but don't forget this is quite late in the evening and the traffic going into Poole is not going to slow them down as it would during the day."
"Fair comment, Tom. So what happened next, did he get a train? If he did, we've lost the bastard."
"Well, this is the thing. He didn't actually go into the station. He seemed to hesitate at first, and then he went into the station and

came out again after a few minutes. Then he walked away from the station and disappeared from the camera."
"Which direction would you say he went?"
"It's very hard to tell as you would have to walk out of the station car park and then take a particular road."
"Damn!" said Alex. "I wonder where the hell he went?"
"Maybe he was aware that there was CCTV and was trying to throw us off the scent. He must have realised that we would trace his movements somehow."
"Right, now what would you do if you were trying to throw people off the scent?"
"I think I'd somehow double back to confuse anyone following."
"Yes, that would be a good move, but how do you travel? By taxi? No, because that can be traced. Where would you go?"
"Just a thought guv; the boat came from Tuckton so maybe there's someone there who is in league with him and can keep him under cover."
"Do you know Tom; you might just have the right idea. I have to say that I've been thinking along similar lines. You say he went into the station for a few minutes and then came out. What does that suggest to you?"
"I don't know, there must be a reason of some sort."
"So how do you travel from Poole to Tuckton? Maybe by train to Christchurch?"
"He could walk to Tuckton Bridge from Christchurch station in about 15 minutes and I'd think that no-one would pay much attention to someone walking by themselves, and he could get a train from Poole to Christchurch with no bother."
"Tom, get on to Poole station and see if he got a ticket to Christchurch. I don't know how late those trains run. Maybe he got a train to Christchurch and we could with a little slice of luck, if they got him on CCTV there."
"Would he get a ticket with a card or could he pay cash at the office?"
"How the heck should I know, I don't travel by train unless it's a long journey and then all the bookings are done by someone else. Just get on to the station master if they have one, but I do know that if he paid with cash, we'll have a job chasing him again. Maybe they have CCTV inside, I wouldn't be surprised. Get on to it pronto."
Tom was straight on the phone to the station master at Poole to enquire about buying a ticket at that time of the evening. He was told that there was a ticket office and yes, a ticket could be bought with cash. Tom had a thought. He said," I know you have CCTV for outside the station, we have that, but I should have asked if you have any cameras inside the ticket office."
"We do, in case we have any disruptive people after they've had a few drinks. There can be trouble sometimes and it's very handy to point out that they are 'on camera'. It soon shuts them up."

"I know we asked you for the CCTV data a little earlier, but could you possibly give us the same time span for inside, as we believe that our man may have bought a ticket."
"That's no problem. If we have a good picture of him, perhaps our sales operative can remember where the ticket was for."
Tom was pleased at this. "That's great; it would help us enormously, thanks."
"Right, just come round and we'll have it ready for you in about half an hour."
Tom went back to Alex and told him about the CCTV.
Then Alex said, "That's great, but didn't you say that he went into the station and came out again in a few minutes? Why the hell would he do that, why not just go into the station and wait?"
Tom said, "I looked up the train times and the last train to Christchurch goes at 10.54. We have him on camera at 10.35. Do you think he had some time to wait and wanted to get away from cameras? He could have gone to a local café and had a coffee or something. They wouldn't have cameras would they?
"Good point Tom. Let's have another look at the video and see if he came back closer to the train time."
Together, they looked more carefully at the video images and at the showing run time of 10.52, there was a figure running quickly with head down, straight into the station.
"That's got to be him," shouted Tom.
"I think you're right. Now let's see what the ticket office have for us. Nip over there will you and get that CCTV video to confirm this and maybe the ticket clerk can tell us more."
Tom was more than happy to drive over to Poole to get more information which would help to move the investigation on.
Alex was thinking over the possibilities now. 'If this man, more than likely the killer of both Yaren and the so-far unidentified man found in the boat, had taken a train to Christchurch, would he have walked back to Tuckton? It's now becoming more than likely that these events began and now have come full circle to the boat auction place at Tuckton. Although nothing is proven as yet, the circumstantial events seem to be pointing firmly in that direction.'
With the information that Alice had received regarding the well-off Mrs Harrington-Thorpe and her previous marriage to Frank Jordan, he was making connections and think along the lines of something far deeper than a 'marriage settlement' of some sort.
Was the house hers? What was the Mr. Harrington-Thorpe up to now, was he still in the picture? What was Olive's real background? If she was with Frank Jordan in earlier times, he, as a scrap dealer, however far removed from the 'dirty fingernails and greasy overalls' of that sort of business, still had the stigma of money not quite legitimately achieved. And he thought ‘we know that he was convicted of fraud of some sort and served time in prison for this. The saying is that 'Leopards don't change their spots', so maybe Frank Jordan is still capable of doing things that are 'beyond the

bounds' and involvement in dealings of the wrong sort. That is not just selling boats and marine equipment, but perhaps using that as a cover for other things. I think we'll have a brain-storming session to bring together all the information we have right now and see if we get some ideas and possibilities'.
When Tom came back, it was getting late, so he called everyone together and told them that in the morning they would have a session where all ideas can be thrown into the ring and see what emerged.

CHAPTER 46

Alex called everyone to the main office incident room for an update on the information to hand.
“Okay Tom, let’s have your findings about our killer suspect.”
Tom had now received the CCTV information regarding the train from Poole to Christchurch Station. "This is the suspect buying the ticket for a train from Poole at 10.52 p.m. to Christchurch." He showed this to Alex, and they both looked over the pictures.
“Put this up on the screen please Tom, so we can all see.”
The CCTV pictures were put through the computer onto the main screen and they could all see the action. His face was clear and would be good enough to circulate for identification.
"Well, I reckon it has to be him," said Tom, "don't you guv?"
"It certainly looks like him, but I'd really like some further confirmation as we have to be sure that we have the right person if we're going to rush in and try to arrest him. I remember you said that it was only a 15 minute walk to Tuckton from the station, so how about you go over there and walk the route to see if there might be any more cameras which could give us a better picture and maybe confirm that he went to the Marine Auctions."
"We don't even have a name for this bloke do we?"
"No, but even if we did it wouldn't help us to find the bugger. Just let's see if he went where we think he went, so that we don't miss him."
Then Anna offered the point that a ‘Mr George’ had been mentioned at some stage as an ‘interesting’ person who had asked Rebecca Connors at the Gallery, for Yarens’ address. Could this be the man who killed her and is now the prime suspect?
“Anna, I think that he could well be the one and we have no other names in the frame, at least at the moment, so we’ll call him ‘George’ until we know differently. Is that okay with everyone?”
There were nods all round.
Tom drove over to Christchurch station, parking his car in the station car park and began to walk the route the suspect might have taken from the station to the Marine Auction buildings. He took the most direct route as it seemed the most likely, crossing into Station Road and taking a right turn into Stour Road. This was a straight road and Tom assumed that as it was the most direct route, it would be the way this man would have taken. There seemed to be nothing along the route except private houses and he didn't spot any CCTV cameras even on the more expensive looking houses. He continued right to Tuckton Bridge and after crossing this, he then saw on the right hand side of the road, the Riverside Restaurant. Right, he thought, I know they've got cameras, so he went in through the main door and was met by an attractive young woman who greeted him as though he were a customer. Caught slightly 'off guard' because he was looking at her, rather than keeping his mind on the job in hand, he fumbled for his warrant

card. He showed this in a surreptitious way to keep it away from general view asking to see the manager on 'official business'.
"Of course Sir," she said, returning shortly after with a rather 'stout' man who had only a little hair but a great expanse of shiny head. He introduced himself as the restaurant manager. "How can we help you officer?"
"I am Detective Constable Peterson of Bournemouth CID. I wonder if you can help us with an enquiry we are making. Can I ask if your cameras cover the car park and show the road crossing the bridge?"
"Indeed they do," was the rather terse reply, if a little obsequious.
"Do you have CCTV data records for the last few evenings up to around 11p.m. to 11.30 p.m.?"
"Of course Detective Constable, we keep data from our cameras for one week."
"And would you have coverage of the car park looking towards the buildings opposite?"
"We do indeed. Our coverage is excellent as to be able to recognise car registration numbers can be quite useful sometimes if there happens to be a scrape or damage to a car, not to mention the occasional trouble from customers who are a little, shall we say, boisterous. Not that this happens too often of course," he said in what Tom thought was a rather 'slimy' tone.
"Of course. In that case, could I see the pictures from that time for the last five days please?"
"Certainly. If you'd like to come with me, I can take you to the office where you can study them without interruption."
Tom and the manager went through the restaurant to his office where he asked one of the staff who was doing some, what appeared to be 'routine' work, to access the CCTV data for the days Tom had requested. This only took a few minutes and very soon Tom was looking through what was indeed very good, clear, pictures across the car park to Tuckton Bridge itself, where the Marine Auction buildings were situated just below the bridge but unfortunately, out of sight.
As the operator scrolled through the footage to the time frame that he was looking for, Tom became aware that there were virtually no pedestrians, simply cars either crossing the bridge or leaving the restaurant. He carried on checking for anyone walking and eventually, he saw the very person he was hoping to see. "Yes!" he said. "Gotcha!" Although it was a clear picture, it did not show this man in enough detail for him to be totally convinced, but Tom was quite sure that the shoes this man was wearing were not 'trainers', but obviously an ordinary 'city shoe' with a thin sole and not the thickness that a trainer or 'walkers' type shoe would have'. That was enough for Tom. He watched as the man slowed down when he neared the Marine Auctions site and looked around him a couple of times and then stopped and stood by the bridge railings for a few moments, as though he were just looking at the river. He looked around to the left and right, then simply vaulted over the railing and

disappeared from view below the parapet. Tom noted that the time was 11.10 p.m. and asked the office worker if he could make a quick copy of that particular view, together with the time caption so that he could take this back to the police station. While this was being done, the young man doing the copying looked at Tom with an interested expression and said, "Is this man a suspect then? What is he a murderer or a rapist, are you chasing him?"
Tom said, "I think you've been watching too much telly chum." If only he knew, thought Tom..."No, we'd just like to ask him a few questions, nothing serious."
"Oh, pity, we could've been on ‘Crimewatch’".
"In your dreams lad - but seriously, if you notice this man again, please would you call us immediately?"
"Well yes of course, but I don't sit here and look at the camera stuff all day and night you know."
"I understand, but I guess you do check the tapes occasionally."
"Yeah, but like I said, we can't check everything. Only when we are asked to do a check because maybe something has happened in the car park."
"So if we ask you to check another time frame, you'll do it for us, yes?"
"Yes, of course."
"Thanks. That would be very helpful. If you could just make a copy of that section we were looking at, we would appreciate it."
The young office worker made the copy requested and handed it to Tom.
“Thanks again, most helpful.”
“If I find anything, we’ll give you a buzz Sarge.”
“Detective Constable actually, but you never know, ‘one day’,” said Tom with a slight grin.
Tom realised that there was nothing more he could do or extract from what he had seen, so he thanked the office chap and made his way back to the station.

CHAPTER 47

The next morning the team, Alex, Anna, Alice and Tom were in the office early.
“Mornin' everyone," said Alex, in a cheery upbeat way which made Alice think that he perhaps had a ‘good night’ as he wasn’t quite a chirpy as this usually, she thought. It’s about time he got himself a new person in his life after what had gone in the past. Alice knew about his previous situation and how it had ended so tragically and she knew that he had been without a steady partner for some considerable time now. He's a nice guy really and she felt glad that he seemed to be a little happier.
"Let's have a run-through of what we know up to now," Alex said. "If anyone has any thoughts just let them out because we need to think 'out of the box', even though I hate that phrase but in this case it may be appropriate as we have lots of little bits of information but nothing which leads to an arrest and that is what we need, pronto."
"Anna, can you have a run-through of what we know so far from your perspective."
"Right guv, well we now have CCTV confirmation that chummy went back to Christchurch via Poole thanks to a lift from Lymington. I guess this was to put anyone off the scent so that he could get back to where we think he has contacts and lie low. The reason he went back there and not just made his escape is not clear at the moment but there has to be a good reason. I think that there is a definite link to actions that take place at the Auctions that are not really concerned with boat sales but something far more lucrative. I also think that Mrs Olivia Harrington-Thorpe is linked in with this somehow through the gallery and now we have Katya's details, I am going to see her to get to know what she does and maybe her connection to the gallery. We have to get some more information on her involvement in the proceedings."
"That's very well put Anna, thank you. Do you have any thoughts Alice?"
"Well, I was thinking that as we have the fact that Olivia, or should we call her 'Olive' now, was married to Frank Jordan, and we know that Mark is a product of that marriage, but then why do we not have any mention of him in our searches? He has not been mentioned, as far as I know, in any interviews apart from the fact that Frank admitted that Mark was Olivia's son but there's something very odd about a mother who wants nothing to do with her son whatever, and that makes me very suspicious, doesn't it you guys?"
"That's a very good point Alice. It is strange and I suppose that we have to accept Frank's story but I do wonder if Mark knows who his mother is?" He looked around at them as he said this, raising his eyebrows as he did so.

"That would be really dodgy, wouldn't it?" said Tom. "I mean if my mum hadn't wanted me to know that I was her son, I'd at least ask my Dad who my Mum was and where was she."
"I think that's a fair point Tom, although Frank tells us that he told Mark that his mother had died or something like that, I don't know. Perhaps we should ask Mark when we get him in, but at the moment he's a slippery little eel."
"He's certainly very secretive. We don't know where he lives and we can't seem to track him down at all."

CHAPTER 48

Anna called the number for Katya that they had found in Yarens' notebook.
"Hello."
"Good morning. Can I speak to Katya please?"
A heavily accented voice answered. "This is Katya, who is this talking please?"
"Katya, My name is Anna. I believe you have a friend named Yaren."
"Yes, Yaren my friend. Why do you want me and who are you?"
"Katya, I am sorry to be calling you like this, but can you tell me the last time you saw Yaren?"
"I sorry, but I not know what you are wanting from me. Why you ask questions?"
"Katya, I am a police officer from Bournemouth."
At this, Katya became very wary. She was from Turkey but had been in England for a few years now; but even so, the mention of police put her on her guard. 'What have I done - what is problem'?
Anna realised from her accent that perhaps she was worried about her status in England, so she sought to put her at ease.
"Katya, please do not worry. I have some news for you of Yaren. When did you last see her, please tell me."
"I am not speaking with you until you tell me what it is you are wanting. You have news of Yaren. What news you have? I not see her for one week or more."
Anna was thinking hard. 'Do I tell her or keep it quiet? If I tell her now she could pass on the information to someone who perhaps should not know'. She reached a decision and drew a deep breath.
"Katya, I know that Yaren is your good friend and I am so very sorry to have to tell you that Yaren was found dead last Wednesday."
There was silence for many seconds, but Anna heard sharp intakes of breath as though Katya was choking, followed by the sound of crying now.
Then there was a long drawn out, 'Ooooh no! Tümçabaları boşagitti '. "She found dead, where, how?"
"I can only say that she was found dead. More than that I cannot tell you at the moment but what was that you said Katya? I could not understand you."
"I say something in Turkish. I shocked by your news." Anna sensed that there was something more to the explosive phrase. She realised that as all her calls were recorded as a matter of course, she could get someone to translate this phrase later.
"I think you meant something more Katya, and I must ask you again what you meant by that phrase."
"It nothing, I just surprised by what you say me. It just a saying we use for surprise. Yaren, she so beautiful and good, very clever, speak very well the English, not like me. I will speak with you about Yaren because she my good friend."
"Thank you, Katya. Can you tell me where you come from?

"I come from Isparta, this not very far from where Yaren live. She live in Antalya. This on sea coast."
"And your friendship with Yaren?"
"How you mean friendship?"
"I mean, I know you were friends but were you close friends?"
“We meet sometimes. We go run together. She work at gallery and give me work sometime to make copy."
Anna almost lost it at that. 'Copies. Now that is *very* interesting'.
"When you say copies, what sort of copies."
"I copy painting and I restore also. Yaren know much about paintings and ceramics, history of these things."
"And are they copies of well-known artists?"
"Most of time, yes, very famous painters."
"Do you do many 'copies' of paintings for the gallery Katya?"
"I do maybe four or five."
"And over what period?"
"I no understand period."
"Sorry, over how long do you to make these copies?"
“I not understand.”
“Over what period of time have you been making these copies?”
“Make copies maybe for gallery for two years or two and half.”
Anna asked Katya how much she was paid for her copies but she was very reluctant to say. Then she asked if Katya knew Mark. Her reply ‘Yes,’ said in the tone of voice which she used, gave Anna pause for reflection. Then she made a decision. "Katya, I am going to have to ask to see you, together with my superior, Detective Inspector Vail, in person. There are points which are too important to be said over the phone. I will make an arrangement for us to meet if you will give me your address and when it will be convenient for us to see you. You must have a job, so perhaps we can see you when you have finished work one day soon. Do you understand what I am asking you?"
"I think I understanding. My painting my working. You want seeing me when I finish working?"
"That is correct Katya. Where do you work, is it local to where you live?"
"I sorry, I not know what 'local' mean. I have work at home. I artist, so can see you anytime."
'More art links', thought Anna. "That is good; we will make a time and come to see you. Perhaps we could come tomorrow if that is convenient?"
"That okay. I not go, I work in studio."
"Very well, we will come in the afternoon. Is that a good time for you?"
"Yes, good time. I start working early in morning as light in studio good for painting."
"We'll try not to keep you too long."
“Okay, I see you in after morning, yes. I give you address."

Katya lived and worked from her home in Crystal Palace, and Anna realised that it was not too far from where Yaren lived.

Back in the office Anna checked the recording of the conversation and found the phrase that Katya had said in Turkish. Using a 'spoken translation' program on the web, she entered the recording and the translation was fairly accurately made. The phrase meant '*Ooooh no! All my efforts went to waste'!*"
'Now, I wonder what she meant by that. It wasn't what she told me. What 'efforts' had she made? Was it connected with her work or with Yaren'?

CHAPTER 49

Yaren Ganim was of Turkish origin. She was 37 years old and had studied Art History at Durham University. After University she moved around to Newcastle working in various low-paid jobs to do with art and design. Unfortunately, with low wages, she turned to a little shoplifting to 'help out' but was caught and consequently charged, found guilty, fined and given a suspended sentence. She then went back to Durham and lived in a rented flat, still working in the Arts. She met and in 2012 subsequently formed a relationship with a man who was on holiday visiting a friend who ran a small business in the Durham area. This man was Mark Jordan who came from Dorset. After a short period, they became 'an item' and whilst Mark went back to Dorset, he came back two weeks later and they had a longer time together. Following this time together, Mark said he had a friend in the art world who needed someone with a good knowledge of art and that he could find her a job in a gallery and suggested that she move down to London. She readily agreed, as her career seemed to be going nowhere in Durham. Mark said he could get her a flat and she was more than happy to move down more or less straight away.
Moving down to London Mark moved her into a flat in South Norwood, where she spent a brief period of being shown around to friends of Mark; going to parties and getting to know London. She frequented a local Turkish run café and she subsequently met a Turkish girl named Katya, who happened to come from the same area in Turkey. They became firm friends as Katya was an artist and Yaren realised that the work she did was of exceptional quality. Katya was a very accomplished painter and worked from a studio at the back of her house near Crystal Palace. This was only a short distance from her own flat, except that although she thought it was her flat, Mark paid all the bills and in fact it was rented. At 33 Mark was slightly younger than Yaren, but that was no problem. Yaren had long raven black hair and was very attractive, slim, with olive skin and dark, almost black eyes which were wide-set. Her symmetrical face was fine-boned with a high forehead, high cheekbones and clear smooth skin. Wherever they went, she garnered compliments and Mark was quite envied for her looks. However, she had a fiery temper which sometimes was quite volatile. Mark could never quite cope with this or understand it, although he had to accept that sometimes, for no apparent reason, she would go 'over the top'. He had learned that whenever her eyes went an 'inky black', trouble was brewing. Mark presumed that this was due to her Turkish roots. However, Mark also had quite a 'short fuse' and sometimes his good humour dissipated like smoke.
Thanks to an introduction, organised by Mark and the help of his father, she was offered a job at an art gallery in Wimbledon. After an interview with a very 'upper-class' lady and her gallery curator Rebecca Connors, she was offered a position as an assistant. This

was based on her exemplary knowledge of art history and her awareness of the respective value of various artists and schools of painting, together with her expert knowledge of ceramics. This fact seemed to have greatly impressed the gallery owner, who said that she would be 'an asset'. Mrs Olivia Harrington-Thorpe, who was the owner of the gallery readily admitted that she didn't know much about art, but relied on her staff for that area of expertise, whilst she had the 'contacts'. She was able to 'talk the talk' to cover her lack of knowledge and she 'persuaded' her contacts' to come to her gallery where they could 'invest' in artworks, following which the chosen piece would usually increase in value. Whether the painting or artwork, be it impressionist, abstract or whatever they were told the school was, had any bearing on their choice has to be left to the imagination. Usually, they were interested in the value and how much this might subsequently increase.

Rebecca, who was the gallery curator, asked Yaren a few well-chosen questions regarding her knowledge of art and art history and due to her education and a degree from Durham University, she was more than able to answer all the questions and impress both Rebecca and Olivia Harrington-Thorpe with her in-depth knowledge, which actually surpassed theirs. Yaren was subsequently offered a position of 'assistant' at the gallery.

Yaren liked the job and she very soon became well-known to many clients and her knowledge was well respected. Her home life was a little strange as Mark was often away 'on business' for two or more days at a time. She didn't know where he went as sometimes, he said he was going to London and sometimes went down to Christchurch where his father was the owner of an auction business selling boats and marine equipment. Sometimes, she would ask Mark where he went or what he did, and when she did, he would become very cold and told her, very forcefully, not to ask questions as it was private. In fact, Yaren never quite knew what Mark did for a living; it was enough for her that he had plenty of money, was very easy-going and fun to be with. He had very good humour and Yaren never knew that Mark had served a 5-year prison sentence for fraud. This was to play a very important part in the subsequent proceedings.

However, Mark and Yaren were having problems. He had asked Yaren to look after a large package for him while he was away in London for a few days. Because she really had no clear idea of what he did for a living and when she asked him, he was always very oblique and just said that he did a few things to 'arrange sales' and things like that. This gave her cause for some concern. She was no fool and was not convinced. Mainly because recently, he'd come back from a trip, and he was uncommunicative and moody for a while. When she asked him what the problem was, he had become quite aggressive and told her not to ask too many questions. 'I just make money, Okay? Is that a problem? I pay for everything and give you whatever you want. Just don't ask too many questions and do what you're good at, you know, finding buyers'.

CHAPTER 50

The next morning, Tom, Alice and Anna were all in the CID office and they were all into their respective favourite morning 'wake-me-up' drinks. Anna had a milky coffee from the machine while Alex preferred a strong cappuccino. Tom was a 'milky tea' man and Alice simply had water.
"I don't know how you can call that a 'wake-up' drink Alice," said Tom, who was looking just a little ‘bleary’.
"One coffee in the morning is enough for me," Alice said defensively, "and I had one before I came to work. I can't even think straight until I've had my coffee hit."
Alex came into the office with a 'determined' expression on his face. "Good morning people. What have we got that's new? Alice had a good day yesterday with some eye-opening news about Mrs Olivia Harrington-Thorpe. I’ll let Alice tell you what she discovered, as I can see she's all cock-a-hoop about it, and after she has shared her finds, Tom, you can tell me about the results of chummy going back to Christchurch."
"Well now,” said Alice with an air of satisfaction, “after digging through the official records, it transpires that Mrs Olivia was not called Olivia but Olive before her marriage to Harrington-Thorpe. He is, or was, by the way, a city trader and that's how he made his money. Or that's what we think at the moment. It's not clear as to who actually owns the house, but that's for more delving into council archives. For now, the real news is that she was formally Mrs Olive Jordan."
At this, both Anna and Tom looked incredulous. "S'truth," said Anna, "now that IS interesting. It just can't be a coincidence, can it?"
"I bloody hope not, said Alex, otherwise we are going to have to go back many squares."
"Surely not," said Tom, "I mean, they both live in the same part of the world don't they?"
"Not really," said Alex, "but in the South of England, for sure. They're not a million miles apart and perhaps far enough after a divorce. What really concerns me is that who actually owns the house. If the present husband does, that's fine, but then does she have any part of it?"
Alice stepped in here. "She's divorced from Harrington-Thorpe but I can't find outright ownership at the moment."
Anna said, "If for some reason he doesn't own it, then perhaps she does. The question then is, how the hell did she come by it? She could not afford that sort of place by herself. If I'm really picky, then I'd suggest that hubby Frank, if he is the bloke, bought the place and lets her stay in it. You know, he owns the house but she pays all the expenses or something like that."
"Or,” Tom said, "If she was given the house by Harrington thingy, then she'd be worth a few bob for sure."

"I somehow don't think that Mister Harrington-Thorpe would leave a house to her, these guys are too money conscious," ventured Anna.
"I wouldn't have thought so either," said Alex. "Do we have any further information on how Frank Jordan made his money?"
"Not really. It's all very much 'off the radar' as far as actual documentation is concerned. I guess that most of it comes from cash transactions and stuff like that, which is obviously untraceable," said Alice.
"Especially from the taxman," said Tom.
"How about the business accounts relating to the Marine Auctions?"
"They all check out and seem to be above board, but it doesn't make much money and the figures really don't support a great big house like he has."
"Okay Alice, thanks for that but please keep on digging around for more information. Tom, what do you have?"
"About the guy going back to Christchurch? Yes, he did. He got the late train from Poole station and we have him on CCTV getting out of Christchurch station at 11.15 p.m. Then he went from view, but we have him on the CCTV camera of the Riverside pub restaurant at 11.30 p.m. It was their car park camera and it only showed a long shot of this bloke, but I'm sure it was him."
"And where did he go, can you see?" said Alex.
"He walked across the bridge and then stopped. Looked around for a bit, you know leant on the railings, and I suppose when it was clear of anyone else, he vaulted over and went straight into the Auctions. I had a look and it's only a short drop to the ground from that point, but he would be out of sight."
"Bingo," said Alex. "Good work Tom. Now we know that this is the bloke and we need to go back to the Auctions to find out who he is. I doubt that he's still there, but we can do some serious questioning."
Alex then asked Anna for her findings of her going to see Katya at her home. "I believe that Rebecca did not know or know of Katya?"
"That's right. When I asked her about Katya, she said she'd never met her although I'm not a hundred percent sure she's telling the truth. She said that she only knew of Katya as the person who did the copies and I think she wanted to cover herself in case there were more questions regarding fakes. I think we'll have to give her a more thorough interview and apply a little pressure."
"That seems reasonable. Perhaps you could arrange this interview shortly, Anna?"
"Will do. Anyway, Katya is Turkish as we know and comes from a town not that far from where Yaren came from. They apparently knew each other some years ago and had lost touch until quite recently. Katya comes from Isparta and Yaren came from Antalya, which is quite a large town in South Western Turkey, while Isparta is a way inland and up in the hills. Rebecca says she didn't know

Katya. I asked her about her friendship with Yaren; she said that she and Yaren sometimes went running together. When I asked her about Mark and if she knew him, she did not seem too happy. I asked her if she liked Mark and she said that although he was nice looking, she thought that, and I quote, "there was just something about him that I didn't quite like." When I asked what she meant, she just said that it was nothing she could be definite about but her 'instinct' gave her cause for concern and that it was as if there was a different side to him that she could not explain, but which worried her."
"She couldn't tell you anything specific then?"
"No, and to be quite honest, when I asked her if she had a boyfriend, the way she answered did make me wonder if Katya was lesbian, but then I could just be barking up the wrong tree boss and doing her a disservice. That's her choice although perhaps it could explain why she didn't like Mark too much."
Alice said, "Perhaps if she wasn't interested in Mark or other men for that matter, she could 'see through' Mark."
Anna said, "You could be right Alice. She would be more dispassionate than Yaren and not be taken in by his outward charm."
"You see Tom," said Alex, "here we go again, these girls see much more than we do. They have these feelings, whereas we blokes see black or white, don't you reckon?"
"Yeah, either a bloke's all right or he's a knobhead, guv."
"So succinctly put Tom," said Anna, with heavy irony.
Alex said, "I'd be interested to know what Yaren saw in Mark that Katya didn't."
"I'm afraid we'll never know what she thought now," said Alice with a sideways glance at Alex.
Anna then carried on, "She obviously knew about Yaren working at the gallery and that she had a good knowledge of painting values. I asked her if she had copied any paintings for the gallery. She said she had done maybe five."
"Five, over what time period?" said Alex.
"I asked her how long each one would take and she said that the five paintings she did each took about two to three weeks and the five were over a two-year span."
"Did she say how much she was paid for each copy?"
"I asked her, but she was quite cagey about this but I guess from what she did say, and from what I have been able to find out, was that it would be around twenty to twenty-five thousand for each one. That's a lot of money, but when you consider what the original might be sold for, its peanuts. She must have a lot of skill if these paintings are going to be taken for the real ones and not be obviously a fake."
"The whole thing is though boss, if a painting is 'copied' and is sold as such, then it is not against the law. It only becomes a crime if it is sold as an original and is, therefore, a 'fake'. If the painting has an

'authentication certificate', then it is to all intents and purposes the real thing, but the buyer has been 'conned'. This also means that the certificate has been issued for the original but switched somewhere along the line."
Okay, so let's say this copy is made and a buyer is found who thinks he is buying an original with the correct certificate, how does he get the copy instead?"
"Any ideas anybody," Alex asked the others.
Tom put in, "Supposing that the copy was put in a crate which looked exactly like the right one and switched somehow' the copy was then delivered in the usual way I suppose, and if it had the correct certification, then the person receiving it would presume that he'd got the original."
"Mmm," said Alex, that's a possibility, but when would it be switched and by whom?"
Alice spoke up, "It could be done if, let's suppose the buyer was told that his purchase would benefit from being cleaned and that cleaning would take anything from a few days to a few weeks depending on the condition and value of the work. This would give the people doing the copying and switching the time they needed. And we know that Katya is a copyist and restorer, so I suppose she does 'cleaning' as well."
"Yes, but where could the switch take place?"
Anna took over, "I talked to Rebecca at the gallery and she said that when someone buys a work, they can take it immediately, but if it's very valuable, it's usually crated up and delivered by a specialist carrier on a specified date. This would give a good opportunity for a switch to take place, especially if the painting is sent for cleaning. With the right connections, I'm sure it could be taken to have a copy made, and who knows, even properly cleaned at the same time, while a copy is made. They could be both crated in identical ways so there would be no suspicion and the original put into storage for selling at a future date, again, and the copy is then delivered to the buyer who has a great looking painting."
Alice broke in. "But surely this means that the person who is getting the original back must know about the scam as the original has just been apparently sold? Oh, but I'm not thinking," she said, "the original is put back into storage, so it's out of sight and perhaps 'out of mind'."
"Now that's a good point of view. This again points to everyone knowing about the copies or frauds, including I would think, the gallery owner."
"But supposing the buyer gets a painting which looks nothing like the one he bought?" said Tom.
"Ah," said Anna, "but the painting he gets will look very different if it had been cleaned. They'd be more than happy that it looks one hundred percent better and they'd not question it as they have the certificate, so they would be content, apparently."

"Until someone who knows a lot more than the buyer about this painting and this artist," said Alice, "and suspects that it's a copy, then what happens?"
"They get it re-examined?" said Alex.
"Then the shit'll hit the fan," said Tom.
"I think you could say that Tom," said Alex. "Hmm, Italian buyer, possibly Mafia. Does that ring any alarm bells?"
"It does," said Anna "and another thought. Just supposing that the copyist is the same person who does the cleaning or restoration. What a wonderful opportunity for keeping everything quiet and no-one knows what's going on. The painting is delivered; the original is put away for re-sale. Buyer is happy. Big profits all round."
"That puts a whole new light on things," said Alex, "but somebody else must know what's going on, don't you think?
"Absolutely, and do you know who I think is in the know?" said Anna, "Olive Jordan, Rebecca and the other part of the picture, Frank Jordan. I am really sure that Katya has no connection and she simply does the artwork and cleaning as a legitimate business. I reckon the others are in it together and Mark is just a go-between doing the real dirty work, with his runs to France. I reckon there are drugs involved as well."
"So where does Yarens's killing come into this and the other chap in the boat who hasn't been identified as yet? And we still don't have a name for the killer."

CHAPTER 51

Alice had been busy with digging into the background of Olivia Harrington-Thorpe or now known to be Olive Jordan before her marriage to the Merchant Bank Trader.
Now divorced, she had been married to Harrington-Thorpe for five years but she and Jordan had divorced some ten years previously. They had recently connected again and quietly, with no-one being aware of the liaison, they would meet.
Through council records and checking of phone records, bank statements and other details which were available via various websites, it was discovered that she and Jordan had communicated on many occasions. The content or meaning of these meetings was obviously unknown at this moment. It was significant that they were still in touch and the connections with the art world through the gallery and therefore connections were being made regarding the possibility of the paintings being sold as originals but were in fact copies.
It was now known that Katya was a skilled copyist and she was also a cleaner and restorer of paintings and was therefore ideally placed to carry out the copying and subsequent fraudulent sale of paintings to unsuspecting buyers for very large sums of money.
It was discovered that the house that Olivia now lived in was actually owned by Frank Jordan and although Mr. Harrington-Thorpe thought it belonged to Olivia, this was not the case. Another link and connection with Frank Jordan.
The speculation was now that Frank and Olive were both involved with fraudulent copies of painting purporting to be originals and sold as such for very high prices.
Back at the CID office, Alex was being brought up to speed regarding the information on the man seen leaving Christchurch station at 11.15 p.m.
"Okay, we have to assume that as he was seen at the Riverside restaurant which is very close to the auctions, that he was going there. Who is at that place who can hide him and who the hell is he? He seems to be the obvious choice as the killer of Yaren together with the unidentified bloke on the boat at Lymington."
"Anna, do we have any further information on him yet? It's been bloody ages."
"Not really guv, we only know that he was around 30 years old and was slightly built. Nothing on him, no wallet, no clothes, no phone, zilch."
"Damn. How about DNA?"
"That's being checked now but you know how long that takes, and they are not hopeful."

"Well, chase them up Anna please, we need to know who he is. Give them a rocket and tell 'em we need this information before any more bodies turn up."
"Tom, go back to Tuckton and see if anyone knows who this mystery man is, but I get the feeling that 'nobody will have seen him' or 'knows who he is'."
"But Guv, if he is the killer, then surely they're not going to tell me who he is even if he is there, are they?"
"Bollocks - you're right. If he is the bloke, they'll be keeping him out of sight, for sure. We still have no sight of Mark, so where the hell is he?"
Alex changed tack and asked Alice, "Can you get onto Interpol and ask if anyone has reported any 'art fraud' or something like that? I'm sure that anyone who has a dodgy picture they'd paid a pile of money for and then found out it was not 'kosher', would be just a little mad."
"Right boss, I'll get onto that right now. Let's just hope they are helpful; they usually are."
Alex called Jack, one of the other constables who worked with the CID department and asked him to go to the Auctions at Tuckton and ask to see the boss on the pretext that he was from a local tax office and needed to talk to both directors of the business.
Very happy to get away from the more mundane work which was the 'norm' for the everyday police work, Jack drove over the Christchurch. Arriving at the auctions, he 'wandered' around for a while before going into the main shed. Finding Keith, he asked for Frank Jordan and was told that the boss was out with his son.
"Would that be Mark Jordan?" said Jack.
"That's right," was the reply from Keith, who had not asked who Jack was or what his business was. He'd simply taken it that Jack was someone who knew the Jordans. "Mark came back from France a few nights ago and he was in a hell of a mood. He reckoned he'd hit some driftwood in the Channel and put a hole in the stern of the boat he was in."
Keith's tone was one of 'exasperation' for some reason. Perhaps it was due to the extra work that Mark had caused him.
"Is that the boat I saw up on the dock as I came in?" asked Jack.
"Yeah, it's gonna take me a while to get that fixed and I've just heard that the owner is coming down in a couple of days to take her out with some friends. That's all I bloody need. If he sees that, he's gonna go ballistic and wonder how it happened when his boat is supposed to be tied up here safe and sound."
"So Mark isn't the owner of the boat then?"
"No, he'd just 'borrowed' it. They do that sometimes and if anything is asked, they just say that was on a 'demonstration run'.
'That will interest them back at the office', Jack thought. Just been to France; someone else's boat without their knowledge or permission. Naughty, I wonder what he was doing chasing off to France.

"When did Mark go over then, Keith? Was he on his own?"
"He had Jason with him and they went on Monday morning. Said he had something to deliver to somewhere called 'Westerham' or something like that. I've no idea where that is. It don't bother me. What does though is that Mr Boat owner will come down on me like a ton of bricks. Bound to blame me for not looking after it, so I just want it fixed as soon as bloody possible. So, if you don't mind, I have to get on."
"Okay, but who is 'Jason'?"
"Oh, that's Marks friend from out Newbury way. That's all I know about him, I've only seen him a couple of times and he and Mark just come in and then they're gone again. But hey, you're asking a lot of questions for a punter."
"I should have said, I'm a tax inspector and we like to know about a company and their activities."
'Oh shit!' thought Keith, 'I don't think I should have said so much. I won't mention his visit to Mark or Frank or I could be out of a job, knowing their tempers'.
"Right, I'll not keep you," said Jack, but just one other thing, do you know who came into the premises last night at about 10.30.?"
"I've no idea mate; I was in the pub enjoying a couple of pints with my mate Ben, the bloke who works here with me."
"All right. Thanks for your time Keith, you've been very helpful."
'More helpful than you know', he thought and he went back to the station to see Alex.
Once back in the Bournemouth Police headquarters, he sought Alex.
"So how did you get on with finding out about the bloke who we are looking for, Jack?" asked Alex.
"Apparently, no-one was there at the time we know he went there, so we still have no idea who he is. But, what is very interesting is that Keith, you know one of the chaps who works there, told me that Mark and Jason went over to France a couple of days ago to, 'deliver something to a place that sounded like 'Westerham'."
'Westerham'," said Alex, but that's in Kent, he can't mean that. If it was France, it has to be on the coast. I'll bet a month's salary that he didn't go there for a cup of tea. That sounds like it could be 'Ouistreham', that's Caen, the ferry port across the Channel. Thanks for that Jack. That information is very useful. Do you think they suspected that you were not a 'Tax Inspector'?"
"I don't really think the guy I spoke to knew much about anything except boats."
"That's good, as we really don't want to give too much away and scare them. Thanks again for your help."
"No problem Guv, glad to help. But I tell you what; I don't think he'll be too eager to tell his boss about my visit."
"Why's that?"
"Because he told me about the boat that Mark and Jason had taken over to France – not his boat, but someone else's, and hit

something or had some damage to the stern and Keith has to fix it in a hurry. I don't think he should have mentioned this somehow."
"Thanks again Jack, great stuff, very helpful."
Alex thought, 'Jason. Now we have a name. Could that be the second body?"
Alex turned to Tom. "What do you think, Tom?"
"I reckon he'd have to have a damn good reason to go over to wherever this 'westerham' place is and that he took a fast boat to get there and back in the day says a lot."
"And what reason do you think?"
"The most obvious thing is drugs. Just nip over there with a shipment, drop it off and buzz back to base. No questions, no customs. Too easy."
"I'd agree with that Tom, at least it would be a good way to get them into the country with little risk as I'm sure that there won't be many customs checks on small boats unless they had a good reason to suspect something was going on. Added to that is that we suspect Mark of storing drugs at Yarens' flat. Can you have a look to find a place that sounds similar to 'Westerham' and we can do some more checking?"
"Yes," said Tom, "I'll get a map of the French coast and see if I can find somewhere that looks like it. It can't be that hard to find as it must be fairly opposite this coast to keep the distance down."
"Good, let me know as soon as you've found something. Try looking for 'Caen', and don't forget, we now have a possible name for the other bloke on the boat; 'Jason'. He seems to be a friend of Marks', so we'll have to ask him when we actually get to meet him. Now I've got to talk to Alice about Frank Jordan and Olive Jordan."
Alex called Alice to his office.
"Alice, do you have any further information about these two?"
"Yes boss, I've been checking Olive's phone records, thanks to the cooperation of the phone company, and I've found quite a number of calls made by Olive to Jordans' number over the last year or so. What they were concerning is anybody's guess."
"I think the fact that they are in touch again tells us a great deal, or at least it gives us a lead and the question is that she needs money for upkeep of that great house and how does she get it? She's hardly on benefits."
"I wonder if she's been down to Christchurch or his house in Sandbanks. That would be interesting wouldn't it boss? Do you think there might be some CCTV records from the area that could prove that she has been to see him there?"
"That's a very good possibility Alice. Can you go down there and see if there might be any places which would have coverage of the local area, roads of course where we could see her car? We can get on to Traffic to see if either his or her car is a regular visitor to the area, either in Shirley where she lives or his house in Poole at Sandbanks."

"I'll get on to the database records at APNR HQ and see what we can get. There must be some cameras on the main roads where they take automatic records and we can get a trawling search to see if their cars are regulars. I'll go down to Sandbanks this afternoon. I'd like some fresh air."

CHAPTER 52

Anna arrived at the address that Katya had given her in Crystal Palace. As she sat in her car, she looked around at the general area. The houses all seemed to be Victorian and they had been either kept in good repair or they had been well renovated. Katya's flat was on the top floor of this once large detached property, which had been converted. She pressed the button on the intercom panel on the wall of the entrance porch. A deep but feminine voice answered. "Yes, who is thees?"
"This is Detective Sergeant Anna Jenkins of Bournemouth Police. I called yesterday to arrange a meeting."
"Oh yes, but please, you come in. I am on top floor."
The door latch buzzed and Anna opened the door, to be pleasantly surprised by the excellent décor and furnishings in the entrance hall. The stairs were heavily carpeted and there was a smell of furniture polish. She went up the flights of stairs and passed two entrance doors, obviously to the other flats. Outside one, were tubs of flowers on each side of the door and they made the landing very attractive. Much better than most places where the building has been converted to flats, she thought. They usually stink of cats and kids with bikes and toys littering the place. This is something really different and just how they should be.
At the top floor, a woman was waiting; this was obviously Katya. She was quite tall and had very striking looks. Olive skin and her dark hair was worn in a bob which came just below her ears and gave her face a very slightly 'elfin' look, although she had a strong face and her eyes, although dark, had a serious look. Anna thought that as Katya was an artist, she saw a great deal more than most people. Artists are trained to 'see' and they usually noticed things that others did not. This would be very useful attribute in a detective, thought Anna.
Katya said "Please to come in. You are alone? You not have your Detective?"
"No, he is very busy working to find the man who killed Yaren. I must talk to you alone."
"I not mind this. I think better we talk just me an' you."
Katya motioned for Anna to enter the flat, and as she looked around, she saw a host of paintings of all types hanging on the walls. There were also some standing against one wall. There were a mixture of impressionist and abstract paintings and also some prints. Anna was very impressed with these pictures. She said, "You have a fantastic collection. Are they your work?
"Some of them, but most of ones you can see here for cleaning or restoration."
Katya spoke with a strong accent, which Anna knew was Turkish as she came from a town near where Yaren came from.

Anna took a line of questioning which would answer a lot of questions that she was mulling over. "So you restore old paintings, Katya?"
"Yes, and sometimes I clean also. This very specialised"
"So I believe. Would it be possible that you also copy paintings?"
"This I do also. I have customers who have very valuable painting but not wish hanging this on show in house. They ask me make copy and then valuable original put away in safe place. I ask why you come to see me. Police, am I in trouble? I am in England many years now, not illegal."
"Not at all Katya, you have nothing to worry about."
Anna had the passing thought that although Katya had been in England for many years, her accent and grasp of English was not particularly good. However, to be fair, as an artist she would not have substantial contact with people as she would if working in an office environment; then it would not be that surprising that her accent were a little 'heavy'.
Katya was becoming a little wary now. Perhaps she was giving away too much, but she knew this knowledge was open to everyone, so she did not see any reason for trying to hide what she did for a living.
"Katya, can I ask if you have seen Yaren recently?"
"I not see Yaren for maybe two weeks now. I have much busy with restoration work."
"But you and Yaren went running together sometimes?"
"That right. Not often but we go for run for keeping fit. She so nice, she come from same part of Turkey as me."
Anna looked at Katya and her expression became very serious.
"Katya, I am afraid that I have some very bad news. " I know I told you that Yaren was found dead and that is very bad, but I am very sorry to tell you that Yaren was murdered sometime around August the 13th. That is last Wednesday."
Katya exclaimed, "Masha Allah!" Anna knew this was the Muslim for 'Oh My God'. Katya looked very shocked as her colour drained. She put a hand out to find the edge of the desk she was standing by and supported herself. Then she sat heavily down on a chair and put her head in her hands.
To Anna, this looked quite genuine as though Katya didn't know that Yaren had been murdered.
"This cannot be true. I know Yaren dead but you tell me murdered. You mean someone kill her? She not have accident?" How Yaren die? Why? Öldürülen, AmanTanrım! amakim buşe kildeöldüre bilir!"
"I'm sorry Katya, what did you say?"
"I sorry. I say who can kill someone in this way?"
"It is a terrible thing and we need to know as much about Yaren as possible so that we can find who did this awful thing to her, and why."
"Yaren not have many friends here as she not in London so long."
"We know that she had a boyfriend, Mark. Did you know Mark?"

"I meet Mark maybe one, two times. I not like him much."
Anna's attention went up a few notches at this. "And why was that Katya?"
"Something about him I not like. He seem okay at first, but he have temper and he always not here many times. Yaren not feel safe when he not here."
"And why do you think Yaren did not feel safe when Mark was away. Was it the area she lived in?"
"I sorry, area? I not know what you mean."
"The place where her flat was. Was it a bad place?"
"It not good. Houses full of strange noisy people. Much cars, nowhere parking. I feel, how you say, 'not good'."
"Do you mean, 'uneasy'?"
"Uneasy. I not know uneasy."
"Not comfortable, we say 'uneasy'."
"I think that the word, yes."
"Did Yaren say what made her feel 'uneasy'?"
"I only know Yaren say he make her hide things in flat. I not know what things."
"When you say 'he', do you mean Mark?"
"Yes, Mark. He make her feel not easy."
And did Mark make you, feel 'uneasy'?"
"Sometime, yes."
"And can you say why Mark made you feel uneasy?"
"I not know, only that he sometime like two people. When he good he funny but when he in bad mood he not nice, not good."
This is interesting, thought Anna.
"When did you last see Mark?"
"I last see Mark when he and Yaren have bad words and he go out and bang door and drive away in his silver car."
"You were there when this happened?"
"Evet, I arrive just as bad words happen."
"I'm sorry, what did you say, 'evet'."
"I sorry - I say yes. ' Evet' mean 'yes' in Turkish."
"I see, said Anna. So do you know what these 'bad words' were about?"
"I only know he say, 'You have to look after them, that's all you have to do'. Then he go out quickly."
"And you don't know what she had to 'look after' for Mark?"
"No, only that Yaren most upset and say to me, not to worry. I will handle this."
Anna was really concerned that Yaren was being asked to look after something which was really not what she wanted to do. Given the drug connection possibilities, it could be that drugs were being kept in Yarens' flat and she didn't like this. She changed tack and said to Katya, "Do you know the Art gallery called 'Arcadia'?"
"Yes, I hear of this. Yaren work there. I not go there but I get work sometime from gallery when buyer need painting cleaned."
"And how do you get the painting?"

"Mark bring it here. Mark not like me much, so he never stay. Just leave picture and take other with him."
"Other?" what do you mean, 'other', Katya?"
"Maybe one I restore or maybe one I copy. I not know. Sometime he take both. I paid for doing work. I not know where paintings go with Mark."
"Can you tell me how much you are paid for these copies?"
"I not like say. This my business, it private. It not wrong for copy paintings. They sold with buyer knowing that work a copy."
"I am aware of this," said Anna, "but as this is a police matter, I must ask you to give me some idea of how much you are paid for a copy. It could be important to our investigation."
"I not see how this important, but money change. Sometimes, lot of money, other times, not lot but I pay tax. All proper, I make list and professional man make list for place who take tax."
Anna realised that she could find out if really necessary. "Don't worry Katya, I'm not here to ask about tax, but have you copied a painting recently?"
"I do one not long ago. A work by Édouard Vuillard. This I copy and restore original because it in bad condition. It very difficult to copy because strange materials painting made with."
"Was this an expensive painting?"
"Yes, this work much money. Very difficult copy. Very difficult clean and restore. Take long time to finish."
"And do you know who bought this painting?"
"I not know this, but it go to Italy I think."
"How did the painting or paintings leave here?"
"Mark come. He take both. They both in box used for sending paintings. I think they called 'crates'."
Now THAT is one for Alex, thought Anna. Confirmation of Mark's participation. "Do you mean that you saw Mark take these paintings with him in his car?"
"One time, yes, but I think other times too, but I not see this, because I here in studio and Mark in car in street but he take down stairs with him."
"I think that will be all, for now, Katya. I may have to speak to you again if you don't mind."
"I think I stop working now. I too upset. This terrible thing happen to my friend."
"I am so sorry to have to bring you the bad news Katya. We will do our very best to find whoever killed Yaren in this terrible way. If you think of anything which might be unusual or different and which seems strange to you, please call me." Anna handed Katya her card.
"I think I understand. I call you if I think anything."
She wished Katya goodbye and made her way back to Bournemouth to see Alex. She was almost certain that Katya was not involved with the fraudulent sale of paintings but simply a very gifted artist who made a very good living from her skills and was not linked to the gallery except for the work she did.

It seemed very strange that Rebecca did not mention the fact that Katya was a copyist and did work for the gallery.

CHAPTER 53

Anna and Alex had been out for another date and this time things had progressed beyond the 'goodnight' kisses.
Following their first date at the restaurant, they had met on several occasions when time and circumstances permitted, given that they were in the middle of what had become a very complicated case.
Subsequent and necessarily 'clandestine' meetings had taken a natural progression and now he had invited her to his flat to spend a very 'close' evening.
Earlier that evening, before they finished work, Alex said, "Would you like to come over to my place this evening – I'll cook us some dinner?"
"You – cook?"
"And why not, may I ask? I can chuck something together which may or may not be edible." He did say this 'tongue in cheek' as he was actually a passable cook. This came from him having been living on his own for some considerable time.
"I'm sorry. It's just that usually men can't cook to save their lives and live on 'junk' food and pizzas."
"What a hoary old misconception madam? I'll have you know that when really pushed, I can rustle up something decent, but if you'd rather not take the chance, we can go to a MacDonald's. How about that?"
"Yuk".
"Is that a 'Yuk' because you like Macs 'Yuk' or you don't like them?"
"I'll give you three guesses."
"I thought so. So will you allow me to make you something special?"
"And what did you have in mind?"
"Something a little different. It'll have to be a surprise for now, but I can assure you that it won't harm you."
"Okay then, I'd love to, and I'll get some wine on the way over. If it all goes in the bin, at least we can get smashed; but I have one condition."
"And that is?"
"That we don't talk about work. Just us and no office chat, no 'how is the case progressing', sort of stuff. "
"Agreed and I think that would be the way things should stay when we are together outside the office."
"Absolutely. So I'll come to your place at about 8, if that's okay, 'cos it'll give me time to get changed into something more comfortable?"
"Just come as you are, you look great to me."
"No way Jose. I need to get out of these work clothes."
"Okay. I'll have something ready for us when you get to my place."
"Surprise me with your culinary skills. I can't wait," she said with a slightly dubious countenance.
"You might be surprised; anyway, I hope so."

"See you at eight then, 'bi for now." Then quite loudly, Anna said for the benefit of anyone who might be listening, "Goodnight guv, see you tomorrow."
"G'Night Anna."

Alex did a little shopping on the way home in preparation for the meal. He called in at the butchers and had two escalopes of turkey cut just the way he wanted. He was going to prepare Turkey Saltimbocca, with Parma ham topping the escalopes and marinated with butter. For the basic sauce, he would gently fry some red pepper and onion with a little balsamic vinegar in the olive oil. After the vegetable were cooked the turkey would be taken from the oven and finished in the open saucepan. This would not take long and to finish the dish the heat would be turned up high to give the escalope's a golden 'tan'. He would make 'Delia Chips' and with fresh French green beans, tossed in butter, he hoped the meal would be well received. For dessert, he prepared baked apple filled with sultanas and prunes, with a few walnuts and these would be put in the oven with the turkey escalopes which had Parma Ham overlay. These were in a foil parcel for the first part of the cooking which he would undo for the final part to crisp up the Parma Ham. He had opened a bottle of Cabernet Sauvignon to 'breathe', but he did not seriously think it made a difference as the amount of air in the neck of the bottle did very little in the time it would stand before being drunk.
***
At precisely eight o'clock his doorbell rang and Alex opened the door. She was standing in the 'half-light' and her eyes were like little coals.
"Hi Anna, spot on time." She was carrying a small case which he took and said, "Come on in. Welcome to my humble abode."
"You sound like a smurf when you say that," she chuckled. "Well, I don't know about you but I'm hungry, so I hope you've been down to the pizza place – she sniffed the aroma filtering through the air and said, "But something does smell rather nice."
"Here, let me take your coat." As they moved into the stronger light, he took her coat and then just stood there, looking at her, saying nothing.
"Is there something wrong?"
"Wow!"
"Sorry?"
"Just Wow! I mean, you look absolutely stunning. You look gorgeous."
"Thank you - one does try you know."
Anna was dressed in a pair of close-fitting black trousers, with a crimson loose-fitting blouse, worn open over a black silk camisole top. Simple but very classy and the whole effect, together with her subtle make-up, which she normally wore very sparingly at work,

accentuated her almost 'elfin' looks. Her brunette hair was immaculate and Alex was completely taken with her.
This was Anna's first visit to Alex's flat and she was clearly impressed with how neat and tidy it was. She thought, 'I expected it to be a bit messy and untidy from my previous experience with blokes, but he's pretty good, although he's probably made an effort'. But when she looked around more carefully, she saw that it wasn't just a special effort but that it was more obvious that it was his normal routine to keep things in order.
"Are you ready to eat madam?"
"Indeed, I am Sir."
"Then, may I offer you a glass of Cabernet Sauvignon?"
"That would be lovely, thanks."
Alex poured them both a glass and handed one to Anna. "Here's to a good evening,"
"And maybe, to a better night," said Anna, looking straight into Alex's eyes, without flinching, while touching glasses.
With that, something deep in him did a quick somersault. He took a deep breath and said, "Shall we eat?" "Yes, I'm ravenous."
Looking her in the eyes, he said: "I think the word should be 'ravishing'."
***
The meal went very well and when they had finished, Anna said "I am well impressed. That was really great. I thoroughly enjoyed the escalopes, they were really tasty and the chips were something else, where did you get that idea?"
"Delia."
"Delia?"
"'Delia Chips'. You know, Delia Smith, the famous cook, always on telly."
"Oh, right, yes of course. They were super. A really lovely meal, thank you so much for your efforts. My doubts are dispelled."
"You had doubts?"
"But of course. It's a well-known fact that most men are rubbish cooks."
"I'll ignore that jibe but have to say that I'm hurt."
"I really didn't mean to criticise but it had to be said, but you have proved the exception to the rule, so I apologise."
"It was absolutely my pleasure. Some more wine?"
"Yes, please."
***
As the evening progressed they spoke about many things, their early days, their schooling, their friends, where they went on holiday; all the things that people talk about to get to know each other.
They were sitting on the sofa and quiet music was playing in the background.
"That's really nice music Alex, soothing and gentle. I've not heard that instrument before, what is it?"

"It's the Kora."
"Kora, I've not heard of that. What sort of instrument is it?"
"The best way I can describe it is that it's made from a large gourd which is cut and a skin put across, rather in the fashion of a drum. On the top they make a frame which takes all the strings. It's a little difficult to describe, except that I suppose it's a sort of harp, but the most amazing thing is that what you are hearing is just one man playing the Kora."
"But if he's playing this with his hands and fingers, it sounds as though he has about twenty fingers!"
"This guy is probably the best Kora player ever, he's fantastic."
"It certainly is, in fact it's quite enchanting. How did you find out about this instrument?"
"I was with some friends a few years ago and they invited me to join them at Poole Arts Centre where this particular virtuoso was playing a gig. I have to say it was probably the best concert I've ever been to. It was so amazing. Actually, when there was a break at the interval, he received a standing ovation which lasted a good few minutes. The audience went absolutely crazy at the incredible playing, and there was no dancing about and prancing females, just one man gently playing the most complicated music, wonderful!"
"Sounds great. Who was this guy?"
"His name is Toumani Diabates."
"I like it," said Anna, and she was just about to snuggle up to Alex, when she said just a 'mo." She slipped off her loose blouse to leave her black camisole top, which was a very soft and silky material. Pretty soon, they were touching and then caressing each other. He reached to her face and gently, very gently stroked her cheek with the back of his hand. This was greeted with a gentle sigh of appreciation. Things soon progressed to kissing, which became more and more urgent.
He was gently touching her body and when he moved his hands to her breasts, he realised that she was naked under her camisole top. As he fondled her breasts through the thin silky material he thought that this was probably one of the most incredibly erotic feelings he had ever encountered. It made his head swim. The softness of the swell of her breast and the firm suppleness of her skin simply made his heart thump so much; he was convinced that she could hear it. He gently caressed her nipples with his thumbs and she was making little murmuring noises as they became erect – and so did he.
Anna said quietly, as she caressed him, "I think you are as turned on as me, so maybe we should move to somewhere softer?"
"What a good idea, I was thinking the same thing. Come with me."
"I'll do my best," she said, with a very cheeky grin.
***
They moved to his bedroom and slowly but urgently undressed each other. When they were naked, he caressed her body with his hands gently exploring her body, all over, everywhere, probing.

He was gently feeling her breasts and in return, she was running her hands across his chest, enjoying the rising urgency they were both feeling.
"I'd like to do something you might enjoy," she said.
"I think anything you'd like to do, I'd enjoy very much."
"Okay, in that case, you can turn over and lie on your back. I feel the need to be promoted, and then I can be higher than you."
He looked puzzled, but he did as she suggested and Anna then moved on top of him. Alex groaned with pleasure as she kneeled above him with her knees apart and lowered herself to him. With very sensuous movements, she began to move slowly back and forth along his very rigid penis. Her lips were glistening and lubricated. The feelings that this produced were sending him into orbit. She moved slowly with very sensuous movements, and he was giving little groans of mounting pleasure.
"Please, now," he said and put his hands up to feel her breasts again. She firmly pushed his hands down to his sides.
"Soon," she said and began to move just a little faster. "Are you ready for me?" she said.
"Oh God, yes please, I'm about to explode!"
"Patience." She reached behind her back and found his hardness. She said, "I think you're ready, it's like an iron rod !" Very gently she guided him into her. As she moved and he drove gently deeper, she arched her back and felt the pleasure of feeling him deep inside her. His hands went to her softly firm breasts now and gently squeezing them in utter appreciation.
"I'm glad you like my breasts," she whispered. They were not large but not small either, 'just right' thought Alex. Her nipples were almost as hard and erect as he was.
She was moving more and more and he was deeper and deeper to the point where her whole body was pressed against him. Their movements became ever faster and very soon they came to an intense climax, both making sounds of intense pleasure and satisfaction of coming together.
***
Later, lying in the intensely satisfying afterglow, she said softly, "That was our first time, but I don't think it'll be the last, do you?"
"I certainly hope not. I can honestly say that I have never had such wonderful sex. No I won't say sex; I'll say 'lovemaking'. Now I understand your 'promotion' to be above me but next time you will have to become subordinate again, sorry."
"No problem, I am sure I'll be quite happy being 'under' you."
"I thought we weren't going to mention work Anna."
"Hey, this isn't work unless you count the effort."
"I'm more than happy to put the effort in."
"I'd rather you put something else 'in'," was her riposte.
"Happy to oblige; turn over, please."

She did, and once again they made love, this time slower and more erotically, with prolonged caresses and kissing to make everything last longer, both exploring each others' bodies tenderly but eagerly. Their lovemaking was urgent and passionate, to say the least, although 'controlled', not wishing to go too fast. They had both been without intimate contact for a considerable time and they both had 'pent-up' passions which were again unleashed with enthusiasm.

***

They slept, eventually, holding each other in a warm and very tender embrace. In the morning, they both lay pleasantly exhausted in the bed and the sun was shining through the curtains. Alex looked at Anna as she was dozing quietly and thought that she was even more attractive than he had realised, while she was so relaxed. Sometimes at work, she seemed to have this quite 'hard' exterior. Probably because she was a very conscientious officer and took her work very seriously, thought Alex. She would also dress in a more 'sober' way which was more appropriate for the work she did. This sometimes belied her softer side which he was now seeing and he was so pleased that they had finally overcome the 'boss/subordinate' problem. They had make every effort to keep their liaison quiet as to let it be known that they were an 'item' would lead to problems. Little did Alex know that Alice had a sneaking suspicion about them but she would never let on? She respected her boss too much for that and anyway, she was pleased for him and her, as she liked Anna a lot and got on well with her. Anna stirred and turned over. He had been awake for quite some time and had been happily just looking at her with intense pleasure. She opened her eyes and saw him looking at her. Smiling, she gave a little purring sound. This had an immediate effect on Alex and he gently stroked her face and gave her a gentle kiss. She responded by reaching down his nakedness and as she gently caressed a particular part of his body, which she had so enjoyed last night, she feigned surprise and said, "Oh, that's nice. Somebody's awake."

"Yes, and he wants to say hello if that's all right?"

"By all means. Good morning 'Sir', nice to make your acquaintance again," she said.

After another bout of intense 'social interaction', they both realised that they had jobs to go to. Luckily, they both worked at the same place, but Alex said, "Perhaps we should arrive separately."

"I think that would be best, yes."

"What would you like for breakfast? I'd like to make it for us. I'm used to doing this for just me but it will be just great to make it for two."

"You're on," she said, "I'll just get a shower then. I'd like some toast and jam and a cup of strong coffee. That'll get me set up for the day."

"Your wish is my command Detective Sergeant Jenkins, but maybe I could call you 'darling'."

"Yuck," she said, "just call me Anna, that'll do for now. Let's leave the DS Jenkins bit for the office eh?" and forget 'darling' or I'll punch you."
"Right," said Alex. "You get your shower and I'll do the toast and stuff."
Alex was about to go to the kitchen to prepare a breakfast for them both. He stopped and turned to Anna. "Can I just say that last night was absolutely incredible? I didn't imagine it would be so good."
"Hey, it was great for me too you know," said Anna. She rose from the bed and as she walked out of the bedroom toward the shower, Alex was looking with a great deal of appreciation at her nakedness. She had a slender figure with all the right things in the right places. As she reached the door, she turned and gave him a very lascivious look on her face. She paused and stood quite still while he looked at her fully naked body with total and complete appreciation.
He groaned, "Will you stop that please, I have to make the breakfast, and I can't concentrate?"
With a little chuckle, she turned and went into the shower. He realised that he probably shouldn't have taken a look at that point, but it really was too tempting and anyway, she didn't cover herself and she did invite his long look. To invade privacy without permission or reason could have been a death knell to their relationship, but as she didn't seem to mind, his mind was put at rest, so he went into the kitchen, cut the bread and put it in the toaster ready for when she had finished. He put the coffee into the cafétiere and was about to put milk into the cups when he realised that he'd not asked her preference. He went to the bathroom door and shouted, "Do you take milk in your coffee? I forgot to ask."
"No thanks Alex, I take it black in the mornings. It helps to get me started."
"I think you were doing pretty well already if you don't mind me saying."
"You didn't do so badly either," she shouted back. "Can you not cremate my toast too much please?"
"No problem. Your wish is my pleasure."
"Thank you, kind sir."
She came out of the shower, and as she had fairly short hair which dried quickly, she was already dressed for work. They sat at the kitchen table and made their breakfast with Anna having some jam on her toast. Alex did the same and he said, "I really had no idea what you would have for breakfast. Do you have this at home or do you have something different?"
"No, I usually have just a slice of toast with jam and a nice coffee, 'proper' coffee, not the instant stuff. I love the smell of that first thing; it seems to start the day properly."
"This must be a good omen because I usually have just toast as well. I don't normally have time for anything more adventurous, but I suppose I've got into the habit now and just like you, I really like

some decent tasting coffee first thing. It makes a great change from the junk we have at the station."
"Do you know, I was meaning to ask you about that? Alice and I were talking the other day and she suggested that if we all 'chipped in' we might be able to get one of those new coffee gadgets where you put in a 'pod' of some sort and it makes some really good coffee. It might be a good idea, what do you think?"
"I think that's a great idea. Can you find out what it would cost and how much we'd all have to put in?"
"Sure, no problem. I'll look into it. I'm sure there must be deals online or from somewhere like Argos or Amazon. They usually have some good prices going."
"That's great, thanks Anna."
"By the way," she said, "that's a great shower you have. I'm quite envious because my bathroom at home is a lot smaller. With yours, you have room to move about and you don't feel claustrophobic at all."
"I know, it's nice isn't it and what's really good is that it's big enough for two."
"Mmm, I'll have to think about that. Okay, I've thought. Great idea, but not now."
"No, you muppet, I was thinking of the next time we get to spend some time together, It might be a good way to get together."
"I think it could be a way of getting 'some things' together."
"I think we should get to work now before I get waylaid again."
"Did you say 'waylaid or just 'laid'"?"
"Enough! We've got to go. You go first and I'll clear up and follow a little later. See you at the office."
"On my way Alex."
"Before you go Anna," he said, "come here please."
She moved over to him and he put his arms around her and held her gently but firmly and they kissed with a lingering, gentle passion.
Anna broke away, reluctantly, and said, "Bi then, if I can have my lips back, see you later."
"A tout a l'heure, ma Cherie."
Taking her little overnight case, she said, "A bientot, monsieur," and was gone.

CHAPTER 54

There was a knock on Alex's office door.
"Come in." Alice entered.
"Hi Alice, come in", said Alex, "what have you got for me?"
"Some more info on our Olive, or should I say Mrs. Olivia Harrington-Thorpe. I have taken a look at the phone records that we could get hold of and they do show quite a number of calls to the Christchurch number of Frank Jordan. Some of them to the office of the Auctions and some to his private address. We know that he doesn't have anyone living with him, but from other enquiries, he does have a number of female 'visitors', from time to time."
"Understandable I suppose," ventured Alex, "given that he is single and has a lot of money. Go on."
"Well, I have also, with Tom's help, been going through some of the ANPR data that we could get when we correlate the times that we know Olive has been out in her car."
"Hang on," said Alex, "how do you get to know when she has gone out?"
"Aha," said Alice, "we just happen to have found a CCTV camera on a shop directly on the road where she would have to pass on her way to the South, and Tom and I have some interesting links to times she had phoned Frank. We were able to correlate the times and dates and check their data. It seems that very soon after some of the calls, she had driven off and we were able to follow her part way on the motorway, enough to verify that she was making her way to the South Coast. It seems fairly certain that she was going to see Frank. For what, we can only guess at this stage."
"Fantastic work Alice. Thank Tom for me will you?" You've obviously been hard at it."
Anna had come into the office a little earlier and was listening to this. To stifle a smile, she quickly turned and bent toward the floor as though picking something up, she thought, 'so have we'......
"Thanks boss. We've still got a lot to do but we're both sure that there is a lot more to tie up between those two, given that she is involved in the art market and this figures highly in our investigations."
"I'm sure that's right Alice. I think we'll have to pursue the copying of expensive paintings by Katya to see where that leads."
Anna said, "Katya told me that Mark was somehow involved and he had collected a painting recently. I wonder who arranged that and where was he taking it?"
"I would think that with the connection to ex-husband Frank Jordan and the art works and copies, I wouldn't be surprised if there aren't some very dodgy goings-on with copied paintings. Do you remember Katya saying that she just copies paintings or restores them?"

"Yes," said Anna, "she said that copied paintings are not illegal as some buyers of very expensive masterpieces have them copied for show, while they put the genuine ones into 'safe-keeping'."
"Exactly, Anna, now what I'm thinking is that just supposing Olivia Harrington-Thorpe, or should I say Olivia Jordan 'as was', is linking up with Yaren through the gallery and their collective contacts and sales abilities. They find a prospective buyer and arrange a sale. They get the original copied by Katya and somehow swop them for the original and then deliver the copy to the buyer who thinks it's the real one. He would be none the wiser unless he became suspicious and had it checked."
"It's a possibility. If Mark had collected a painting from Katya, where would he have taken it?"
"Could be as simple as taking it to a company who despatches high-cost pieces of artwork or sculpture for them to forward it with the appropriate documentation. I don't see that it would be difficult, as if the painting was properly protected and ready for shipment, nobody would query the contents, if the documents were in order. Or maybe it was even taken back to the gallery and it was shipped from there. Who knows?"
"I think you could be right Anna. Let's get on to Katya and see where her last copy went, so that we might have an idea of the trail."
As Anna was leaving the office, Alex said, "Annie, can you find out who might do the packing because if there's someone else in the chain, they could help."
Anna turned, looked back at Alex and said, "I will, but it's Anna, not Annie. I hate that." She left the office without a further word.
'Bugger', thought Alex. 'That's a "brownie" point dropped'.

Later, Anna saw Alex sitting in his office poring over some paperwork. She knocked on his door and he looked up. Seeing Anna, his face broke into a big grin. This brought a little tingle to Anna, and she smiled back. She went in as he said, 'Hello gorgeous, have you got anything for me?"
Anna began to colour slightly and said, "Yes, but not here. You'll have to wait."
"Stop it you muppet, you're making certain things uncomfortable I'll have you know."
Anna just smiled, raised one eyebrow but saying nothing, raised the hem of her skirt very slightly and gave him a really long, sexy look. That'll come later."
"I'm sure you will," said Anna," with a giggle.
"Will you behave? We're supposed to keep this quiet. If someone opens that door without knocking, they'll be trouble we don't need. To business, we have a lot to do."
"Sorry guv. You're right. I've had another word with Katya and she tells me that the last painting she copied was an 'old master' by ÉDOUARD VUILLARD."
"Never heard of him."

"Nor me, but then I don't know much about art."
"Like a lot of people, I think Anna. How much was that worth, did she say?"
"She could not give a definite figure, but I've researched it a little and I reckon it would have been worth around two hundred and fifty thousand."
"Bloody hell," said Alex, "that's a load of shekels."
"Yes, and if the buyer discovers it's a fake, he's not going to be very happy."
"You can say that again," said Alex.
"He's not going to be very happy."
Alex looked at her with a resigned expression, "Will you get out of here?"
"Going," she said and left the office with a smile.

Tom and Alice found more details concerning the despatch of a recent painting to a buyer in Italy. They had traced the company which transported the painting and the address of the purchaser.
"What do you have Tom?" said Alex.
"It seems that the latest painting to be sent was taken to an address in Tuscany. A villa called Castiglioncello, only I can't pronounce it. It is owned by a Signore Tosco Scarpetti. The paintings are normally carried by a specialist company but this particular one was taken by two blokes in a white van which called at the gallery. Apparently, they had a letter of authority to collect it and the gallery phoned the buyer to confirm this and they took the crate and drove all the way to Italy. It's a bloody long way to take one painting, but I suppose if it's that valuable it'd be a good idea.
"How did you find that out then?"
"We asked Rebecca who did the shipping and how many they shipped through this company, and she gave us all the delivery details for the last six shipments."
"So, there was no effort made to hide the delivery addresses?"
"No, none. She was most helpful in fact. This tells me that she thinks there was nothing to hide."
"That looks like it yes, but forgive my suspicious mind, but if she were good, she might seem as though she is as pure as the driven, said Alex, "Do you have any details on this Signore Scarpetti?"
Alice spoke up. "Yes, we have traced him through Interpol. We asked them if they knew of him through any criminal activities."
"And did they?"
"They certainly did boss, he is known to them as a member of the Italian Mafia, and quite high up it seems, in fact they think he is a 'Don'. Although he has no convictions, they keep an eye on him as his involvement in various dodgy dealings always seems to mention him, but he is clean."
"Typical Mafia tactics apparently," said Alex, "they always get someone else to do their dirty work while they stay clean."

"One day they'll get it wrong though," said Tom, "and then they'll get what they deserve, with a bit of luck."
"Tell you what, you two can get back to Interpol, because they handle criminal investigations and see what they can give us in the way of lines of enquiry we can follow up, and also contact Europol because they handle intelligence. They might have our friend Scarpetti on their radar."
"Right'o," said Tom, "we'll get straight on to that. Who knows, he might be involved with something other than collecting art and stuff."
Alice said, "It's the 'stuff' that will help us. We know he collects art and he's got a painting which we now know is suspect."
"And," said Alex, "I don't suppose he'll be too chuffed if he discovers that he has a dodgy painting. What do you think he'll do?"
"I reckon, if he's mafia, he'll have someone come looking for revenge and restitution, don't you?" said Tom.
"I reckon that's a fair bet."
Later, Alice found Alex deep in thought in his office.
"Boss, I've got some details on Mark Jordan which might help."
"Great, what have you got?"
"Well, it seems from Rebecca that Mark collected the painting from Katya as he was near her place and he apparently arranged for the packing and took the crate to the gallery."
"Was it normal for Mark to do this?"
"I don't really know, but it seems that it may have happened before. When Katya has made a copy, she usually returns both the original and the copy to the Gallery and they handle them from there. Occasionally, Rebecca said, Mark would collect the painting and take it to the shipping company, if he was in the area. She also says that what normally happens is that the original is sent on to the customer as arranged, together with all the documentation and the copy is retained in the gallery for future sale, or simply to be stored in 'safe keeping'. She told me that they keep the copy in storage for some time as it would not look good if the buyer were to see their lovely painting back on the wall straight away."
"I can see that," said Alex. "So this time, Mark did the handling. Do you think he might have done a switch and the copy has gone to the buyer as the original?"
"I think it's a strong possibility boss."
"Right, get on to the shippers and find out the address details and if possible, contact the buyer to see if this is a proper job. Maybe you could go 'undercover' again."
"Do you mean pose as a journalist, like before at the Marine Auctions?" said Alice.
"Maybe," mused Alex. "I suppose if you were a journalist from some art magazine asking about a recent purchase, they might buy it. Worth a try, don't you think?"
"I could give it a try. I'll look up some art magazines and find a suitable title. I just need to ask them what they thought about the

service and were they pleased with their purchase from the gallery, that sort of thing. Do you think that would give us some information?"

"Yep, give it a whirl and see what you can get."

CHAPTER 55

With the information from the bank accounts which had been brought to light, it was becoming obvious that due to the large amounts of money which were being transferred across all the accounts, that something very big and lucrative was going on.
Alex said, "To me this looks like it's to do not only with the paintings which we now know could be forgeries, or as Anna says, 'copies' which have been sold as originals together with completely authentic Authentication Certificates, but also dealings involving drugs. Here we don't have enough evidence to make it to the prosecution stage but the fact that the resulting amounts of money have been moved from one account to the other suggest something really big is happening. However, from what we understand, Olive Jordan or as she would rather be known as 'Olivia Harrington-Thorpe', has been transferring large amounts to Frank Jordan and then again there have been similarly large amounts transferred the other way. My instincts tell me that a large amount of this money has been stashed away in 'Offshore Accounts' to keep it out of the taxman's way, but we obviously can't get the full information on this. It is only conjecture."
"We know that Mark is involved in the copying scam don't we?" said Anna.
"That's true. We have information that Mark actually collected a 'copied' painting and took it to the gallery for onward transport to the address in Italy. It would be quite easy, I would think, to switch crates containing paintings at this stage and send it on its way. So Mark then gets the money for the painting which has been sent to 'an address' in London where he collects this and takes it, we don't know where, but we suspect it was used to buy a supply of drugs. Again, we have no proof, but the facts seem to support the supposition. The problem could have been that the killer was involved or even employed by the buyer of the painting to get some sort of restitution from Yaren as she was the one he thought he had paid and that she would have the money. How does that sound?"
Anna said, "I think that is a very strong possibility and we must surely be able to prove this somehow."
Alice put forward a point of possibility. "How about Rebecca at the Gallery? She must have known about the copies and the sales to all the various buyers. Can we really believe that she was completely unaware of the subterfuge going on?"
"I suppose it is possible that she didn't know Alice, however unlikely, but until we have actual proof of this, we cannot take the slim supposition to a point of arrest. I also think you're right and she did know, or at least suspected that there was collusion between Katya, Yaren and Olivia Harrington-Thorpe. If they all knew, then

they were all liable to keep things very quiet to save their own skins. However, this is going to be very hard to prove until we have, as I have said many times, more hard evidence. So, people, let's keep working at winkling out all the relevant facts so that we can put a case together."
There was another point from Alice. "How about Katya. She says she knew nothing about the 'switching' of the paintings. Do you believe this? I would have thought that she realised only too well that it could, and did happen. In which case, she is in on the scam and is just as guilty as the others."
Anna took over. "I have to say that I really get the impression that Katya is not in on this. She earns a shed load of money and seems to be quite happy with what she does. I definitely got the impression that she was telling the truth and not trying to hide anything."
"Point taken Anna, I hope you're right."
"So now Guv, we have Olive and the others on the art side and Frank, Mark and whoever else on the drugs side, all earning shed-loads of money, but we can't prove anything at the moment. All we actually know is that two people have been killed but we don't know who did it or where the killer is."
"Well, thanks for telling us that we actually know bugger all Anna, but essentially, yes that is the situation. Until something happens that opens the case or we can catch 'mystery man', we are pretty well 'in the dark'. We may well suspect Mark of drug dealing and supplying, but quite frankly, until we actually catch him in the act, we don't have enough evidence to even arrest him."
Tom then put in a suggestion. "How about pulling him for 'questioning' relating to suspicion of involvement with the supply of drugs, and see how he reacts. He might give something away that we could use."
"A good thought Tom, but I don't really know what that would give us except a clue, but what it would give him would be a reason to keep his head really down and then I don't think we'd ever get a good result. We'd have to wait for him to make a mistake and that could take a heck of a long time. What do you think people?"
"I'm inclined to agree with you sir," said Alice.
Anna said, "Me too. We'd like to think we could get him but the problem with being forewarned is that they are also forearmed and he'd be even more careful than he is already."
"Right then," said Alex, "we keep on going with our enquiries as we are, but we'll still try to catch our killer which anyway is our main case."

CHAPTER 56

How could they discover the two men in a white van who took this painting by road, all the way to Italy and why was this not taken by the usual shippers? She could ask the question of the buyer possibly. Going back to her desk to look up some appropriate magazines, Alice finally decided to become a freelance 'journo' who wrote pieces for magazines like 'Apollo' which handled all types of international art. Suitably vague, she thought.
Researching the buyer of the painting, she found from Rebecca at the Arcadian Gallery, that the buyer was a Signor Tosco Scarpetti. She also received the address of his villa in Tuscany.
She put in a request to Interpol regarding 'Tosco Scarpetti'. To see if any more information was known about him. When she had the reply, she was quite shocked to know that although he was 'known' to Interpol, he had never been arrested although he was actually a member of the mafia and was known as a 'Don', or head man. The source at Interpol said that although he was a Don, he was not at the top of the tree but very high up and had many contacts.
Alice had contacted the shipping agent normally used by the Arcadian Gallery, but they said this time it was carried privately and they were not involved.
She was quite worried about having to talk to a mafia boss and she had to try to control her nerves. She said to herself, I think I'll just have a little wine tonight and give him a try in the morning. She had obtained the address and contact details of Tosco Scarpetti and after her nerve quelling drink the night before, called the number. Her call was answered by a female Italian voice. It was Rosina, Scarpetti's maid who had answered.
"Ciao, questo è la residenzadel signor Tosco Scarpetti. Chi stachia mando per favour".
"I am sorry, but I do not speak Italian. Can you speak English please?"
"Si, sì, ma io parlo solo, I spik only very leetle Engleesh. Ooiz callin pleez?"
"I need to speak to Signore Tosco Scarpetti, per favore."
That's as much Italian as I know, thought Alice. I hope he speaks English or I'm lost.
"Un momento per favore". The phone went quiet.
After a few moments, a voice spoke in very good but heavily accented English.
"This is Scarpetti. To whom am I speaking please?"
Taking a deep breath, Alice said, "Buongiorno, Signore, My name is Abigail Lawrence. I am a journalist writing an article for a well-known London Art Magazine, called 'Apollo.' As an art collector, perhaps you have heard of it?"

"Well, Miss Abigail Lawrence, may I presume that it is 'Signorina or perhaps Signora'."
"It is Signorina Lawrence."
"Very well, perhaps you can tell me why you are calling me, and yes, I have heard of this magazine. It is an international publication, is it not?"
"That is correct, Signore. I happen to know through a friend of mine, that you recently purchased a very wonderful impressionist painting by Eduard Vuillard. As I am writing an article for this magazine concerning the gallery system for purchasing works. I am asking how you found the service by the gallery from which you purchased this work and how satisfied you are with your purchase. I also understand that it had been cleaned before being sent to you."
There was a definite silence at the end of the line; as though the person were considering his answer.
Scarpetti was thinking hard. Should he tell this woman what had happened, but then this might lead to suspicions and with the current state of the situation, that would not be good.
After this pause, he said, "Signorina Lawrence, I have to tell you that I am not particularly pleased that my details have been given to you, but I will let that pass for now. What I can say is that the painting which I purchased through the gallery Arcadia was a masterpiece and a wonderful addition to my collection. The service was what I expected and what I received looked superb. I cannot fault the gallery as everything was carried out to my specification and I received a painting which looked wonderful."
Alice detective mind clicked on and she was on her guard. He had said that the gallery performed everything as they should but, 'I received a painting which looked wonderful'. What he might have said was 'The painting was wonderful'. Also, he'd said 'What I received looked superb'. Strange phrasing, but perhaps this was just the accent, but then he did not sound like the sort of man who did not use the English language extremely well. He was obviously highly educated and had a suave manner.
Hang on; thought Alice, this guy is a Mafia Don. Suave he might be, but the Mafia have some nasty habits, don't they?
"May I quote you Signore Scarpetti, in my magazine?
"I would rather you did not my dear, I would be more than happy to be quoted as 'The recipient', or something similar, but I value my privacy and would not like to think that I might have uninvited people calling me to discuss my acquisitions."
"I completely understand, of course. If I may ask you just one more question?"
"Of course, but I may not give you an answer."
"I understand from the gallery that you did not use the normal shipping company, but had a private carrier who took your painting directly by road. Can I ask why you did this?"
"This was done by one of my employees. That way, I was completely sure of the security."

'So, 'one of his employees',' thought Alice, does that mean that this 'employee' lives in England'?
"But of course I understand that. Does this employee actually live in England, Senor?"
"That is no concern of yours Signora. I think I have answered all your questions now."
Alice realised that things had taken a sharp turn and quickly decided to end the conversation.
"Thank you so much for your co-operation and I can assure you that you will not be mentioned in my piece. It would simply be part of an article to encourage others to use the Gallery system and services."
"Thank you for your understanding. This is appreciated." This was said with a definitely 'clipped' voice.
"Signore Scarpetti, please enjoy your paintings. I will bid you goodbye."
"Arrivederci, Signorina."
***
She went directly to Alex with the result of her subterfuge.
"What are your results Alice, did you get anything worthwhile?"
"I don't know to be honest guv, but a couple of things did strike me as rather odd, the more I think about it. One thing he said was that 'The service I received was what I expected and what I received looked superb.' "Don't you think he would have said something like 'was wonderful' or 'was superb'? He also said 'I received a painting which looked wonderful', again a strange phrasing rather than 'I received a wonderful painting'. I think he was being very cautious and there was a long pause after I'd said that I understood that the painting had been cleaned before delivery. I think now that he was being very cagey and if perhaps he had discovered that the painting was a copy, or in his eyes, a fraud, then he was choosing his words very carefully. One other things, when I asked him why he had had a private delivery he said that It was done by 'one of his employees'. Does that mean that this employee lives in England? I asked him that, but he said it was 'no concern of mine'. I think I'd pissed him off, so that was the end of the conversation."
"That could very well be the case and if we could get a description of this man, it might be useful. I think you are very astute Alice," said Alex. "This does seem to fit into our findings and suppositions. Great stuff, a nice bit of undercover work. I just hope he doesn't realise that he was a victim of might be loosely termed "entrapment," but he didn't say anything incriminating. Just gives us a possible reason for a Mafia man to take action for revenge of some sort."
"I'll get on to Rebecca right away and see if she can give me a description.

CHAPTER 57

Alex called his team together and they gathered in his office for another briefing. "I'm going to fly a few kites here and try to get some ideas to link together. Let me know if anyone has and information or input over and above what we already have. We know that Mark collected the painting, no, let's say paintings, from Katya. He pays her for the copy, or perhaps she is paid directly from the gallery. We think around fifteen to twenty thousand pounds. That seems to be the going rate for a really good copy of a masterpiece of the type we are looking at here.
He takes the paintings together with the documentation and so on, back to the gallery. Somewhere he switches the crates containing the paintings, with the result that the gallery gets the original back, which they think is the copy, and he arranges for the copy to be despatched to Scarpetti in Italy."
"Or perhaps they don't think it's the copy but actually know it's the original they have back," said Anna.
"Good point."
"Scarpetti hangs it and sometime later, he is led to believe that it might be a copy and has this verified, who wouldn't?" The copy is confirmed and he obviously goes ape. What does he do now? How does this sound so far?"
The team all seemed to be in agreement.
Anna said, "I think this is quite plausible, but what does he do for revenge? He wouldn't do anything himself, he's a Don and they don't get their hands dirty, do they? How about his 'employee'?"
Tom puts his thoughts into the pot. "We know that Yaren has been murdered, so maybe he has sent someone to do the dirty work. It also seems that her connections with the gallery and to Mark and Katya are too much of a coincidence to be anything else, don't they?"
"Right, I think you're pretty well on the mark there Tom, but let's just take this a little further. Let us suppose that this copying scam has been going on for some time, with or without Katya's knowledge, who else could have been conned with a copy and not the real McCoy, what sort of people would buy these?"
"I reckon that they might be politicians," said Anna, "big business people or celebrities. Anyone with money and good taste, and perhaps people without the taste, just loads of cash, who want to show off. There are plenty of those around. Just look at the papers to find the 'tasteless tycoons'. I really don't think some of them would know a real masterpiece from an inkblot."
"Not impressed with celebrities then Anna," said Tom.
"Let's just say that good taste comes from knowledge amongst other things, and some of these so-called 'celebrities' have the IQ of an amoeba."
"What the heck's an 'amoeba' when it's at home?" said Tom.

"Something with an IQ one below yours, Tom," she said with a cheeky grin.
"I'll take that as a compliment then," he said.
"Come on, you two, let's get serious," said Alex. "If Mafia Don sends a 'hit-man' to take revenge, could this 'hit-man' have been the employee who collected the painting because we have to presume he lived in England. The revenge would be on Yaren, as she was the one who completed the sale and possibly was given the money. What did she do with it?" And, not only that, but surely Mrs Harrington-Thorpe or Olive would know about what was going on. Surely she can't have been so naïve as not to know what was going on. She may even be part of the whole scam."
"Maybe she gave it to Mark. We suspect that he has been into drugs and he used this to fund the drugs to be sold on for more profit. But then again, surely if Olive was party to all this, she wouldn't be involved with financing drugs? That seems to be way off the scale of probability for me."
"Possibly, but let's hang on to that thought for now."
"Alice, can you get on to Rebecca at the gallery and see if anyone actually went to Italy to finalise the sale?"
Alice phoned the gallery and spoke to Rebecca, and she was very helpful. Telling Alice that although the Italian buyer had not met Yaren, they had spoken on the phone to clarify some specific questions that he had. Scarpetti had come to London to look for a suitable work to hang in his Tuscan villa collection. He was advised that the painting he had chosen had deteriorated somewhat over the years, especially due to the materials used in the painting which were quite unusual and that they advised him to have it 'cleaned and restored'.
"And these were the points that he discussed with Yaren, over the phone?"
"Yes, and Yaren advised him that the painting should be 'cleaned and restored' to bring out its full beauty and definition."
"And he agreed to this?"
"Yes," said Rebecca. But remember that he never actually met Yaren."
Mental note here, thought Alice. "And how was the payment to be made?"
"After speaking to Yaren, he and I discussed payment and he suggested that this would be made slightly prior to the delivery and to be collected in cash from an address in London.
"Do buyers usually pay that way Rebecca?"
"Actually, no. It did seem a little unusual, but then our buyers often have little 'quirks' as they are sometimes very private people and we never seek to intrude or change their methods."
"But why did it seem strange to you?"
"Well, to be paid in cash is rather unusual, although it does happen, but to be paid before the item has been delivered is certainly different."

"And the money was paid as arranged? Do you have the address of where it was collected from?"
"No, but I believe that Mark actually collected the money as he was in London on business."
And may I ask what the amount was?"
Rebecca said, "We don't usually give out this information, but I suppose in this case it is very different. The amount was £250,000."
'Whew!' thought Alice. "That is a lot of cash to be collected by a 'third party' don't you think Rebecca?"
"Well, as the sale was actually down to Yaren and she agreed to let Mark collect it on her behalf, we thought it was acceptable."
With this, Alice had some serious misgivings regarding this payment. She was thinking that Mark had collected a vast amount of money in cash. Why cash? From an Italian Mafia man? I'll bet he didn't know that he was a Mafia man. Did this amount to 'money laundering'? Where did the cash come from? It didn't really take much of a guess to think of the ways of getting large amounts of cash. Also, how did the money get to 'an address' and why was it not through a bank, for instance? How was it taken from Italy to England? Perhaps there were other ways of arranging for cash. I must have a chat with the DI thought Alice. I must ask how Mark had acquired the money for drugs shipments, although she remembered that it had been suggested that Yaren had allowed this money which Mark had collected, to be used, and this could be the reason why she had been murdered.
She also thought it quite strange that Rebecca had at first, denied knowledge of the connection with Katya and she appeared no to know her. She had now changed her story.

CHAPTER 58

George had stayed very close to Frank after returning from the boat trip which ended up at Lymington Yacht Haven. George wanted the money which he had demanded from Mark, and Frank had been in contact with Olivia (Olive) Harrington-Thorpe. He had told her that he was coming to her house on a very important matter. He would be demanding that she supply a large amount of money to enable the repayment to Scarpetti. This would 'bail out' Mark who was going to have to repay the money for the painting which had been discovered by Tosco Scarpetti to be a fake. The alternative did not bear thinking about as George had already killed both Mark's girlfriend and his close friend Jason. George was a 'Hit-Man' for the mafia and would not hesitate to inflict pain and death in pursuit of his given task from Scarpetti.
Frank had gone to see Olive at her house in Shirley Hills and George had insisted that they should both go so that he would know what was happening and also to 'ensure' that the money would be available. Frank had explained to Olive that one of the 'copied' paintings had been discovered to be a fake and the buyer was not only extremely displeased but he wanted all his money returned 'with interest'. Not only that but as he was a member of the Mafia, he was ensuring that his wish was fulfilled. Since Mark did not have sufficient money available, this was the only way that George could get and take the money to Tosco Scarpetti that he had demanded.
They were in the large house in Shirley Hills that Olive had been living in since her split from Harrington-Thorpe some years ago. The situation was actually quite unusual in that although she and Harrington-Thorpe had separated, they had not actually divorced. This was due to the fact that Olivia didn't want to give up the money which he passed to her on a monthly basis in the form of cash. It appeared that as he made an obscene amount of money from 'dealing' at his merchant bank, he was able somehow to filter off some of this money to offset his tax liability. How this was managed could only be guessed at but the reality was that there was no way in which Olivia would agree to a divorce, whatever he did with whoever he did it. She liked wealth far too much, and her 'monthly' handouts. With her refusal, this 'blackmail' situation would continue.
When Frank had called on Olive, he had George with him. George did not want to let Frank out of his sight to prevent he tried to contact anyone that he thought might compromise him.
Frank said to Olive, "This man is someone you must pay very great attention to. Believe me, I would rather this meeting was not necessary but please listen very carefully and do exactly as I say, because the alternative is not something you would like, trust me

on this. The situation is that this man needs to have £300,000 to take back to Italy to his boss.
"What!" she exploded.
"Now you and I both know that you have made a great deal of money through the sale of 'copies' of paintings which have been passed off as originals. I need to get my hands on this cash in a hurry and don't forget that I know you and your methods. You'll have kept large amounts of cash that won't be in the bank."
"But why should I give anything to you?"
"Simply because one of your paintings which was copied and sold as an original has been discovered by the buyer in Italy. He is not at all happy, to say the least and he has sent this man to collect the money, with interest, I might add. Right now 'I'm not in a position to argue the case. All I can say is that this man is with me to make sure that we get the cash. Oh, and something you might like to think about. This man's boss is a Mafia 'Don' and I think even you know very well what that means.
He let that little piece of information 'sink in'.
"Mark has been dealing and supplying drugs, again something we both know. The problem is that Mark has just lost a great deal of money through several mistakes and that means that he needs funds pretty damned quick."
"But that's not my fault," said Olivia. "You've made a load of money as well from the paintings. This is not my problem."
"Olive, let me put it this way. If you don't come up with this cash right now there are two things that can happen. One is that I will inform the police about the paintings scam and give them a list of the clients who have bought copies thinking they were originals, through your gallery."
She interrupted, "But if you do that you will incriminate yourself, so you can forget that."
"I don't think so. Maybe you think I'm completely stupid, but there will be no link to me whatsoever. There will be no trace of my involvement as everything was done by 'word of mouth' which you know very well cannot be proven. Anyway, that is not the real problem. I know that you have a safe here and I want the key to that."
"No bloody way Frank, that's my money, not yours, and you'll not get any of it. This is my house and everything here is mine."
"Olive, my dear, it's about time you knew some home truths. This house is not actually yours. In fact, it's mine."
She looked incredulous.
"I bought the house and you signed a number of documents at the time. I suspect that you were so overawed at being about to live in a house much bigger and better than you had known before, that you didn't check all the papers properly. One of those papers was actually putting the house solely in my name, so in fact you own nothing. You only stay here because I let you and you obviously pay all the usual expenses as if you were the owner. That's fine by me,

because when it comes to a sale, this is going to be worth a small fortune."
Frank was smiling whilst he said this, but Olive was most certainly not. She had firstly turned as white as a sheet as the information sunk in, and then changed to a rather deep shade of pink when the full import of her situation had dawned on her. She was, for once in her life, thought Frank, speechless.
"You absolutely despicable fucking bastard," she said through gritted teeth. "All this time I've been under the illusion that you had done something decent but the fact is that you were just the same deceitful and cunning shit that you always were."
"There is no need to give me compliments," he said with a grin.
Her 'upper-class' accent had slipped a long way down the scale of 'socially acceptable speech', together with her choice of words.
"Shut the fuck up Frank. You are a disgusting hypocrite and I hope you rot in hell."
"Never mind all this, I want the money which you have stashed away from your banker money-bags. I will tell you that you'll more than likely get it back when Mark gets back on his feet, although it may surprise him to know that his mother has actually bailed him out."
"Don't you dare tell him!" she screamed at him.
"No need to worry, I won't, for now, providing I get the cash. We don't have much time and we need to get back, so get a move on. And the second thing, I'll tell you why you'll give me the money. This man here has actually done something which has convinced me that he will not take 'no for an answer when he says he wants this money."
So far, George had not spoken, simply looked on with a nondescript expression on his face.
"Oh, so what's that then?"
"He has killed two people."
"What!?"she exploded.
"That's what he does for a living for his Italian boss. You have heard of the Mafia?"
"Yes, but I can't believe this. You're making it up."
She looked over at George at this. He looked directly at Olive and his eyes were like steel balls, very hard and direct. His expression now was decidedly 'evil', she thought.
"Madam, I can assure you that Frank is not making this up."
As his words sunk in, she felt as though there was iced water running through her veins.
"Olive, this man has killed Marks' girlfriend and another man who was a friend of Marks."
"Oh my God! What sort of monster are you?"
"It is what I do. I am a professional." As he said this, he pulled out his gun so that Olive could see that he was not bluffing. "I leave no trace of my actions. Nothing can be proved."

When these words had finally sunk in, Olive became extremely fearful. With good reason.
"Perhaps now you understand," Frank continued, "so just go to your safe and get this money before things become more serious. In any case, you can always replace this money with the other paintings that are in the process of being copied. Let me just say this; if there are any complications, the police will be handed a list which I have prepared of all the politicians, celebrities and other so-called 'important' people who have bought your paintings thinking they were the real thing. They will find out that they have worthless copies and I don't think either they or the police will think this very funny. So perhaps you can just get that key and we can be away from here. Nevertheless, perhaps you should consider the alternative which could just as easily happen, Olive. George here is a killer and please believe me when I say that he has absolutely no qualms about doing it again."
Olive had realised by now that she was in a completely untenable situation and the only way would be to hand over the money.
"There is a problem," she said. "I don't have that much cash here. I only have about half that."
"But you can get more; you'll have it in your accounts in the bank Olive. I know you have it."
"I do, but it will take a day or so to get access to that much. They are very cagey about large withdrawals without prior warning."
Frank was not impressed but it was a fair point which he understood. "So call the bank and get the arrangements made and get them to tell you exactly when the funds will be available, in cash. We'll just listen in to make sure that we know what you are saying."
She had no choice but to follow the instructions. All three went to the telephone while she albeit reluctantly made the call.
Calling her bank, she asked to speak to the manager and when he was called to the phone, she said, "This is Mrs Olivia Harrington-Thorpe speaking. I need to withdraw a rather large amount in cash very quickly. Can you arrange this please?"
"And how much do you wish to withdraw Madam?"
"I need three hundred thousand pounds."
There was a definite pause as she said this.
"May I ask the purpose of this withdrawal Mrs Harrington-Thorpe?"
"You may not," she said in her best 'posh voice'.
"I am so sorry and I do not wish to be intrusive, but our procedure tells me that we need to have a particular or specific reason for such a large withdrawal," said the manager.
"Very well, I need this for the purchase of a very special artwork for my gallery. As you know, we often have extremely expensive works and this is one purchase which I need to conclude urgently."
"Very well Madam, I will authorise this, and if you can give me a few minutes I can verify this and when the money will be available."

There was a slight delay before the manager came back to the phone to tell Olivia that this withdrawal had been authorised and he gave her the details of when the funds would be in the branch. Following the conversation, she said, "The money will be available in two days."
Frank then said, "In that case we'll stay here until the cash is available and we can stay with you while you collect it, just to make sure."
Olivia had no choice.
Frank and George would now have to 'sit it out' and be with her continuously to make sure that she did not make any further phone calls or leave the house.
"Olive, give me your mobile phone please," said Frank.
"Why?" she said in a petulant voice.
"Again, you're thinking I'm stupid Olive. I just want to make sure that you don't tell anyone about our presence here, and to make sure, I'll just cut the phone wires. With that, he said to George, "I expect you know more about cutting phone lines that I do, so maybe you'd like to do it?"
"Yes, I'll make sure that we are here 'privately', so I'll put your car in the garage and see to the phone lines. This way, we will be untraceable."
"I thought you'd say that somehow," said Frank. Now Olive, just make sure that we have some food and drink, it's going to be a long two days. Then we'll come with you to the bank and just to be sure that when you're there, please don't think of mentioning our visit to anyone because George will be close by you and I can assure you that blood, especially your blood, will be spilled, and that is after something similar happening to you as happened to Mark's girlfriend."
"Oh yes, and what was that then?" she said with bravado which she didn't feel.
"The word 'torture' is one word I could use but believe me you really do not want to know the details, but it does involve a great deal of pain, or so I understand from Mark after he had seen her body. And that's before he blew the back of her head off."
"Oh my God," said Olive quietly.
George was outside in the process of garaging the car and cutting the phone lines into the house.
"Do you understand Olive? Nothing said, no-one else gets hurt. The money is taken back to Italy and everything can get back to normal."
"I think I understand, but this man is nothing but a monster."

CHAPTER 59

After looking carefully at the CCTV of George on the bridge, 'Gotcha!' said Alex. "Great. Now we know that he went there and all the time slots add up to him being the killer we are looking for. I think you're right about the shoes and that just about clinches it as far as I'm concerned. What I really want to know is where the hell has he been since all this began? He must have been hiding somewhere and I suspect that he's been with Frank Jordan or perhaps Mark. We'll have to mount some surveillance on the Auctions to see if he turns up there again. We know that he went there the night he went on the train, but where the hell has he been since then, and why has he disappeared? I think we might need a brain-storming session to see what ideas we all have."
Alex called for a briefing just after lunch with Tom, Alice and Anna to throw some ideas around regarding the whereabouts of the suspect since the investigation began.
When they were in the main office, he said, "Now this is going to be very quick. To re-cap, we now have confirmation that he went by train from Poole station, where he was dropped off by Bob Parsons after the lift from Lymington, to Christchurch station. He then must have walked to the Marine Auctions buildings, as he had no transport and to confirm this, we now have CCTV pictures of him standing on Tuckton Bridge at exactly the time we expected. This was confirmed by Tom actually walking the route to check for any other cameras."
"So what happened after he was seen on the bridge?" said Alice.
"He just leaped over the railings and disappeared. I think it pretty definite that he went into the Auctions Buildings but we can't confirm this. We are going to get some surveillance organised and try to get him and anyone else, especially Frank Jordan and Mark Jordan together. Then we can start some interviews. I'll get that organised right away. Now, the main reason for getting you all here. What do you think he, the suspect, might have been doing since he was seen on Tuckton Bridge? Any ideas?"
Alice was looking a little pleased with herself.
"I've been on to Rebecca and she gave me a description of the 'employees' who collected the painting and one of them pretty well matches this 'George' character."
"Great. That's confirmation of what we were thinking. It shows that we are on the right track. Tom?"
"Maybe he has some place he can 'doss down' until he can make his escape. He must know that he will be hunted."
"Why would he know that he would be hunted, Tom? Perhaps he doesn't know that we are trying to trace him."
"Yeah, but if he's killed two people, you'd think that he'd be off like a shot and not still in the area."

"Exactly, and that's why I think there must be a very good reason as to why he's still here."
"I think he might have been with Mark," ventured Alice.
"Why's that? Alice."
"Well, we know that Mark is very hard to find as we don't even know where he lives. He goes to London and back very frequently and maybe he has somewhere to keep this bloke out of sight."
"Okay Alice, good point, that's a possibility and we really have to redouble our efforts to find out where Mark actually gets to. I think he must have a place somewhere in this area."
"Anna?"
"I have a feeling that he might be with Frank Jordan. I can't really explain why I think this but Frank lives in this area and we haven't kept a watch on his place but it must be easy to keep someone out of sight in a place such as his house, it's pretty big and private. Also, as we know there is a 'tie-up' somewhere along the line with copied and fraudulent paintings, I think this is all linked to someone discovering a dodgy painting and getting very pissed off and demanding some form of restitution. I know it's all hypothetical at the moment, but the circumstantial evidence is mounting up that someone either came over here from Italy or at least was 'employed' to get this retribution."
"I think you're as close as we can get Anna and that seems to me to be the most likely scenario."
"One more thing guv, I have to wonder about Olivia Harrington-Thorpe's link in all this. After all, she has the gallery, the paintings are copied with the full knowledge of the gallery, and Rebecca let's not forget, and we know that Mark has moved or carried some paintings, so he must be involved in some way. Furthermore, we know that Mark is most likely involved with drugs running to France, thanks to the photos from that 'twitcher' in France who took the photos of the floating bags. That puts him right in the frame and I'm sure we can use this as a lever when we get to see him.
"Good point Anna. Okay I think that's as far as we can go at the moment so the next thing is to actually get Frank and Mark in for an interview to see what they have to say. If we can get the main suspect as well, that would be a bonus but so far he's like the 'Scarlet bloody Pimpernel'."
Alex arranged the surveillance teams to keep watch for as long as they could according to the constraints of their budget to find the ones he wanted.

CHAPTER 60

Thanks to the CCTV data from the cameras at the restaurant near the Marine Auctions, the suspect for the murder was seen crossing the road outside the Riverside Restaurant and heading in the direction of the Marine Auctions. This was after he had travelled from Poole to Christchurch station. With all the information that was to hand, Alex felt that the time was right to make some arrests. He suspected that not only was Mark Jordan involved with the art forgery but it was more than likely that Frank Jordan was linked together with Olive Jordan, as was. More investigations were necessary, but with a suspected murderer on the loose, time was vital in catching this man before he disappeared. Perhaps he thought that he had not been seen after leaving the boat at Lymington and making his escape. However, good police work had discovered the CCTV data which showed him at Poole station and obtaining a ticket to Christchurch, together with the timings and subsequently going back to Tuckton where he leaped over the bridge parapet and disappeared, probably to the Marine Auctions buildings.

Alex told his team that they would keep a close watch on the Marine Auctions as the suspect was believed to be there. "As soon as he is confirmed as being present, we'll close in and make an arrest. It's not going to be possible to make a 'dawn' raid as there'll be no staff there but perhaps he had stayed there overnight, so we'll keep surveillance and keep in radio contact."

At 8 a.m. the next morning, 'Alpha One' and 'Alpha Two' were in position. Alex and Anna were in an unmarked Vauxhall Corsa, parked in the Riverside Restaurant car park and they had a clear view of the entrance to the Marine Auctions. Tom and April were in a similarly nondescript car in Wick Lane, parked in a conveniently clear space overlooking the 'Tea Gardens', but which gave them a clear view of the opposite end of the Marine Auctions buildings. The Firearms Unit were also in a white van parked just ahead of Tom and Alice. Their code name for action was 'Response One'.

Alex and Anna were to be in one car and Alice and Tom in a second. Alex said '"We'll be 'Alpha One' and the other car will be 'Alpha Two'."

"Ooo, goody," said Anna, "just like a TV cop show."

"Will you behave yourself Anna, this is bloody serious."

"I'm sorry, you're right. It's just that we don't do much 'close contact surveillance' with inter-car communications around here, it's usually just routine boring sitting around waiting."

"I know, but this one is really serious. Don't forget he's killed two people and we must assume that he is still armed."

"In that case, shouldn't we have the 'Firearms Unit' on standby, in case things go 'tits up'?"

"I think that was a 'no-brainer Anna. It's all arranged. Can you see that white van just along the road, out of view of the auction buildings?"
Anna craned her head and saw the van. "Yes, I can just see it."
"That's the ARU. They'll be ready as soon as we give them the word. We have a pretty good photo of chummy, so we should be able to spot him if he turns up. Let's hope we're not wasting our time."
"If he doesn't show Alex, at least we can get a coffee. Look behind us, they're opening up."
"Let's keep our minds on the job shall we, and our eyes open?"
"Yes guv. Right, guv. Eyes open guv."
"I may remind you, Sergeant Jenkins that this is a very serious situation, and I am beginning to regret that we are not in separate cars."
"I'm sorry. You're right. I'll behave. It's just that I'm excited."
He gave her a very direct look, saying "There's a time and place to be excited, but just now is not that place, "When the shooting starts, that'll be a good reason to be a little tense, otherwise let's just keep a sharp watch, is that clear?"
Anna was very quiet.
After 8.30 a.m. there was a call on the radio. "Alpha Two to Alpha One."
"Alpha Two, go ahead."
Anna was trying desperately to stifle a giggle.
"Alpha One, Keith has just turned up closely followed by Ben. They came in by the back entrance to the boat shed."
"Alpha Two, copy. Thanks Tom, keep a close watch as we're expecting either Mark or Frank to turn up very soon. Alpha One out."
Alex turned to Anna, who was smirking almost uncontrollably and said, "This is stupid. I know what you mean, I think we'll keep the "Alpha One and Two stuff for another time, don't you?"
"I think you're right Alex, it does seem a bit childish. How about just 'Guv or Tom'?"
"Sounds good to me." Alex then keyed his radio and said, "Tom, we'll just use Tom or Guv, is that okay with you?"
"Sure is Guv. Much easier."
"Right, keep your eyes open then."
"Wilco."
"Oh God, now he thinks he's bloody Biggles!" said Alex.
Anna was chuckling quietly.
"However, 'Alpha One to Response One, are you receiving, over'?"
"Response One to Alpha One, roger that."
With this Anna really burst out laughing.
"I just had to do that, you little minx."
Just then, Alex spotted a Silver Porsche driving into the entrance to the Auction building.
"We're on," said Alex. "That's Mark Jordan."

“Guv to all cars, leave the Porsche alone. That’s Mark Jordan and we leave him for now but keep watch.”
“Tom to Guv, received.”
Alex turned to Anna, "Okay let’s wait and see who else turns up before we get him. At the moment he’s not our number one target. We’ll save him for later when our enquiries have given us some more concrete information. If we take him now, we might miss the other players."
They waited for another hour before Alex said, "I don’t think our suspect is going to show. I wonder if he’s with Frank Jordan at his place. I suppose it’s more than likely that he spent the night there and can make a getaway when he thinks the coast is clear. Let’s give it another half hour and then call it a day. I don’t think he’ll make a run for it in broad daylight, so maybe we’ll mount another surveillance at night.”
After passing on the timing to the other car and the response unit, they decided they would retreat for the day.
As they were leaving, Anna said, "Mind you, we have to find out where Mark goes to. We don’t have an address locally and all we know is that he ‘goes to London’. Maybe he usually stays at Yaren’s flat. We just don’t know. Maybe we’ll have to have him in for interview."
"Reckon you’re right. Shall we go out for a meal or something tonight?"
"Which would you prefer?"
"Both," said Alex, with a grin.
Anna didn’t need to answer.
He called the other cars and told them to stand down and subsequently, they all returned to base with no arrests of suspects.

CHAPTER 61

Some more information had come to light which referred to the possibility of a drugs connection. Apparently a bird-watcher on the shore at Ouisterham had watched the customs boat approach the 'Lady in the Mist' bearing both Mark and Jason on their trip across the Channel with drugs. He had seen the two boats and watched the proceedings with usual curiosity. Then he had seen the white packets floating away from the stern of the boat with Mark and Jason. He thought this to be intriguing and took some photos with his telephoto lens, giving a very clear shot of the packets being carried away towards the open sea on the outgoing tide.
When he got home, he had downloaded the photos he had taken that day and among the shots, he saw the five or six frames of the packets together with the shot which included the 'Lady in the Mist', with her name clearly showing together with the packets which were very close to the stern.
He realised that this was something which was possibly of interest to the Customs as they were obviously investigating that boat for some reason and he assumed that it was to do with checking craft from illegal cigarettes or drink and perhaps drugs. He simply thought that he would do his duty as a 'citizen' and report this, so he loaded the relevant pictures to a 'memory stick' on his computer and the next morning, went to the local Gendarmerie.
There he explained how and where he had taken these photographs and because the camera automatically records the full details of time, date and all relevant camera details, they were of the opinion that the Customs would be interested.
This was indeed the case when the photos were looked at by the Port Customs Officers. They recognised that the packets were probably drugs, either Heroin or Cocaine. They were instantly suspicious and because the boat was English, the information and suspicions which they had were communicated to their colleagues in England at the UK Border Control Office in Southampton. They correctly surmised that the boat 'Lady in the Mist' had come from the South Coast of England. The UK Small Ships Register of the UK government contained all the details of boats under 25 metres and a simple search of that register by the English Customs soon revealed that the 'Lady in the Mist' was registered to an owner based in London. His name was Michael Fortune and Alex phoned him.
"Good morning Mr. Fortune. My name is Detective Inspector Vail and I am currently involved in an investigation and we believe that you own a boat which is currently berthed at the Marine Auctions in Christchurch. Is that correct?"
"Yes, it is a Jeanneau cruiser, called 'Lady in the Mist.'"
Alex was actually trying to hide a small smile over the previous reference to Fortunes' 'companions' when he went out on his boat during his visits to Christchurch. The boat was colloquially renamed

as 'Lady on the Piss' due to the state of some of his female passengers.
"And have you given permission for this boat to be taken to France recently on a demonstration run as I believe your boat is up for sale at the Auctions?"
"The only time the boat can be taken out is for a short demonstration run and the auctions must seek my permission for this and I have certainly not received a request for this. But why are you asking me these questions, has the boat been stolen or something?"
"No Sir, the boat is at the auctions but we do believe that it has recently made a trip to France as it was seen and photographed at Ouistreham and we are trying to find the reason for this. We thought that perhaps you had some knowledge of this, which is why we have contacted you."
"There is no way I would sanction a trip to France for whatever reason. Thank you for letting me know. I will be down to the auctions to inspect the boat for any damage as soon as I can."
"That would be a good idea sir," said Alex as he bade Mr Fortune goodbye.

CHAPTER 62

Subsequently, the police at Bournemouth were contacted and the details revealed by the photographs were transmitted to them by the French Customs.
Alex received this information and immediately called Anna to his office.
Anna walked in and saw that Alex was actually beaming. "Just look at these Anna and tell me what you think they are."
Anna bent over and took a close look at the various photos on the desk and chose the one showing the boat called "Lady in the Mist" with the packets floating close behind. She looked up at Alex and said, "I'm pretty sure that they could be packets of drugs which have been thrown over the side from that boat being approached by the customs boat. I can't think that they'd be anything else, can you?
"That's exactly what I thought Anna. I bet you can't guess where that boat came from."
"Don't tell me that it came from the Marine Auctions."
"Abso-bloody-lutely! I've checked with the Small Ships Register and they confirmed that the owner, a Michael Fortune lives in London. He has already been contacted and confirms that this boat is, or was at the auctions, but he had not given permission for it to be taken across the channel. Do you realise the implication of this Anna?"
"I think I do. If that boat was taken from the auctions without permission and if those packets were drugs, which can only mean that a person or persons from the auction have taken at least one or possibly more trips to France to deal in drugs."
"I think you're spot on there. I've been giving this a little more thought and it occurs to me that If we link up other factors, then perhaps, just perhaps Mark is involved not only with the paintings scam but if he were using the money from that to finance drugs, then this could be the motive we've been looking for. Maybe the killer is linked to a person who had bought a painting which was found to be fake, who wanted some restitution or other and traced it back to the place it came from. Yaren was employed at the gallery who sold a dodgy painting, they found out where she lived and went there to get some money back. We know the rest. The connections are beginning to click into place, don't you think?"
"It all sounds very plausible Alex. We know that the mystery man is probably the one who killed Yaren; in fact we are almost certain. And, Mark is connected with the paintings as he has moved some of them, then who is best placed to do the 'swopping' of copies for the real ones?"

"Also, Anna, let's assume that this is the case, then he has had access to a great deal of money. Now if that money has been used to purchase drugs, that he's then taken them across the channel to sell on, we can see that there must be collusion between the various parties."
"Yes, he has, but why was Yaren tortured and killed?"
"Well, we know that a painting was fairly recently shipped to Italy, through the Gallery. Do we know who this Italian buyer was or what he was?"
We know that this painting was bought by Tosco Scarpetti, who is a known mafia 'Don' and he lives in a villa in Tuscany. If perhaps he's found out that the painting is a copy and not an original, he's going to be very unhappy, wouldn't you say?"
"Actually Anna, I'd say that he'd be extremely 'pissed off', to say the least, and we know what the Mafia can do. Let's assume that this 'Don' wanted some revenge or restitution, how would he do that? I would imagine that he'd have someone who could 'request' the money back or some form of restitution, someone who would do the 'dirty-work' so that his hands stay clean. After all, that's how they work I believe."
"So, do you think he sent someone over here to do that and that person goes to the person who sold him the painting to get the money paid returned to the buyer?"
"I think that's a very distinct possibility Anna, but perhaps this person was already here?"
"So this person comes here, and we know that a strange phone call to Rebecca at the gallery was asking for Yaren's address which she obtained authorisation for and subsequently goes to see Yaren. And could he possibly be the mafia 'employee' who lives in England who took the painting in the first place?"
"Another strong possibility."
"She says she hasn't got the money. Why hasn't she got the money, where has it gone?"
"Now we bring Mark back into the equation. Let's say that he has used the money to buy some drugs which he takes to France for selling on. Yaren doesn't have the money so she can't give it to the Mafia man. He probably won't take that and tries to persuade her to tell him where the money is. She can't or won't tell him, so he tortures her but still she can't tell him. He's running out of ideas, loses his temper because he can't find any money."
"And," said Anna, "he ransacks the flat so he probably thought it was hidden there somewhere, but can't find it. Even more annoyed."
"To the point at which he kills her."
"So what next?"
"We just don't know that, but supposing she has told him about Mark, you know where he is or might be, that would give us a link down to Christchurch wouldn't it?"

"Yes," said Anna, "that would make sense. But then there's a body which will be found. How would that link down to Christchurch?"
"It wouldn't at first, but once a link is made if the killer turns up looking for Mark, there will be a traceable connection with the body which any police investigation will turn up. It follows then, that the body will have to be 'disposed of', or they'll find out how everything is connected and the people involved will inevitably talk. I'm sure that anyone capable of killing on the orders of someone else is going to want himself, or herself for that matter, kept very secret and they'll take all precautions to keep their head down."
"Right Alex, if what you say is true or even partially true, how do we find this person? We have traced the man who dumped the boat at Lymington and who undoubtedly shot the unnamed person on that boat, and who very probably dumped the body in the harbour, to someone who got a lift from there back to Poole and then back again to Christchurch. He was seen going into the Marine Auctions but since then, we've had no sight of him. So where's he been hiding? Maybe he's gone back to Italy or wherever he comes from, we just don't know. Also, how did the body get back to Christchurch? Did Mark bring her as he would have probably found her?"
"As you say Anna, and a question which needs answering."
"As this 'George' is tied up with these murders, we can assume that he is known to or known by either Mark or Frank Jordan or both. In that case, if it were me, I would make sure that as I'm still trying to get restitution or repayment, that either one or both would be 'lent on' very heavily to cough up the money. He must think that as Yaren didn't have it, then her boyfriend did. And who's that but Mark?"
Anna then looked up and, holding one finger in the air, said, "And how about these photos taken at Caen. This only happened recently didn't it? Supposing the boat had been carrying what we think are packets of drugs, to France, to be sold. We know the boat came from the Marine Auctions and we know that Mark had just been to France on this boat, and crossing the Channel would be nothing to them. If that's the case and obviously the drugs were not meant to be in the sea, then they've been lost somehow. If all the drugs had been either lost or dumped overboard because of the Customs boat, then money from the sale would have been lost."
"Great!" said Alex, "Another piece of the jigsaw pops into place. Good thinking Anna. They wouldn't be taking just a few quid's worth of drugs over there, probably multi-thousands of pounds worth. If they were lost or dumped, then they'd be very short of readies to hand. Chummy comes looking for a refund of a big lump of money which ain't there and it doesn't take much to imagine the outcome."
"So what would come next?"
"I'd say that someone has to cough up the money PDQ or more heads will roll, wouldn't you?"

"And if and when he’s got it, what does he do now? He gets it back to his boss as soon as he can I suppose," said Anna.
"Right. And what’s the best way, given that he doesn’t want to leave any clues?"
"Cross the Channel again, probably by night, no-one sees him, he’s not gone through any Border Control points. He doesn’t exist."
"Exactly Anna. Now I think he is still in the country and about to do just what you’ve suggested. This time we have to put an ‘all-night’ surveillance on the Auctions because that is where he will no doubt leave from. We know that he’s more than likely to be based there now. We’ll get him this time."

CHAPTER 63

Alex called Anna to his office. "Anna, I want you to call Rebecca and ask her to come here for an interview. Do you think she'll come?"
"I don't see why not but I think she might ask for 'transport' as it's quite a way from Wimbledon."
"I suppose you have a point. I think she might just drop some of her 'hoity-toity' voice knowing that we know she actually comes from lesser beings and give us some good information regarding these paintings. I'm sure she knows more than she lets on. Do you have those feelings Anna?"
"I do. I'm sure that there is far more to these 'copies' than is evident at the moment."
"Right then, get her booked in for an interview and arrange the transport if you will. In the meantime, I think I'll do the same for Olivia Harrington-Thorpe, better known to us now as 'Olive'. I am, absolutely certain that she knows a damn sight more than she has told us. Not only whose house it is but why she has been in touch with Frank so often, and why Mark doesn't know that she's his mother. That's very strange to say the least."
"For sure, that's going to be interesting Alex."
Anna called Rebecca.
"Rebecca, this is DS Anna Jenkins from Bournemouth Police. You will remember we have met before."
"Yes, of course. How can I not forget the news you brought of the death of Yaren. She was a lovely person and she will be sadly missed. Have you found the person who killed her?"
"I am sorry to say that we have not completed our enquiries at the moment but we are getting very close to finalising everything. We have to cover every avenue and consequently, I have to ask you if you will attend the Bournemouth Police Station for an interview as soon as possible please."
"But what can I tell you that you don't already know?" she said.
"I know this is inconvenient but as I say, we have to cover everything in great detail and there are a few questions which we have to ask you for our records."
"But it is a long way for me to have to travel. Can you not conduct the interview here?"
"Unfortunately, it has to be done with a recorded statement at the station, so that everything is verified and nothing is missed or misconstrued. I am sure you understand how these things work. We will of course supply a car to bring you here and take you back when we have concluded the interview."
"You make it sound very serious. Should I be worried?"
"Not at all, it is simply procedure."
"Very well, I will arrange this with Mrs. Harrington-Thorpe. I'm, sure she will understand."
"Would it be possible for you to arrange this for your day off and not to inform Mrs Harrington-Thorpe, It may be better that way?"

"Well, possibly. My day off would be better I suppose. It would save having to ask her as she is rather 'tetchy' about such things and I would rather she didn't know that I was 'helping police with their enquiries' if you see what I mean."
"I think that would be a very good idea. We can make the arrangements right now if you don't mind, then we can get on."
"Of course."
The interview was set for the next day as it was actually a scheduled 'day off' for Rebecca.
A car was arranged to go to collect Rebecca.
While Anna's call was progressing, Alex had actually phoned Mrs Harrington-Thorpe and to his surprise, she was at home.
She answered his call with, 'Good afternoon, this is Mrs Harrington-Thorpe speaking. May I ask who is calling?" Her accent did not quite match with what Alex actually knew of her background. She seemed quite 'polished' but he let that be as it may. For now.
"Good afternoon. I am Detective Inspector Alex Vail from Bournemouth Police. We are making enquiries and we would like you to attend an interview here at Bournemouth Police station so that we may ask you some questions relating to our enquiry."
"Why on earth would I be asked to answer questions relating to a crime in Bournemouth?" Alex knew from her tone of voice and the way she had already assumed that it was 'crime related', that she was rattled.
"I did not mention a crime, madam, but we do have some serious questions which need to be answered here with us. Are you able to come to Bournemouth Police station in the very near future?"
He sensed that she was already "on her guard" as she mentioned ""crime"".
"But I don't understand why you are asking me Inspector."
We understand that you own the Arcadian Art Gallery in Wimbledon. Is that correct?"
"Yes, that is correct," she said, the tone of her voice rising a little. "But what is it to do with my gallery?"
She's getting really rattled, thought Alex. I'll just let her stew on this for a while. The more unsettled she is, the more she is likely to make a mistake, especially when she finds out what we know.
"Then you are the person we need to speak to regarding our enquiries. We will explain everything. Are you able to make your own way here or should we send a car for you?"
Alex thought that perhaps she wouldn't want to be seen in a police car, in case her neighbours saw her and then she might be asked some awkward questions.
He was right. "If I must, I will make my own way there. I have no wish to travel in some a police car which probably smells of cigarette smoke, or worse," she said, her haughty voice returning.
"As you wish madam. In that case, can you come in tomorrow morning? Would that be convenient for you?"

"Actually it is most inconvenient; however, I will change my important arrangements and make my way there tomorrow. It will have to be in the afternoon. The morning will be most impossible."
Alex was thinking, I'm sure it would be. I bet you don't get up until late and probably spend the morning pampering yourself.
"Tomorrow afternoon will be fine thank you. We will expect you sometime in the early afternoon."
"This is most inconvenient Inspector. I do hope there is nothing wrong with my gallery."
"As I say madam, we will explain everything when we see you tomorrow, thank you."
"Very well, goodbye."
'Goodbye to you Mrs. Harrington-Thorpe. Olive'.

CHAPTER 64

Rebecca was duly brought to the station by police car from her address in Wimbledon. Her interview would be conducted by Anna. When she arrived, she was taken to an interview room where the décor was, to say the least, Spartan. There were two plastic chairs on one side of a Formica covered table with metal legs. This was screwed to the floor, a point which Rebecca had noticed as she entered the room. She looked around with distaste.
"Why am I in this room? It is horrible, I feel like a criminal." She had also noticed that there was a recording machine on one end of the table. "And that makes it worse," she said.
"I really am sorry Rebecca, but this is the only room we have available right now. The others are being used for rather more serious matters. We only need to ask you some questions and we have to take a recording of this interview just so that everything is on record and there are no mistakes or misinterpretations. I hope you understand this."
"Am I under arrest or something?"
"Of course not. We just have to clarify some points which are part of our enquiries about an ongoing situation. Now, if you are ready, we can begin."
"Yes, carry on."
Anna pushed the appropriate buttons on the recording equipment and said, "This is an interview with Miss Rebecca Connors, employed at the Arcadian Art Gallery in Wimbledon. Present is Detective Sergeant Anna Jenkins".
"Now Rebecca, you are Miss Rebecca Connors, employed by the Arcadian Gallery in Wimbledon?"
"Yes."
"And your duties at the gallery?"
"I manage the gallery and see to most of the day-to-day running. I also make arrangements for exhibitions and for the forthcoming works to be put up for sale. I also arrange for some paintings to be moved to other galleries."
"And why are they moved to other galleries?"
"Sometimes the paintings might be in one place for too long and our customers really don't like to see the same works being shown for too long a period. They can be exchanged with other galleries so that customers see changing works."
"I understand. I believe also that your gallery undertakes to have paintings "cleaned and restored", is that correct?"
"That's right. When a painting has been sold, the customer is sometimes asked and sometimes they ask, to have the painting either cleaned or restored, depending on the condition."
"And who does this work, the gallery?"

"Heavens, no. It is far too specialised for us to undertake. We have a highly skilled artist and restorer who does this. She is a lady from Turkey called Katya."
"Do you have her surname?"
"Katya Sadik."
"Thank you. Does Katya only clean and restore paintings or does she do other things as well?"
"What do you mean, 'other things'?"
"I mean, is she an artist in her own right, or is she just a 'technician'?"
"Oh no, she is a very talented and competent artist in her own right."
"And does she produce her own paintings for sale in the gallery?"
"Sometimes, yes."
"And does she sell them for a very high price?"
"I think that is for her to tell you, not me. I'd rather keep that information private if you don't mind."
"That's okay Rebecca, I understand. So does Katya do anything else for the gallery?"
"What sort of thing do you mean?"
"I think you know what I mean Rebecca," said Anna, giving her an unblinking stare while she said this and the look on Rebecca's face became very different. She knew very well what Anna was getting at. She was silent as she considered her reply.
"I think you know very well what I mean Rebecca. I'd like you to tell me what other things Katya does for the gallery."
Rebecca was very uncomfortable now. She was now thinking that there was no point in keeping things quiet as from the way that Anna had spoken and the look she had given, meant that the police probably knew anyway.
She said, "Sometimes Katya did make a copy of an original painting."
"And what happened to the copy after it was completed?"
"The copy was put back in the gallery where it was kept in storage for a considerable time."
"And the original sold I presume?"
"Yes."
"And why was the copy kept in storage?"
"I would have thought that was obvious. A customer who has just bought an original really doesn't want to see the same work in the same gallery straight away. It would be rather like buying an expensive designer dress that cost a great deal of money, only to see the same design of dress in TK Maxx the next day."
Anna completely understood this. "I can see your point, she said with a wry smile."
Rebecca said, earnestly, "You know it is not illegal to make a copy of a painting."
"But that is providing that the fact that it is a copy is made to clear to the possible purchaser."

"But of course, otherwise it would be fraud."
"Exactly," said Anna. "Did Katya get paid a lot of money for making a copy?"
"Again, that is something that I am not at liberty to divulge. It is her business and to be quite honest, I really don't know what sort of payment she receives."
"And yet it would be the gallery who paid her, is that correct?"
"It would, but that would be completed by Mrs Harington-Thorpe."
"I see, so when a painting has been copied, the original goes back to the gallery. How is that taken?"
"Sometimes it comes by a shipping company who usually move our paintings. They are very reliable and careful. Some of the works we sell are enormously valuable. Also, sometimes we send this on to other galleries to be displayed."
"And other times?"
"Sometimes they are brought by someone else."
"Someone else? Who would the 'someone else' be? Can you give me a name?"
"Sometimes it was the boyfriend of Yaren"
"Would that be Mark?"
"Yes, he brought them sometimes."
"I am still in shock over Yaren and the fact that she was murdered, it was so terrible."
"Yes, I am sorry about Yaren. It was a horrible way to die."
I was never told how she died. Why was it a horrible way?"
"I really shouldn't say this, but she was tortured before she was shot."
"Oh my God, but that's so awful."
"Indeed it was, but as Yaren was employed by the gallery, you can see why there is a link to our investigation and why we have to ask all these questions, to find anything that can give us a clue as to the killer and why she was murdered. Now can we get back to Yaren's boyfriend?"
"Yes, Mark. Sometimes he would collect the copied painting and bring it back to the gallery. He was often in London and it did save a great deal of time and expense with the shipping company."
"And how was the painting protected?"
"It was usually in a wooden crate. We use a crate which is quite a standard design and is the normal way of protecting something so valuable. It is completely sealed so that it can withstand being moved around."
"So that no-one could tell what was inside the crate?"
"No. The only way one would know would be by the documentation which was attached to the crate giving details of owners, addresses, recipients' etcetera."
"And would there be any other documents with this crate?"
"Perhaps a sealed envelope with an Authentication Certificate."
Anna was getting somewhere.

"Let me suggest a possibility to you Rebecca. If an original painting had been copied and both the copy and the original were crated in the same way, would it be possible for them to be 'swopped' so that the copy was actually sent to the person who had bought the original?"
"No, of course not!" That would be impossible. This document would be properly attached to the crate in such a way as to be secure.
"Are you absolutely sure? If both crates looked identical, then surely it would be possible to exchange them at some point?"
"Well, that could only happen if someone who is...not...our...usual...carrier..."she said slowly, obviously realising the possibility of the Authentication Certificate Document being 'switched'.
"Do you mean, if the carrier were not the ones you usually use?
"Yes. And now you put it like that, the only person who could do this would be Mark, Yaren's boyfriend. He is the only one who has carried paintings of ours for about two years now. Will this get him into trouble?"
"That depends entirely on what we uncover about copies and originals and the opportunity to possibly exchange paintings. On our previous meeting, you did say that there was 'Something about Mark' that you couldn't quite place. Can you expand on that for me?"
"Well, not really, because I didn't see that much of him. He never stayed long enough to actually 'chat', if you know what I mean. He was usually in some sort of a hurry and just dashed in and dashed out again."
"But what was your impression of him as a person?
"As I say, I didn't know him at all well and as he is not my type of man, I never tried to engage with him. Although I can say that I had just a feeling that he might have been a little difficult to reach, if you know what I mean."
"Can you expand on that, I mean how do you mean 'reach'?
"As a woman, I'm sure you understand that intuition can form some sort of idea but nothing that can be too solid if one doesn't talk with that person, so it is very difficult to form a proper view."
"I think I understand but you have not any factual things which you can state about Mark?"
"No, it would not be correct to do that. In fact, no, there is nothing I can truthfully say against him, I only know that Yaren had said in the past that he has a quick and sometimes quite aggressive temper, but then she also said that she did as well which led to some quite heated 'exchanges' between them."
Anna wondered if these 'exchanges' were the result of his business dealings or connected with them.
"Very well Rebecca, I think that is all I have to ask you for now. If you do think of anything that has happened recently or even over a period of time, that does not seem quite right, in the light of what

you know now and the possibilities raised, then please give me a call."
"I will of course."
"Oh, there is just one other thing. Did Mrs Harrington-Thorpe know of the copies that were made of these originals?"
"Do you know, I imagine that she had to know that a work was being copied, and as she handled the payment for them. I only handled the sale and the documentation, delivery and so on."
Anna already knew that Katya did not seem to either know or care what happened once the copy had been made and it was also known that Mark had taken the copies in his car, presumably to the gallery, but perhaps he was forwarding the copy to the buyer, what they thought was the original.
Now that was very interesting. If Olivia Harrington-Thorpe knew of this, then a lot of links were beginning to come together.
"Thank you for coming in Rebecca. I'll call for the car to take you back to Wimbledon. If you could just wait in this horrible room just a moment longer, your car will be ready. I'm sorry it must have ruined you day off, but as I'm sure you're aware, this is most important and we need all the information we can get regarding the death of Yaren."
Anna then said, 'Interview with Rebecca Connors terminated at 12.02 p.m'. Anna left the room, rather pleased that all that was on tape and she could let Alex listen if he wanted, just to bring certain facts together.

CHAPTER 65

Alex knew certain facts about Olivia Harrington-Thorpe. For instance, she was formerly 'Olive Jordan', married to Frank Jordan. They had divorced some 10 years previously and had subsequently married Jonathan Harrington-Thorpe, a city trader, separating after 5 years of their marriage.
Olive was actually Mark Jordan's mother although Mark had no idea. He had been told at a very early age that his mother had died in a car accident and Mark had accepted this. Olive really should not have borne a child as she was very selfish and could not cope with nursing a baby. She left the marriage very soon after the birth with Frank having a 'nanny' to raise Mark mostly, although latterly, he and Frank had become very close. They both raced large powerboats, but even though Frank had a lot of money from his past as a 'scrap dealer', powerboat racing was exceedingly expensive and both he and Mark had found ways of filling their bank accounts. Mark through drug dealing and recently, art fraud and Frank through various so-far unknown methods, although collusion was suspected.
Olivia Harrington-Thorpe arrived at Bournemouth Police Station at about 3 p.m. Her car number was relayed to Alice for her to link to Traffic Division to trace via their database of any traces of her travelling to or from Christchurch from her address in Shirley Hills, during the past year. When Alice had asked her contact at Traffic to do a search for this information, she was greeted with a derisive snort. 'You must be joking Alice, you little sweetie.' This annoyed Alice intensely, but she knew that the information was quite integral to this investigation, so she said, "Don't call me sweetie, you little shit. I'll report you if I hear that again. That's sexist harassment. It's just a good job that I know you Fred, or you'd be in for a bollocking from your boss."
She and Fred had both worked in the same department some years ago, so the exchange was quite light hearted, but Alice really had meant every word.
"Okay love, I'll see what I can do," said Fred.
"And don't call me 'love' either."
"Sorreee."
Olive, as Alex now thought of her, was shown into the same interview room as Rebecca. Olive almost literally turned her nose up as she looked around the room. She noticed the tape recorder unit and looked hard at Alex.
"And what is that for? She asked.
"It is part of procedure Mrs Harrington-Thorpe. It is an important part of our information gathering and it ensures that nothing is either missed or misconstrued. You will understand that as one of

your employees has been murdered recently, and the connection with your gallery, as you are the owner, makes it imperative that we have correct information."
Her so-called 'upper-class' accent had been 'acquired' as had Frank Jordan's, according to Anna's observations.
Switching on the tape recorder, he said, "This interview is taking place in the presence of Detective Inspector Alex Vail of Bournemouth Police and Mrs Olivia Harrington-Thorpe. Do you agree to this interview being recorded, Mrs. Harrington-Thorpe?"
"Yes. I have nothing to hide, so please go ahead."
"Very well, thank you. You are Mrs. Olivia Harrington-Thorpe, divorced from Jonathan Harrington-Thorpe, now living in Bishops Walk, Shirley Hills, Surrey?"
"No, we are separated not divorced."
"You are the owner of an art gallery in Wimbledon, Surrey, called 'Arcadian Gallery'?"
"Yes."
"Prior to your marriage to Mr Harrington-Thorpe you were Mrs. Olive Jordan, having been divorced from Mr. Frank Jordan?"
Olivia went deathly white. She said, "What do you mean?"
"I mean that we know that you were divorced from Frank Jordan some 10 years ago and that you were married to Mr. Harrington-Thorpe for some five years."
"My God. You have been into my private life. That is scandalous, that is unacceptable."
"I have to tell you that as we are investigating the murder of one of your employees, namely one Yaren Ganim, our investigations have to include all avenues which may have some bearing on this crime. I am sure you can understand that?"
"I understand this but surely it is an intrusion into my private affairs?"
"Unfortunately, when it comes to murder, we have to uncover all the facts which may be relevant but I can assure you that we do not divulge any details which are not related to the facts of this case."
"If I can be sure that my private life will not be put in the hands of the press."
"You have my word that we will not divulge any details unrelated to this investigation."
"Very well."
Alex thought, 'We won't divulge them, but it's a pretty fair bet that the press will get their slimy little hands on some tasty bits of information through other means, in the same way as we've found them, in the public domain if they look hard enough'.
"To continue; in the course of business at your gallery, you sell some very highly priced works of art to 'influential' customers both here and abroad, is that correct?"
"We do indeed. Some of our customers are highly regarded politicians and we also have many celebrities."
This was said in a very condescending tone.

Alex really felt like 'putting her in her place'. "By 'celebrities', do you mean some people who are in the public spotlight, such as singers, actors and television personalities; those people who often spout ill-informed rubbish which is then reported in certain newspapers, whose journalists seem to have lost the ability to either spell correctly or use grammar let alone actually report true facts?"
"I take it that you don't have a very high regard for celebrities?"
"Forgive me, I deal in facts and correct information, that is my job and I follow this to the best of my ability. You are right in thinking that I don't think much of celebrities or reporters. Their reports seem biased, full of inconsistencies and ill-informed opinion, so, no I don't. My opinions aside, I have digressed. These 'celebrities' for want of a better description, do they buy expensive paintings?"
"Sometimes yes, because they amass a great deal of money sometimes and some of them actually want to invest this money where it will appreciate in value."
"So would you say that they buy paintings for the possible value increase rather than their appreciation of the work and the skill of the artist?"
"I think that is certainly the case sometimes. They usually ask the price before discussing the artist of the integrity of the work."
"And do you know these facts, such as the artist or their history and their work, their inspiration and so on?"
"I must be honest, I don't know enough to give opinions on these expensive works, I just leave that to the people who do, such as Yaren and Rebecca."
"I must ask you for a complete list of sales of high priced original paintings which have been copied and the documentation accompanying them, covering let's say the last three years."
"Why on earth would you need these details?" Olive had become a little nervous now and her demeanour had changed somewhat. She was definitely on the defensive thought Alex. That's shaken her tree, especially at the mention of 'copied'.
"Just part of the investigation as I have said. You must be very sad that Yaren is no longer with you."
"Yes, I was absolutely devastated when Rebecca told me. I couldn't believe it. To be murdered, that is so terrible and one cannot begin to guess why she was killed like that. What possible reason would there be?"
"That is what we intend to find out and who did it, to bring them to justice. Also to uncover all the details surrounding the motive. We have many different avenues of approach and we need to link these up to form a coherent train of events and reasons to take this case to a satisfactory conclusion, as I am sure you appreciate."
"Of course."
"One other thing, we know that Katya Sadik is a skilled artist and she is the person who has copied a number of original paintings for you. Is that correct?"
Olive realised that denial would be fruitless.

"Yes. She has copied a number of these. I don't know how many. She also cleans and restores works of high value.
'I'll bet you do know how many', thought Alex. "We can ask Katya, as she will have full details of them I'm sure. Can you tell me what happens to the copy once she has done them?"
"They are taken back to the gallery."
"And what happens to them then, are they put back on display for instance?"
"Heavens no, if they were put back on display directly, and spotted by the purchaser of the original, they would not be very happy to say the least, so the copy is either put into store for future sale or perhaps passed to another gallery at a distance or perhaps in another part of the country where there would be less chance of that happening."
"I see that it would be rather inconvenient." Alex was thinking, yes, and let the possibility of a fake being discovered become less and less and then the 'exchanged' original be sold on, perhaps overseas. Who knows how that part of the art market works, it's sure to be kept rather quiet.
Alex changed tack somewhat now. There were details that he knew that Olive didn't know that he knew and he was about to exploit these details to put her on the 'wrong foot'.
"Moving on, can I ask who owns the house that you live in? Is it yours or does it belong to Mr. Harrington-Thorpe?"
"It is mine. It was bought when I was married to Frank. Jonathan knows it was mine when we married."
Here we go, thought Alex. "Our enquiries show that the house you now live in is actually owned completely by Frank Jordan."
He was right. Olive went as white a sheet. It's mine, mine," her voice rising considerably.
This outburst confirmed to Alex the impression that had been mentioned that she was very selfish and self-consumed.
"I have to tell you that it is indeed the case that the deeds are held in totality by Mr Frank Jordan, who now lives in Sandbanks, Dorset."
Olive then said between tightly closed teeth, "I know where he lives, the bastard. He lied to me all those years ago and I've been living there thinking that the house was mine. Anyway, he said it was mine and I could live in it when we divorced?"
"We have confirmation from the Land Registry that the deeds do indeed state that he has full title and the documents referring to this were actually signed by you."
Her demeanour had changed completely and it did seem as though she were back in the 'scrap yard' days. She said in a venomous voice, "The scheming shit. He must have got me to sign something together with all the other documents I had to sign when we divorced. I was confused and it was a bad time. He has taken advantage of me. I'll see the fucker in hell for this!"
'Her 'upper class' accent and demeanour had taken a sudden downturn', thought Alex.

He let her simmering hate settle just a little, while she took this information in. After all, she seemed to have lost what she thought was her 'pension', not to mention her control.
Again Alex changed tack. "We understand that you have been communicating with Frank Jordan by telephone many times and fairly frequently over the past two years. Furthermore, we have CCTV evidence of your car travelling the same route and for just a short time. This suggests to us that you have been actually meeting Mr Jordan on numerous occasions.
"No we haven't," she said hastily.
"We have telephone records that show there have been a great many telephone calls between your two telephone numbers, together with the dates and times and duration of the calls."
Once again, the wind was taken out of her sails. She said, "Well we may have spoken occasionally. Perhaps I was asking about Mark."
"Mark, why would you talk about Mark? We understand that you have had nothing to do with him since his birth. We understand that you left the marriage when he was very young and did not want to bring up a child. Is that the case?"
"This is totally unacceptable; you have been snooping into my private life. I will sue!"
"Unfortunately, when it comes to a crime as serious as murder, no stone is left unturned, as you have just found out."
"Well, it is true, but I still take an interest in him and what he does."
Mrs Harrington-Thorpe, or should I call you Olive, I am of the opinion that you not only take an interest in him, albeit that he perhaps doesn't know that you are his mother, but that you are involved together with Frank Jordan and Mark, to have copied original paintings 'exchanged' and the copy then sold to buyers who think they have purchased an original."
"She blustered, "How dare you suggest that I am dishonest. The gallery is perfectly legitimate."
"I'm sure the gallery is legitimate as you say, but it our belief that behind the façade of this, paintings are switched around by either you or Frank or Mark and then sent to the new buyer who is completely unaware of the fraud. The painting is accompanied by an 'Authentication Certificate', which itself is correct, but is not with the correct work which was purchased. With the list of customers which we have, we will suggest that these people have their purchases re-examined by experts, and then we will know the true situation. I think a great deal of money has been made and this in turn may provide a motive for far more serious crimes to take place and when this information is to hand, we can discover where the large sums of money actually are. Do you understand just how serious this is?"
Olive now realised that she was in really deep trouble and the trail of deception would be uncovered. After what she had just learned from Alex regarding her house and the deception of Frank, she was determined to make sure that he would suffer just as much as she

might, if not more. During the course of her marriage to Harrington-Thorpe, she had made friends of a number of very 'high-flying' legal people and she would turn to them as soon as she could.
"That it all for now Mrs Harrington-Thorpe, although perhaps we should call you by a different name, but that is your choice. Thank you for your time. We may well need to interview you again, so please be available and we will contact you in due course. We will inform the Surrey Police of our interest so that they are aware of the situation. Thank you for your time."
'Interview completed at 3.50 pm.'
Olive left the station a much more subdued person than when she arrived.

CHAPTER 66

George Manion had returned to the Marine Auctions and was together with Frank and Mark. Unbeknown to them, the police had seen CCTV date showing Manion about to enter the Auction buildings after returning from Christchurch station. They were waiting for their chance to find him but so far had been unable to catch him there. Frank and George had actually gone to Shirley Hills to see Olive and had returned two days later, as had Mark. As the police surveillance had not had sight of them after waiting for a long time on the previous surveillance, they had given up and returned to the station, with the intention of returning again to try to catch the 'unknown' suspect whom they now called 'George' and Frank Jordan. Mark had been nowhere to be seen during this time as he had been to a friends' house to keep out of sight.
They were sitting in Frank Jordans" office and Manion said, "Now you have the money, I want you to take me to France. You will have a fast boat available. You can take this and we can be in France in a short time. This way, there will be no trace of me and I can get the money to Scarpetti then the matter will be resolved. I will return to England in due course and you will never see me again. Everything will be settled."
Mark thought to himself, 'You may think so pal, but don't you be so sure. You killed my girlfriend and my best friend and you calmly say 'everything will be settled'. He didn't know how, but he was desperately trying to think of a way seeking retribution for these callous murders.
"What, so now you want me to be a taxi-driver so that you can get away? said Mark.
"Exactly Mark. It will be easy for you because you are used to crossing the Channel, are you not? You have made many journeys with your drugs trafficking I understand."
"How the hell do you know that?"
"I didn't, but as you have not denied it and asked how I knew this, you have just given yourself away. You are too easily fooled young man. Anyway, enough of this, you will do as I say or perhaps you have forgotten that I have the means and the opportunity and of course, the ability to silence you for good. I am sure that you will keep everything to yourself as you have so much more to lose."
Mark kept silent at this.
Frank said, "I think the best thing is that we just do as George wants and we can get things tidied up and be back to making some progress. We have that 'Dive-Tender' out on the dock don't we? That's probably the fastest boat we have here."
"What boat is that?" said George.
"It's a boat with a Hamilton Jet drive; she'll do about 45 knots."

"Hamilton Jet, what's that?" said George.
"It's a Jet drive, where the propeller is inside a kind of tunnel under the boat. The water is taken up from below the hull and the propeller is contained in this tunnel and the jet of water from the stern gives the propulsion."
"And this gives 45 knots? It must be very powerful."
"I don't know the exact thrust pressure but it's extremely high and the boat is very manoeuvrable."
"All I need to know is that it'll get me to the French coast as quickly as possible and leave no traces. Can it land me on a beach?"
"Yes, it can work in almost zero depth of water, so I could take you right to the shore and you wouldn't even get your feet wet."
"So if the propeller is in a tunnel, does that mean that it is safe from damage like we had the first time?"
"Yes, the only problem could be if it sucks up some seaweed, but that is very unlikely where we would be going."
"Right, that's what we'll do then, just as soon as I have the money safely stowed and you say that there'll be no propeller damage this time. You had better be right," he warned.

CHAPTER 67

"I think we have to assume that he will take some sort of action to take retribution in some form or other, don't you guv? Probably money."
"I think you're right Tom, and we know that the murder of Yaren is linked to this revenge, that this guy was sent over here to sort out the mess. What does that suggest anybody?
"That he came looking for Yaren and when she didn't have what he wanted, he killed her anyway and then came down here to look for his retribution,"
"That's just about what I'm thinking Anna, and he went off in a boat from the Auctions and killed another bloke who was probably just 'in the way."
"But we don't know that do we? I mean we haven't found him and he hasn't been spotted at the auctions so can we assume that he is still around?"
"Maybe we can, so let's go with that for a moment. If he's still here, surely he'll want to get away as soon as possible, so how would he make his escape?"
"I don't suppose he'll want to go via any airport or ferry as he'd know that can be traced, so perhaps his only way is to cross the Channel and once he's there he could easily get to Italy, if that's where he's going, by train, and the chances are that he would not be followed. We can't alert every police force and I don't suppose they would be too keen on keeping a lookout for someone we only have a sketchy description of and no name."
"So what's our next move then guv?" said Tom.
"I think it's entirely up to us to catch this guy before he makes his escape. It's about time we put a round the clock watch on the auctions, if it isn't too late by now. I'll arrange the coverage and you three can be ready to get in position so that this time we don't miss him."
"But where do you think he is at this moment guv?" asked Anna.
"I think if I were him I'd be keeping my head well down and waiting for the best moment to get off. We've alerted all the airports and ferry ports so with their cameras we should be fairly certain that he'll not get past them but my money is that he still is around locally and if he made a quick cross channel dash, he'd be home free."
"Yes, but where is he though? Now, I mean."
"What would you do Tom?"
"Well if I was him and I didn't know anyone locally, I'd stay close to the people who can help me get away and that has to be Frank or Mark."

"Good lad," said Alex. "My thoughts exactly,so maybe he's with Mark in his flat, but of course we still don't bloody know where that is, except somewhere in Poole. Surely to Christ we can find him somehow? Have we no information on that front anybody?"
Alice spoke up. "Not so far, and yet Tom and I have been really trying hard but there is just no record of him on any official lists, no electoral details, no records of him so we have to assume that he is using a different name altogether."
They were all rather dispirited at this stage of the investigation and Alex said, "Right, time to stop dicking about and take some action before it is really too late. Tonight we start surveillance again. Tom and Alice, you watch from the Riverside Restaurant, and Alice, no sneaking in for a cake or two."
Alice coloured up at this. She hadn't realised that she'd been so spotted when she'd been there before on her visit to the Auctions to see Frank.
Anna and I will take a position at the back with the view as before from the road just over the car park. That way we can see who arrives without being too obvious. We will only use radios when necessary and only then. None of this 'Biggles' stuff, understood? It could well be a long night people."
The all nodded, knowing full well that it had been Alex who had started the 'Alpha One to Alpha Two' nonsense before, but they had the sense to keep this to themselves, even if it was correct procedure.
"Do you think we should take a look at Frank's house guv, just in case he's there? You never know, he could have this suspect with him."
"Why do you think that Alice?"
"If the suspect is waiting for money for instance, he wants to keep out of the way and maybe Frank can keep him there out of sight."
"Good point, but I think Frank knows that we know his house and that we'll be keeping an eye on it, so I'm pretty sure he's somewhere else, such as Marks' flat. I honestly think that by now we should have found out this place but I'm buggered if I'm going to sit around and wait. We have to get them at the Marine Auctions because that is where I'm convinced he'll try to make his escape. I just wish we had more bodies for extra surveillance points but with all the restrictions that we have on manpower, we just don't have the resources, so we'll just have to do our best.
The others seemed to go along with this, and were quite happy with the arrangements for the surveillance.
As Alex went into his office, Anna looked around the door and smiled at him, saying quietly, I'd rather be with you somewhere else than sitting in a cramped old car waiting for something to happen."
"So would I Anna, but when we get this bastard sorted and nicked, we'll be somewhere else, I can assure you."

CHAPTER 68

After the suspect was seen on Tuckton Bridge, a fruitless overnight surveillance was mounted to try to arrest him and although they knew that he had jumped over the bridge railings and disappeared, it was fairly obvious that he had gone to the auctions. They wanted to catch Mark Jordan there as well because so far they had been unable to find him or trace his movements or whereabouts. He was suspected of involvement with not only drugs but the shipment of copied paintings which had been sold as originals. A dossier was being prepared prior to the arrest warrants. Alex had decided to wait until he was sure that Mark was there in the buildings before attempting an arrest.
"But if we don't get him now guv, he might get clean away," said Anna.
The further surveillance was organised and was due to start at 11pm.
The warrants for arrest which contained all the customers on the list of recent sales covering the last 3 years were being prepared. Recipients of paintings bought from the Arcadian Gallery in Wimbledon, ostensibly originals, had been contacted and their purchases re-examined by specialists to ascertain their authenticity. This resulted in several copies being found which had been supplied purporting to be originals, together with Certificates of Authenticity. Although these were apparently genuine, the sale was fraudulent. The sums involved sometimes amounted to hundreds of thousands of pounds.
***
As a result of these findings, a prosecution was being prepared covering the gallery owner, together with the gallery manager who were both suspected of complicity and also, Mark Jordan and his father Frank Jordan. With the combined evidence and testimony obtained from Katya Sadik, the 'copyist' who was not actually involved in the fraud, this prosecution was now awaiting the arrest of Mark Jordan and his father.
The suspect in the murder of Yaren Ganim, who was also involved in the fraud, was still being sought as thus far, he had managed to evade capture, but it was suspected that he was now at the Marine Auction premises and consequently it was hoped that the 'all-night surveillance' would ensure their arrest.
***
It was 11 p.m. and both the police cars and the Armed Response Unit, were positioned as before. One car was in the car park of the Riverside Restaurant overlooking the buildings of the auctions and the other in the road behind the buildings but with a view of the entrances. The ARU were out of sight but ready for action.
The surveillance was to be carried out right through the night. In one car, Alex and Anna were again together, in the side road behind the buildings, with just a slight view of the river.

Anna said, "We must stop meeting like this Alex."
"I know, but where do you suggest then, somewhere we can keep an eye on our suspects and do something really special?"
"I know where I'd like to be," she said with a knowing glance.
"Me too but I think we're in with a chance tonight. They have to come here as all the signs indicate that chummy is trying to make a getaway. He's taken very great care to try to cover his tracks in going from Lymington to Poole and then back to Christchurch. He's not been seen anywhere else locally until we saw him on the bridge."
"I'll tell you what Alex, I reckon he's been holed up either with Mark or Frank somewhere and if you're right, he'll make his move very soon and we'll get him."
"That's what I like, a positive attitude; I damn well hope you're right Anna. I had the 'Super' on to me this morning asking why the hell we haven't caught this suspect yet. I tried to stall him but he's very not happy, I can tell you, but then neither am I."
***
Unknown to Alex and his team was that George Manion - and they only presumed that his name was 'George', as he had been the most likely suspect after he had obtained Yaren's address from the gallery – had actually been hiding in a small building within the auction rooms and he had spent the time there since he had jumped over the bridge railings, hiding and waiting for an opportune moment to make his escape. The money had been collected from the bank by Olivia Harrington-Thorpe and all was ready for the escape run to France. This had come as the night drew in and the police cars were watching'
George walked from his hiding place within the auction rooms and crossed the main shed and went through a small door which led out onto the dockside. It was very dark as all lights were unlit as usual at that time of night. There was sufficient light to see the river quite clearly but not so much that he would be visible from a distance. He crossed the little pontoon bridge and entered the auctions office where Frank and Mark were waiting. Because he was on the 'riverward' side of the buildings, he was out of sight of the police cars.
***
Mark had arrived by a different car, unknown to the police. This was obtained by Frank earlier that evening and now they were ready to get under way on the crossing to France to make Georges' escape.
Again, the boat they were to use was not under observation as this would have been impossible due to the lack of places from which the pontoons could be seen and the fact that it would have been out of sight anyway because it was hidden by the main building.
"I was thinking Anna that perhaps we should have had someone watching from those flats on the other side of the river. They'd have a good view of the dockside wouldn't they?"

"Yes, but whoever was watching would need night-vision binoculars to see anything, it's very dark on the riverside."
"A good point, except for two things. One, we don't have the available officers, thanks to budget cuts, as we all know, and two, we can't afford those special binoculars, they cost an arm and a leg. They're only for 'special ops' I believe."
"A bit late now anyway, isn't it?"
"Thanks for letting me know Anna."
***
They had been sitting there quietly observing all that went on around the auction buildings. Out of sight to all the cars observing, a boat was quietly leaving the far end of the auction pontoons in the darkness This was a fast boat driven by a high-powered "jet-drive". It was capable of around 40 knots and it was carrying two men. George Manion and Mark Jordan.

CHAPTER 69

After Frank and George had both stayed at Olives' house for two days and then accompanied her to collect the money, they had arrived back at the Marine Auctions buildings at night, and were not captured on CCTV. Had the police asked the Riverside Restaurant to re-align their CCTV camera to take in the entrance to the Marine Auctions, they would possibly have seen them arriving at around 10.30 p.m. Mark had also returned after keeping well out of the way for some days, this time in a different car.
Frank was inside the large building which housed the smaller boats and all the chandlery which was ready for the auction. He was talking to Mark.
"At least we have the money so now we can put an end to all this," said Frank. "George told me to give Keith and Ben the day off so that he wouldn't be seen."
"So you're taking orders from him now are you?"
"Never mind that, it makes sense. Just let's do what he says and not annoy him. Which boat are you taking?"
"Like I said before, we're taking that 'Dive-Tender' that came in to the Auctions about three weeks ago. I know that the owner is on holiday in Barbados for a month, so he won't be back yet and with 45 knots I can be there and back in less than seven hours."
"Right, let's get on with this. I hope it's ready to go when you are."
"I did all that as soon as I came this evening." The boat was tied up and waiting at the far end of the pontoons.
"What time is it now?" said Frank.
"It's about ten past eleven."
"What time do you reckon to leave then?"
"I reckon if we leave about dawn, I should make it back around dusk providing nothing goes wrong."
"Just you make sure that nothing goes wrong. So far you're not doing much of a job. You'd better get some sleep so that you're alert."
"Good idea."
Just then, George shouted over to them. "We've got company!"
"What do mean?"
"I mean there are at least two unmarked police cars outside. One is on the lane behind the sheds here and the other I noticed parked over by the restaurant."
"Shit!" said Mark. "That's all we need."
Frank did some quick thinking. "Right, change of plan," he said, "can they see the river from where they are?"
"They might see a bit but only at quite a distance, and it's dark so I doubt they can see much at all."

"What I suggest is that you leave right now and slip quietly down the river and get to a spot in the harbour where no-one can see you. Run it onto the shore so you don't drift. I wouldn't trust the anchor in the soft sand with a current running. You can go before anyone is awake and anyway, it's very away from any roads. Get some sleep before you go at dawn."
"We could go now, couldn't we?" asked George.
"Are you completely mad? The last thing you need is to be belting across the channel at night, because not only can't you see the wave patterns but it could be disastrous if you hit some big ones really fast. Plus, as you know there are quite a few semi-submerged containers which 'fall off' ships in the Channel."
"Yeah, I know, we've seen them during some of our races," said Mark.
"I agree," said George. "I don't really fancy ending up sinking in the middle of the channel."
Mark simply nodded. "Okay, let's get on the way. Everything's ready. It won't matter if we're seen by anyone. It'll look like we're just going out on a pleasure run. Nobody will notice us."
"But if the police see us, they'll be on us like a ton of bricks," said Mark.
"Hang on; I'll just take a quick look from the side of the shed. There are enough gaps in the woodwork to give me a clear view of them if they're on Willow Way." Frank then walked over to the far side of the large shed and looked through the gap in the wooden siding of the building. This gave him a good view of the police car with two occupants, parked on the road. 'Couldn't be more obvious if they had their 'blues and twos' on', he thought.
He walked back to where Mark and George were waiting. "It's okay," he said, "they can only see the river at a long distance and I actually doubt that they'd see a boat at all in this light and at that distance."
"Right," said mark, "that's it, we go. Down to the Harbour and we'll do as you suggest and beach the boat. I know exactly where to do this where it can't be seen."
George and Mark walked down the pontoon to where the boat was waiting. They boarded the craft and Mark checked the fuel gauges and the engine instruments. The boat was propelled by a single Hamilton jet unit, which gave enormous speed and agility from the powerful engine and jet drive which was thankfully very quiet. Mark was not at all happy with the last-minute arrangements, but then he had accepted the inevitable.
Mark started the engine and while it warmed up, George got aboard and looked around. He noticed a large anchor right at the bow.
"There's a bloody great big anchor on the bow."
"That's where anchors usually are."
"Why does it have such a big anchor Mark? Are we going to stop on the way over, for a cup of tea?"

"Do you think I want to stop? I just want to get you off this boat as soon as possible." Mark thought, 'That's as close as I've heard him to come to humour, but I'm going to wipe the smile off his face.' There was a very large anchor on the port side of the bow, tied off to cleats just next to the small door in the bow, which allowed divers quick and easy access to the water without having a long drop.

"It's a big anchor because this is a diving boat. When the divers are down, the last thing anyone wants is for the boat to drift away, so they use a very big anchor, just to be sure it doesn't."

At just after 11.15, they slipped the moorings and moved off into the river where there was little current. Cruising very slowly and quietly towards Christchurch Harbour they passed Stanpit Marsh, negotiating the bends in the river until they entered the harbour proper. Mark said, "We'll go over towards Hengistbury Head and slip into the shallows there. There are no roads anywhere near that part of the beach. There'll be absolutely nobody there at this time of night and we'll be safe until dawn. At least this way 'plod' won't catch us."

"Good. I've been hanging around here for long enough and now that I've the money to give back to my boss, I want to get everything tidied up and get paid. I've had enough of chasing around after this money and what I've had to do to get it. This wasn't my intention."

"And I can't wait to see the back of you either. "I can't believe what you've done and what I'm doing now. I've lost a huge amount of money, you've killed my girl and my best mate, you have pressured us to give back the money for the painting and now you are going to get paid for murder. You're just an evil fucker."

"I know, but it's all been said before. It's what I do and get paid for. But you don't need to know this, so just shut up and accept it, unless you really want to try something else," said George.

Mark was thinking, 'If only', but just looked the other way and said nothing.

CHAPTER 70

Frank Jordan was requested to attend a further interview at Bournemouth Police station and as he had previously agreed to participate in their enquiries, he was in interview room 1.
"Present in Interview Room 1 are Detective Inspector Alex Vail and Detective Sergeant Anna Jenkins."
Alex switched on the recorder and as he did so, Jordan said, "But this is only an interview. Am I under arrest?"
"Not at all, Mr Jordan. However, we are anxious that all information is collated correctly and nothing is open to either negotiation or misinterpretation. You will of course understand for that reason, we systematically record all official interviews."
"I do."
"Mr Jordan, thank you for coming in again. We have a few more questions for you relating to the sale of paintings to various buyers both here in the U.K. and abroad."
"I know nothing about any paintings; I leave all that to my ex-wife Olivia Harrington-Thorpe who has a gallery in Wimbledon."
"Oh, we think you do, Mr Jordan," said Anna, with a very slight smile and a look towards Alex. "We have made enquiries based on the information given to us by the gallery manager, a Miss Rebecca Connors, whom you have met on a number of occasions. We know that you have introduced several 'buyers' of paintings through the gallery. We also know that some of these paintings are very expensive originals and some of them have been subsequently 'copied' by a specialist who was employed by the gallery to produce perfectly legitimate copies. However, from enquiries that we have made, several buyers have been contacted and subsequently checked by art specialists. An as yet unspecified number have been declared to be illegally sold copies. These copies were sold by the gallery with accompanying 'Authentication Certificates' which had been taken from the actual original painting and delivered with the copy. As I am sure you are perfectly aware, this is totally illegal and although the original painting was copied which is not illegal, it is to sell this copy purporting to be an original."
"But if I have only 'introduced' these buyers, I cannot be held responsible for a copy being delivered to them which is not the one they bought."
"That is true Mr Jordan, but if you had been party to this deception in knowing what was taking place, then you are an 'accessory' to the crime. In which case you are liable for prosecution in the same way as the person or persons actually carrying out the deception."
"This is crazy. You have no proof that I was involved."
"We have to tell you that we do indeed have proof and this will be passed to the Crown Prosecution Service at the appropriate time."
"Your involvement is purely 'incidental' at this time, but a particular painting was sold to an Italian man who just happens to be a member of the Mafia. When he discovered that the painting he

bought was a fake, I'm sure we don't need to tell you what his reaction was."

"Do I need a lawyer?"

"That is entirely up to you Mr Jordan, but as we said, we are not arresting you at this time. However, there are other issues that we need to cover." "What issues are they?"

"Firstly, we know that your son Mark recently crossed over to France on a boat bearing the name, 'Lady in the Mist'. This boat is actually owned by a Mr Michael Fortune and berthed at the Marine Auctions in Christchurch, which you own. We understand that this boat was apparently reported stolen from your premises. We now have proof that Mark did in fact go to Caen and was inspected by the French Customs at the time. Nothing was found on the boat, but very suspicious packages were seen floating from the stern of the boat and photographs were taken at the time, clearly showing these packages and the name of the boat. Subsequent investigations have linked these details and we have every reason to believe that these packages were drugs which were intended to be delivered to a dealer in France. Further investigations have uncovered the fact that this boat, which was at your Auctions waiting to be sold, was damaged underwater and when our specialist carefully inspected the damage, the conclusion was that the damage was caused by a metal object being smashed against the hull. It was the opinion of our expert that this may well have been caused by a metal canister, probably containing the drugs. For this to happen it would probably have been caused by this container being suspended by a rope, under water to escape detection, and this rope being taken into the propeller. This would certainly cause the rope to be wrapped around the propeller shaft. The result of which would have been that the metal tank would have been flung into the hull with the ensuing damage."

"This is all supposition, you have no actual proof."

"Well, actually," said Anna, "we do have the testimony of one of your yard workers who pointed out the damage and when it happened, to one of our officers who visited your premises recently."

"If a police officer came to the yard and spoke to one of my employees, he must have been doing this covertly. This would constitute 'entrapment', I would suggest."

"Actually, Mr Jordan, our officer was not asked who he was nor did he offer this. He was simply taken to be a member of the public looking around the auctions as would anyone simply taking a look at what was on show. Your employee offered this information without any prompting on our part."

"Again, this is supposition."

"Perhaps we don't have actual proof, but our specialist evidence and opinion would be extremely convincing to a jury, which is why you are not under arrest at this time, but we do have other issues which are far more serious."

Jordan was looking considerably less relaxed now as Alex took over. "We have been trying to trace your son Mark without success. As you are well aware his girlfriend Yaren Ganim was found dead on a small island in Christchurch Harbour on August 30th. A boat was seen at your auction site prior to the discovery of her body. This boat, which is known as a Fairey 'Christina' was reported to the police as 'stolen' and subsequently found abandoned at the Lymington Yacht Haven. Two men were seen on this boat exiting the harbour late in the evening of that day. We think that the body of Yaren Ganim was taken on board this boat and it was placed or dropped into the water from this boat."

The look on Jordan's face was simply 'stony' and was giving nothing away.

Alex continued, "The body was dropped where, what we are sure these two men did not know, the water was very shallow. At the time this deposition would have happened, it was a high 'Spring Tide' but by the same token, spring tides are the highest and the lowest. Consequently, when the tide was lowest, it uncovered a small island which is very rarely seen. It was on this small island that the body was found. What we would really like to know is how the body came to be brought from London to Christchurch."

There was still no change on Jordan's face.

"As the boat was about to go out of the harbour entrance, it was seen by witnesses to apparently hit something, which we believe to have been a sandbar near the exit from the harbour, which would have caused propeller damage. Because of this damage, the boat made its way to Poole Harbour where it was seen to take a mooring in the middle of the harbour. The propeller was removed and taken to Poole Quay where this was repaired. This would have been replaced and the boat then exited Poole harbour and made its way to Lymington Yacht Haven where it was found abandoned. Two men were seen on this boat at Christchurch but when it was found at Lymington, only one man was seen leaving it and the body of a naked man who was in his late twenties was subsequently found on board. He had been shot in exactly the same way as Yaren Ganim had been killed."

Anna then said, "We have never found the killer of Ms Ganim, but we are convinced that one of the men who were seen on the boat in Christchurch Harbour was in fact the killer of both individuals. The other man is unknown to us and we are wondering if you could shed any light on who he might be."

"I really have no idea," said Jordan. As he said this, Anna was watching his eyes and detected a look which gave her pause. He knows something, she thought. He actually looked 'shifty', which was not usual for him, as he normally had complete control. This time, she thought, he almost looked guilty.

Alex was very serious and he looked hard at Jordan. "We think you know far more than you are telling us Mr Jordan. If you know anything, it would be seriously in your interest to tell us now before

we obtain more proof. When we do, and I say 'when' and not 'if', your situation will become a great deal more difficult. Is there anything you wish to tell us?"
Jordan was silent for long moments and then he said, "Okay, there is something I should tell you. A man came into the auction office recently and he said his name was 'George', nothing more. He said he was instructed by his 'boss' to collect some money which he had been defrauded out of. I understand that a painting which you referred to earlier had been bought by this man, who lives in Italy, and he had discovered that it was a forgery or at least a copy which he believed to be an original which he had paid a large amount of money for. He had employed this man to recover the money and take it back to him in Italy. As the painting had been obtained from the gallery which my wife owns, he was approaching them for restitution. He was apparently told that the sale had been concluded by a Yaren Ganim, who was employed by the gallery and the money was paid to her, in cash."
"And do you have a full name for this 'George'?"
"I only know him as 'George'. As I said, he never gave another name and he was most aggressive when I asked him. He told me that he had killed Yaren and he also had a gun, so I was not about to argue with him. He was given her address by the gallery manager calling Mrs Harrington-Thorpe for permission to give him her address."
"We know from the gallery manager how he came to obtain her address, so we must assume that he went there and subsequently tortured and then killed her, presumably because she would not, or could not tell him where this money was."
Alex was laying out exactly the situation and he was hoping that Jordan would realise just how much was known and how deep in the proceedings he was.
"If you say so," said Jordan.
"We know so, Mr Jordan," said Anna. "Perhaps you realise just how this case is covering all the members of your family and that you would really be strongly advised to tell us everything, before charges are brought when we finally apprehend the killer, including those involved. So where did the cash come from that this 'George' wanted?"
"As I said, he was very aggressive and threatened us with this gun, saying that he had no compunction whatever in killing and would do it again if this money was not produced. He and I went to Olivia Harrington-Thorpe's house and waited for two days while she obtained the cash from her safe and her bank."
Anna moved her head close to Alex and said very quietly, "This explains why we had no sight of anyone for a couple of days."
Alex nodded.
"And how much money was it that 'George' wanted to take back to Italy?"
"£300,000."

Anna and Alex exchanged glances which explained what they were both thinking.
Changing tack slightly, Alex said, "Can you confirm that it was your son Mark who actually found Yaren and it was him that brought her body to Christchurch?"
"Yes."
And was it this 'George' who took the body for disposal?"
"Yes."
"And who was the other man on the boat?"
"This was Jason Chandler, a friend of Marks."
Anna looked again at Alex who said nothing, but she knew what he was thinking.
"Would that be the naked body which was found on the boat in Lymington?"
"Presumably, yes."
"We can verify this because we have fingerprints found on beer cans on the boat which are those of Jason Chandler, arrested for burglary some years ago in Newbury, together with dental records from the same area."
"Mr Jordan, do you know where either Mark or 'George' are now?"
"They are taking the cash to France."
"Do you mean they are on the way now?"
"Yes."
Alex then said, "Did they take a boat from the Marine Auctions?"
"Yes."
"At when did they leave?"
"Yesterday evening, late."
"Why did they leave at night? That would have been very dangerous surely?"
"They left because they knew that you had surveillance on the boatyard. Your cars were seen."
"And did they cross the channel at night?"
"No, the intention was to lie over in the Harbour at Christchurch and start the crossing at first light."
Anna said quietly to Alex, "Can I have a quick word guv?"
"Interview paused at 3.50 p.m."
***
They went outside into the corridor. Anna looked at Alex and with an earnest voice, said, "That means that they must have left just after our surveillance began yesterday. They would have taken a boat but we didn't see one. Why's that?"
"Because we weren't looking in the right bloody place Anna! - *Shit!* - Why didn't we have someone watching the harbour entrance down at Mudeford? I should have thought of that."
"Even if we had guv, we just don't have enough manpower to watch all these points."
"But we should have seen them leaving the Auction premises, shouldn't we?"

"Just how much of the river could we have seen from where our car was? I know I couldn't see much and it was so dark when we set up, I'm not surprised we didn't see anything."
"But if they'd not had any lights on we wouldn't have seen them anyway, would we?"
"Maybe you're right Anna, but that's no excuse. I'm going to get a real bollocking from the 'Super' now. If we'd had someone there they may have spotted them, but let's get back to Jordan, he should know when Mark should be back."
***
They both went back into the interview room and Alex started the recorder. "Interview re-commenced at 3.58 p.m. Mr Jordan, do you know exactly when they left yesterday?"
"They left the auctions just after 11 p.m. They went into the harbour and waited there until dawn this morning before crossing the Channel."
"So, they went across the Channel at dawn, so presumably this is to drop 'George' off and Mark will return?"
"That is the idea, yes."
"And what time do you expect him back?"
"The trip to France would take around 4 hours so if they left at dawn which was around 6 a.m. he should have been back around 2 p.m., but he isn't back yet."
Jordan was now looking quite concerned and he had a frown on his face. He had a considerable knowledge of sea conditions in the channel after many powerboat races and although he was sure of Mark's knowledge and ability in powerful boats, he was now becoming more and more worried as there had been no phone call from Mark to confirm his return. 'Still', he thought, 'there could have been a tide change which caused a delay in the expected return trip, so maybe I shouldn't be too worried. There's no chance of a mobile phone link while he was a distance from the coast, so maybe I'll hear soon'. He hoped.
Alex looked at his watch. It was now just after 4 p.m. "Are you worried that he isn't back yet, or perhaps you have not been back to the auctions where he would return to?"
"Not really, as he knows the water well and currents can have an adverse effect on timings, but I did say to him to call me as soon as he was back." Actually, Jordan was more worried, than he looked but he kept his cool.
"Can you tell us what boat he will be in?"
"He was in a Red 'Dive Tender' which is quite recognisable as it is a jet boat."
"Anna said, "We'll ask Andy at the RNLI station at Mudeford to keep watch. Even if he's not watching, he'll have someone keep a lookout. I'll ask him notify us as soon as it comes past and we can meet Mark at the auctions."

CHAPTER 71

They entered the larger part of the harbour and made their way across towards Hengistbury Head. This was a site of an Iron-Age settlement back in 'pre-history', but now they thought it was a good place to beach their boat, out of sight of anyone. It was extremely doubtful if anyone was walking there at that time of night, as it is quite remote and very dark and forbidding.
The boat moved slowly to the sandy shore and with a slight scraping noise, the bow rode up the beach a little way and stopped.
"This is fine. The boat will go nowhere but I'll just put the anchor in as the tide will rise by just a half-metre but it'll stop us floating away," said Mark.
***
Mark had been thinking over his options before getting only a little sleep. As the first light of dawn broke over the harbour, he pulled on his waterproof gear and shook George awake. "Let's get it over with," he said. "I'll just bring the anchor in." Mark retrieved the anchor and carefully tied it off to a cleat in the bow of the boat. Coffee from the thermos jug they had brought and a sandwich from the supply they had put on board the previous evening, constituted breakfast.
"Are you ready to go," Mark growled, "because I for one can't wait to dump you off over there and get back here."
"There's no need to be like that," said George. "You sound bitter."
"Bitter? You mad bastard. You're nothing but a sadistic, evil minded psychopath. You've just killed my girlfriend and my best friend, and you say I sound bitter? If only you had lost two people you liked. I think you'd feel 'bitter'."
"If she'd told me where the money was, she would still be alive today."
"I don't think so. You are just a really nasty fucker with no feelings. In fact I think you actually like killing people and torturing them as well I'll bet."
"Actually you are quite right, but I've heard that before, George said with the hint of a grin. I have lost people. In fact they were shot by police when there was a robbery which went wrong. This happened years ago."
"And I suppose you got off scot free again," said Mark.
"Oh yes. With no traces."
George was carrying a small metal case containing all the banknotes which just about fitted into the case which had toggle catches on the front. There was no real need for locks. The gun which George had, as Mark knew, was the only protection the case needed.
Mark had prepared everything and was ready to go. They set off toward the exit from Christchurch Harbour. They passed Mudeford Quay where George had had the problem with the propeller in the boat used to dump Yaren's body. Mark was unaware of this location

and the only other person who had known this, apart from George, was Jason. All eventualities were covered in George's mind.
Having passed Mudeford Quay they carried on through the Run and turned towards the French coast. Mark pushed the throttles to 'full ahead'. The boat surged forward with tremendous acceleration which pushed George to the back of his seat. The boat leaped over the waves with the grace of a craft designed for high-speed use in all weathers. The powerful engine producing the enormous thrust from the high-pressure water jet at the stern, was roaring away at full speed. The waves were not particularly high but there was quite a swell running which made the motion of the boat quite 'elegant' and Mark was actually enjoying the feeling of a fast and powerful boat which he knew well from his powerboat racing experience.
They were nearly half-way on their 150 mile run to France when he said to George, "You know that anchor that's on the bow George?"
"Yes, what about it, are we going to stop for a cup of tea now?"
"Ha, bloody ha. We're not stopping for anything. The sooner I can see the back of your repulsive body the better, but actually the anchor is working loose with all the wave action and if that happens the damn thing is going to bounce over the side and cause all sorts of problems. The hull is fibreglass and a loose anchor could punch a hole in the hull. Can you get up to the bow and tie it down again, just to be sure?"
"You should have tied it better; you're supposed to be the boat expert."
'I am', thought Mark.
"Okay, I suppose it wouldn't be good to sink out here." George made his way to the bow and trying to wedge his knees into the space between the seats, began to make fast the anchor which was indeed becoming loose.
***
One of the very special things about a 'jet' boat is that it has incredible manoeuvrability. It can turn very sharply but Mark knew it had another speciality which he intended to exploit. A water-jet propulsion unit has a 'deflector' shield over the jet outlet for the purpose of re-directing the jet. This enables the boat to stop by deflecting the jet downwards in much the same way as a jet aircraft slows on landing by deflecting the thrust downwards.
***
Mark quickly throttled back, deployed the deflector plate and then re-applied full throttle. The effect was to powerfully lift the stern of the boat and cause the bow to dig really deep into the water, bringing the boat almost to a complete stop in about thirty feet.
This action catapulted George over the bow and with a large splash, he went head-first into the sea. This gave Mark a great deal of satisfaction because he thought, 'Now try to swim to France you bastard. This is for Yaren and Jason'.

What George hadn't known was that Mark had purposely tied the anchor loosely, giving him the chance to move George to the bow, ready for his manoeuvre.
However, there was a problem for Mark, in that he had not taken to heart Franks' comment when he had said that the Italian Mafia boss would only find another way; he was only thinking that he still had the money and he could turn round and get back to Christchurch to get the drugs situation finalised with the 'cash in hand' and George would cease to be a problem.
Mark was looking at George who was treading water, grinning with evil satisfaction as the boat drifted slowly past. 'Restitution for the murder of Yaren and Jason'. Looking hard at George, he raised his arm and pointed toward France and shouted, "*It's that way*."

CHAPTER 72

George still had the gun tucked into his belt. He quickly drew this as the boat was now almost stationary. Shaking the gun to get as much water out of the barrel as possible, he aimed as best he could while treading water and fired at Mark. His first shot missed and Mark was taken by surprise. He ducked down below the gunwale of the boat and George fired again. His second shot was far too low and missed Mark but actually went through the hull and pierced one of the twin fuel tanks.
The fuel vapour exploded with a deep 'Whump' and a gout of burning fuel shot towards Mark. The fireball engulfed him, covering his chest and face with burning fuel. Mark was screaming with the pain as he burnt, desperately trying to smash out the flames with his hands; but that was completely useless. The whole of his upper body was drenched with burning fuel and this was searing his flesh. He actually inhaled some fuel and this turned to flame deep in his chest and his breath turned to liquid fire. Then the screaming stopped and he was silent, collapsing on to the deck.

The flames seemed to be confined to the stern of the boat and were actually dying out as most of the fuel had been dissipated. The fire did not spread and George thought he could still get back onto the boat and he was thinking that if he could get back onto the boat, there was just a chance that he could send up a flare which would be spotted by one of the many ships using the Channel. As he was very close to the boat, he quickly grabbed at the gunwale. This proved to be too high for him to reach. He floundered round to the stern by using the ropes on the sides of the craft as handholds. Reaching the stern, he held on to the jet unit and with great difficulty, managed to scramble into the boat. There he stood and looked dispassionately at Mark who was by now a terrible sight with his body charred and blistered.

Was he dead? Looking at the blackened upper torso of the body it was quite obvious. George really didn't care. He smiled. No problem. He was glad that there would be no connections and no traces. Just get over to France and to the shore and he would make his way to his destination somehow.
He thought.
What he didn't know was that the explosion had also blown a hole through the hull below the water-line and the stern section of the boat was filling with water. The engine was somehow still ticking over due to the second fuel tank on the opposite side of the boat. He found a bucket and quickly filled this and threw it over the dying flames. He eventually succeeded in quenching them and went back to the helm position, shoving Marks body away with his foot as though he was a piece of driftwood.

He managed to push the throttle forward and the engine sprang into life. As he had no real idea of how to operate the controls of the boat, he soon realised that the boat was not moving forward, but backward. This threw him off balance and he fell to the deck, beside Marks' body. Quickly standing up, he struggled back to the helm position. Throttling back he looked again at the controls. After a couple of moments it dawned on him that there must be a control for reversing which Mark had used to stop the boat so quickly. Eventually this became evident and he managed to change the setting to 'forward' and pushed the control to 'full ahead'. The boat leaped forward with the immense thrust from the jet unit. So much so, that he had to hang on very tightly to stop being thrown back over the stern of the boat.

He looked around for a flare but had no idea where they were kept. Leaving the boat to hopefully steer itself on a relatively straight course, he checked all around for a flare, but again couldn't find one.

Going back to the helm position, he realised that something was not quite right. Looking back toward the stern, it became rather obvious that the boat was actually taking on water. The stern was much lower in the water especially due to the heavy weight of the engine and jet-drive unit, causing a very steep angle.

The boat was slowing dramatically and very soon the engine flooded and died.

The boat stopped moving. It was sinking quickly.

By now the boat was becoming nearly vertical, with the bow high in the air and it was slipping backwards, deeper and deeper.

Marks' body was partly wedged into the hatch leading to the small cabin and as the boat went down it took his hideously charred body with it.

The metal case with the money slid down the deck disappearing from sight.

As the boat finally sank and slipped quietly beneath the water, George was back in the sea.

The water temperature was around 16 degrees and it would take around 20 minutes or so for hypothermia to begin to take effect. Muscles begin to weaken, strength lessens, co-ordination goes as blood moves from the extremities to the central body core.

He was treading water.

He did not swim well.

He was about 75 miles from either shore.

Alone.

He left no traces.

THE END.

CHAPTER 73 - Epilogue

Following the interview with Frank Jordan, it was realised that Mark was not going to return from his trip to France. The intention was to take George Manion and the money for him to return this to the Italian buyer, Tosco Scarpetti. It was suggested that perhaps he had simply stayed in France, but this idea was instantly rejected as extremely unlikely. The probable scenario was that something had happened to them during the journey but it was impossible to know the exact outcome.
The police investigation was finalised with the impending prosecution of Frank Jordan, Mark Jordan in absentia, Olivia Harrington-Thorpe and Rebecca Connors for their parts in the fraudulent sale of 'copied' artworks to various buyers over a period of five years previously. A comprehensive list of these buyers had been furnished by Miss Connors and subsequently, these buyers had been contacted and their purchases examined by experts. The result of these examinations revealed that the majority were indeed copied and not the originals which had been ostensibly purchased from the Arcadian Gallery.
As Mark Jordan was never found, he was declared 'missing, presumed drowned at sea', together with the unknown 'George' who was presumed to be the killer of both Yaren Ganim and Jason Chandler.
This outcome was interpreted as a 'bad outcome' by the higher Police Authorities, as it was also for the Senior Investigating Officer, Alex Vail, as the two main players were never apprehended and now it was impossible to arrest either of the two main suspects.
The court case involving Jordan, Harrington-Thorpe and Connors, resulted in a custodial sentence for Jordan as an accessory to murder, borne out by the fact that he was instrumental in disposing of the body of Yaren Ganim and aiding and abetting the death of Jason Chandler. Harrington-Thorpe was also given a custodial sentence for her part in the fraudulent supply and sale of copied works of art over an extended period, together with Jordan who was complicit in the deception who received a further sentence for his part in this fraud. Harrington-Thorpe was also given a very heavy fine, due to the amount of money which had been made from these crimes. Both Jordan and Harrington-Thorpe had assets seized as part of the Criminal Restitution proceedings.
Connors received a suspended sentence. The Arcadian Gallery was subsequently sold and the profit from this sale was sequestered to the Criminal Restitution procedure.
DI Vail was summoned to a meeting with Superintendent James Gordon to provide an explanation as to why no suspects had been apprehended during this case.

The meeting did not go well.

Printed in Great Britain
by Amazon